The Rise of the Dark Lord

The Rise of the Dark Lord

GARETH PRESCOTT

Contents

Aerinthos
GRALTUM
Ma'Yan
HENT-TAUI
(The kingdom under the mountain)
HENT-TAUI
(The human settlement)
Graul
NORTH ARUNA
ANTHER
Ganth
CAPITAL
Santelana
Anuris
URIAS
Toftek
CAERATHEON
Harton
Baldus
SILVERWOOD
SOUTH ARUNA
STONEHELM
BATLON
CERVIA
ANHAI
Alesia
Decan
Candleford
STRADA
Leath
ASERIUM
YAGER
MOR'DAN
Seket
Charun

Chapter 1

The soft glow of antique lamps filled Will's study, where ancient books and arcane relics were arranged with meticulous precision on fitted shelves made of rich, oiled hardwoods. As usual, he shunned the company of the hoards of lackeys and sycophants who hung around since his meteoric rise to fame, instead finding himself once again drawn into the quiet embrace of his studies. Before him lay an ancient Norse script, its brittle parchment inscribed with their most forbidden rituals. His pen scratched feverishly across a notepad as he parsed the cryptic language and jotted down potential interpretations.

Beyond the heavy wooden door, the rhythmic thumping of music pulsed from the party that was proceeding in his absence at the far end of the house. Will had long since tuned out the sounds, focussing entirely on the mysterious contents of the script, until a soft change in the soundscape behind him caught his attention. A door creaked open gently, then closed quickly, allowing the sounds of revelry from beyond to spill into his sanctum of calm for the briefest moment. As the door clicked shut, it was immediately followed by the distinct, measured clicking of heels on the hardwood floor.

Wendy stood behind him with a playful yet insistent smile. "There's a party going on, you know. A lot of people have come here to celebrate your birthday with you... It might be good for you to step out for a bit, at least for some fresh air."

Will looked up, irritation momentarily flickering in his eyes. "Really, Wendy? I'm sure no one has even noticed I am missing," he murmured, his tone dripping with undisguised disdain as his eyes lazily slid back to the text in front of him. "They're only really here for the free booze and the chance to say they were at Will Preston's fiftieth birthday party."

Wendy's gaze softened as she looked over his desk, taking in the scattered papers and the intense focus in his eyes. "I can see you're busy," she said softly, stepping closer, placing a hand gently on his shoulder. "But perhaps a little break might do you some good."

Before Will could protest further, Wendy lightly squeezed his shoulder, an unspoken plea for him to rejoin the world outside his self-imposed seclusion, before heading back to the party. With a sigh, he returned his gaze to the script, his mind blotting out the distractions from the other side of the house.

He tried to reapply himself to his study, but in the wake of the interruption, he couldn't focus. Eventually, he sighed and put the book down, glancing towards the door as he realised that Wendy was probably right, and that he ought to make an appearance at his own party. He stepped out of his study and locked the door behind him. In the brightly lit hallway, he paused a moment in front of a mirror, focusing on the familiar stranger that stared back at him as he forced his face to adopt the mask that the party guests would be expecting.

Finally, when he was satisfied that he had applied enough in-sincere enthusiasm, he stepped away from the mirror and made his way towards the thumping music. He'd become quite adept over the years at wearing the persona the public expected, so much so that he sometimes almost forgot the haunted soul that resided within. With the practised ease of a seasoned celebrity, he stepped into the crowd, greeting guests with familiar pleasantries and light banter, perfectly playing the role of the jester in his own tragedy, watching the moments unfold with an absolute lack of interest.

It was amid this carefully curated performance that a subtle anomaly caught his attention. Standing a few paces away, in a quiet corner of the room away from any of the groups of half-drunk party-goers, was a woman unlike the rest. There was some-thing about her. Maybe it was the way that she stood apart from anyone else, yet seemed the most interesting person in the room. Maybe it was the way her eyes had sought him out and locked onto him the minute he had walked into the room. Or maybe it was because, despite the stifling heat that forced most guests to remove any additional layers, she wore a hood pulled firmly over her head. The style and fabric of her garment seemed outlandish, but there was a familiarity that Will couldn't quite put his finger on.

His practised smile wavered slightly as she moved towards him across the room. "Excuse me," she said in a soft, melodic voice, "are you Will... Will Preston?"

For a brief moment, his mask slipped, revealing a spark of guarded curiosity beneath his cool exterior. "Yes," he replied, "and who might you be?"

The woman paused, as if weighing the right words, then continued, "I'm Athtar Morran. I've been trying to reach you ever since I read your book. I've sent letters month after month." Her eyes, momentarily visible as her hood shifted, locked with his in an intensity that belied the casual words.

For a moment, Will's hackles went up. He had come across his share of stalkers since his return to his own world, and he was immediately on the defensive. "Fans aren't supposed to be in here," he said, backing away slightly. "You can see my agent, Wendy, for a signed copy of my latest book on your way out."

Athtar's eyes, however, shone with a burning determination that held his gaze. "You don't understand," she said softly, stepping forward. "I'm from Silverwood. Ever since the curse broke, we've been stuck here... cut off, stranded, and we need your help."

The words struck him like a chord to a song he'd long thought silent. His mask slipped, and the ache beneath it that he'd fought so hard to bury surged up. But scepticism still bubbled beneath the surface, slowly reasserting itself in the front of his mind.

Sensing the shift, Athtar's gaze softened, realising that her next words might determine the course of the remainder of their encounter. "I know how this sounds," she said, "but I've been trying to reach you because I believe you hold the key to understanding what happened... and perhaps, to finding a way back."

For a moment, the noise of the party blurred into insignificance, leaving the two in a suspended, fragile dialogue of possibility and doubt. Will's heart pounded with anxiety as a long-suppressed hope bloomed in his chest, the kind that stirred every time he recalled the lost warmth of his past; of Lyra's smile, her touch, the magic of a time when his life had meaning.

Scepticism gradually burned away the holding effect of the shock, as he realised that a stalker would have no trouble knowing this information. "Come now," he said, his tone rising slightly as he started to fear that this person might actually be dangerous, "anyone who's read my books would know of Silverwood and the curse of Shadowmoor."

But just as Will was about to usher her back to the main foyer, Athtar reached up and pulled back her hood. As the fabric fell away, a flash of pointed elven ears was revealed, set against a cascade of dark hair.

Glancing around to ensure no one else had seen this, Will reached out and gently pulled Athtar's hood back up. "Let's talk somewhere more private," he said, still glancing around as he led her away from the party and back towards his study.

Back in the study, he went over to his drink cabinet and took the stopper from a crystal decanter to pour himself a large glass of whiskey. He lifted the glass and looked inquisitively at Athtar, but she shook her head as she took a seat.

"I know how impossible this must sound," she began softly, "but when the curse collapsed, it didn't just send you back here."

Will swirled the amber liquid in his glass, suspicion clouding his features. "Earlier, you said we. Does that mean there are others?"

Athtar nodded. "At first, I thought I was alone. For years, I convinced myself of it. But then I found another elf working in a bookshop. A dwarf working as a porter at a hospital. As time went on, more and more joined us. We recognised each other, even before the words passed between us."

Will leaned forward slightly despite himself. "And you... you stayed in contact?"

Her eyes softened with a distant ache. "We try. Once a month we gather at a nearby community centre. We tell stories of home, and share the difficulties we've faced here. It helps to have a place to talk freely."

The weight in her words stirred an ache he'd buried under years of detachment. He tried to resist it. "If there are so many of you, why hasn't anyone reached out before now?"

Athtar's expression faltered, a flicker of bitterness breaking through. "Some did. Letters were sent, messages left. But they never reached you. We got polite replies with printed signatures. You were always too busy, always on another tour."

Will's grip tightened on the glass. A flicker of shame crossed his face, quickly masked with irritation.

Athtar let it linger for only a breath before she added, "We found each other, Will. But we are trapped. You're the one who crossed the veil once before. We're hoping that you will be the one who can lead us back."

The night stretched on as they continued to discuss the ones Athtar referred to as 'the refugees', and Will discussed his study of the arcane and his tireless hunt for a way to return. As the last echoes of distant laughter and music faded into silence, Athtar and Will eventually made a promise to continue this conversation soon. After exchanging details, Athtar left for home. Will sat alone in his study, digesting what had just happened, his mind racing with possibilities and a sense of destiny that he had not felt in nearly a decade. In that quiet moment, with Athtar's revelations still reverberating through his mind, a question took root: if the collapsing portal had ferried living people to this world, might it also have carried with it relics of magic from the other side, too? The thought sent a shiver of excitement through him.

He wandered through his house, casually picking up discarded drinking vessels and moving them to the kitchen as his mind raced with a million thoughts all at once.

The world saw him as a successful author, living a life filled with glamorous parties and endless travel. But in the solitude of his private moments, the pages of his new manuscripts lay unfinished, his thoughts adrift in memories of his time in Aruna. He had gradually stopped writing, his creative spirit eroded by a relentless quest for something far more elusive than literary acclaim. His fortune, that he had once considered the measure of his success, had instead become the fuel for a desperate, all-consuming desire to gather obscure ancient texts and relics. Every penny spent was part of a singular mission: to decipher the secrets of any long-dead civilisations of this world that held tales of the arcane, in the hope that those studies would yield any tangible evidence of real magic, and a way back to Aruna. It was a visceral need, an ache in his soul, the deep burning desire to return to the only life that had ever held meaning. And so, even as his world celebrated his success, Will's heart was tethered to the place where he had found and lost love. To the place his heart remained.

As he stepped over two sleeping guests on his living room floor to retrieve some more dishes, he stopped to look around. He really was thankful for everything he had built here, but the meeting with Athtar and the prospect of being one step closer to understanding the magical connection between his world and Aruna had left him feeling an unfamiliar sense of euphoria.

He glanced at the clock on the wall and realised it was already well on the way to sunrise. Looking down at his uninvited slumbering guests, he smiled, a genuine smile, and muttered, "You've got the right idea, haven't you?"

Chapter 2

Will was jolted awake late the following morning by his phone vibrating against the surface of his nightstand. Glancing at the screen, he tried to focus his blurry eyes on the text message:

Athtar: "There's a meeting tonight at eight. Meet me there, I know they'll be excited to meet you."

This message was promptly followed by another ping from his phone with a pin of the location. He placed his phone down on his chest, smiling up at the ceiling.

That evening, Will input the location Athtar had sent into the navigation system in his car and, with an unfamiliar mix of elation and apprehension stirring inside him, wound his way through the city.

As he followed the route laid out by his sat nav, he found himself moving away from the more familiar parts of the city, finally pulling into a cracked and worn car park. The building itself was an unassuming, weathered structure with peeling paint and a light on the wall that flickered as the bulb inside tried to hold on to life just a little longer. The street was lined with cracked pavements covered in rubbish, neglected by the street sweepers who frequented the more affluent areas of town, and was lit by a scattering of orange streetlights that cast pools of amber light, doing little to dispel the shadows between. A chill wind rustled the detritus along the curb, carrying with it a faint scent of damp concrete and city decay.

A few figures lingered outside the community centre, their silhouettes stood outlined in the pale, flickering light. They turned occasionally towards the door, watching a clock on the wall inside as they finished their cigarettes.

Inside the foyer, there was a notice board covered with faded posters for events that had long since passed, and the door to the main hall stood propped open with a wedge of timber. The floor of the main room was filled with worn-out chairs, and several people were already sitting around in quiet conversation, waiting for the meeting to begin.

Athtar greeted Will at the entrance with a knowing smile, exuding an energy of anticipation. "I'm glad you came," she said quietly.

The meeting began with soft introductions and tentative stories. An elderly man recalled the vibrant festivals of Caeratheon, his voice trembling as he recounted the celebrations that would go on for days at the lord's birthday. A female dwarf stood up next, weeping over the loss of her whiskers. She had taken to shaving them to avoid the stares of the intolerant people of this world, who would openly mock her appearance. Will sat quietly at the back of the room and listened, his heart filling up with empathy for these poor souls, trapped, so far from home.

The meeting continued for some time as people shared stories and reconnected, finding solace in that connection that would sustain them in this strange, hostile world. Eventually, everyone broke off into smaller groups. As Will was considering getting up to leave, Athtar came over in the company of a tall, aged man with long, silvery hair. There was a powerful presence about the man, a serene confidence that carried with it an air of grace.

"This is Thuridian Chaelen," she said to Will, gesturing to the silver-haired man. "He is our community leader, as appointed by the people. I spoke to him about our meeting last night, and he insisted on meeting you."

Thuridian's eyes searched Will's face for a moment before he spoke. "Many here regard you as something of a saviour," he said, his voice probing, as though he were gauging Will's reaction. "Your book... became a beacon to many of us in our darkest hours, keeping us connected with home. Some of our number have even begun talking of it as a sacred text, and revere you as more than a man, speaking of you with an almost religious fervour."

Will shifted uncomfortably from one foot to the other under Thuridian's scrutiny, unsure how to react to that. "I am no hero," he said, "and my book is just my story... nothing more."

Thuridian seemed satisfied with his response, nodding approvingly.

Will didn't know what to make of Thuridian, but he saw the way his people looked at him, their faces filled with absolute reverence and trust. Moreover, his own instincts were at ease in the man's presence. He reached out a hand in friendship. "It's a pleasure to meet you. I didn't hear you speak tonight... where are you from?"

Thuridian reached out to shake Will's hand. "I was a member of the Order of the Burning Torch."

Will leaned forward, his curiosity piqued. "You were a magic user?" he asked softly. He paused a moment before asking the question that really burned in him for an answer. "Have you... have you tried to use your magic since being here?" he blurted out finally.

Thuridian's gaze drifted to the worn floor. "I tried a few times in the early days after my arrival. But I could no longer bear the sting of disappointment, and so after a while, I stopped trying."

They talked together for some time, and Will found it quite cathartic having people with whom he could discuss his time in Aruna. They spoke of Silverwood and of Thorn Island. Will spoke of his time in Aruna, of his friends, and his adventure.

They spoke for so long that they didn't realise they were the last ones left in the building, the others having turned out the light in the main room before leaving.

As he was leaving, Will stopped just inside the door, hesitating a moment as he decided whether to share something with them. Finally, he drew in a short breath and turned to them. "I think there's a way back to Aruna."

Athtar and Thuridian turned to one another, a small smile tugging at the corners of Athtar's mouth. They turned to look back at Will. "Go on," said Athtar.

"I've been digging into arcane rituals from this world. There's a lot of our history that suggests the old civilisations had some sort of connection to magic, but many of them were just superstition," he said, warming to his point.

Thuridian and Athtar were now waiting in expectant, rapt silence.

"There have been a few promising leads, though. I have recently been studying an old Nordic ritual that seems to have some merit, but it requires a relic of the destination realm," he said.

Thuridian's brow raised, "And you have no such relic?"

Will shook his head. "No. That's where I was hoping you could help. Could you ask around to see if any of your followers might have brought something through with them... anything that might contain even a trace of the energy of Aerinthos."

Thuridian nodded, looking intrigued. "I'll ask," he paused for a moment, studying Will. "I had a good feeling about you. A real sense of destiny."

Will's eyes narrowed as the memory of Elysande saying those exact same words to him awakened in response to Thuridian's words.

Thuridian noticed his reaction and tilted his head to the side inquisitively.

Will chuckled. "It's nothing... You just reminded me of someone back in Aruna for a moment."

Athtar stepped past them, holding the door open to the night, letting the sounds of the city spill in. "Can we meet again tomorrow, Will?" she asked.

Will thought for a moment and then shook his head. "I have a meeting with my publisher tomorrow. They want a progress update on my latest work in progress," he said, looking uncomfortable.

"Maybe after then?" Thuridian said. I'll check with those most likely to have knowledge of any items of power that may have journeyed to this realm before we meet. Hopefully, we'll have a clearer picture by then.

As he drove away from the community centre, Will's mind buzzed with everything he'd witnessed there that evening. When he was about halfway home, the sound of his car's entertainment system cut through his silent reverie with the sound of a ringtone announcing an incoming call.

A glance at the dashboard revealed the familiar icon of his mum's caller ID. With a smile, he answered. "Hi mum... how are you—" he began, but his words were quickly silenced by the sound of her uncontrollable sobbing.

"Mum?" he said, his heart dropping.

Through intermittent gasps, she managed to stammer, "It's your dad... can you come to the hospital?"

Will felt sick with worry, but he quickly changed his destination, heading back into the city. "I'll be there soon, mum. Text me the info on where I can find you when I get there," he said, trying to remain calm despite his quickening pulse.

He ended the call, increasing his speed as much as he dared. He knew the route to the hospital well, and the roads weren't too busy at that time of night.

The main door of the hospital was surrounded by a pall of smoke as hordes of visiting family members clustered nearby, trying to calm nerves with heavy doses of nicotine, worried looks on every face.

Will moved quickly past them, knowing the hospital's layout quite well from many past visits, and quickly found the accident and emergency department. Through the glass in the door, he spotted his mum in the waiting room, her eyes red and her cheeks wet from a recent bout of tears.

She looked up as she saw him approaching and her eyes welled up again, spilling a fresh wave of tears down her cheeks as she threw her arms around Will's neck, burying her face in his chest.

"What's going on, mum? What's up with dad?" Will asked as he wrapped his arms around her, pulling her close.

She didn't move for a moment, finding relief in his presence, but eventually the sobbing subsided, and she was able to answer. "They think he had a stroke," she said in a shaky voice, choking up again at that last word.

Will didn't know what to expect, but he'd always thought his dad was invincible. This news totally winded him and he found he suddenly needed to take a seat, staring distantly at nothing in particular as the background sounds around him became muffled and distant.

His mum took the seat next to him, still holding his hand, and for a moment it felt like they were the only two people in the world as the news sank in. Eventually, though, the sound of voices echoing in a distant part of the building and a persistent cougher nearby intruded themselves back into his awareness.

Still feeling quite numb, Will almost didn't notice his mum standing up as a doctor approached. He barely heard the mumbled words that they exchanged, but when his mum turned back to him, she looked a lot more optimistic. "Come on... we can go and see him now," she said, throwing her handbag over her shoulder as he'd seen her do a million times.

Will slowly got to his feet, the weight of the recent developments pressing down on him. As he followed behind, he overheard snippets of conversation between his mum and the doctor as they walked down the sterile hallways towards the wards. There seemed to be a consensus that they were hopeful for a good recovery, but the doctor kept reiterating that the first three to five days would be critical.

They were shown through to a room where several beds lined the walls. A few of the beds were occupied, but Will barely registered them as his eyes scanned the room, looking for his dad. He spotted him in the far corner of the room, near a window. He was lying back in bed, his eyes closed, a nasal cannula delivering oxygen as an array of machines monitored his vitals. Will went over to his dad's bed and gripped his hand gently, his mum remaining by the door, talking to the doctor a moment longer.

His dad's eyes slowly opened, and although he looked slightly dazed, he smiled as he looked up at Will. "So this is how an old man gets a visit from his son, then, eh?" his dad said, only half smiling as the effects of the facial paralysis still lingered.

Will let out a little burst of laughter that was as much fuelled by relief as mirth. "Yeah... let's try a phone call next time, eh, Dad? I am sorry I haven't been around as much. This recent book has been taking all my spare time," he lied, although his voice was heavy with regret.

"Don't be daft, I was only teasing," his dad said, throwing Will another half smile. "Your mum and I are very proud of you."

Will squeezed his dad's hand again, not knowing what else to say to that. They just stood there in comfortable silence for a moment until the clacking of his mum's heels cut a path towards them.

Will decided to give them some privacy for a moment. "I am just going to grab a coffee from the vending machine. Does anyone want anything?"

His mum shook her head, not removing her eyes from his dad's face. His dad looked over at him, "I'll take a pint if you can sneak one past the nurses," he said, winking.

Will chuckled, pleased to see his dad in such high spirits. "I'll see what I can do," he said with a smile.

His Mum's head whipped round, her eyes squinted in mock ferocity. "Don't you dare, William!"

He laughed again as he strolled off down the hall in search of a vending machine, digging into his pocket for some change. He hadn't really known what to expect. His mind had raced with every single worst-case scenario he could imagine, but seeing his dad awake and cracking jokes put his mind at rest a bit. However, as he reached out to put a coin in the vending machine, he realised his hand was shaking. He stopped and took a moment to sit and do some breathing exercises, feeling the faint, fluttering edges of an anxiety attack, but he was able to control it.

When he got back, his mum was sitting on the far side of his dad's bed, holding hands and talking quietly. Will cleared his throat as he approached to announce his presence, and his mum looked up and smiled at him.

"Pub closed?" his dad said, a look of disappointment on his face.

"Sorry Dad," Will said with a little smile.

His mum stood up then. "The doctor says he needs his rest, but we can come back in the morning. Can you pick me up tomorrow, Will?"

Will nodded, remembering his meeting, but deciding that he would have to call and cancel. The publisher would have to wait. Some things were just more important.

His mum leaned down to give his dad a hug and a kiss, promising to return the following morning, her voice still quivering with emotional exhaustion. Will patted his dad on the shoulder, "Get some rest, Dad. I hope you feel better soon."

His dad reached out with his own hand, placing it on top of Will's, smiling. "Thanks, son."

As Will and his mum turned to leave the ward, his dad turned sharply. "Can you hold back a second, Will?"

Will looked back at his dad, then turned to his mum. "I'll meet you downstairs," he said.

She nodded and carried on ahead.

His dad looked at him seriously as he approached. "I needed to say something. Just in case... You know..." he left it hanging there.

"I need you to promise me that if I don't make it out of here, you'll take care of your mum," he said seriously.

Will didn't know what to say. "Don't be daft, Dad. You'll be home in no time."

"I'm serious, Will," he said. "I need your word."

Will was choked up with emotion, but nodded. "Of course, Dad. You know I would."

His dad relaxed and closed his eyes at that, his breathing becoming less laboured.

Will grabbed his hand again, making him open his eyes. "Was that all, Dad?"

His dad shook his head. "One more thing," he said, although his voice was starting to get drowsy.

"I'm listening, Dad," said Will.

"Life's short, Will... shorter than you think. I don't want you—" he coughed, trying to catch his breath so he could continue. "Don't waste time. When love comes... or a chance for happiness... grab it. Don't let it slip past."

Will was stunned. His dad had never really been one for talking about feelings, but here he was speaking words that resonated so deeply with Will that he found it knotting into a lump in his chest. "I hear you, Dad. Rest now... I'll be back in the morning."

His dad smiled, his eyes now closed in exhaustion. "Goodnight, son," he mumbled.

"Goodnight, Dad."

Chapter 3

Over the next few days, Will spent his time driving his mum back and forth to the hospital, timing visits around the allocated visiting hours, and the ebb and flow of his dad's energy. The hours there blurred into a mix of quiet shared moments, drinking bad coffee from paper cups, and half-finished conversations cut short by ward rounds. His dad, even with slurred words and a crooked smile, still found ways to tease the nurses and make his mum roll her eyes, giving them hope for his continued recovery.

For Will, it was strange how comforting the routine became. Sitting beside them, he found himself listening more than talking, watching his parents with an attention he hadn't given them in years. It struck him how rare it had become to simply exist in the same room with them, and he promised himself that once his dad was home, he wouldn't let so much time slip away again.

When the doctors finally declared his dad well enough to return home, relief washed over them all. Will carried the bags, made sure the heating was on and the cupboards stocked, and only when his parents were settled back into their familiar armchairs did he finally let himself exhale. Driving towards his home, he felt lighter, but also more aware than ever of how fragile the days ahead could be.

He parked close to the front door, exchanging a brief wave with the gardener, and paused to check his mailbox, retrieving a half-dozen envelopes that had accumulated during his absence before heading inside.

Stepping inside, he powered on his phone for the first time in days, and he realised that whilst he had been preoccupied, his messages had accumulated at an alarming rate. He quickly sorted through the bulk of them, deleting some, moving past trivial ones that could wait, and then working his way through the urgent ones that demanded his immediate attention. The first wave of messages came from Wendy, in incremental degrees of irritation as she demanded to know why he had missed the meeting with the publisher. He silently cursed himself for having forgotten to call and let her know, deciding to make her the first person to call.

Following that, Athtar's message arrived, bearing disheartening news. Despite their best efforts, neither she nor Thuridian had found anyone aware of relics from Aruna that had made the journey to his world. The disappointment stung; he had really been hoping that this new resource would yield fruit.

Absently, he navigated through the hallway leading to the kitchen as he continued reading messages and opening mail.

With an instinctive motion, he turned on his espresso machine and began grinding fresh coffee beans, pausing briefly to inhale the aroma of what would be the first good coffee he had enjoyed in days. Finally, coffee in hand, he walked towards his study and began dialling Wendy.

After only a single ring, the call connected.

"Where the bloody hell have you been? I've been trying to reach you for days! You can't just drop off the face of the planet like that, mister... You have obligations, you know?"

Will held the phone away from his ear, squinting as the ear-splitting tirade spilled forth from the earpiece. The angry words finally tapered off into a tense silence. With an air of amused nonchalance, he lifted the phone back to his ear. "Hello, Wendy. How are you?"

A deep, shuddering breath came from the other end as Wendy gathered herself. "You know," she began, her tone wavering between exasperation and hurt, "you left me looking like a fool at that meeting."

"I know, I'm sorry, Wendy. It really was unavoidable," Will replied, his voice heavy with genuine regret.

A brief pause followed before Wendy interjected, "Well? I assume you have a good excuse... as usual?"

Will sat down at his desk, his chair creaking slightly as he leaned back, running his fingers through his hair. "I was with my mum and dad. My dad was rushed to the hospital with a stroke."

A soft gasp and a momentary silence followed. "Oh, Will... I'm so sorry. Is he...?" Wendy's voice faltered with concern.

"He's okay...I mean, he's going to be okay. He's back home now, anyway," Will reassured, though his tone carried the fatigue of the past few days. "But I'm knackered. Now, how was the guy from the publishers... Steve, isn't it?" he asked, trying to steer the conversation back to work.

Wendy paused again, the sound of her contemplative silence filling the space between them. "Well... he wasn't happy," she finally said. "We had no idea what was going on with you, obviously. They're eager to know when they can expect the book. I tried to smooth things over as best I could, and I've managed to buy you a bit more time, but you're really going to have to do what you need to do to get this one over the finish line. Go to a retreat, do some drugs... do whatever you need to do."

Will looked at his laptop screen where the manuscript stood open, the cursor blinking at the end of a lifeless line of dialogue. The exact spot it had lived for the last couple of weeks. He sighed, resting his head in his hand. "Okay... leave it with me. I will have something to submit soon. Was there anything else?"

He could hear Wendy's discomfort in the silence that followed. "What is it, Wendy?"

"I know you hate doing interviews, but it was the only way I could get them to agree to the extension. They said the fans are getting restless waiting for the sequel and that an interview might appease them for a while. You have a ten-minute segment on tomorrow morning's breakfast show down at the radio station," she said.

Will considered it. He really didn't like doing interviews, but he acknowledged that Wendy had probably done the best she could, given the situation he'd left her in. "Alright, I'll be there. I'll be sure to wear my smiley face."

"Thanks, Will. I'll see you there in the morning, then. Be there for 7 a.m."

He hung up the phone, fidgeting with the handset as he stared off into the distance, trying to find the inspiration to finish writing this damn book. Finally, when inspiration didn't arrive, he looked back at his phone and the message from Athtar. Reading over the message again, his shoulders slumped. "Another dead end," he muttered to himself wryly.

He slid his thumb to the reply button, quickly typing out a message: *Sorry for not getting back to you sooner. Something came up. I'll give you a call tomorrow.*

* * *

Will squinted his eyes, not wanting to wake up and face the world just yet, but the alarm on his mobile phone persistently sounded off, until eventually, he rolled over with a deep groan to silence the noise. He rubbed his eyes, trying to recall what could have possessed him to set an alarm for such an ungodly hour. He rubbed his face, clearing the sleep from his eyes as he ponderously surfaced from the depths of slumber. Just as he was about to sink back into the comfort of his bed, the memory of why he set the alarm struck him. "Shit!" he said, jumping out of bed as though it were suddenly on fire, getting ready in record time, and quickly grabbing a coffee in his travel mug on his way out the door.

This early in the morning, the traffic into the city wasn't too bad, and he made it to the station ahead of schedule, parking close to the door. He quickly drained the last of the coffee from his cup and looked up at the grey, unassuming building that was home to the most popular commercial radio station in the city. He quickly pulled down the sun visor and checked his reflection in the mirror on the back of it, carefully setting his mask in place, before stepping out of the car.

The car door shut with a muted thud, sealing off the last pocket of quiet. The moment Will stepped out, the city hit him full in the face. Engines growled at lights, tyres splashed through last night's rain, and the shuffle of countless feet drummed a steady march along the pavement. A bus screeched to a stop at a nearby bus stop, brakes hissing, doors clattering open to eject another knot of bleary-eyed commuters. The air was thick with petrol fumes and the sour tang of yesterday's rubbish, a reminder that the city never really slept. It just changed shifts.

He stepped into the warm reception area, waving at Sarah, the young girl who worked the reception desk there.

"I'll sign you in and let them know you're here, Will," she said, her tone familiar.

"Thanks, Sarah," he replied.

A few moments later, she came around the front desk with his ID lanyard and passed it to him. "Wendy is already upstairs. Did you want me to walk you up?"

"It's okay, I know the way," he said with a smile.

He hung the lanyard around his neck as Sarah awkwardly returned to her desk, casting a shy look over her shoulder at him as she did so. He made his way upstairs to a small waiting area outside the recording studio, where he found Wendy nursing the cold remnants of her cup of coffee, and she looked up as he approached. "Morning, sunshine," she said.

Will sat down on the sofa opposite her and leaned back, "Morning," he said, groggily.

She held up her sad-looking coffee in a polystyrene cup. "Did you want me to get you one of these? Fair warning, it tastes like shite," she said with a grimace.

Will shook his head. "I'm alright, thanks. I had one on the way over."

He looked at the clock on the wall. Only five minutes to seven, at least it would be over soon. Wendy had immediately picked up her phone and sat ignoring him, so instead he passed the time planning what he would do with his day after he'd finished here, prompting him to lift his phone and shoot off another quick message to Athtar: *Free for coffee in about an hour?*

Over the speakers that quietly piped the show in from next door, he heard DJ Dave announce his next segment: "Coming up after the next song, we have a special guest. Local author Will Preston will be joining us in the studio to give us the lowdown on his upcoming book, so stay tuned, folks."

The next haemorrhage-inducing no-talent pop artist started playing, and through the window, Will saw DJ Dave remove his headphones and stand up, approaching the door.

"Looks like I'm up," he said to Wendy, who looked up briefly from her phone, giving him a smile and a thumbs up.

The door opened. "Will, my man, how have you been, bro?"

Will smiled. He liked Dave. He liked his energy and his eternally optimistic seeming outlook. "Yeah, not too bad. Yourself?"

"Can't complain," Dave said with a little chuckle. "And no one is listening if I do, am I right?"

Will laughed. "Right."

Dave ushered him towards the booth. "Come on, let's get you settled in. This track only has about another minute left on it."

As the final notes of the song faded, DJ Dave's voice returned, bursting with more energy than anyone ought to have at that time of the day. "Welcome back, listeners! You're tuned into DJ Dave's breakfast show, and we're thrilled to have local author Will Preston here in the studio. Will, it's great to have you back on air."

Will settled into the booth, a wry smile playing on his lips as he leaned in towards the boom mic. "Thanks, Dave. Always a pleasure."

"So, Will, my man," Dave said, leaning into the microphone with mock solemnity, "new book on the horizon. Give us the scoop. What's it all about, and is it gonna keep us up past bedtime again?"

Will smiled faintly, leaning forward as though confiding something. "Well... I don't want to give too much away, but let's just say that this time, my adventurers leave the familiar islands of Aruna behind and set off for the mainland. They'll face a struggle that's far more intense than anything they've encountered before. The stakes are higher, and the challenges will test them more than ever before."

Dave clapped his hands together. "You heard it here first, folks. Clear your diaries and stock up on strong coffee."

He wagged a finger at Will with mock accusation. "Now, tell me... did you ever think, when you scribbled down that first book, that you'd end up being such a big-shot bestseller?"

Will chuckled nervously, brushing off the praise. "Honestly, I'm still very uncomfortable with it. I'm just a guy with a story to tell, but I'm truly grateful to every single reader. I love reading the reviews online and hearing people's personal experiences of their journey to Aerinthos."

"That's wholesome, mate," Dave said, leaning back with a grin. "And here I was expecting you to say you wrote it all for the yachts and champagne!"

The studio erupted in a ripple of laughter from the production crew. Will gave a small smile, letting Dave carry the energy forward.

"Alright," Dave continued, eyes narrowing as though he were about to crack a case wide open, "be honest with us. Do you write like clockwork, or are you one of those night owl 'midnight genius' types with coffee stains all over the desk?"

"I'm a routine kinda guy," Will replied. "I always sit down to write at the same time every day. That's not saying I always get something written, or that it's any good."

"Hey, that's the magic, right?" Dave shot back. "Staring at the page until it gives in! I call that the author's workout plan... lots of sitting, plenty of caffeine, occasional crying."

Will let out a laugh despite himself. "Sounds about right."

"Right, lightning round," Dave announced, drumming his fingers on the desk. "No thinking, just fire from the hip. Tea or coffee?"

"Coffee."

"Early bird or night owl?"

"Night owl."

"Pen or keyboard?"

"Keyboard."

Dave pointed at him like he'd just won a prize. "Boom! There you go, folks. Will Preston: powered by coffee, cursed by midnight, enslaved to the keyboard."

The laughter had barely subsided before Dave leaned in again, his tone shifting just enough to catch Will off guard. "Now, people have noticed it's been a little while since the last book. Be honest, mate... was it writer's block, or were you just living the high life too much to pick up the pen?"

Will hesitated, a pause that stretched a fraction longer than was comfortable. His mask wavered. Finally, he said, "Sometimes, if something's worth doing, it's worth doing well. This next book is going to be bigger and better... and that has just taken a little longer than expected. But I promise... it will be worth the wait."

Dave's grin widened like a man who'd just landed a winning hand. "Ooooh, that sounded dramatic. Bigger, better, worth the wait... You heard him, people. And if it isn't, I'll personally demand a refund for everyone..." He threw up his hands quickly. "Joking, joking!"

The laughter carried them into the next segment, Dave's easy banter sweeping over the brief crack that Will's answer had left exposed.

"Thanks for joining us today, Will," Dave said, wrapping up the segment with his trademark exuberance. "And thanks to all our listeners for tuning in. Stay with us... There's more coming up after this short break!"

With that, their monitors filled with the sounds of the commercials running.

Dave and Will stood up again. "That was great, Will. You're a real natural on air. We should get you in for a regular spot sometime," Dave said, his face shining with enthusiasm.

Will laughed. "Maybe if I get a minute to spare. I'll look you up after I get this next book released."

Dave held the door open for him, patting him on the shoulder as he left. Wendy had already left when he got out of the booth, and Will couldn't help but wonder if she had only been there to make sure he actually showed up. He felt bad that he had put her in such a position and made a mental note to make it up to her soon.

Will waved a quick goodbye to Sarah as he stepped back through the radio station's reception and out into the car park. He sank into the soft leather bucket seat of his car, feeling the familiar comfort of the luxury upholstery wrapping around him, and almost immediately, his phone vibrated in his pocket. On the screen, a notification from Athtar blinked up: *Sure, where do you want to meet?*

He hesitated, thumbs hovering over the keyboard. Finally, he tapped out, *How about my place? I can pick you up if you like.*

As he waited for her response, Will started his engine with one hand while cradling his phone in the other. The powerful, smooth rumble of the engine turning over filled the air, the low growl soothing. A moment later, the phone vibrated once more in his hand.

Glancing at the screen, he read the new message: *Okay, pick me up outside the community centre. I'll be there in about ten minutes.* He stowed his device safely away in his pocket again and swiftly punched in the community centre's address into his navigation system.

With a last-minute check of his mirrors, he slowly pulled away from his parking spot, merging into the stop-start traffic of the morning rush. He thought back to a time when this kind of drive would have set his blood boiling and smiled, recognising his growth. Instead, he selected his favourite music streaming app and his playlist started chiming out his favourite songs. Before long, he had moved away from the city centre and the worst of the traffic and in no time pulled up at the community centre where Athtar was already standing waiting, absorbed in whatever she was scrolling on her phone.

He honked his horn and waved as she noticed him there. She smiled and walked over, climbing into the passenger seat.

Will waited as she got buckled up, turning down the music so they could speak. "You didn't take long to blend right in here," he said, looking pointedly at the phone still clutched in her hand. "Do you think you'll be able to give up the lifestyle if we manage to find a portal back?"

She laughed. "It was quite overwhelming when I first got here, I'll be honest. I couldn't fathom this strange magic, but I have to be honest, I will probably miss it... a little. But compared to what we left behind..." her eyes went distant.

He pulled off and started the drive back towards his place on the outskirts of the city. "So you had no luck with any of the other refugees?" he asked.

Athtar shook her head. "I'm sorry, they arrived with nothing but the clothes they were standing in, and have seen nothing of our world since."

Will sighed deeply as he paused at a traffic light. The light turned green, and he continued the journey. "I suppose it was a long shot," he said. "There were only a handful of relics powerful enough to enact this enchantment anyway, and they probably wouldn't have been just lying around in Shadowmoor."

Athtar looked at him with concern, "I really am sorry we didn't have better news, though, Will. I know you were really hoping this would be the key."

He smiled. "It's okay. I am sure we'll figure something else out," he said, as much to comfort her as himself.

Lost in conversation, the miles back to his place passed quickly, and they were soon inside, where Will made them both a coffee and showed Athtar through to the sitting room. She sat first, and as he leaned over to put her cup of coffee down on the table beside her, his amulet fell forward, away from his chest. She gasped as it glinted in the sunlight that flooded in through the floor-to-ceiling glass wall. "Is that...?" She was in such shock that she could barely breathe.

He smiled as he held the amulet between his thumb and forefinger, remembering the quest to the Heart of Eryndor to claim the amulet of purity. "It is," he said, nodding gently, still half lost in the memory.

She looked at it in awe. "May I?" she asked, reverently, her eyes filled with wonder.

He pulled back a moment, not really wanting to relinquish the amulet. It was the last remnant of his time there that he had, and it had never left his chest since his return. The flinch was fleeting, though, and he reached up to release the clasp, removing the amulet and passing it to Athtar, who took it with trembling hands, that same look of reverence verging on worship on her face as she studied the intricate patterns etched into the amulet's surface. Suddenly, she caught her breath and looked at Will sharply. "You idiot!" she said.

Will blinked. "What?"

"All this time you have been seeking a powerful relic of Aruna, and you had one resting against your chest the whole time."

He closed his eyes and tilted his head back to rest on his shoulders as the realisation hit him. "You're right… I am an idiot!"

She held out the amulet, passing it back to him. "Do you have everything else you need to enact the portal enchantment?" she asked him, suddenly very excited.

His eyes darted around nervously as his mind scrambled to take stock of the moment. "I think so," he said after a moment.

She lifted her phone and, after selecting a number from her contacts, pressed the call button, putting it on speaker. The phone only rang a couple of times before Thuridian's voice answered, "Hello?"

"Thuridian, it's me," Athtar said, her words tumbling over one another in her excitement. "How quickly can you gather the others?"

Chapter 4

The energy inside the community centre buzzed with a suppressed tension as Will and Athtar stepped inside. Will smiled at first, mistaking it for excitement, but as they moved deeper inside, the fragile calm snapped. A scuffle broke out across the room as bodies became tangled in a sudden brawl. Shouts erupted, sparking more arguments as tempers flared and the murmurs gave way to chaos.

Thuridian emerged from his office, eyes dark with weary anger. He waited a moment, watching the chaos unfold before him, but when the uproar only grew, he raised his voice, cutting through the din. "Enough!" he bellowed, the echoes of his words reverberating off the walls. The raised voices slowly settled, first to scattered protests, then to silence.

Thuridian strode into the centre of the room, his face like thunder. "What is the meaning of this?" he demanded, his voice dangerously low.

There was a moment of awkward silence before an elderly dwarf stepped forward from his group. "Sorry for the disturbance, Thuridian. It's just... some of us have been talking, and..."

Thuridian raised his eyebrows, his face set in an expression of expectation. "Go on."

The dwarf was now looking down at his feet and squirming uncomfortably, but one of his fellows stepped forward. "Some of us think that the risk of stepping through a portal is too high. We have a life here now... and there are no guarantees that this human you mentioned can actually get us home."

The disagreement between the opposing groups threatened to erupt once again, as voices began to rise in anger. Thuridian simply raised his hand this time, and the murmurs settled down as he gazed around at the group, a thoughtful expression on his face.

Finally, he looked up. "You're right, of course, Durirdir. There are no guarantees... but, for the first time in a long time, there is hope, and for me, that is enough."

Thuridian began pacing in front of them as he weighed up how to continue; all eyes in the room locked on him, waiting for his next words.

"It will, however, be up to each one of you to search your souls to decide what is best for you. This may be our only chance at a return home, but some of you have made this your home now, and whilst we will miss you dearly, the rest of us *will* respect your decision," he said, emphasising that last part as he gazed around at those assembled there.

A hush fell over the room as his words sank in. Thuridian gave them a few moments before he spoke again. "Now, my friends, I present to you someone that many of you have heard of. The hero who lifted that Shadowmoor curse... Will Preston."

A heavy stillness fell over the room as one and all turned to face Will and stare, with unabashed awe on almost every face. Will noted a few peculiar reactions in the crowd. With no apparent pattern, some of those assembled took a knee, their heads bowed towards the floor, and adopted a peculiar gesture with their hands. Athtar leaned in close and whispered in his ear as she spotted him noticing them. "Those are the zealots we mentioned last time."

Will was troubled by that behaviour, but moved on without addressing it further. "Hi everyone," he said, waving his hand at them and smiling, unsure how to begin.

His easy-going approach seemed to put the crowd at ease, though, and a couple of them responded to his greeting.

"I heard what Durirdir was saying about your concerns," he said, pausing for a moment to take a sip of water. He had never been really comfortable addressing groups. "You have every right to be cautious, and I won't try and convince you otherwise."

"What makes you think you can get us home?" came a soft elven voice from the back of the room.

"That's a really good question," he said, casually strolling over to the table where a pile of books and relics sat, and resting one hand gently on them. "Our world is no stranger to magic, but over the years those who practice it have dwindled to the point where it may as well not exist at all... but it's my belief that it is still there, simmering beneath the surface, waiting to be found. I have been studying the arcane beliefs of our world, exploring their mythology and stories that may contain clues, and I found one a few years back in a Norse text about something they refer to as Bifröst."

The room was in absolute silence now, every face locked on his. He took another sip of water before clearing his throat to continue.

"Most of the texts I read referred to Bifröst as a rainbow bridge to Asgard, the home of the gods, but one I read spoke of it as though it were a ritual to summon a portal to any world for which you have a powerful relic in your possession."

A murmur of excited chatter rippled through the crowd, and Will paused to let that sink in for a moment.

Durirdir stepped forward again, bowing respectfully to Will before awkwardly clearing his throat. "Forgive me, but just two days past, Thuridian approached me to ask if we knew of any such relic. And I assume he asked others?"

There was another ripple of agreement that ran through the crowd before Will replied. "That is true... but I neglected to take into account that which has been with me since my return. Behold...The Amulet of Purity," he said, lifting the amulet from beneath his sweater and holding it aloft.

There was a notable gasp from those immediately around him, and much jostling from those further back who were trying to push forward for a better look.

Will gestured to the table and the assorted relics and ingredients there. "As you can see, I have come fully prepared, and for those who wish to return home, I will be attempting the ritual within the hour. Gather what you need for a journey and say your goodbyes to those who are staying behind."

Will stepped back, lifted the artifacts and books from the table, and led the way back to Thuridian's office with Athtar and Thuridian close behind him.

As she closed the door behind them, Athtar turned to Thuridian. "Will they be ready?" she said, her tone concerned.

Thuridian moved around to sit behind his desk, exhaling heavily as he rubbed at his tired face. "I don't know. But ready or not, we're moving forward. What do you need me to do, Will?"

Will was looking down at the Norse text in front of him, double-checking everything one last time. After a moment, he looked up. "I will need to be at the centre of the ritual, holding the amulet, so I will need you to read the ritual scripture."

Thuridian nodded. "I can do that. Is everything else ready?"

Will looked over everything one last time. "I think so," he said.

* * *

Over the course of the next hour, most of the refugees returned with their belongings. Some of those who weren't planning on travelling with them also turned up to offer their support and say their farewells to those friends who would be leaving.

Will moved nervously to the centre of the main room; his footsteps, muffled by the worn carpet, seemed very loud in the silence. All around him, the faces of the gathered refugees shone with anxious hope, each one silently praying that his ritual would finally allow them to return home. He began to mark out intricate, arcane designs on the floor. His hand moved carefully over the worn carpet tiles, tracing lines and curves with painstaking precision as he compared each stroke against the faded images in the ancient text clutched in his hand.

Once the designs were completed, Will set about placing candles and relics at their prescribed locations. Finally, satisfied with his work, he flipped through the fragile pages of the book one final time, locating the passage that Thuridian was to read. It was written in Old Norse, and though the language was archaic, the words were simple enough, and Thuridian had studied them whilst they were waiting for the others to return.

With one final glance around the room, Will nodded to Thuridian, and everyone in the room fell completely silent. Will placed himself in the very centre of the arcane sigil, taking his pendant off and holding it aloft as Thuridian began to chant the spell. His words rolled with an archaic cadence that reverberated off the walls, the echoes taking on a life of their own. The edges of the room seemed to grow darker, and the flames atop the candles stood perfectly still, as though time itself was holding its breath.

As Thuridian reached the final words of the incantation, Will carefully placed the amulet onto the ground at the heart of the sigil. The instant the amulet touched the centre of the sigil, the room was plunged into absolute blackness. Will's heart pounded wildly as the strain of the anticipation gripped him.

Then, as suddenly as it had descended, the darkness was expelled. The candle flames erupted into life, leaping upward and reaching an unnatural height, their light throwing wild, dancing shadows across the walls. Will could feel the energy of the spell fill the room, flowing outward from the amulet in waves of pure light. He stood there for a moment, rejoicing in the exhilarating touch of magic that he'd resigned himself to never feeling again.

But just as hope began to well up inside him, the magic faltered. The towering flames flickered and sputtered a moment before extinguishing entirely, and the feeling of energy ebbed away, leaving the room exactly as it had been a few moments earlier. A stunned silence fell over everyone present. Will stood motionless, lost in the brief, disorientated hope that the ritual had worked. Slowly, a ripple of disappointment began to spread through the gathered refugees as the realisation washed over them.

Will had given himself over wholly to the idea that he was leaving this world and remained kneeling at the centre of the sigil in denial. "No... it cannot be! I felt it... the magic was there," he said, patting the ground as though he could locate the missing magic.

Athtar came over and placed a comforting hand on his shoulder. "It's okay, Will... we were really close, we'll get there."

The disappointment grabbed him by the throat so tightly he could barely breathe, let alone respond. Crushing despair pressed down on him until it seemed to fill his lungs with lead. He turned to face the crowd of refugees, their eyes still clinging to him with desperate hope, and the sight hollowed him. The failure paralysed his throat, leaving him mute before them, caught between shame and sorrow. For a moment, he simply stood there, choking on silence, the weight of their expectation bearing down on him.

At last, as bitter tears threatened to spill, he forced out a strangled apology in barely more than a whisper, before his feet carried him away. Athtar called his name, sharp with concern, but her voice seemed to come from a distance he could not cross. He pressed blindly forward, needing escape more than air.

The streets blurred past in a haze of headlights and shadows, fragments of the journey slipping from memory as if his mind refused to hold them. When awareness finally returned, he found himself once again in his study, hunched over his desk with a lukewarm cup of coffee cupped between his hands. He blinked, taking in his surroundings. He looked around at his huge collection of the arcane. He had dedicated so much time and so many resources to this endeavour, and for what?

He looked over at the blinking cursor on his unfinished manuscript, which also seemed to be attempting to mock his failure, but that just irritated him. "Shut up, you... Get in line," he said angrily, laughing in spite of his heavy heart at the absurdity of his outburst.

The remainder of the day slipped by in a blur of meaningless tasks, his mind unravelled by disappointment. Musings of reassurance flickered in his thoughts, reminders to himself that there would be other chances in the future, but in the end, they felt empty.

He tried to get an early night, hoping that sleep would offer some kind of escape from his self-inflicted torture, but it too eluded him, slipping through his fingers like the sands of time. By just after midnight, after another long stretch of staring at the ceiling, he glanced at his phone's screen, the harsh glow flooding the room with a pale light.

He pressed on a message notification and found a message from Athtar: Are you alright?

Will stared at the words for a long while, thumb hovering above the screen. A dozen replies formed and faded in his mind, none of them adequate. In the end, he set the phone aside and switched it off, telling himself he would answer tomorrow. Tonight, he had no strength left to explain.

He sighed deeply, realising that frustration was keeping sleep at bay, but that thought only served to frustrate him further. Deciding to give up on it altogether, he threw off the covers and dragged himself out of bed. The night was still and empty around him, but at least in his study, he would have something to distract him, even if only for a little while.

For a fleeting moment, Will considered spending some time writing, but he quickly dismissed the idea. His creativity was always at its most elusive when his mind was so heavily burdened. Instead, he reached for the box that had arrived today from his usual rare book supplier. With a swift motion, he sliced the tape with a letter opener, the gentle scrape of steel on cardboard breaking the silence. Carefully, he opened the lid and peered inside.

At the top of the pile was an old book, its leather cover darkened with age, its texture unlike anything he'd encountered before. He ran his fingers over the raised pentagram embossed on the cover, and the image of Baphomet within it burned into his mind, searing itself into his thoughts. It was difficult not to recoil as his hand traced the contours of the pentagram, an overwhelming sense of wrongness emanating from the book's very presence.

With a growing sense of unease, he moved to a nearby lamp, hoping to cast enough light on the book to avoid having to turn on the ceiling light. He settled into an armchair, and he gingerly opened the first page, feeling the fragile paper crinkle beneath his fingers.

As he scanned through the opening paragraphs of the book, he came to realise it was a grimoire of a coven from the American Midwest, its origins tracing back to the 1800s. Will had leafed through countless books like this, his eyes now able to recognise the key signs of something valuable, but after skimming a few more pages, he'd sensed this one didn't hold much promise. With a resigned sigh, he snapped the book shut, the sound cutting sharply through the silence. He stood up, about to return the book to the box, when something... just one word, flashed at the corner of his vision from the last page he'd turned, that stopped him in his tracks. A wave of disbelief swept over him, and for a split second, he thought he was mistaken, or perhaps the dim light playing tricks on his eyes. Shaking his head, he opened the book once more, his hand trembling almost imperceptibly as his curiosity began to overpower his hesitation.

He scanned down the page, moving his finger across the lines until he found the last passage that he'd read... and there it was.

—Hearken, ye seekers of forbidden lore, and attend unto these words. In the year of our Lord 1812, when the night was as black as the abyss and the stars hid their countenance, I, Elinora, servant of shadow and hunger for power, did resolve to transcend the frail

limits of mortal ken. With trembling hand and heart resolute, I did prepare the rite most dire, that I might summon forth the dread demon Moloch, whose name is writ large in the infernal registers.

Will was shaken to his core. Not by the nature of the satanic ritual described, for he had read many grimoires from that era, and they all followed the same kind of patterns, but the mention of the demon lord Moloch, whose name he had only ever heard uttered previously by the mages of Thorn Island, when describing the deal Malakar had made with the lord of the underworld. Could it be that this was the same demon? Will continued reading, now fully engrossed.

By the ancient incantations, drawn from the tongue of perdition, I invoked his presence. Lo, the veil betwixt our world and that of eternal damnation did wane, and there, in the midst of unholy flame, Moloch did appear, his visage both terrible and seductive. He spake unto me in a voice that chilled the marrow of my bones, offering power beyond measure in exchange for that price most grievous: my very soul.

As he continued reading, Will's mind began to construct an idea. One born of the dangerous combination of exhaustion and desperation, but the more he read, the more he considered it his only hope. He looked down again, eager to read more.

Thus, in a covenant sealed with blood and fire, I did bind my essence to his dark dominion. Henceforth, by the mark of this infernal pact, the forces of night and fury bend to my command, though the weight of eternal damnation ever lurketh upon my spirit. Let all who read these pages beware: ambition pursued through the exchange of one's soul is a peril no mortal should ever court.

Will finished reading the last passage and exhaled sharply, unaware that he had actually been holding his breath. He carefully turned the next page, not wanting to damage the extremely dry and brittle paper, and as he'd hoped, there was the summoning ritual. The witch had carefully detailed everything he would need and written the incantation in spidery script.

His immediate instinct was to put the book away, but as he went to place it on the bookshelf, he paused as an idea slithered into his sleep deprived mind and took seed. He absently ran his finger over the spidery script on the spine of the book as the idea grew into a compulsion. His whole being recoiled, screaming at him to stop, yet the longing to return to Aerinthos rose louder still, smothering every instinct. With his father's stroke, the failed portal, and nights starved of rest weighing on him, the call of that lost world was impossible to ignore. It felt less like a choice than a sentence, as though fate itself had steered his hands to the page and left him no way back.

Once he had gathered everything he needed, he moved out into the garden. He didn't know what kind of damage a demon summoning would cause inside the house, and it was a warm night anyway.

Under the watchful gaze of a pale moon, Will carefully began marking out the sigils on the ground, the pentagram containing symbols specific to the ritual. He placed the necessary relics at the prescribed locations, laying a bronze bowl at the heart of the design where he began mixing the herbs. As a precaution, he laid out a ring of salt around the summoning circle before stepping inside one last time, kneeling in front of the bowl. Taking a knife and running it down the palm of his hand, Will prepared the necessary blood sacrifice required for the ritual before igniting the contents of the bowl and speaking the words of the incantation out loud:

"Moloch, audi me. Veni ad me, daemon inferni. Per sacrificium huius Sanguinis, te invoco."

The words reverberated within him, a coil of ancient energy that wrapped around his soul and surged into the very bowels of the earth. The ground trembled, gently at first, then with growing insistence, while the air thickened and warmed, carrying an overpowering scent of sulphur. A metallic taste filled his mouth, and his nostrils burned with the acrid sting of brimstone.

Then, from the murky shadows at the edge of the circle, she emerged... a vision of haunting beauty. Her dark hair cascaded like silk over porcelain skin, and her presence exuded an otherworldly seduction that rendered Will momentarily mute. Her eyes, glowing with an amber light that seemed to hold centuries of secrets, locked onto his with an unnerving familiarity.

She glided forward gracefully until she stood before him. Brushing a cool hand down his stubbled cheek, she murmured into his ear in a purring voice, her hot breath disturbing the small hairs on the side of his neck, "What are the odds of this chance encounter? I have been looking for you. We had a deal, and it's time for you to pay."

Her words sent a shiver through him, and as if sensing the turmoil beneath his stoic exterior, she reached out and seized his chin, tilting his head from side to side. Her gaze bore into him, probing the depths of his soul. "Wait… you're not Malakar… Or at least not entirely. What trickery is this?" she demanded.

Will's mind raced. The hairs on the back of his neck stood on end as he recognised the danger he was in. He explained, haltingly, that Malakar was but a fragment. A fractured aspect of his own soul, now reluctantly reunited. Her expression shifted subtly, irritation dissolving into a seductive purr. "Well, it seems that unless you separate again, I can't settle my debt with you… or him… unless," her voice trailed off into a suggestive murmur. "…there's a deal you need to make?"

Will swallowed hard, trying not to show how much his skin was crawling as he pulled his face away from her and attempted to project a confidence he didn't feel. "I need a way back to Aruna," he said simply. She reached out and placed a hand on his forehead, and images began flashing through his memory. Images of his time in Aruna, of his life since his return, and finally of the failed Norse portal enchantment. Finally, she released him, and his shoulders slumped, leaving him feeling drained and violated.

"I can help you," she said. "But I will require payment."

He had been prepared for this. He knew the cost, and he nodded with only a slight reluctance. "My soul is yours."

A wicked chuckle escaped Moloch's lips. "By the seven circles, no. Why would I want such a tarnished prize? Besides, the technicality of Malakar already owing me a soul leaves the acquisition of your essence in something of a grey area."

He gazed at her, confused. "So, what then? What would you have from me as payment?"

A sly smile slid across her face. "A trifling thing, really. All I want is a favour."

"A favour?" he said, parroting her words numbly.

"That's all," she said, her eyes burning with the hunger of sealing the deal.

He considered this for a moment, recognising the danger in her eyes. "And what if I can't help you when you call in your favour?"

Her smile vanished as if cut away, and for an instant the illusion of beauty faltered. The air rippled, the candle flames guttering as something vast and malignant pressed close. Her eyes burned with a feral hunger, and her voice dropped to a guttural rasp that vibrated through the marrow of his bones.

"Break our bargain," she hissed, "and I will take one you hold dearest. I will strip them apart, piece by fragile piece, until their screams are sewn into the fabric of your dreams. You will wake every day already broken, until the only comfort left to you is the thought that at last I will come for you... and when I do, there will be no end to it."

Then, as quickly as it had surfaced, the distortion melted away. Her beauty reasserted itself, smile languid and alluring once more, as though the slip had never happened. "But that won't be a problem, will it? It's just a little favour."

Will wavered for a moment, unsure of what to do, but then an image of Lyra rose in his mind, and his resistance wavered. "Okay," he said. "How do we do this, then?"

She placed a hand on the side of his face. "You've already made the blood oath in summoning me. All you have to do now is seal the deal with a kiss."

Will squinted. "That's it? I am not sure what I expected, but that wasn't it."

She leaned in close, bringing her lips close to his. He closed his eyes and leaned forward, pressing his lips to hers. He felt an energy pass between them as they exchanged a kiss, something dark and foreboding, but he was committed now to this path, and the prospect of being reunited with Lyra overrode all his other senses.

Every instinct screamed that he was making a dreadful mistake, but he pushed those voices down, wilfully ignoring them. Moloch pulled back after a moment, and the sensation he had felt moments earlier was gone, replaced by an oppressive stillness that felt like the earth itself was standing still in disbelief at what he had just done.

Shock held him in place for a brief moment, but he soon regained his wits and looked up. Moloch was standing before him, a victorious smile playing about the corners of her mouth that left him wondering if somehow she'd gotten the better end of the bargain. "So what now?" he said, breaking the silence.

She paused a moment longer, savouring the moment of victory, before speaking. "Tomorrow, call your little group of refugees together. Tell them that you missed a key part of the portal spell last time you tried it. When you attempt it again, use my sigil and add a blood sacrifice to the spell. I will hear your call and ensure the portal opens. As far as anyone else is concerned, the great hero, Will Preston, will have saved the day... again."

Without another word, Moloch gazed directly at him, snapped her fingers, and folded back into the shadows, the flames in the bowl snuffing out in response to her absence.

Will stood shivering in the centre of the pentagram despite the warmth of the night air for some time. He knew that he should probably try and go back to bed for a while, but the sun was already painting the eastern sky with the gentle blush that indicated dawn was approaching, and his racing pulse meant that any kind of meaningful rest was probably not his to have this night.

Chapter 5

Through gritty eyes, Will watched the sunrise with a quiet sense of farewell that morning. He realised he had rarely taken the time to appreciate the small enjoyments like watching the sun rise in a long time, and it felt fitting. He left Wendy a message, saying he was taking her advice and going on a retreat to get the book finished, and would be unreachable for some time. As an afterthought, he also sent his mum and dad a message to the same effect.

Later that morning, he reached out to Athtar and Thuridian, arranging another meeting at the community centre. The events of the previous night left him feeling oddly detached, a sense of disconnection he hoped was merely the result of a sleepless night, rather than a residual effect of his unholy communion.

He gathered everything he needed for the ritual and drove to meet them. The centre buzzed with an air of renewed anticipation. He noted with relief that more faces had turned up this time; the delay having afforded them the chance to reconsider their choice, rather than regret their decision when it was too late.

As Moloch had instructed, Will began to reconstruct the Norse portal spell, with the additional, subtle changes that would allow her to intercede and activate the portal for them. He could see Thuridian consulting with the book out of the corner of his eye, shaking his head, his face perturbed, but Will kept his head down and continued working.

He was so engrossed in his task that when Thuridian spoke from just behind him, he nearly jumped out of his skin. "I think you've done that part of the sigil wrong, Will."

Will tried to look nonchalant as he continued marking out Moloch's sigil. "No, it's right," he said, finalising the last part of the design.

He looked again at Thuridian's troubled face. He didn't like lying to him, but the others could never know the truth. Finally, he gave Thuridian the enchantment to read, mostly to placate him, knowing it was now a meaningless part of the process. Once everything was ready, he knelt at the centre of the sigil with the amulet in his hand. The cut he had opened up in his palm last night was still fresh and barely healed over, so as Thuridian approached the last part of the incantation, he squeezed the amulet really tight, feeling the hard metal edge slipping between the folds of skin and reopening the wound. As he pressed the blood-soaked amulet into the carpet where the sigil of Moloch was marked, the candles flared, and a darkness pressed in from the edges of the room. This time, though, Will could feel Moloch's heavy, malevolent presence in the room. The sigils started to glow with a bright green fire that pulsed in time with the throbbing in his freshly opened wound. After a moment, the candles extinguished, and with a whoosh, a pulse of light energy burst forth from the far wall, quickly retreating to form the event horizon of the portal that stood there like a vertical surface of water, casting a gentle glow across the faces of everyone there as it moved in sluggish rotation.

With the success of the portal, a cheer went up from everyone, but even though they were itching to head through the portal, every face turned to Will, looking for his instruction.

He almost resented their trust. He hadn't earned it, and given the devious manner in which he had managed to succeed, he was quite sure he didn't deserve it. He was, however, adept at wearing the mask that the occasion demanded and looked out at them all with a wide grin on his face. "It looks like we're going home, friends!" he said.

A ripple of excited chatter ran through the room, and everyone grabbed their packs and formed an orderly line. Will turned to Athtar and Thuridian. "Shall we?" he said, turning and facing the portal as a growing wave of excitement built inside him at the prospect of returning to the place that, somehow, felt more like home than the world he'd grown up in.

Will squared his shoulders and stepped up to the portal. He tried to suppress the feeling of dread that had settled in his chest as he walked confidently forward, passing through the surface. The familiar sensation of portal travel gripped him as he felt his body pass through the event horizon. He felt pulled in a million directions, his mind filled with a flood of thoughts and emotions, as though witnessing the birth of a thousand worlds in an instant. As they were ejected from the portal on the other side, there was a momentary weightlessness before they were surreptitiously deposited on the rough stone platform.

He had no idea where their journey would lead, but his face broke into a wide grin as he looked around and saw a familiar sight. It looked different under the light of the moon, but the distant crashing of the waves on the nearby bluff, and the sight of the carved stone pillars that he had seen so many years ago, flooded his mind with memories, both happy and painful, as he remembered those fateful final days of the journey into Shadowmoor. In small groups, the refugees began appearing behind them and spreading out into the ruins to make space for everyone arriving. They all remained quietly reverent, recognising this place as somewhere deserving of respect. For a moment, they stood still, letting their eyes adjust to the sudden darkness as the portal behind them flickered briefly, before collapsing into itself with a faint rush of wind.

Will looked around, taking a quick head count, although in reality, he had no idea how many were in the room back in the centre. "Did we all make it?" he said, cutting through the silence in the wake of the portal closing.

There was a slight murmur of confirmation from those around him, and he grunted in satisfaction before sitting down on the stone platform, tugging at some grass as his mind sank into an exhausted numbness.

He could see Thuridian and Athtar exchanging a worried glance and looked up at them in irritation. "What's up with you two?"

Thuridian stepped forward, gesturing to the frightened faces of those who stood nearby, huddled in small groups. "Do you have any idea where we are? We could do with putting their minds at rest that we have arrived at the correct destination."

Anger and resentment rose in Will at this request for a moment. These people were not his responsibility; why should it be his place to put their minds at rest? But as that thought ran through his mind, he looked around in shame, realising that they were indeed his responsibility. It was Malakar who had created the Shadowmoor curse that had trapped them, and his defeat at Will's hand that had banished them to another world. He rubbed at his face, trying to rub away some of the fatigue that was clouding his senses, before wearily pushing himself to his feet. "Good news, folks," he said, loud enough to be heard by everyone, "We are, by my estimation, some distance to the north east of the farm town of Candleford on South Aruna."

There was a notable easing of tension amongst the group at this news, and a gasp of relief rippled through the air as voices rose in joyous celebration. Will removed himself to sit apart from the others as they chatted amongst themselves, unaware of his absence.

The group lingered in the ruins for much of the remainder of the night. Though excited to be home and eager to reunite with long-lost family, they also cherished the bonds and connections they had forged over the past ten years and were reluctant to part ways with old friends. After much heartfelt reminiscing and shared tears, the refugees gradually began to peel off into smaller groups, each heading in a different direction.

Thuridian opened the temple's portal, creating a path for those who needed to return to North Aruna. Finally, when the last few refugees began their farewells, shaking Thuridian's hand and thanking him for his leadership during their time in Will's world, he approached Will, who was still sitting apart from the others, alone with his troubled thoughts.

"It seems this is where we part ways, my friend. Though we have only recently met, I feel as if we have known each other for a lifetime," Thuridian said, his gentle voice cutting through Will's brooding.

Will looked up at him, a genuine smile splitting his features, despite the inner turmoil he felt. "I feel the same way," he replied, standing and reaching out a hand in friendship.

Thuridian clasped Will's hand firmly, his eyes lingering a fraction too long. "You've done what few others could. Whatever path lies ahead, you've given us a chance."

But the warmth in his words didn't quite reach his face. There was a weight behind his gaze, as though he was studying Will for something unseen. After a pause, he added quietly, "Take care of yourself, Preston. And of those who walk beside you."

He released Will's hand and turned back to Athtar, who was nearby overseeing the departure of the last group heading north toward Stonehelm. "Well... will you join me, Miss Morran?" he asked as he opened the portal to Thorn Island. "Or will you be going home to Silverwood?"

Athtar glanced at the swirling portal as it burst into existence within the stone archway behind Thuridian, then back at Will, pausing for a moment as she considered the question. "I will return home in due time, but I have a strong sense that my fate lies to the south. I will journey with Will for a while," she said.

Thuridian nodded in approval. "Then farewell, my friend. We have been through much together. Until we meet again."

Athtar waved softly, smiling as he made his way towards the portal. "Bye for now, Thuridian."

With that, Thuridian stepped through the portal, and moments later, it collapsed upon itself, plunging the area into silence once more.

For a long, quiet moment, Will and Athtar sat on a crumbling wall at the edge of the ruin. The only sounds were the distant crashing of waves against the shore and the gentle murmur of the night as the horizon slowly emerged from the darkness.

Without warning, Will slapped his thighs and sprang to his feet, startling Athtar. "I suppose we should get going then," he said, leaving no room for discussion as he turned south-west and strode away into the night. Athtar simply nodded, standing and brushing the debris from her clothes as she turned to follow him from the ruins.

It wasn't long before the sun crept over the eastern horizon, painting the sky in soft pastel hues that lit their path. Despite the weariness that seemed to make every step he took a chore, the journey stirred a torrent of emotions within him. Emotions that flickered across his face like the pages of an open book caught in the breeze. Athtar observed him in silence for a moment before softly asking, "Are you okay?"

Will glanced at her, a hint of confusion in his eyes as if he were noticing her presence for the first time. He paused a moment, wondering whether he really wanted to share this deeply personal moment, but finally he smiled. "The last time I travelled this way, I was on my final journey to Shadowmoor... to confront Malakar. I was in the company of Lyra and our dear friend Lolmig, who sadly perished defending us from one of the creatures of that cursed realm."

She gazed at him, sympathy furrowing her brow. "I am sorry to hear that. I can tell that he meant a lot to you."

Will nodded, stopping for a moment to look around and get his bearings. "He was like a father to us. I have no idea what happened to him after I left, but I left instructions with those who remained to take care of his remains."

Athtar looked at the distant hills, now bathed in the warm morning sunlight, as the landscape came to life with the start of a new day. "We can rest for a while if you like. I know you've had a long day. But it is only a few more miles, if I am not mistaken."

Will shook his head. "I can rest when we get there. Let's push on."

They continued on, every landmark releasing a fresh wave of memories, but underneath all the bittersweet emotions that were being rekindled by his return home was a growing excitement that was building inside him with each passing mile. He had missed her so much this past decade. He had often wondered what she was doing over the years, but now, for the first time in all those years, the question seemed more important than ever. It suddenly crossed his mind that she may have moved on. She may have settled down with someone, perhaps had a family. That thought almost stopped him in his tracks.

It was nearly noon when they crested the hill where Will had first laid eyes on Candleford, the very spot where he had first witnessed the devastating effects of the Shadowmoor curse. Today, the town stretched out vibrantly across the valley, alive with the hustle of its farming community, surrounded by patchwork fields of golden crops. As he took in the scene, a disturbing flicker seized his vision, and an ominous feeling of dread settled in the pit of his stomach. For a fleeting moment, the idyllic town was overlaid by a grim, cursed vision of what had been. The dark, cursed town that had teemed with monstrous creatures, and where no sunlight touched the land.

Will's heart pounded as he rubbed at his eyes, desperate to dispel the unsettling image. His sudden motion and pained expression drew Athtar's concerned gaze. "Are you sure you're okay?" she asked sharply.

He shook his head, re-examining the vista until the sinister overlay dissolved back into the familiar, lively townscape. "Just tired," he replied, straightening his shoulders and taking a deep, steadying breath. As his heart rate slowed and his breathing resumed a normal rhythm, the same concern that had been nagging him all day intruded into his thoughts once more... *had the darkness of his deal with Moloch begun to infect him?*

"Let's head into town," he said, his tone weary, but the prospect of seeing Lyra lifted his spirits once more.

It was almost impossible not to enjoy their stroll that afternoon despite the weariness in his bones and the dark thoughts that troubled his mind. As they ambled through the rolling fields, the idyllic sounds of birdsong filled the air. The warm afternoon sun bathed the landscape in a comforting glow that salved all of Will's lingering worries. He smiled, breathing deep, as if he might absorb every ounce of that revitalising energy, letting it seep deep into his soul. Memories of Lyra's tales of this place played in his mind, and he smiled as he recalled how her face had lit up with joy as she described every detail.

There were several farms scattered throughout the valley, and Will wasn't certain which one belonged to Lyra's family. Rather than walking the entire Valley searching for them, he and Athtar made their way into the town, seeking information. The outskirts of the small town were mostly reserved for the modest homes of the town's residents, but at this hour, everyone was out and about. There were a few neighbours chatting on front porches and children laughing in the streets, but Will decided to continue on toward the town centre rather than bother them.

As they rounded a corner that led to the small plaza at the town centre, Will was once again afflicted by the same, flickering visual anomaly that had troubled him when looking down on the town. For a moment, the white stone fountain at the centre of the market square flickered, and in its place stood the tormented, twisted onyx version from the curse, oozing dark ichor that stained the cobbles. The haunting image flickered in and out of focus, moving in and out of his vision as though the nightmare was trying to reassert itself on the landscape. He instinctively rubbed his eyes, and once again the vision faded when he looked back up.

The town centre was buzzing with activity. A bustling market encircled the fountain, where traders enthusiastically sold locally grown produce and artisans traded their handmade goods. The rich scents of fresh herbs and ripe fruits filled the air, and somewhere nearby, Will could smell a bakery where the sweet aroma of baked pastries lured nearby shoppers. On the far side of the plaza, the rhythmic ringing of a smith's hammer echoed throughout the square, punctuating the friendly hum of conversation and laughter that filled the air. The smith, a sturdy man with soot-stained hands, worked diligently on repairing broken farm equipment and shaping horseshoes, his friendly face ruddy from the heat of the forge.

Will nudged Athtar to get her attention. "Let's ask him," he said, pointing at the smith, "If they have a farm, no doubt they will use his services."

Athtar nodded, her expression approving. "Makes sense," she said.

They slowly made their way through the market square, the noise from the smithy growing louder as they approached. When they got there, they waited for the smith to finish working on the piece he was hammering, not wanting to interrupt. After a moment, he stopped hammering, inspecting the piece critically, before moving it over to the forge to put it back in the heat again for a moment.

Turning around from the flames, his face broke into a wide grin as he saw them waiting uncertainly by the entrance. He rubbed his hands down his apron a couple of times to take the bulk of the grime off and then thrust out his hand in greeting. "Gregor, the smith. How may I help ye today, friends?"

Will took an immediate liking to this man who stood head and shoulders over both of them, grinning from ear to ear. He was the kind of soul who embraced life fully and put all that positive energy back into the world around him. He reached out and grasped Gregor's hand, giving it a friendly shake. "We're just looking for information, friend. My name is Will Preston, and this is my friend Athtar Morran, and we're looking to locate a farm nearby where someone I used to know lives," he said.

The smith's face had changed to one of suspicion at the mention of their names, but he quickly glanced at the amulet at Will's neck, and his eyebrows raised, his mouth dropping open. "You'd be looking for Miss Lyra's farm?" Gregor said, his voice trembling in awe.

Will raised one eyebrow, looking at Athtar with a confused expression, who just shrugged.

He looked back at Gregor inquisitively. "I am, but how did you—?"

"She talked about you a lot, Mister Will. After... you know... we all returned. I almost feels like I knows you, sir."

Will smiled, warmed by this development. "Well, Gregor. It seems you have me at a disadvantage. But if you could direct me to their family farm, I would be most grateful."

"I can go one better than that Mr Will. See that there piece of equipment? Well, I am due to deliver that to them this afternoon after I finish my work here. I can give youse a lift on my cart if ya like?"

"You're too kind, Gregor. Is there some place we might get a meal nearby whilst we wait for you to finish your work?"

Gregor pointed across the square with a huge hand. "Next street over... The old Ox. Best inn in town...well, it's the only inn in town, but it's bloody good food they do at any rate."

Will thanked Gregor, and he and Athtar left to go in search of food and rest, promising to return later that afternoon.

Athtar grinned at him as they strolled casually through the market square. "Seems you're something of a celebrity here," she said, nudging him with her elbow.

He looked down at his feet, looking slightly abashed. "It seems that way, doesn't it?"

They made their way to the inn and sat down, ordering hot stew and a fresh, crusty loaf. The inn was quiet at this time of day, but when asked about that, the server told them they should return after the farm hands were in from the fields. Will and Athtar loitered for some time after they had eaten, chatting, their bellies full and the calm atmosphere of the inn almost lulling them to sleep. When they noticed the sun lowering in the sky, they approached the bar to settle their tab, only to be informed that there would be no charge. Word of their arrival in town had raced ahead of them, and the innkeeper had left strict instructions that their meal was on him.

Once again, Will was left feeling that strange sense of unwanted celebrity that he had been shunning in his own realm, but he was grateful for the food and rest.

They made their way back to the smithy just as Gregor was checking the ropes that tied down the load in the back of his cart. In the front, the cart was pulled by a huge beast of a horse, who stood snorting impatiently.

"That's a big horse, Gregor," Will said as he approached.

Gregor looked up at the sound of his voice. "You know what they say about dogs resembling their owners? Well, Yellin here is like my dog."

"I see that, now you mention it. The resemblance is uncanny," Athtar said, chuckling as she laid an open hand on the side of the horse's neck.

"What do you need us to do, Gregor?" Will asked.

Gregor had his back to them as he secured the forge with a huge padlock. "Just climb aboard, my friends. It won't take us long to reach the farm."

They both climbed up and sat on the hard oak bench behind Yellin, and waited for Gregor. A moment later, he climbed in from the other side and filled the remainder of the bench, holding the reins negligently in one hand. "Are you ready?" he said.

They both nodded, and he snapped the reins sharply. The horse gave a withering look over his shoulder before begrudgingly moving forward.

Will gave a short laugh. "It seems your horse has a bit of an attitude."

Gregor shot a wide grin. "Again, he is very much like his owner."

Gregor steered their little wagon through the wide market square and then out through the tighter residential streets, eventually making his way onto the dirt road at the edge of the town that led out into the farmland. The lowering sun cast a golden glow that framed the edges of every blade of grass and ear of corn in the fields to the sides of the road, and cast long shadows across the landscape. Will found himself leaning back on the cart and closing his eyes, more relaxed than he'd felt in ages, listening to the creaking of the cart and the final farewell songs of the birds as they settled in for the night ahead.

He was suddenly jolted awake as the wheel hit a particularly hard tree root that lay exposed across the track, rousing him from an extremely deep, if short, nap. As he rubbed his eyes, trying to refocus, he realised that they were on a farm track. His heart fluttered with excitement, clearing the last of the groggy feeling from his mind, as he realised he was just moments away. "Is that their place?" he said, turning to Gregor.

Gregor nodded, his eyes fixed ahead as he continued winding the wagon up the dusty track. The road was intermittently shaded by the long, languid shadows of ancient trees that lined the road leading to the house.

As they approached, a man, about Will's age, stepped out of the front door, wearing simple clothing that was marked and worn by the heavy use of someone who toils in the fields. He stood on the raised wooden porch that wrapped around the house, peering down the lane, shielding his eyes from the lowering sun with a hand pressed to his forehead. When he recognised Gregor, he smiled and waved, making his way down the steps to the yard, standing amongst the fowl who were strutting around, scratching at the dirt.

"You've repaired that plough already, Gregor?" said the man in an easy tone.

Gregor jumped down from the wagon and started untying the ropes that held the load in place. "You know me, Jacob, I can't see a job sitting around for too long."

Jacob moved forward and started helping to untie the ropes as Will and Athtar jumped down from the wagon. A sinking feeling had developed at the pit of Will's stomach at the sight of the man in front of the house. Was this Lyra's husband? Had he made the trip here for nothing?

Jacob looked over to where Will and Athtar were standing, looking uncomfortable. "And who are your friends, Gregor? You're not from Candleford, are you?"

Gregor slapped his forehead. "How forgetful of me. This is Will Preston and Athtar Morran," he said apologetically.

Jacob's face dropped, looking back and forth between the two of them for a moment and then back at Gregor.

Gregor continued on with the introductions. "And this," he said, gesturing towards Jacob. "is Jacob... Lyra's—" Will could barely contain the tension as he waited to find out who this significant man in Lyra's life was. It seemed that the pause went on indefinitely, so much so that when the word was finally spoken, he didn't hear correctly.

"I'm sorry, I missed that," he said. "Jacob is Lyra's...?"

"Brother," said Jacob, striding towards Will. "And our family owes you a great deal, my friend."

Jacob reached Will and pulled him into a tight embrace. "Come, let us go inside and have a drink. We can unload the wagon in the morning. You will all stay here tonight. There's hay and feed in the barn for Yellin, Gregor," he said, gesturing towards a large barn, some distance away.

They followed Jacob as he pushed through the creaky front door and into the kitchen, where the golden glow of the setting sun bathed the room in warm light. The air smelled faintly of woodsmoke and something rich cooking in the oven. Jacob kicked off his dirt-caked boots by the door, so Will and Athtar followed suit, leaving their footwear beside his.

"Sit, sit," Jacob said, gesturing to the sturdy farmhouse table in the centre of the room. As they settled into the worn wooden chairs, Jacob busied himself gathering a bottle of whiskey and a few glasses. He paused to wipe the worst of the grime from them with a rag before setting them down on the table.

Before sitting, Jacob leaned toward the open doorway that led to the hall and bellowed, "Darius! We've got company… get your ass in here!"

With that, Jacob dropped into his seat at the head of the table and poured five generous measures of whiskey. "So, Will," he began, sliding a glass across to him, "I've heard so much about you I feel like I know you already. But Lyra said you'd gone back to your own world. How is it you're back?"

Will's heart lifted at the mention of Lyra's name, a flicker of warmth swelling in his chest. He smiled as he considered how to answer.

"Well, it wasn't easy," he said, fingers tracing the rim of his glass. "I have spent years searching for a way, until just the other day, Athtar here found me, and—" He paused, interrupted by the glass pane in the door shuddering violently.

Gregor stomped in, boots thudding against the floor. "Oh, sorry, friends," he said, realising he'd interrupted.

"Not at all, Gregor. Come and take the weight off," Jacob said, sliding another glass his way.

Gregor took a grateful sip, exhaling as he eased back into his chair.

"So," Jacob prompted, "you were saying?"

Will took a breath, choosing his words carefully. He described his years spent hunting for relics in his world, how he had stumbled upon the Norse ritual, carefully omitting the dark bargain he'd struck with Moloch. Between them, Will and Athtar recounted the failed first attempt and their eventual success in forming a portal as Jacob continued to keep their glasses topped off.

In the comfortable silence that followed their tale, Gregor's gaze drifted to the untouched glass of whiskey still sitting on the table. He turned to Jacob.

"Will Darius not join us?" he asked quietly.

Jacob's eyes shifted to the fire, the dancing flames reflected in his distant stare. His face tightened as though the question had struck a nerve.

"No," he said at last, voice low and tired. "I guess not... You know how he can be."

Gregor nodded, his expression heavy with sympathy. "It's been some time now. Is he no better?"

Jacob let out a long breath, his shoulders slumping like a man buckling under unseen weight. "He has some better days," he admitted. "But he's not much help around the farm anymore. I'm exhausted... trying to keep everything running while he just..." He paused, simply gesturing towards the door. He clenched his jaw before continuing. "I am having to stay strong for both of us. When do I get to mourn?"

Will felt his chest tighten as a wave of sympathy overwhelmed him. He knew what Jacob was going through. He opened his mouth to offer some words of comfort, but something else struck him. A slow, creeping dread took hold, twisting his stomach.

"She's not here, is she?" he asked, his voice quieter than he'd intended. "Lyra... I mean."

Jacob turned back to him, and the look in his eyes confirmed what Will already suspected.

"No," Jacob said, his voice almost a whisper. "It's just me and Darius now... though most of the time, I feel like I'm here alone."

Will's world tilted. The room suddenly felt colder despite the fire's warmth as a deep, resounding fear gripped his heart. How had he not considered this? Ten years... How had he been so naïve to believe everything would be as it was?

"Where is she?" he asked, barely able to get the words out. The question clung to his throat, as the fear that asking the question out loud might somehow make his worst fear a reality made the words hard to get out.

Jacob drained the last of his whiskey, the glass hitting the table a little too hard as he set it down. He grabbed the bottle again, topping up his own glass before pouring another round for everyone else.

"Not long after our parents were killed... bandits on the road back from Decan," Jacob began, his voice tightening again, "she got a visit from an old mage... Eldran, I think his name was. He didn't stay long, but when he left... she went with him. She said there was something important she needed to help with and that she'd come back when she could."

His gaze dropped to his glass, but the flickering light of the fire betrayed the pain in his eyes.

At first, he was deeply relieved. He had feared the worst when Jacob was talking of grief and loss, but in the immediate wake of his relief, his mind began racing with a dozen questions all at once. Why would Eldran have been here? What could possibly have been so important to pull her away from the family farm at such a critical time? He was snapped out of his spiralling thoughts by a light touch on the arm by Athtar, who was looking at him, concern written all over her face.

The evening wore on, and eventually Jacob found them all blankets before retreating to his room for the night. The house soon fell quiet, save for the faint crackling of the dying fire and the occasional creak of wood settling in the cooler night air.

Will lay on his back, his eyes fixed on the dim shadows dancing across the ceiling. He hadn't anticipated this turn of events. In his mind, he'd imagined their reunion a thousand times. He'd pictured her smile breaking through the crowd, her arms flung around him, the warmth of her presence washing away all the doubts that had gnawed at him these past years. But instead, there was only this hollow ache that seemed to deepen the longer he lay in the dark.

He'd been so wrapped up in his single-minded drive to return to Aruna that he hadn't considered what might await him when he arrived. He'd clung to the idea that if he could just get back, everything would make sense again.

The shadows shifted again, and for a fleeting moment, he thought he saw a figure standing in the corner of the room. His breath caught, but when he blinked, the figure was gone, leaving only a cold unease coiling in his gut.

He sighed heavily, closed his eyes, and turned onto his side, pulling the blanket tighter around himself.

Chapter 6

Will tossed and turned restlessly, neither awake nor truly asleep, as his overactive mind wrestled with the day's events. When his mind eventually released him from the waking world and allowed him to sink into slumber, it offered no rest or relief.

He found himself standing in a hellish landscape. A twisted, nightmarish realm that seemed to seethe and writhe as though the land itself were alive with every act of malice ever conceived. The earth beneath his feet was cracked and blackened, its jagged surface oozing a thick, tar-like substance that clung to his boots, making it hard to walk. Gnarled, skeletal trees twisted skyward, their bare branches reaching like clawed fingers toward a sky choked with smoke and ash. The air was heavy and stifling, thick with the acrid stench of sulphur that burned his nostrils and coated his tongue with a metallic tang.

All around him, tormented souls wandered aimlessly, their twisted faces etched with agony. They wailed and wept, their cries forming a twisted symphony of suffering that withered his soul. Some knelt in the scorched dirt, their skin peeling away in strips, raw and blistered, while others stumbled blindly, hollow-eyed and hopeless. Their faces flickered in and out of focus until they almost seemed to merge into one.

A jagged cliff face loomed in the distance, glowing red as molten rivers carved blazing scars into the rock, sending up clouds of steam that billowed like smoke from a dragon's maw. From within those clouds, dark shapes moved, barely visible through the haze, their glowing eyes flickering like embers in the gloom.

A sudden shriek rang out, so sharp and piercing that it sent a chill down Will's spine and set the hairs on the back of his neck on end. He turned sharply, only to find himself face to face with one of the tortured souls. The withered figure whose face was frozen in a mask of unbearable agony simply stared through him, saying nothing.

Will stumbled back another step, his boots sticking to the tar-soaked earth. The twisted figure reached for him, its lifeless, skeletal fingers grazing his arm, and suddenly the world lurched, plunging him into darkness.

He awoke with a sharp gasp, his body slick with sweat and his heart hammering in his chest. The room was dark and still, but the echo of screams lingered in his mind. The acrid taste of sulphur clung stubbornly to the back of his throat as he fought to get a grip on reality.

He lay there in the darkness for some time, his arms wrapped around his knees, waiting for his pulse to slow and his breath to steady. Finally, his heart rate slowed and his breathing resumed its normal rhythm, but the air felt heavier than before; stifling and stale. He knew he should try to sleep, but whilst his body had calmed, his mind remained in turmoil after his ordeal.

Across the room, faint slivers of light were creeping in through the shuttered window as the first blush of dawn began bleeding into the sky.

As he sat and watched the imperceptible changing of the light, he wrestled with questions he couldn't answer. Was it simply the result of an over-tired mind, feverishly stitching together fragments of the day's events, as it tried to process everything that had happened? Or was it something more? Something more sinister, clawing its way into his thoughts?

He turned his head, glancing across the room at Athtar and Gregor, both still wrapped in the comfort of sleep. For a moment, he envied their peace, their stillness.

Quietly, he pushed back his blanket, careful not to disturb the others. The cold air wrapped around him as he dressed, his shirt clinging stubbornly to his still clammy back. He crossed the room on silent feet, slipped through the door, and made his way to the kitchen.

The room was dimly lit by the pale glow of morning, and the lingering scent of last night's fire drifted faintly in the air. Will moved to the hearth, seeking comfort in its warmth, but the embers were barely glowing. He sighed and turned instead to the shelf where Jacob kept his tea. His hands still shook faintly as he reached for the tin, and as he spooned the dry leaves into a pot, he realised that he would still need to light the fire.

He threw a fresh log on and stoked the embers, waiting for the flames to begin curling, before setting the kettle over the flames and moving in close to warm himself. The warmth of the flames and the hot tea finally dispelled the last of the tremors inside and calmed his racing mind.

Just after dawn, Will and Athtar left the farmhouse behind, the scent of damp earth and morning mist clinging to the air. Jacob prepared some supplies for their journey and then watched them go from the doorway, offering a final wave of farewell as they made their way down the tree-lined path.

Athtar walked beside him, her pace steady, her step graceful. Though she hadn't spoken much since their departure from Jacob's farmhouse, her presence comforted him.

Realising that Will clearly had a destination in mind, Athtar finally broke the silence. "Why North? Where are we heading?"

Her words snapped him out of his thoughts, and he looked at her, smiling as though seeing her for the first time that day. "Sorry, I thought I had said. If she went with Eldran, then someone in the order will know where she is... I hope."

"To Thorn Island then?" she asked.

He simply nodded as he continued to trudge on.

They continued north for the remainder of the day, retracing their step from the day before. As they neared the coastal bluff where the temple ruins stood, Will glanced over at Athtar, his voice lamenting. "I thought… when I came back, I'd just find her here," he said, taking in a deep breath as he gazed at the horizon. "I never thought beyond this moment. I have been adrift for so long, and I knew that she was my anchor."

Athtar gave a small nod, her face creased with empathy. "She's out there, Will. And if she's anything like the woman you've described, she is probably doing great things. You *will* find her."

Will nodded absently, but his mind was still struggling with the disappointment. He had thought returning to Aruna would be the final step. But now, standing here, he felt no closer to finding Lyra than he had been when he first set foot on this strange, foreign world.

"But… I'm here," Will continued, his voice gaining a slight hint of optimism. "I'm a step closer than I was yesterday."

By late afternoon, they arrived at the temple ruins under a brooding sky. The air carried the unmistakable scent of approaching rain, carried on the salty coastal breeze. Will stepped up to the portal's frame, sensing the power coursing through its runes, waiting to be activated. His hand hovered over the pedestal, where the smooth, polished stone lay, and he paused, suddenly aware of the subtle shift within him.

Almost as much as being reunited with Lyra had been his main driving force for returning, he was also eager to be back in a world where he could access the light once more. But as he reached out to touch the strands of energy that he could feel pulsing through the portal, he could immediately feel that something was different. The light felt distant. The connection that had been so strong, so immediate when he'd first come to Aruna all those years earlier, was now strained, like a rope pulled too taut.

He quickly dismissed the unease that crept in. *No,* he told himself, shaking the thought away. *It's just been too long. I'm just out of practice.* He didn't want to dwell on the possibility that his connection to the light might be shifting because of his foray into the darkness. He pushed that thought aside, burying it deep beneath the surface.

With a deep breath, he forced himself to focus, reaching once more for the flow of magic, willing the portal to respond. Finally, reluctantly, the magic flowed into the portal.

The runes flared to life.

The portal responded with a sudden, blinding flare as the ancient runes carved into the stone pulsed with energy. The familiar deep, resonant hum filled the air, building in intensity as light coalesced in the archway. Then, with a deafening *whoosh*, the energy surged forward, forming a shimmering veil of swirling silver and blue.

Will exchanged a glance with Athtar, who gave a small, reassuring nod, straightening the strap across her shoulder as she stepped forward.

Will fell in step beside her, and they both stepped through the portal's shimmering surface. He felt the strange, familiar sensation of his body stretching and pulling as the magic enveloped him.

But something was wrong.

Where he was expecting to rematerialise in the huge, vaulted portal chamber on Thorn Island, instead, a suffocating darkness pressed in around them, thick and absolute. An intense cold seeped into their bones as if they had plunged into the depths of an abyss.

Will stumbled as his boots hit uneven ground. Beneath his feet, the surface felt unstable, like shifting shadows given form. His breath came in short, panicked gasps, as the very air around them became thick and heavy, smothering any sound.

"Athtar?" he called, but his voice was swallowed by the void, the completely dead air muffling the sound.

"This isn't Thorn Island," she said, her voice sounding muted.

Will turned in a slow circle, his pulse pounding in his ears. The thick, suffocating darkness pressed in on them from all sides, shifting like smoke. There was no sky, no horizon, only a vast emptiness stretching infinitely in every direction. A sickly, flickering half-light barely illuminated their surroundings, casting distorted shadows that wavered and bled into the blackness.

"We need to find a way out of here," said Athtar, pulling Will back from the edge of panic.

He nodded and they pressed on, cautiously.

Every movement in this place felt sluggish, as if unseen hands dragged at their limbs. Will's head throbbed with an unnatural pressure, as though the realm itself resisted their presence.

Then, as they crested a jagged outcrop of what passed for solid ground, the chasm came into view.

It yawned before them, an abyss of absolute blackness that stretched endlessly in either direction. A vast, open wound in the landscape, it pulsed with something deeper than mere emptiness, something hungry. And on the far side, distorted through the haze of the shadow realm, was their salvation. Standing on a rocky outcropping on the other side of the chasm stood what appeared to be another portal, a perfect inversion of the one they had stepped through.

"There," Will breathed.

Athtar frowned. "And how exactly do we—" She stopped short, following his gaze downward.

Floating stones drifted in the abyss, shifting lazily, as though carried by unseen currents. Some were small, no wider than a man's step; others were large enough to hold them both... if they could trust them to remain stable.

They exchanged an uncertain glance before Will shrugged, stepping forward. As he moved towards the edge, he began gathering magic, instinctively thinking to form the floating rocks into a stable bridge. He reached inward, calling upon the light, expecting the familiar surge of power—

Nothing.

A sharp, unnatural absence met his summons. The warmth of the light, the ever-present flow of magic through his veins, was simply *gone*. His stomach lurched at the realisation. He tried again, straining, pushing against the silence within him.

Still nothing.

"I can't—" His voice wavered. "My magic isn't working."

Athtar looked at him, but before she could respond, something shifted. A whispering sound slithered through the silence. The temperature plummeted further, and the shadows *moved*.

Will turned sharply, his gut twisting with a primal dread.

Figures emerged from the darkness.

Half-formed things, barely distinguishable from the gloom, wreathed in tattered wisps of shadow. Their eyes were mere empty voids, bleeding malice. Their whispering voices grew louder, clawing at the edges of Will's mind, leeching warmth from his body.

"Athtar—" Will's voice cracked, high and tight.

"I see them," she said, stepping closer, her stance shifting.

The spectres surged forward.

Will instinctively raised his hands, reaching for magic that once again refused to come to him. Panic flared, but before he could react further, *fire* erupted beside him.

Athtar's hands moved in a blur, a searing wave of flame blooming to life between them and the advancing shadows. The fire flickered hungrily, its golden light casting an unnatural aura in oppressive darkness.

Will barely had time to process Athtar's pyromancy before she grabbed his arm and pulled him toward the floating stones.

"Move!" she barked.

They both leaped onto the first stone, Athtar keeping one hand outstretched, hurling bursts of fire at the encroaching figures. The spectres recoiled, writhing and shrieking, but they did not retreat. Instead, they gathered, coalescing, as if testing the limits of her flames.

Will stumbled onto the next platform, feeling it tilt precariously beneath his weight. Athtar followed, spinning mid-air to send another arc of fire into the darkness before landing beside him.

The rocks ahead twisted and rolled, shifting unpredictably. The portal was still distant, flickering faintly through the abyss.

"We're not going to outrun them," Will said, panting.

"We don't need to," Athtar shot back, eyes ablaze. "We just need to hold them off long enough to make it through."

The spectres surged again as Athtar's wall of flames diminished under the weight of the darkness, whispering their nameless horrors as they closed in.

Will forced his terror-locked limbs to move, leaping from one shifting stone to the next, his breath ragged and his balance unsteady. The void beneath them yawned hungrily.

Athtar was right behind him, moving with elven grace despite the treacherous footing. She turned mid-stride, her hands ablaze with fire as she hurled a stream of flames at the advancing shadows. The spectres shrieked, their forms twisting in agony as they plunged into the abyss, but still they came, surging forward in waves.

The next jump was farther than the rest, but the platform was larger. Will barely made it, stumbling as the platform wobbled beneath his feet. Athtar landed beside him a moment later, just as the creatures reached them.

The spectres *poured* onto the platform, their insubstantial forms shifting and stretching as they reached for them.

One of them reached him.

An elongated, wraith-like hand passed through his arm, and agony flared through him like fire and ice colliding. A strangled cry escaped his lips as his strength threatened to leave him entirely.

A furious *whoosh* erupted beside him as Athtar flung a massive fireball at their feet. It hit the platform with a deafening roar, detonating in an explosion of golden flame that sent a shockwave rippling outward. The spectres reeled, their shrieks lost to the void as they were blasted backward, their insubstantial forms burning away even as they tumbled over the edge.

Will staggered, gasping, his vision swimming.

Athtar grabbed his wrist and yanked him forward. "Keep moving!"

The last few jumps blurred into a frantic rush. The shifting stones were growing more erratic, twisting and spinning beneath their feet. Will's legs burned with exertion, his body trembling from the lingering cold of the spectres' touch.

He nearly collapsed as his feet hit the solid ground on the far side of the chasm, but Athtar landed beside him, flames still crackling in her hands, grabbing him by the arm and lifting him towards the waiting portal.

Through the shimmering event horizon, they could see the torch-lined walls of the portal chamber at Thorn Island.

Will and Athtar locked eyes, and then, without further hesitation, they hurled themselves through the portal.

Once again, Will felt the familiar pulling and stretching sensations of portal travel, but this time it concluded as it should have before... they were ejected from the portal in the grand portal room.

They both stood gasping as the portal sealed behind them, their hearts still hammering.

"What the hell was that?" Will said, his voice sounding shrill in his own ears, his eyes a bit wild.

Athtar simply shook her head, unable to answer. She stood looking around in wonder at the incredible sight of the underground realm of the order. The room was bathed in the light of the torches that lined the wall, as though it were already waiting for them. They only took a few moments to catch their breath, before Will strode confidently forward, making his way towards the great chamber. Will expected to feel the familiar warmth of his connection with the Nexus of light overwhelm his senses as it had last time they were here, but he was troubled to find it wasn't the same. He could feel... something, but it was less intense, less familiar.

As they approached the archway leading to the great chamber, a figure stepped forward from the shadows, his grey robes marking him as one of the Acolytes of Thorn Island. He was a lean, pale-skinned man with sharp features and a solemn expression, his hands tucked into the wide sleeves of his robes. His eyes flickered with recognition as he regarded Will and Athtar, though his face betrayed no surprise.

"The council has been awaiting your arrival," the Acolyte said, his voice a measured monotone.

Their uncanny ability to know of his arrival before it happened always left him feeling quite uneasy. He cast a sidelong glance at Athtar, who was still glancing around with a look of undisguised awe written all over her face.

The Acolyte turned on his heel and strode into the great chamber without further explanation, leaving them little option but to follow.

The vast, familiar space stretched out before them, an awe-inspiring convergence of knowledge and power. Towering shelves of intricately carved wood lined the walls, cradling countless ancient, leather-bound tomes and scrolls. Between the shelves, mechanical devices and arcane artifacts gleamed under the chamber's ethereal glow. White-robed mages moved about the space, some poring over texts at long wooden tables, others murmuring incantations as they studied artifacts of unknown origin.

The ceiling arched high above, formed from the natural rock of the island itself. From that rock protruded an enormous, writhing mass of thorned vines, their tendrils seamlessly fused with the stone as they wove through the fabric of the island. At the heart of the tangled mass, a radiant sphere of pure light energy pulsed in steady, rhythmic waves.

As Will regarded Athtar's speechless awe at seeing this place for the first time, he finally understood Eldran's amusement when Will and his group had passed through these halls all those years before. As that memory flitted through his mind, he felt a tentative push from the Nexus as a wave of bittersweet memories threatened to overwhelm him. When he had arrived here in the company of Lyra, Valenor, and Lolmig, he couldn't have known that he was about to lose each one of them over the coming days. Each loss was unique in nature, each bringing a unique suffering, but each had fortified him, strengthened him for what must happen next.

Again, he felt the energy of the Nexus brush, tentatively against his consciousness, and he felt hope that his connection to it wasn't entirely lost.

The Acolyte came to a halt at the base of the dais and inclined his head respectfully before stepping aside, leaving Will and Athtar standing before the assembled Elders.

Will's gaze swept across them, their heavy robes and emotionless expressions lending them an air of impenetrable wisdom. The chamber was silent save for the soft rustling of robes as the Elders shifted in their seats, observing him with an intensity that made the back of his neck prickle.

The Elder of Empathy, seated to the left before the green banner, regarded him with kindness in her wise, weathered eyes. Next to her, the Elder of Balance sat with hands folded in his lap, his silver banner behind him shimmering faintly in the ethereal glow of the Nexus.

To the right, the Elder of Justice watched him with a piercing stare, his lips pressed into a thin line as the red banner behind him rippled slightly. Beside him, the Elder of Integrity sat poised, her indigo-clad form upright and composed, dark eyes searching his face for truths unspoken.

But when Will's gaze settled on the central figure upon the ornate throne, he faltered.

This was not the Elder of Light he had met before.

The man who now sat beneath the golden banner was younger than the kind-eyed elder of light Will had once known. He was still aged, his silver-streaked hair cropped close, and his face bore the weight of his years, but there was a strength to him. His eyes, though not unkind, were sharper, shrewder, cutting through Will as though peeling away his defences layer by layer.

The Elder's voice, when he spoke, was rich and confident. "You have returned to us, Will," he said, as his gaze flickered briefly to Athtar. "And you are not alone."

Will took a breath and stepped forward. "No," he said. "This is my travelling companion and friend, Athtar Morran."

A long silence followed as the Nexus pulsed softly overhead, and the elders simply regarded them, as though weighing them up.

Then, finally, the Elder of Balance leaned forward slightly, breaking the silence. "Tell us," he said, "why have you come?"

Will cleared his throat. "I have come seeking Lyra, who I am informed travels in the company of Eldran. I know not what business he has with her, but if you know of their whereabouts, I would appreciate your assistance."

There was a slight murmur from the few mages who had begun gathering in the galleries that surrounded the elders' thrones. The elder of light steepled his fingers as he weighed Will's words, leaning back in his throne and casting his eyes up towards the ceiling, as though seeking the guidance of the Nexus. Finally, he looked back at Will.

"There is much that you need to know, Will. Much has changed since you were last here. Significant events are afoot in the world, and Eldran and Lyra are at the heart of that."

When it looked like that was all the elder was going to say on the matter, Will started to protest, but the elder held up his hand to stop him. "I know... You have many more questions. But now is not the time or the place. If you can show your friend here through to the Hive, your chambers have been prepared. Please... go and rest, refresh yourselves. I will find you soon and answer whatever questions you might have."

Will considered this a moment. There was something in the intense gaze of the elder of light that made him realise there was more going on here than he could say in public, so Will gracefully nodded. "Thank you, Elder—?"

"Lucian," replied the elder of light.

Will nodded again. "I could use a bath and some food. We will talk more later."

Knowing that these formulaic rituals of hospitality were very important to the Order, he felt it was the quickest way to move things along, so he led Athtar away towards the next chamber, where the living quarters were found.

He stepped through the smooth archway, passing from the great chamber into the Hive, and a familiar warmth settled over him. The Hive sprawled across multiple levels, a vast, honeycomb-like

structure carved into the very rock of the island. Spiralling staircases lined the structure, and arched walkways wove between the
tiers, connecting private alcoves, libraries, and communal spaces.
Soft golden light emanated from crystalline sconces embedded in
the stone, their steady glow illuminating the space in a calming
light.

Will exhaled, feeling the tension ease from his shoulders. The air
here carried the familiar comforting scents of incense and ember-
warmed stone, mingled with the faint sweetness of beeswax candles.

Athtar, however, was motionless beside him, her gold eyes wide
as they roved over the towering structure before them.

"You'll get used to it," he said with a smirk, nudging her forward
as he led her deeper into the chamber, towards a large, familiar alcove at the base of the monolithic core of the hive.

They took the opportunity to bathe and change into the comfortable garments provided, relishing the simple luxury of clean,
soft fabric against their skin. A meal was delivered soon after, by
a silent acolyte, consisting of fresh bread and a hearty stew infused with fragrant herbs. They ate in companionable silence at
first, the warmth of the meal settling deep in their bones, soothing them after the cold unease of the shadow realm.

As they lingered over the remnants of their food, talking in quiet
tones, Will found himself unsettled by a strange sense of repeti-
tion. The familiarity of it all should have been comforting, but

instead, it left him feeling oddly detached, as if he were caught in a cycle he had already lived through.

He shifted in his seat, rolling his shoulders as he tried to shake off that unseen weight. Athtar, seated across from him, caught the motion and hesitated for a fraction of a second, her golden eyes studying him carefully.

Will exhaled slowly, forcing a small, reassuring smile. "Not a bad welcome, all things considered," he remarked lightly, setting his empty bowl aside.

Athtar nodded, but he noticed the way her gaze flicked around the chamber, drinking in every detail with barely concealed wonder. "I have never seen anything like this place before."

Will remembered the first time he had walked these paths, the awe he had felt at the thought of what the Order's founding members had accomplished through sheer force of will and magic.

He leaned back, letting his eyes drift toward the ceiling, where faint veins of luminescent energy pulsed within the rock, feeding the Order's sanctum with an ever-present flow of magic. It should have been soothing, but instead, it only reminded him of the disconnection he had felt upon arrival.

Suppressing a sigh, he pushed to his feet. "We should rest. Lucian will call on us soon enough."

Chapter 7

Will awoke to the familiar sensation of the Nexus probing his mind, and as his consciousness pushed up from the depths of slumber, he smiled. But as consciousness took hold, the presence slipped away again. His smile faltered into an expression of frustration, and he called out to the empty room, "Why do you recoil from me?"

A voice from the main chamber startled him. "I have come to talk with you."

Will sat up, shame creeping in at the thought that his outburst had been overheard. He splashed water on his face from a cold, stone washbasin nearby before stepping into the next room.

Lucian stood waiting, his expression calm, offering no indication that he had heard anything. As Will entered, he smiled warmly and inclined his head. "I hope you had a chance to rest, Will. I fear your journey is only just beginning."

Will let out a short, dry laugh. "I think one day they will carve those words into my headstone."

At the sound of conversation, Athtar emerged from the adjoining chamber, rubbing the sleep from her eyes. She crossed the room and began pouring tea from a steaming pot set among the breakfast spread. She glanced at Will, lifting the pot in silent offering, and he nodded in thanks before turning back to Lucian.

The elder settled into a chair, gesturing for Will to do the same. "I imagine you were surprised not to see Elder Rhylen upon your return."

Will exhaled, leaning back. "It was unexpected. I remember him well from my last visit and think of him fondly for the guidance he offered me."

Lucian nodded solemnly. "Rhylen served the Order with wisdom and dedication for decades. But when the weight of recent events grew too heavy, he chose to step down. He lived his final days in quiet contemplation before passing peacefully not long after."

"And you were chosen as his successor?" he asked, glancing at Lucian over the rim of his cup.

Lucian inclined his head. "The Order needed a strategist during these uncertain times. As is the tradition, we cast a ballot, and a significant majority placed their faith in me."

Will studied him for a moment. Lucian carried himself with an unmistakable strength.

"You hinted at these 'uncertain times' yesterday, when we spoke in the nexus chamber. What is going on?" Will asked, getting straight to the point.

Lucian nodded, his expression grave. "There has been a disturbance in the light-source for some time now. It is my belief that the ley lines have shifted, their balance disrupted by a powerful new force somewhere on the continent. We have been investigating the source of the disturbance for some time now, and our search has led us south."

Will's gaze drifted as he tried to process what he was hearing. As his mind worked through Lucian's words, a thought suddenly surfaced. "Does this disturbance in the light source have anything to do with what happened with our portal yesterday?" he asked.

Lucian nodded slowly, his face looking weary as he went on to explain. "Our understanding of portal magic is that we travel through the shadow realm every time, but the entry and exit points of the portals align perfectly, so that a traveller never perceives their transition through the realm in between," he paused, his gaze drawn with concern. "but more frequently, we've been receiving reports of exit portals shifting out of alignment, materialising some distance away from their intended locations, forcing travellers to traverse the shadow realm itself."

Will shuddered at the memory of the place. He almost didn't ask the next question, afraid of what the answer might be, but in the end, he blurted it out, "I tried to summon the light when I was there, but I couldn't. Could that be connected?"

Lucian hesitated, looking at Will and then averting his gaze uncomfortably before replying. "It's possible," he paused. "I haven't heard of anyone else having the same issue, but we can explore that a little more later if you would like?"

Will nodded gratefully.

Athtar took advantage of the break in conversation to ask a question. "You hinted yesterday at trouble between the kingdoms?"

Lucian looked over to her. "That's right. I don't think the two issues are unrelated. What do you know of the politics of the Aerinthos mainland?"

"I have lived my whole life in Silverwood, but when I was younger, my family travelled to the crystal city in the great north woods to visit our ancestral homeland. I recall trouble with the neighbouring kingdoms at the time, but I was very young and don't remember much," Athtar replied.

Lucian folded his hands on the table, his voice measured. "The balance is shifting. The human kingdoms of Anther, Urias, and Cervia still cling to their uneasy alliance, but their kings squabble like children, and eye one another with suspicion."

Will gave a short, dry laugh. "The leaders of nations are ever the same."

"Perhaps," Lucian said. "But what really concerns me is not the north, but in the south. Strada and Yager have set aside their feuds. For the first time in a generation, their banners gather together in Mor'Dan. A people so long divided now moving as one..." He shook his head. "It is a storm waiting to break."

Athtar leaned forward, frowning. "And the clans of Anhai? Have they chosen a side?"

"They remain behind their gates," Lucian replied, tone clipped. "Neutral, as ever... Though their silence grows louder with each season."

"And the elves of the great north forest?" Athtar pressed.

A shadow flickered across Lucian's expression. "The Elves have ever been aloof from the affairs of men, as you know, Athtar. They send words of sympathy, but little else. Do not expect them to stir quickly."

Will exhaled sharply as the scale of the situation hit him. "So the north bickers, the south unites, and the rest look the other way. Sounds like the perfect storm."

Lucian met his gaze. "It is why the Order must prepare... and why your return could not be more timely."

He paused for a moment, drawing in a deep breath. "So what I need now is reliable intelligence from people whom I could trust. That's why Eldran and Lyra have gone south."

Will got irrationally angry at that. He knew that Lyra would be the first to volunteer for such a mission... that's just who she was, but he was still angry that they had put her in that position. "Why Lyra?" Will's voice was sharper than he intended. His frustration surged, irrational but undeniable. "She has nothing to do with the Order."

Lucian regarded him with quiet amusement, as though he had been expecting this reaction. "Will," he said, his tone gentle, "she joined as an acolyte under Eldran years ago."

Will felt like the ground had shifted beneath him. How much had changed in his absence? For a fleeting moment, the realisation stung more than the thought of her being sent into danger.

Noticing the flicker of unease in his expression, Athtar smoothly took over. "So, what's next then?"

Lucian turned his attention to her. "Until Eldran and Lyra return from the south, we wait and prepare. We've been conducting combat training with a select group of mages," he paused, regarding Athtar with interest. "I understand you are a pyromancer? Your knowledge would be invaluable in our training sessions... if you're interested?"

Athtar glanced at Will, seeking his opinion. He had recovered his composure a little, and he met her eyes and nodded.

"If there's anything we can do to help, we're at your disposal, Lucian," Will said.

Lucian smiled, slapping his knees as he stood. "That's settled then. We train daily from noon. I'll meet you both in the great chamber and lead you to the Sanctum."

He paused just as he was about to step out into the hive, turning back to face them. "I have something for you too, Will," he said. "Something you left behind last time.

Will squinted, intrigued, but said nothing.

After seeing Lucian out, they sat back down in comfortable silence for some time as they grappled with the revelations they had just heard.

Will began drumming his fingers against the table, staring at the wood grain as if it held answers. "I can't believe Lyra became an Acolyte."

Athtar studied him for a moment. "You don't like that she's changed."

Will looked up sharply, a look bordering on indignant outrage on his face. "It's not like that, I just—" he started to protest, but stopped himself, sighing. "No, you're right. I've spent so long trying to find my way back, and now that I'm here, it feels like

I'm the one who's lost. Everything here has moved on, and I fear it's all left me behind."

Athtar nodded, but there was a distant look in her golden eyes. "I understand that more than you know," she said wistfully, but Will was so caught up in his inner turmoil that he missed the subtle change of tone in her voice and the pensive stare.

She paused a moment before changing the subject. "What do you make of what Lucian said about the southern clans?"

"It's hard to say," Will said thoughtfully. "It could be that there's something to it. I guess we'll find out more when Lyra and Eldran return."

Athtar nodded, taking another sip of tea.

Will found himself brooding once again as he absently turned his amulet over in his hands, running his fingers along its smooth surface. He traced the contours of the design with his thumb, as if willing it to stir, to react, to prove his magic hadn't slipped beyond reach.

Athtar, meanwhile, meticulously checked her daggers, spinning one idly between her fingers as she moved around the room. Despite her composed demeanour, Will could sense the tension in her movements, as though something had changed. She seemed to be on the verge of telling him something a few times, drawing in a sharp breath, before releasing it and continuing with what she had been doing.

The arrival of the grey-robed acolyte came as a welcome distraction, who entered and informed them that Lucian had requested their presence in the great chamber.

Excitement flickered in Will's chest, and he realised he was quite looking forward to seeing Lucian's mages in action. Whatever else was happening, whatever doubts lingered in his mind, one thing remained certain: he had always been drawn to magic, and the prospect of seeing Lucian's team of trained battle mages in action brought a genuine smile to his face.

Will and Athtar quickly found Lucian, standing beneath the glow of the nexus. He greeted them with a nod, his expression as excited as Will's own. "Come," he said. "I can't wait for you to see."

He led them through an arched doorway at the far end of the great chamber, descending a flight of stone steps that twisted deeper beneath Thorn Island. Will could feel the energy shifting around them, as if they were passing through an invisible threshold.

At last, they emerged into a vast cavernous space. The underground sanctum was unlike anything Will had seen before. Thick thorn vines wove across the ceiling, pulsing faintly as they drew magic from the Nexus. The air vibrated with latent power that resonated at Will's core.

Lucian gestured around them. "This is the Sanctum. A place designed for us to hone our craft. It's protected with warding so we can practice freely, without concern that the magic might spill out, or have unwanted side effects beyond this space. Here, we learn to wield our gifts."

Will and Athtar took in the scene before them. Around the sanctum, small groups of mages were engaged in training, each practising a unique form of magic. Some worked alone, while others coordinated their efforts in small groups.

Lucian led them toward a gathering of mages near the centre of the chamber. "These are our specialists," he explained, gesturing toward the group. "Each focuses on a different discipline, harnessing the elements in their own way."

An older, broad-shouldered man stepped forward first. His robes were earth-toned, and his hands bore calluses from years of channelling the raw strength of the land. "This is Marek, one of our finest earth mages," Lucian said in introduction.

Marek inclined her head toward Will and Athtar. "We earth mages shape the world beneath our feet," he said. As he spoke, he raised a hand, and the ground trembled. A jagged pillar of stone erupted beside him, coiling like a serpent before settling back into the floor. "We can turn the battlefield itself into a weapon."

Another mage, a younger man with a quiet intensity in his gaze, stepped forward. He carried no weapons, his presence calming. "And I am Dain," he said, "an Empath. We channel our energy into the recovery of others. We can ease pain, mend wounds, and even bolster the abilities of our allies, lending them strength, clarity, and resilience."

A sudden crack of thunder drew their attention to another part of the sanctum, where a group of storm mages were practising. A woman with streaks of silver in her dark hair strode toward them. "I am Vaelis," she introduced herself, a faint smirk playing on her lips. "Storm mages command the skies. We summon the winds, call down lightning, and turn the weather itself into a weapon."

She extended a hand, and a small thunderhead materialised above her palm, flickering with energy before dispersing. "A storm is a powerful force, but uncontrolled, it can be as dangerous to us as it is to our enemies."

Lucian turned back to Athtar. "We have specialist forces in most elements," he said. "But you are the first pyromancer we have encountered. I had hoped you might be able to share your knowledge. Maybe inspire a new generation of young mages in a new discipline."

Athtar's expression remained unreadable, but Will noticed the way her fingers twitched, as though resisting the urge to summon flame on instinct. After a moment, she inclined her head. "I will do what I can," she said simply.

"You look like you're preparing for war," said Will, looking around in wonder at the small groups, feeling the crackle of raw energy in the air.

Lucian followed his gaze, looking proudly at them. "We are preparing for whatever comes."

Athtar wandered over to a group of younger mages who seemed not to have chosen a speciality yet and began talking to them and carrying out simple demonstrations as they watched her intently. Will and Lucian watched her for a moment. Finally, Will turned to Lucian. "Have you had any further thoughts on my, um...problem?"

Lucian regarded Will for a moment before speaking. "I have some theories," he said, "but yours is a fairly unique situation, so it may take us some time to fully understand."

He began walking slowly through the training area, gesturing for Will to follow. Will fell into step beside him, listening to the distant rumble of a summoned thunderhead and the rhythmic thuds of earth magic shaping the stone. "Go on," Will prompted.

Lucian exhaled slowly, folding his arms as they walked. "The Light is complex and requires a deep understanding of our own alignment within the universe. It relies heavily on our personal state of mind. When you first came to our world, you were... different. The magic flowed through you like water finding its course... not because you understood it, but because you were part of something larger. The prophecy. Fate's plan, perhaps."

Will's brow furrowed as he tried to grasp what he was hearing. "Okay... So what's changed?"

Lucian stopped, looking at a group of earth mages working on a training exercise nearby. "For most mages, the Light demands years of study, clarity, discipline. When you were here last time, you were fate's instrument. Now? You're just a man. And the Light may be waiting for purpose before it answers you again."

Will let out a heavy sigh, rubbing a hand over his face. "What if... what if this isn't just a matter of my attunement... or state of mind?" His voice was quieter now, almost hesitant as he gently probed around the edges of an idea that had worried him since his deal with Moloch. "What if the Light is rejecting me because of something I did?"

Lucian looked at him sharply. "What do you mean?"

Will hesitated. He couldn't tell Lucian the truth... he would never understand. Instead, he shook his head. "I just... Did things that I don't know if the Light would approve of."

Lucian studied him for a moment, then exhaled through his nose. "Will, the Light does not judge the way mortals do. It does not abandon those who lose their way... it seeks to guide them back."

Will huffed a humourless laugh, but said nothing more.

Lucian tilted his head slightly, his expression thoughtful. "I wonder..." He folded his arms, gazing toward the softly glowing roots that pulsed with the light of the Nexus. "Perhaps the answer lies in something else entirely."

Will raised a brow. "Such as?"

Lucian turned back to him. "Throughout history, there has only ever been one Lightbearer at a time. When you left, the Nexus chose another, as has always been the way. You were no longer here to carry the Light's will, to be the champion of light, and so it selected another."

Will looked at Lucian with deep interest. "And who is the Light-bearer now?"

Lucian nodded. "Since you left, I have been burdened with that responsibility. When you returned, however, it may have disrupted that balance. The Nexus has never had two Lightbearers exist at once," he paused, considering his next words carefully. "I don't think it is rejecting you, Will. I think it is struggling to understand what you are, and how you fit back into the design."

Will frowned, his face contorted with confusion as he grappled with that. "I don't understand," he said finally.

Lucian spread his hands. "You left this world, Will. And yet, here you stand. The Light works within the framework of this world, of its order. You stand outside the pattern the Light knows, and it may be trying to reconcile that paradox."

"Okay," he said slowly, "so what does that mean for me?"

Lucian gave him a reassuring smile. "That is what we must figure out. And until we do, we will train you in whatever way we can. You are not alone in this, Will."

Will wanted to believe that. But as he stood there, he couldn't shake the feeling that something deeper, something darker, was at play. Since his deal with Moloch, his soul felt sullied, his spirit overshadowed by something murky, and he worried that the Light-source could not coexist in such an environment.

They remained there in the sanctum for the remainder of the afternoon. Athtar seemed to be in her element, teaching the young mages, and in turn, they lit up in her presence. In just a few short hours, she had helped a few of them summon and maintain their first small ball of flame in the palm of their hands. "You have to draw the heat from all around you," she would say as they concentrated on the small area of energy starting to ripple above their outstretched hands. "Focus all that heat into one single point and then contain it."

Will watched from a short distance away, leaning against one of the stone pillars that ringed the training area. Athtar's passion was infectious, and he couldn't help but admire the way she guided the young mages with patience and confidence.

The young mages hung on her every word she said, their brows creased in concentration as they attempted to mimic her technique. Some managed only faint flickers of light, while others conjured unstable flames that sputtered and fizzled out within moments. But there was progress, and with each tiny success, their excitement grew.

Lucian, standing beside Will, smiled as he watched. "She's a natural teacher," he observed.

Will nodded. "Yeah, she is."

Lucian turned to him. "And what about you? Have you ever considered taking on a student?"

Will let out a short laugh. "Me? No way. I'm barely keeping myself together as it is."

Lucian tilted his head. "Perhaps. But you have more experience than many. You may be struggling with a disconnect right now, but your experience has value for the novices and acolytes."

Will sighed, crossing his arms. "You mentioned earlier that you had something for me," he said, suddenly remembering Lucian's words.

Lucian smiled mysteriously. "That's right, I had almost forgotten, it's just over here," he said, leading Will towards the back of the sanctum that seemed to be home to a collection of old relics.

As they approached the final row of shelves, Will's heart skipped a beat and he stood still in his tracks, as if seeing an old friend for the first time in years.

"When we recovered it and brought it back here for safekeeping, we had no idea you would ever return, but it seems only right it should be returned to you," said Lucian, gesturing towards the sword of light, with the stone of wisdom resting on its pommel.

Will looked at him, and then back at the shelf, before reverently picking up the sword. It felt right in his hand, like a familiar glove that fit perfectly.

"Thank you, my friend," he said in a choked voice to Lucian. "This means a lot to me."

The moment was interrupted by a cheer going up from the other side of the room, where Athtar had just helped one of the students conjure a perfectly steady flame. She beamed at them, offering quiet encouragement, and the young mage's face lit up with pride.

Will looked down at his own hands, flexing his fingers. He wasn't sure he even remembered what it felt like to wield magic properly, and he sighed.

Lucian seemed to sense his thoughts. "The Light is still there, Will. We will find a way to help you reach it again."

Eventually, Lucian called an end to the training session, speaking a few words of encouragement to the trainees. As Will and Lyra slowly walked back to their alcove in the hive, Will brought up something he had been meaning to talk to her about. "When we were talking this morning... I was saying that I felt like everything here had moved on in my absence."

Athtar nodded. "I remember."

Will considered his words before continuing. "There was something in your response that made me think there was more to it, and I realised I had never asked you about what you left behind."

Athtar's steps slowed, her gaze dropping to the stone floor of the corridor, and he immediately regretted asking, but before he could take it back, she exhaled softly and spoke.

"It was not by chance that I was in the south when Shadowmoor took me," she said, her voice distant. "My husband, Elarion... was dying."

Will glanced at her, catching the way her jaw tightened as she said the name.

"I had gone south seeking a healer," she continued. "Someone beyond the usual talents of those at Silverwood. Someone with the ability to save him from the illness that was consuming him, and I had heard of one such healer in the southern town of Decan."

A sharp pang of sympathy struck Will. He had lost people before, but to be wrenched away like that... to never even get to say goodbye?

Athtar let out a quiet, bitter laugh. "For all these years, I wanted nothing more than to come home. I ached for it. I dreamed of it. And now that I'm here..." she hesitated, shaking her head. "Now that I'm here, I realise home was never a place. Home was the life I had with him, and by now he must be..."

Her eyes shimmered, tears welling but refusing to break as her grief remained locked away behind a mask of composure.

Will's heart ached for her loss, and he wanted to say something... anything, to ease it. But no words could ever be adequate, so he simply wrapped his arms around her, allowing her to bury her face into his shoulder for a moment.

After a moment, Athtar straightened and dashed away the un-shed tears with the back of her sleeve. "That's why I haven't gone back to Silverwood," she admitted. "I don't know if I can face it."

Chapter 8

The days on Thorn Island settled into a comfortable routine, each continuing to immerse themselves in their roles there as they awaited the return of Eldran and Lyra. Will would spend his mornings poring over ancient texts in the great chamber, studying the fundamentals of magic that all trainees and acolytes would learn during their novitiate, hoping to learn something that would help him. Afternoons were spent on drills in the sanctum, where Athtar became an invaluable member of the team, respected and admired by her students.

Lucian worked tirelessly to guide him, offering theories and re-assurances, but no matter what they tried, Will's ability to control the light was feeble at best, but quite often completely eluded him. With each failure, the knot in the pit of his stomach tightened further, and his mood soured. It became a cruel spiral of frustration and resentment that began taking a severe toll on his well-being.

Every morning, he found himself loitering on a large table near the entrance to the portal room, often glancing up from whatever text he was studying to peer down the length of the room for any sign that a portal might be forming, for any sign they were back. Every night, he told himself it would be soon.

As time marched on, the nights, too, were becoming unbearable.

It always began the same way.

He stood upon cracked, burning stone, the air around him thick with sulphur and choking smoke. The sky overhead was a furious, roiling mass of crimson and black, streaked with veins of fire that pulsed like living wounds. Great rivers of molten rock carved jagged paths through the landscape, illuminating the skeletal remains of what might have once been cities, the twisted spires of blackened stone, leaning like broken teeth against the horizon.

And the wailing. The endless, ceaseless wailing.

Moloch's voice curled through the heat and smoke, low and coaxing. *"You are weary, Will. How long will you bleed for a world that recoils from you? How long before you see that resistance is futility?"*

Will clenched his fists, willing himself to deny it, but the words cut through his defences. The terror was familiar, yet laced now with the all too familiar feeling that he was an unwilling puppet on a predetermined course. The more he tried to fight, the heavier it grew, as though his own strength was feeding the thing that sought to break him.

About three weeks after their arrival, an acolyte rushed in to interrupt their afternoon drills. She approached Lucian and whispered a message directly into his ear. Will watched intently, hope building as Lucian looked up and met his eyes, nodding briefly. His face broke into a wide grin as he walked over to meet Lucian.

"Eldran has returned and been shown directly to my study. I assume you will be joining me?" he asked, a smile hovering about the corners of his mouth.

Will didn't need to answer. He was already moving, his pulse racing as he strode toward the exit. Athtar fell into step beside him as they hurried through the stone corridors.

The three of them ascended the spiralling staircases of Thorn Island's central tower, their footsteps echoing against the ancient walls.

Lucian led them through a heavy wooden door into his study, a warm and cluttered room lined with tomes and maps, where Eldran sat by Lucian's bureau, looking travel-worn and deep in thought. Lucian's study was one of the only parts of the structure that was above ground, and had a panoramic window that looked out over the unique landscape of Thorn Island, and the raging sea that hurled itself against the rocks below, but Will barely registered the view, his mind honed on one thing alone.

Eldran turned at the sound of their entrance. For a heartbeat, he only stared, his expression vacant, but then his eyes widened, disbelief breaking across his face. "Will?" His voice cracked, half-whispered as he stammered out. "By the Light... it cannot be."

Will froze, the old mage's astonishment only half-registering. "It's me," he said quickly, his words rushed, almost desperate. "It took me a while, but I made it back."

Eldran's dazed wonder gave way to a rare, unguarded smile, lines at the corners of his eyes deepening. "After all this time... my friend, I never thought I would see you again." He stepped forward as though to embrace Will, but Will was already searching the chamber, his eyes sweeping every corner.

"Where is she?" The question tore out of him, sharper than he intended. His heart hammered as he scanned the shelves, the chairs, the shadows, as though Lyra might be waiting there with her mischievous smile, ready to leap out and surprise him.

But there was only silence.

His breath came uneven, fear scraping at the edges of his voice as he turned back to Eldran. "Where is Lyra?"

Eldran's smile faltered, the weight in his eyes returning as he glanced toward Lucian before answering. "She did not return with me."

The words hit like a blow. Will shook his head, frantic. "No... no, that doesn't make sense." His gaze darted wildly about the room, as if refusing to accept it. "She has to be here... she *has* to." His voice cracked, fear bleeding through, until the sympathetic faces around him left no room for denial.

At last, his shoulders sagged, and his voice dropped to a hoarse whisper. "Why? Why isn't she with you? What happened to her?"

Eldran shook his head, his eyes full of sincerity that he earnestly tried to convey to Will in a glance. "As we were preparing to depart, an opportunity arose for her to infiltrate the headquarters of the occupying force in Alesia and gather more intelligence."

Will looked up sharply, cutting across Eldran. "...and you let her?"

Eldran leaned back in his chair as if suddenly overcome with the exhaustion he was carrying, but he let out a low chuckle before responding. "If you think anyone has the power to allow, or stop that young lady from doing anything, then I question how well you really know her Will."

Lucian stepped in then. "Maybe if we hear Eldran's report, it might clear a few things up?" he suggested, looking around at the others before resting a hand on Eldran's shoulder and walking around his bureaux to his chair on the other side. "I know you are tired, Eldran, but if you wouldn't mind telling us as much as you can before resting?"

Eldran nodded wearily but adjusted himself into a more upright sitting position and rubbed his face, as if preparing for what would be a long story.

"The south is broken," he began. "We walked through towns where hunger gnawed at every face, where children begged in the dust, and whole families lived under patchwork canvasses. Strada and Yager have been left gutted by the war. Their people have nothing left... except anger."

He paused, his eyes drifting as though still seeing it. "And into that ruin stepped Oberith. He appeared less than a year ago, a stranger at first... but his words lit a fire. He speaks to their hatred, their desperation, and they rise to him. What is forming in Mor'Dan is no mere army, but a fanatical movement of two nations."

The room fell still. Even Lucian's composure strained at the edges.

Athtar shifted herself into a more comfortable position. "How did you come by this information down there? It sounds like the people would be hostile to northerners."

Eldran nodded. "In Alesia, we found allies, few though they were. A young woman named Surah risked her life to bring us word. She knows the streets, the mood of the people. If not for her, we might have learned nothing, but Lyra befriended her, and she opened up. It's through her that we learned that Oberith is a powerful magic user. The superstitious and gullible have begun to revere him as a god, further fuelling the zeal in certain areas."

Will felt his stomach twist. "And Lyra? How is it she remained?"

For the first time, Eldran faltered. His gaze dropped. "When the time came to return, she told me to go on without her. She believed she could infiltrate the city hall, the headquarters of the military occupation there, and learn more from within. She made me promise to return in two weeks," he said earnestly, his voice growing softer. "I left her there, Will. By her choice, not mine."

Will's chest tightened. He wanted to argue, to demand why Eldran hadn't dragged her back by force, but as he looked at the sympathy in every face around the chamber, he could see that no one would take his side.

Eldran's shoulders sagged. "That is what we found in the south: a people weaponised by despair, a leader who feeds their rage."

The room fell quiet.

Lucian leaned back in his chair, steepling his fingers as he pondered Eldran's words. "Given that Oberith's people seem to be stirring the old hatreds against the north, we have to assume that their eventual goal is to march against us."

His face took on a pained expression as he realised what their next move must be. "I think it's time we call a conclave. The rulers of the Northern Alliance need to be informed of this. It's time to see if they can put aside their petty bickering."

He pulled a long slip of parchment from a drawer in his desk and scribbled a note on it, and then rang the small silver bell beside him. A young, bright-eyed acolyte appeared at the door within moments.

"You summoned me, Elder Lucian?"

Lucian handed him the parchment and began speaking. "You are to take this message and make five copies. Have one copy sent to each of the Northern Alliance rulers. The message is to be marked urgent, under the sigil of the order of the burning torch."

"Yes, my lord," the acolyte said, already turning.

Eldran looked wearily over at Lucian. "Do you think they'll all come?"

"They'll come," Lucian said. "Their petty jealousy wouldn't allow them to exclude themselves when the others might attend. Whether anything productive comes of it, we shall see."

9

Chapter 9

Over the course of the next few days, they prepared for the arrival of the northern rulers. Under Lucian's direction, the great chamber was prepared for the approaching conclave. Earth mages gathered with quiet reverence, summoning stone from beneath the island's surface and coaxing it upward in swirling arcs until it formed a broad, circular table of veined crystal. It stood directly beneath the radiant pulse of the nexus.

Ten chairs were carefully arranged around the table's edge, each one carved from rich, dark wood and upholstered in deep crimson velvet. Behind five of the high-backed thrones, the banners of the Faith had been unfurled, each representing one of the five elders. The remaining five chairs stood bare of heraldry for now, awaiting the arrival of the monarchs.

Lucian was notably absent from their normal daily routines in those days. Will knew that he was locked in near-constant conference with the other four Elders, strategising how best to present the growing southern threat. They knew they would have to carefully control the narrative of the meeting to ensure that the tensions that always bubbled just beneath the surface didn't get in the way of the task at hand.

On the eve before the gathering, Will found himself in a rare moment of quiet. He and Athtar sat together in their quarters. Eldran was with them, his long frame slouched comfortably in a padded bench by the large opening at the front of the alcove, recounting a dry observation about the rookery keeper's dramatic opinions on inter-kingdom avian protocol.

They were laughing at a particularly funny re-enactment when a young acolyte stepped inside, bowing slightly.

"Elder Lucian requests your presence," he said, his eyes scanning the room. "All of you. He asks that you come at once to his personal quarters."

Eldran raised his eyebrows after that acolyte stepped out. "We are honoured. He doesn't often invite company."

Will stood, wondering why Lucian might need them. "I've never been up there."

"I have," Eldran said, straightening. "I'll lead."

Eldran led them up through the hive, steadily climbing up the spiral staircase and crossing the arched walkways that spanned the open areas between, passing countless personal living spaces of the mages who called Thorn Island home. As they ascended, the corridors narrowed and grew quieter. Rope bridges spanned the air between the higher combs, swaying gently under their weight.

As with all personal quarters in the hive, there was no door on Lucian's personal quarters. As they entered, they saw him standing, hunched over a table, looking at a map with his back to them. He was so engrossed that he almost didn't notice them enter, but as they approached, he tilted his head towards the sound.

He rolled up the parchment map slowly, as though drawing his thoughts back from some far-off horizon. A rare, almost sheepish smile tugged at his lips.

"I thought you might like to join me for dinner," he said, gesturing toward a low table already laid out with steaming dishes. A pitcher of clear, citrus-scented water sat at the centre, beside four ceramic cups.

Will exchanged a glance with Athtar, who nodded with a small smile. The three of them settled onto the cushions around the table.

As they began to eat, Lucian reclined slightly and exhaled, the sharp edge of his usual intensity softening just a little.

"I wanted to speak with you all privately before tomorrow," he began, tearing off a piece of bread. "To share the approach that the council of elders has agreed upon... and to prepare you for what we'll be dealing with."

Will raised an eyebrow. "You mean besides the fact that we're trying to convince five ruling powers to unite against an enemy they can't yet see?"

Lucian gave a dry chuckle. "Exactly that. And the fact that they're not particularly fond of one another... or anyone else for that matter."

Lucian set his goblet down, rolling the stem lightly between his fingers as though weighing his words. "You'll meet them all tomorrow, but it's better you aren't blind-sided."

He leaned back, the candlelight catching the faint lines at the corners of his eyes. "Torvahn of Cervia will be the loudest voice in the room. Hot-blooded, brash... he thinks with his sword arm before his head. Once, during negotiations, he pounded the table so hard it split in half. Claimed it was to 'make his point clear.'" Lucian gave a wry smile. "The man is a hammer, and every problem looks like a nail."

He turned his goblet, considering. "Marella of Anther is another matter. Cold, precise, sharp as shattered glass. She remembers every slight, no matter how small. If she leans forward tomorrow, it won't be out of interest, it'll be because she's found a weakness to press."

Lucian's expression softened slightly. "Edarn of Urias... seems to be a decent man, in his way. More cautious than bold, but that caution has kept his kingdom intact while others bled. He measures twice before cutting once, but sometimes that means he never cuts at all. His people respect him, yet they suffer for his hesitation."

He took a sip of wine, then gestured with the goblet. "The rulers of the elven kingdom in the great north woods will arrive together. Haelyn and Ildeanra rule as one. You'll find them inscrutable, speaking more in riddles than answers. They've lived centuries longer than us, and they'll remind you of it at every turn."

Finally, his tone grew flat. "And King Dhongrolir of Graltum, who rules from Hent-Taui. The dwarves dig deep and keep their gates closed. Dhongrolir wears caution like a crown. He'll speak of stone walls and tradition, but what he means is: 'Leave us out of your wars.' Behind him always stands Gissumir, his older brother."

Will looked confused. "Older brother? Should the line of succession not have gone to him?"

Lucian chuckled. "Indeed it should, but Gissumir always shied away from the spotlight, and when their father, King Dandrul, passed away, Gissumir refused the crown. A noble refusal, perhaps, but one that has left their nation with a lesser ruler and done the dwarves a disservice, and caused some dissent within the dwarven nation."

Will frowned. "And we have to somehow convince them to work together?"

Lucian snorted. "They barely tolerate being in the same room. Past skirmishes and old insults fester like open wounds between them. We will have to handle them very carefully."

"Were the rulers of Aruna not invited?" Athtar asked, frowning as she noted their absence on the list of names Lucian had mentioned.

Lucian's expression darkened. "Invitations were sent," he said quietly, "but their replies were... curt. They no longer recognise any political tie with the mainland... not since we turned our backs on them during the Malakar crisis."

Will gave a slow nod, shrugging gently. "Hard to fault them for that," he said. "If I were in their place, I'd have done the same."

Lucian sighed. "And yet, divided as we are, we may all pay the price."

"So what's the plan?" Eldran asked between mouthfuls.

Lucian looked each of them in the eye, his expression now serious again. "We will try and remind the rulers of the historical importance of the alliance, and appeal to their self-interest. If they see the war coming to their own borders, their own thrones... then we might have their attention."

Athtar gave a small, tight smile. "Nothing simpler."

Lucian raised his cup. "To unpleasant company and impossible tasks, then."

Will clinked his own cup against Lucian's, and chuckled.

They chatted and laughed well into the evening, but eventually, Lucian stood and stretched, muttering something about early mornings and fragile egos. They took the cue and made their farewells, slipping out one by one to seek their own beds.

Though none of them said it, their impromptu gathering left them all feeling ready to face the challenges the following day would inevitably bring.

* * *

That night, he once again found himself in that infernal place. The same place that had haunted him for weeks now. The air was thick with sulphur, acrid smoke curling like ghostly fingers across a charred and broken landscape. The ground cracked and smouldered beneath his feet, and the cries of the damned echoed faintly on the wind.

He had grown accustomed to this hellscape, if one could ever truly grow used to such horror. But tonight, there was a subtle, but significant difference.

She stood at the edge of a blackened rise, shrouded in swirling ash, her white cloak somehow untouched by the filth around her. She was facing away from him, her form faint and flickering, like a mirage barely holding its shape.

Will's breath caught in his throat. He would have known her any-where, but of all places, he did not expect to see her here.

"Lyra!" he shouted, but his words stubbornly refused to project in this twisted nightmare realm.

She didn't turn. Not one flinch of acknowledgment touched her.

"Lyra!" he yelled again, louder this time.

He began to run. His limbs felt heavy, as if wading through oil. With every step forward, the dread within him deepened. Cold, coiled fear wrapping tight around his ribs, squeezing his heart. He needed to reach her. He had to get her out of this place. She did not belong here.

But the earth beneath his feet had other plans.

Dark, skeletal hands erupted from the ashen soil, clawing at his ankles, calves, thighs. They grasped at his limbs, pulling, holding fast. He stumbled, screaming her name at the top of his lungs as she walked slowly away, vanishing into the distant haze.

"No! No, no, no... please!" he screamed frantically, tears of frus-tration cutting paths down his cheeks.

He thrashed, ripped at the hands, tore skin and flesh away from bone, but they kept coming. Holding. Dragging. Slowly pulling him down into the earth to join them.

And then... release.

He burst free of the grip, lunging forward, gasping for air like a drowning man breaking the surface.

But she was gone.

Nothing remained but the smoke, and the fire, and a voice that filled the world.

Moloch's laughter.

It began as a low, rasping chuckle, swelling into a raucous, gleeful mocking cackle that echoed through Will's skull like the tolling of a great iron bell.

He dropped to his knees, fists clenched in ash.

"Why do you torment me?!" he screamed at the uncaring sky. "This was not the deal! Set me free!"

The laughter faded. Slowly, deliberately.

And then, from somewhere deep inside him, the voice came again. This time, low and Intimate. Whispered like breath against his ear.

"Soon enough, Will. Soon enough."

* * *

Will rose late the next morning, but even then, his head felt as though it was filled with sand. As he dressed and stumbled toward the Nexus Chamber, his mind played over the dream, wondering what it meant.

Moloch had haunted his nights for weeks now, always waiting, always whispering. Will had grown almost accustomed to it, to the idea that he belonged in that hellscape. As if his mistakes had earned him a place there. But Lyra... the image of her trapped there, her innocence being corrupted by that awful place, that was different. Wrong.

Yet even as he recoiled from it, another thought whispered at the edge of his mind. He realised that always seemed to be the way that fate worked. Simply punishing him for his mistakes was never enough. It always seemed to reach for the ones he loved, dragging them down with him. The notion burrowed into his mind and began slowly eroding his sanity.

Will found the nexus chamber bustling with an unusual level of activity. He asked a nearby empath mage where he might find Lucian, and was directed to the portal chamber, where the elders were waiting to greet their royal visitors.

Lucian had coordinated the arrivals of the royal delegations down to the minute. The mages had arranged staggered portal schedules, allowing each delegation to arrive without crossing paths to avoid any chance of tensions rising before the conclave had even begun. It also allowed each ruler their own moment of grandeur, which was very important to high-born people with superiority complexes. Dozens of mages lined the hall, and the elders stood near the dais, ready to greet the arrivals.

Will joined Athtar and Eldran at the chamber's edge as the first portal flared to life, casting the stone floor in ripples of pale blue light. A warm breeze followed, carrying with it the scent of lavender and citrus on a sea breeze.

King Torvahn of Cervia emerged first, a tall, broad-shouldered man with a square jaw and a sweeping crimson cloak embroidered with gold thread. His expression was that of a man who expected admiration and was seldom disappointed. Behind him trailed a line of liveried retainers. Lucian and the other elders greeted him with deep bows and a flattering welcome, thanking him for gracing the conclave with his presence. Torvahn responded with a stiff nod and a vague smile, clearly appreciating the deference, but fighting the urge to appear too impressed.

Next came King Edarn of Urias, thinner than Torvahn and with a hawkish face and sharp eyes that missed nothing. He spoke little, offering a clipped thanks before accepting the ceremonial drink offered and striding off toward the guest quarters that had been prepared for his party.

Queen Marella of Anther was the last of the human rulers to arrive, resplendent in shimmering green silks and crowned with a circlet of platinum and emeralds. She smiled graciously, but her eyes were hard and calculating. Her entourage was smaller, more refined, and her brief speech of thanks sounded rehearsed, and carried all the warmth of a crypt.

Each monarch was led to their private quarters, which were lavishly prepared and stocked with delicacies and rare vintages, all designed to please their individual needs. Will watched all of it unfold with quiet bemusement. The amount of effort it took just to manage their egos before a single word of diplomacy was spoken was staggering.

The portal flared once more, and through it stepped the elven delegation, led by Haelyn and Ildeanra, rulers of the Crystal City and the elven nation. They came with no guards, no fanfare, and a simple retinue to tend their needs. Their presence was calm and unhurried. Every motion and effortless grace made even the most elaborate of the human arrivals feel somehow overdone.

The elven king and queen greeted Lucian and the gathered elders with warm smiles and courteous nods. Haelyn clasped Lucian's forearm in greeting, and Ildeanra hugged him. These acts of mutual respect were more of an informal gesture than the stiff protocols of the humans. Will noted how even the elders seemed to ease in their presence, as though a subtle pressure had lifted from the room.

Finally, as the elves were led away to their quarters, the air changed once again. The portal flared a deep orange, and with it came the heavy stomp of boots.

The Dwarves of Graltum had arrived.

King Dhongrolir emerged at the head of a tight column of ceremonial guards, all clad in burnished bronze and black steel. The king himself was exactly as Lucian had described. Squat, squirrelly, his scraggly whiskers barely concealing a weak chin. His crown looked slightly too large for his head, and his eyes darted around the chamber as though expecting an ambush.

Lucian stepped forward with a formal bow, his tone polite but clipped. "Your Majesty, such a guard was not necessary. Thorn Island is—"

"The guard is non-negotiable," Dhongrolir interrupted, voice thin and nasal. "Standard precaution."

Lucian inclined his head, offering no further argument, though the faintest twitch of irritation passed across his features.

Beside the king stood a far more striking figure of Gissumir, Dhongrolir's brother. Taller by nearly half a foot, broader in the shoulders, and far more relaxed in his bearing. His beard was neatly braided, and his eyes, unlike the king's, did not flick about in suspicion. He nodded cordially to Lucian and the other elders before slowly gazing about the room, taking it all in through eyes that shone with intellect.

Once the monarchs were tucked into their private suites, segregated with surgical precision, Thorn Island buzzed with final preparations. Once preparations were complete, runners were dispatched with scrolls bearing gold-inked invitations from the Order of the Burning Torch to each ruler.

The Elders of Thorn Island respectfully request your presence in the Grand Chamber for the opening of the Conclave.

In the Great Chamber, Will and Athtar sat in the observers' gallery, nestled among acolytes, mages, and other members of the order. Only the elders and the delegations from the ruling nations would be present at the meeting. All others who wished to witness this momentous occasion were seated in the galleries.

Lucian stood near the large table, his white robes radiant in the light of the nexus. To either side of him sat the other elders, patiently awaiting the arrival of the monarchs. His hands were clasped before him as the last of the monarchs were escorted to their places.

The human rulers entered one-by-one, each taking their seats without once dropping their stoic masks. Once seated, they barely looked at one another. When they did, the glances were sharp and short-lived.

Haelyn and Ildeanra sat next with dignified grace, their faces betraying no emotion beyond mild curiosity. They looked around the room with feigned interest, but never once met the gaze of the other rulers.

Finally came Dhongrolir, shuffling into position, flanked by two guards. He perched at the edge of his seat, shoulders hunched, whiskers twitching. His beady eyes flitted about the table as he gauged the strength of his position. Gissumir stood behind him, back straight and expression alert, leaning toward his brother every so often to whisper something beneath the ambient murmurs.

When they were all finally seated, the room fell into reverent silence.

Lucian raised both arms.

"Lords and ladies, monarchs of the North, guardians of your people... I welcome you to Thorn Island, sanctuary of the light, and seat of the Order of the Burning Torch. It is no small thing to gather so many crowns beneath one roof, and we are grateful for your presence."

His voice rang clear, smooth, and solemn. He continued, invoking ancient pledges of cooperation, recounting victories of the alliance from generations past, and the sacred responsibility each ruler bore in the preservation of peace on the continent. He had spent days working on his speech, and Will was impressed with the artistry, the craftsmanship that had gone into each carefully curated phrase, designed to set the tone for what was to come and give it the best chance of success.

As he continued, most of the faces around the table responded with carefully arranged expressions: some polite, some weary, some outright bored. Torvahn barely concealed a yawn behind a clenched fist, while Marella picked invisible lint from her sleeve.

But beneath all that manufactured, faux civility, Will could sense the building tension. The cracks that lay just below the surface of the thin veneer of civility began to expand under the strain of that pressure.

"And so," Lucian concluded, "let us turn now to the reason we have called you here."

He gestured to Eldran, who stepped forward and bowed to the assembly. When he lifted his face again, he raised his voice to fill the chamber.

"My lords. My ladies. I bring troubling news from the southern nations of Strada and Yager."

The room went silent. Even Torvahn, who had been murmuring to an aide, looked up.

Eldran stepped into the circle of light, bowing briefly before lifting his voice so that it carried to every tier of the gallery.

"In the south, a new power rises. Where once the clans of Strada and Yager fought one another, they now march together. Where once their villages starved and turned on themselves, they now march with purpose. I walked their streets... I saw children begging in the dust, and women chanting the name of the man they believe will deliver them."

He let the silence hang for a heartbeat before driving on, his eyes sweeping the assembly.

"They kneel willingly. They swear oaths. And they march north beneath a single banner. One man has done this. A powerful dark mage, whose name they speak like a prayer: Oberith."

A ripple stirred through the gallery. Eldran pressed the moment, his voice rising.

"He has taken a people broken by despair and turned their hunger into fire. Life has taught them not to fear death... they welcome it. They believe that by dying for him, they will rise into a new age. That zeal is more dangerous than any sword."

He fixed his gaze directly on King Edarn.

"Urias lies closest to Strada. Your fields, your villages, your people will be the first to feel the storm when it breaks. They are not coming to raid and scatter... theirs is a quest of annihilation."

Edarn stiffened, but Eldran held his gaze before sweeping on.

"Even now, Oberith's recruiters press north, spreading his message: *Morda il ka mueras kalla.*" His voice dropped to a rasp. "Death to the Northern Alliance."

The words echoed like a curse in the vaulted chamber. A rustle of robes swept through the gallery, and chairs scraped stone.

Eldran drew himself up, shoulders heavy. "This is no rumour, no phantom. I have seen it. I have heard it. The threat is real, and it comes sooner than you dare imagine. We have slept while the south mobilised under our noses, and that Dark Lord, Oberith, has created something formidable."

He bowed once more and stepped back, leaving his words to settle like ash in the stunned silence that followed.

The monarchs sat with stiff backs, eyes glittering in the light of the nexus, each of them measuring the others before daring to speak.

It was Queen Marella who moved first, fingers drumming once against the polished arm of her chair. "So we are to act on the word of the south? Desperate tribes who have never once troubled our borders. Until now, they have torn at each other more than us." Her lips curved into something colder than a smile. "Forgive me if I am unconvinced."

Torvahn bristled immediately, pushing half out of his seat. "Unconvinced? Did you not hear him? An army gathering in Mor'Dan, swearing death to us all? It won't wait for polite debate, Marella."

Her eyes flicked toward him, sharp as a dagger. "And you would have us march our armies south at the first rumour, burning coin and blood, just to prove your valour? Your impetuousness will kill us faster than any Stradan blade, Torvahn. If your brain was even half as big as your bicep, you would still be a halfwit."

The tension spread like fire across dry grass. Dhongrolir cleared his throat, his voice weak and snivelling. "The dwarves will not be dragged into another war. We remember the Hundred Years' slaughter. If this threat comes, the gates of Hent-Taui will hold. Besides, what proof have we of this... god-man? Hearsay and whispers?"

At his side, Gissumir leaned in again, speaking quickly into his brother's ear. Will couldn't hear the words, but he saw the quiet pleading in Gissumir's eyes. Dhongrolir merely frowned and waved a hand dismissively as if swatting away a fly.

A murmur rippled, half agreement, half outrage. Edarn sat forward, his face drawn, hands clasped so tightly the knuckles whitened. "Enough." His voice was calm, but the strain beneath it showed. "My kingdom lies closest to Strada. If this Oberith truly marches, my people will be the first to suffer. But even I cannot move Urias alone. To commit, I would need proof... I cannot move my armies based on shadows and campfire tales." He glanced at Eldran with genuine regret before shaking his head.

Haelyn of the elves finally spoke. "You speak of proof as if it can be gathered like berries from a hedge. War leaves proof only when it is upon you. Until then, what you call rumour, others call prophecy." Ildeanra, at her side, inclined her head in agreement, eyes unreadable. "However, we elves do not concern ourselves with the squabbles of men. We will offer our wisdom, as ever. But we will not intervene in a human war."

The chamber broke then, voices rising in accusation, denial, suspicion. What had begun as measured debate slid into squabbling, the monarchs speaking over one another, each voice raised not to persuade but to drown out the rest.

Will shifted in his seat, taking a deep breath as he watched the conclave devolve into chaos before his eyes. The room pulsed with rising heat as rage barely leashed behind velvet words spilled out in waves of malevolence.

He looked to where Lucian was seated, his gaze drifting slowly from one monarch to the next, his face shifting from disappointment to realisation.

Finally, Lucian rose once more, and when he spoke, his voice had taken on a harder edge. "We have brought you information today. Oberith seeks to destroy us all, and our only chance is to stand together. Your petty bickering will not delay what is to come. I just hope you come to your senses before it's too late."

Will's fingers tightened on the rail in front of him. From beside him, Athtar whispered, "They won't act. Not until the flames are at their door."

Will nodded grimly. "Then we'd best prepare for fire."

Chapter 10

The remainder of the conclave had devolved into bitter bickering and thinly veiled accusations. The moment Eldran's solemn warning was met with scepticism, the fragile diplomacy holding the chamber together began to unravel. Each monarch, spurred on by pride, paranoia, or plain stubbornness, had retreated into self-interest. Voices rose, fingers pointed, and alliances frayed before they had ever truly formed.

One by one, the rulers withdrew from the chamber, their escorts trailing behind like shadows. No resolution had been reached. No pact signed. Only empty courtesies and the faint stench of failure hung in the air.

Will and Athtar had slipped out before the worst of it, making their way back to their alcove in the hive.

"I have never in my life had the misfortune of being witness to such a vile display of self-centred behaviour," Will said softly, rubbing his temples. "Unless they can put their petty bickering behind them, Oberith will simply walk in through the cracks and make himself at home without any resistance."

Athtar murmured her agreement.

Eventually, footsteps approached, and Lucian and Eldran emerged from the corridor, their faces drawn and weary.

"No change?" Will asked, already knowing the answer.

Lucian shook his head. "They've all gone to their quarters. Preparations are being made for their departure. Not one has offered aid."

"They're afraid," Eldran added quietly. "Too much bad blood between them has made them afraid of letting their guard down, afraid of showing weakness."

"So what now?" Will asked. "If they won't stand with us, what's left?"

Lucian's gaze hardened. "We must prepare for what is to come. With or without them."

He paused for a moment, tapping his fingers on the back of a chair as he considered what must be done.

"We need to know where he intends to attack first," Lucian continued. "If we can figure that out, we can start planning a defence. I should say, our first priority should be to extract Lyra from the south and see what she has learned."

Eldran nodded gravely, then turned to Will. "I assume you'll be joining me?"

Will looked up, eyes burning with intensity at the prospect of continuing his search for Lyra. "Wild horses couldn't keep me away."

At that moment, an acolyte stepped into the room, his hood slightly askew. He made his way to Lucian and whispered in his ear. Lucian's brow arched with curiosity.

"See him in, then," he said, gesturing toward the door.

Moments later, Gissumir was escorted into the chamber, his broad shoulders wrapped in a travelling cloak, his axe strapped across his back. He removed his gloves absently as he stepped in, then bowed his head respectfully.

"I wanted to speak to you before I depart, and to apologise for my brother's behaviour at the conclave," he said with a rueful half-smile. "If Dhongrolir found out I'd said this, he'd have my beard pulled out from the roots."

Will exchanged a glance with Eldran and Athtar.

"You've no need to apologise," Lucian said. "But your words are appreciated nonetheless."

"It was plain to see your heart lay elsewhere," Eldran added. "You were the only one in that room who seemed to be listening."

Gissumir gave a tired shrug. "I tried. But my brother's as stubborn as a mule. Logic won't sway him, fear even less so."

"Is there any chance you could convince him to reconsider?" Athtar asked, her tone gentle.

Gissumir shook his head. "Not a chance. Not unless the battle lines were already at his doorstep. But... there might be another way."

He paused a moment, his eyes going distant as he played out a scenario in his mind.

"The Ma'Yan clan of north Graltum. They're governed by my cousin Kasarlum and his wife, Dula. They've always kept their distance from Dhongrolir's politics, and Kasarlum has a clearer head on his shoulders. If I send word, there's a chance they might march to your aid when the time comes."

"Your countrymen have a fearsome reputation in battle," Eldran said. "If you could secure us that support, it could make all the difference."

Gissumir smiled, a bit of pride in his eyes. "Aye, we do."

He paused then, looking around the room. "What are your plans now?"

Will felt at ease in the company of this earnest dwarf. He didn't know if it was because he had a similar bearing to his old friend Lolmig, but he felt comfortable opening up to him. "We're going south. There is someone there very dear to me, who will hopefully have more answers about Oberith."

Gissumir nodded once. "I'll send word to Kasarlum with someone I trust from my brother's retinue. But if you'll have me, I would like to travel with you. I need to see with my own two eyes what's really happening down there."

Eldran extended a hand in friendship. "We don't know what we'll face in the south, but an extra set of hands would be appreciated."

With a respectful nod, Gissumir excused himself to begin his preparations, leaving the others in a brief silence.

After a moment, Lucian stepped away from the table. "Come," he said. "The monarchs will be leaving shortly. We should be there to see them off. Diplomacy, even when strained, demands its rituals."

The great portal chamber was filled with a tense energy as the mages prepared to orchestrate the complex schedule of portal travel for the departing monarchs.

First to leave was Queen Marella, her velvet cloak trailing behind her like a plume of midnight smoke. She spared Lucian the briefest of glances. "My thanks for the hospitality, Elder," she said, her voice icy and formal. "May the light guide your path... whatever it may be." Without waiting for a response, she stepped through the portal and vanished.

King Edarn followed, his jaw tight with something more than anger as the mages reassigned the portal to travel to Anhai in Urias. "I cant afford to waste soldiers on ghost stories and rumours, not when half the capital's ready to burn if I so much as blink wrong," he said, standing at the portal's edge. He paused, gaze flicking briefly toward the group. "If it turns out you're right... Then I pray we'll still have time to rally a defence."

He looked like he was about to say more, but instead, turned and stepped through, the echo of unspoken regret trailing in his wake.

Will met Lucian's eyes, both of them having caught that flicker beneath Edarn's words, the whisper of a man not entirely lost to their cause.

King Torvahn was the last of the humans to depart. He gave Lucian a long, unreadable look. He looked as if he was about to speak, but simply nodded curtly before stepping forward, the light of the portal swallowing him and his entourage.

When the elves stepped forward, the mood shifted slightly. Ildeanra inclined her head to Lucian. "We honour the invitation and the warning," she said, her voice smooth as moonlight. "But the affairs of man often burn themselves out without our intervention." Then, with no further comment, they disappeared into the light together.

Then, from the rear of the hall, a sharp exchange of voices cut through the din. The Dwarven contingent had entered, their heavy boots striking against the stone in a steady rhythm. At their head strode Dhongrolir, his expression grim, his crown glinting in the glow of the portal's light. Beside him, Gissumir walked at a slower pace, his face pale.

"You would stay here?" Dhongrolir's voice boomed, carrying easily across the chamber. The surrounding conversations faltered into uneasy silence. "Among surface-dwellers who will drag you into their quarrels? You would turn your back on your kin... on your blood?"

Gissumir stopped short, standing his ground, though his eyes wavered with hurt. "I serve not their quarrels, brother. I believe I serve Graltum best by assisting in this matter. The threat that rises in the south will not stop at human borders. You know this."

Dhongrolir's nostrils flared, his beard bristling as he stepped closer. "You speak with their tongues now. The Order has clouded your judgment."

"I see clearly for the first time in years," Gissumir replied softly, but his voice carried a note of iron beneath the pain. "I will remain to aid Lucian and his mages. The world is changing, and Graltum cannot hide behind its gates forever."

For a heartbeat, neither moved. Then Dhongrolir gave a contemptuous snort and turned away. "So be it. I will not call you brother again. You are no dwarf of Graltum... you are a blood traitor."

Without another word, Dhongrolir mounted the steps to the portal platform, his guards falling in behind him. "This... was a waste," he grumbled. "Let the surface realms bicker and burn," he said, barely acknowledging the others, pausing only long enough to give Gissumir a frosty look as he stepped through the portal.

As the last ripple of light faded, silence fell in the chamber.

Lucian exhaled slowly. "So much for unity," he said.

The bitter taste of disappointment lingered for some time after the conclave, its echo colouring every quiet moment with frustration and unanswered questions. Despite their best efforts, the monarchs had left Thorn Island with more suspicion than unity, each retreating behind their own borders as they clung jealously to old prejudices and fears. But Lucian had been right about one thing... they had done what they could.

At the very least, they now had a clear path forward. Lyra was still out there, and the Order of the Burning Torch would prepare for war. And perhaps... just *perhaps*, they had planted an idea, or a sliver of doubt. Something that might grow in the minds of the monarchs as whispers turned into reports, and unease bloomed into realisation.

The day after the conclave, Will and the others prepared for their journey south. With Eldran's guidance, they packed appropriate clothing and what supplies they might need for the road.

"King Edarn is a reasonable man," said Lucian in a weary tone as they all gathered in the portal room, ready to embark on their quest, "He may not have been persuaded to help fortify the north, but he will offer you whatever aid you need once you are beyond Thorn Island."

Eldran nodded, adjusting the satchel at his side. "He was most accommodating the last time I passed through. If he allows us, once again, to travel south with a trade caravan, that will be enough."

They turned to watch as Eldran began the portal sequence. His fingers danced over the rune stones, selecting the coordinates for Urias. A surge of magic pulsed through the room. The air cracked and shimmered, and with a burst of brilliance, the portal whooshed to life.

Once Eldran was satisfied they were ready, he pulled his hood up and gave a single nod. "Stay close. Move quickly. And whatever you do... don't get separated." Then, without hesitation, he stepped into the portal's light. One by one, the others followed.

The air was intensely oppressive as they stepped into the shadow realm. Every breath felt like inhaling water, leaving them feeling immediately breathless. Sound died on their lips, muffled at the source.

Then the wraiths came. Faster than before. More frenzied.

They coalesced out of the darkness like ink in water. Will turned to strike, instinctively calling on a power that didn't respond like it used to. Athtar was faster. Her eyes flashed with light, and flame erupted from her hands, sweeping through the air in a blazing arc. The wraiths scattered, reforming further back, hissing silently.

Eldran raised his arms, and arcs of lightning burst from his fingers, dancing in blue bolts across the stones and into the air, leaping from wraith to wraith in chains. He spun the current into a swirling cage of electricity, encircling the group, the light giving them a temporary reprieve, but the strain of holding the enchantment in place showed immediately in the beads of sweat that formed on his brow.

More wraiths emerged. Dozens. Then hundreds.

Distracted as they were by the attacking wraiths and their intense need to traverse the distance to their exit portal, there was a sense of something massive watching. It loomed, hidden, a silhouette just beyond vision, slithering through the gloom. The air shifted. The stones groaned. And for a moment, Will was certain that whatever it was had begun to descend from above.

"Move!" Eldran barked, his muffled voice breaking through the stifling silence.

They ran, stumbling over the slick, swaying stones. In the rush, the group began to splinter, the space between them growing. Gissumir slipped behind, nearly swallowed by a swarm of shades. Will darted after him, heart pounding, while Athtar shouted after them, her fire flashing.

Will reached Gissumir and hauled him forward. A crack of lightning carved through the path beside them, Eldran's warning shot driving back a second wave.

They regrouped at the edge of the platform. Athtar, breathing heavily, turned and launched a final wave of fire, scorching the last few wraiths clinging to the edges of the trail. Eldran stood in the centre of the group, arms trembling.

They could make out their destination portal ahead, standing on a promontory.

One by one, they leapt through.

Will landed hard on the stone floor beyond, blinking in the bright sun streaming in through the arched windows. Athtar came through next, dragging Gissumir. The moment Eldran stumbled out behind them, the portal snapped shut with a thunderous pop.

Eldran hit the ground hard, his skin pale and clammy, chest rising in rapid bursts, and then slumped sideways, his staff clattering to the stone floor of the Urias portal chamber.

"Eldran!" Athtar exclaimed, throwing herself to her knees by his side, lifting his head off the floor.

Eldran's breathing was shallow. Sweat soaked his brow. His robe was scorched along the right shoulder, fabric clinging to something beneath that glistened wetly.

Will reached forward, gently peeling the cloth away, recoiling at what he saw.

The wound was jagged, a raw slash torn through flesh, black veins spidering out beneath the skin like a web of poisoned rivers. The edges pulsed unnaturally, each throb pushing a slick of dark miasma from the wound that hissed faintly as it touched the air.

"Gods," Will breathed, horror blooming in his chest. "One of those things must have got him."

"It's spreading," Athtar murmured, looking at the inky tendrils that were spreading slowly across his shoulder. "It will need to be purged...and soon if he's to be saved."

Eldran stirred, groaning faintly. His eyes fluttered open, unfocused.

"We have to stop it from spreading," Athtar said. "If it reaches his heart..."

"Do something!" Will urged, looking from her to the wound again, feeling useless.

Gissumir had already risen to his feet, scanning the chamber. A pair of guards who had witnessed their arrival stood on the far side, watching uncertainly.

"You!" he bellowed, waving his arms. "We need a healer.. *now!*"

The younger of the two guards turned on his heel and sprinted from the room, his cloak billowing behind him.

Athtar's hands hovered over the wound, flame crackling between her fingers. She met Will's eyes briefly. "I might be able to purge it with flame... but I have to be careful. If I push too hard, I'll hurt him more than help."

Will gave a tight nod. "You've got to do something...he's fading fast."

Athtar knelt beside Eldran, her hands hovering just inches from his corrupted shoulder. The miasma writhed and pulsed just below the surface, recoiling from her warmth.

Fire blossomed in her palms. Tiny tendrils of flame, like molten threads, delicately extended from her fingertips and wove their way into the wound with surgical precision.

Eldran twitched violently as the fire found the infection.

The flame threads moved like seekers, weaving into his flesh, chasing the black veins that spread from the wound like roots. Wherever they met the darkness, they hissed and sparked, purging it in bursts of searing heat. The miasma responded, retreating, darting deeper into Eldran's body as if it could outpace the cleansing flame.

Athtar's face was serene, her expression focused and calm despite the toll it was clearly taking on her. Sweat dripped down her brow, her fingers trembling slightly as she pushed her power deeper. Will had never seen magic wielded with such precision, with such intimate control.

Suddenly, Eldran began to thrash under her hands. His skin flushed pink, then red, his entire body glistening with sweat. His breathing became ragged, gasping as if he were being burned alive from the inside.

Will flinched, fighting the urge to pull Athtar back. He knew she was helping, but seeing Eldran in such agony twisted something inside him.

Athtar's eyes narrowed. "Almost there..." she murmured.

Then Eldran's eyes snapped open, and he *screamed*.

It was a raw, primal howl. The kind of cry that made your soul shrivel and the hairs stand on the back of your neck.

The scream echoed back from the stone walls of the portal room...then, silence.

Eldran collapsed, unconscious once more. His head lolled to the side, lips slightly parted, body sagging as the last ounce of strength left him.

Athtar let the fire fade from her palms, her hands trembling as she caught her breath. The wound was still there, but the black veins were gone. The miasma had been destroyed.

Moments later, a team of Uriasan healers arrived, accompanied by robed attendants and portal guards. One knelt beside Eldran immediately, pressing two fingers to his neck and nodding to another. "Stable pulse. Let's get him moved."

They worked quickly, applying salves and bandages to the shoulder, murmuring incantations as they worked. A stretcher was brought, and within minutes, Eldran was being carried away, a slow procession winding its way toward the palace infirmary, with Will, Athtar, and Gissumir following closely behind.

Will's eyes never left Eldran's motionless form.

If I still had my light magic...

The thought cut deep. It was one he'd had too many times in recent weeks, but never with such guilt attached. Would Eldran have been hurt if he still carried the power within him? Could he have shielded him? Cured him before it took root?

The pit of despair and self-loathing opened wide in his chest again; cold, gnawing... familiar. He wrapped his arms around himself as they walked, suddenly feeling very insignificant.

Chapter 11

Two full days passed while Eldran recovered. He lay on a narrow cot in one of the healing chambers, his body cocooned in soft linens. Thick poultices clung to his injured shoulder, releasing the sharp scent of crushed herbs and oils. The healers came and went silently, in steady shifts as they cleaned wounds and refreshed salves. By the end of the second day, some colour had returned to Eldran's cheeks, and the lines of distress on his face had begun to soften.

Will, Athtar, and Gissumir stayed close, taking turns at his side. When one watched over Eldran, the others rested, sleeping in short bursts on a couch provided in the next room. Their time passed in gentle silence, broken only by the occasional murmured question to the healers or the subtle shift of blankets as Eldran stirred in restless dreams.

On the morning of the third day, Will entered to find Eldran propped up against a bolster, a bowl of broth in hand, talking quietly to Gissumir.

"Well," he said, voice raspy but laced with amusement, "I must look dreadful if the look on your face is anything to go by."

Will chuckled, the knot in his chest loosening just a little. "Better dreadful than dead. It's good to see you up."

Eldran set the bowl aside with care and swung his legs over the edge of the bed. "The healers are very skilled. I feel... so much better already."

"We were worried about you," Athtar said softly from the doorway, arms folded. "We did what we could to fight off the dark infection... but we weren't sure if it would be enough."

Eldran met her eyes, seeing the relief. "Then it seems I owe you my life."

Athtar stepped inside, offering a faint smile. "I'm just glad to see you're doing better."

As he stood watching the other three chatting quietly, Will was reminded of those days spent in the hospital with his parents after his dad's stroke, and wondered, with a slight pang of guilt, how his dad was doing.

Eldran had no memory of anything after leaving Thorn Island, which was probably a blessing, but as they chatted and the broth warmed him through, they almost imagined they could see him visibly improving.

"That reminds me," said Will, interrupting the flow of the conversation as a memory struck him. "Edarn popped by on the day we arrived. He was quite concerned for you, and he ensured you had the absolute best care available."

Gissumir grunted from the other side of the bed, where he was sitting in a comfortable chair. "Yes… He's been the perfect host. Quite the gentleman when not in the company of the other monarchs."

"He did ask, when you're up to it, that we present ourselves in the throne room, though," said Will, gently gauging Eldran's condition.

Eldran immediately threw the covers off and swung his legs over the edge of the bed. "Well then," he said. "Let's not keep his majesty waiting."

He insisted on dressing himself, though the others lingered nearby in case he faltered. With some effort, he exchanged the loose healer's robes for the clothes he had arrived in, now cleaned and mended by the palace staff.

Eldran's complexion had paled somewhat by the simple act of getting dressed, and Will looked at him with concern. "Are you sure you're up to this, my friend? We can go and see Edarn without you."

Eldran waved his hand dismissively. "I have been in bed for days. I need to stretch my legs."

As they stepped out into the halls beyond the infirmary, Will was finally able to take it in. When they had arrived, he had been far too distracted by Eldran's condition to absorb much of anything.

The palace was constructed of red sandstone, and unlike architecture further north, tended towards more external openings, covered with the most intricate latticework that cast beautiful patterns across the corridors. Open walkways lined with stone pillars curved around lush courtyards brimming with flowering vines and still pools of water. Warm shafts of morning sun spilled into the halls, gleaming off intricate gold inlays and jewel-toned mosaics that adorned every surface. The cool touch of the palace's heavy ancient stonework tempered the blazing heat pressing in through the wide balustrades that separated them from the outside.

When they reached the great doors of the throne room, the door guards saw them approaching and stepped aside, as attendants opened the doors and announced their arrival.

The throne room of Urias was a marvel of opulence. Vaulted ceilings inlaid with delicate filigree, and grand pillars carved with ancient stories in looping, interwoven script. But it was the morning light that gave it life. It poured through the intricately carved lattice-work of a massive arched window behind the throne, casting golden patterns across the mosaic floor and gilded walls. The warmth of it softened the grandeur, making the room feel almost intimate.

King Edarn stood before that window, and his bearing was markedly different than the one he had presented at Thorn Island. The guarded, sharp personality had been replaced by that of a man more at ease. His hands were clasped behind his back as he stood staring out through the window, the patterns playing over his face like moving shadows.

"I am truly grateful to have the chance to meet you all properly," he said without turning. "To speak freely, away from the political bickering of the conclave." He turned to face them, offering a weary smile, before slowly walking to stand before his throne, the hem of his cloak brushing lightly across the sunlit floor.

His eyes found Eldran first, noting that he was leaning heavily on his staff. "How are you feeling, my friend? Would you like a chair brought?"

Eldran waved a hand dismissively. "I am doing much better, thank you. Your healers are very skilled."

Edarn beamed at that. He seemed to be a man who wore his emotions plainly when his guard wasn't up, and the notion that he had been of service pleased him. "From what the healers say, they would not have had a chance, if not for the actions of your friends here," he said, gesturing at the others.

Eldran shifted with a wince, then inclined his head respectfully toward the king. "We're bound south again... to find and retrieve the young woman who accompanied me before." He paused, his gaze steady. "But before we depart, I must ask, Your Majesty... at the Conclave, you seemed troubled when you withheld Urias's support. Was it distrust of the others that stayed your hand, or the weight of your people's fears?"

"I wish I could have committed aid, but it was impossible," Edarn said. "Here at home, I am dealing with something of a sensitive matter. My cousin, Lord Malrec, has begun to... test the boundaries of loyalty."

Will remained silent, not quite letting his guard down, but wanting to hear more.

Edarn exhaled sharply through his nose, as if expelling his own frustration. "I suspect he's building toward something bigger, but I have no proof. And if I'd pledged military support, it would have given Malrec the excuse he needed to name me unfit and make his move."

He stopped pacing and looked them each in the eye. "So please, believe me when I say... I am not your enemy. I want to help. But I must tread carefully."

Will considered the king's words for a moment, absently pulling at his beard. "What makes you think Malrec is planning something?"

Edarn's expression tightened, and for a moment, he looked again toward the patterned sunlight spilling through the arched window.

"He was once a contender for the throne," the king said, his voice quieter now, as if speaking the words aloud pained him. "When my father died, the council debated succession for weeks. Malrec was the other name whispered in those meetings. He was a charismatic and ruthless young man, possessing many of the qualities that would have made him a great ruler. He had the support of several key houses, but the council ultimately upheld my claim... and my father's will."

He turned back to them, eyes a little darker now.

"But his followers were less than satisfied by this outcome. Over the years, they've opposed nearly every major reform I've tried to pass at court. Always just within the bounds of protocol. Never enough to accuse them of treason... but always enough to slow progress. Enough to remind me that I don't sit on this throne unopposed."

Athtar looked at him, intrigued. "I take it they've grown louder?"

Edarn nodded. "More than that. Reports have started to reach me with a growing frequency, indicating that Malrec is making appearances in places he hasn't visited in years. Rural estates. Merchant quarters. Outlying forts. Stirring old loyalties back to life. And when his supporters speak in council, there's a new kind of edge to their words. A certainty."

He paused, his voice dropping.

"So, to answer your question… I have no hard evidence, but I sense it in my gut. It's a problem that's been simmering for years, and it feels like it's ready to boil over."

Will exhaled heavily as he realised the position Edarn was in. "And if you'd pledged forces at the conclave, Malrec could've used that as fuel for rebellion."

"Exactly," Edarn said, his gaze heavy with regret. "He would've painted me a fool, wasting Urias's strength on foreign affairs, while the 'true king' stayed to defend our people. He's not just ambitious. He's smart. And he's patient."

Gissumir grunted. "Dangerous combination."

Edarn nodded grimly. "Which is why I must walk this line carefully. I can't challenge him without hard proof. But waiting for him to strike seems equally foolish."

He looked at the four of them with something like hope buried beneath his fatigued expression. "But if I had allies I could trust… discreetly… maybe we could change that."

Will shifted his weight, suddenly hyper-aware of the silence in the room. He glanced at the others, who all nodded in turn.

His own thoughts, however, were anything but calm. Lyra was out there, waiting for them to come and extract her from Alesia, and any kind of delay felt fundamentally wrong to him.

But Edarn was right. If Urias fell into civil war, or if Malrec seized power and plunged the country into turmoil at this critical juncture, this first line of defence against the south would be like low-hanging fruit, ripe for the picking. And Edarn, for all his faults, still stood on the right side of this fight.

Will exhaled slowly, closing his eyes a moment as he tilted his head back, battling his own instincts to refuse.

"I didn't come back to play politics," he said quietly, "and I didn't come here to get drawn into someone else's war."

Edarn's face fell slightly, and he opened his mouth to respond, but Will held up a hand.

"But I also didn't come back to watch the world fall apart again."

He straightened, eyes firm now despite the reticence behind them.

"If Oberith is coming, we can't afford to let kingdoms like Urias tear themselves apart. If Malrec is a threat, then we need to deal with him, quietly and efficiently, before he has a chance to turn that threat into something real."

He hesitated again, the thought of Lyra once more clawing at him like a wound. But he forced it down, locked it away, and met Edarn's gaze.

"What can we do?" he asked. "I take it you have an idea?"

Edarn's mask of royalty slipped away momentarily, and gratitude flooded his features. He gave a slight bow of the head, a rare gesture from a monarch.

"Thank you. All of you. I won't forget this."

He paused, then glanced toward the throne at the far end of the hall, his mind putting together the last parts of his plan.

"There's a state banquet tonight," he said finally, turning back to them and beginning to pace, "to mark the start of the summer festival. All the noble houses of Anhai will be in attendance... including Malrec's key supporters."

He stopped pacing, looking directly at them and lowering his voice conspiratorially.

"Malrec's supporters will be guarded around anyone they know to be loyal to me, but I will present you, Will, as a foreign dignitary; Lord Alric of Batlon, here on a diplomatic mission from King Torvahn. Your companions will pose as your retinue. I have received credible intelligence suggesting that Malrec will be using tonight's event as cover for a gathering of his key players. I need you to see if you can identify them."

Will's brow furrowed. "And once we know who they are?"

"I act," Edarn said simply. "Once I have proof, I can organise a coordinated sweep before dawn. Every known supporter will be arrested before they can react. These players are the head of the

snake. I hope that by removing them, the entire uprising will falter and collapse."

Edarn straightened, suddenly assuming the role of king once
more. "There's much to prepare. I've had rooms prepared for
you in the western wing, and my staff will see that you're properly clothed for the occasion."

He inclined his head with genuine warmth and a glint of excitement in his eye. "Rest for now. Tonight, the game begins."

With that, Edarn swept from the room, leaving the four of them
alone in the sun-drenched throne room.

Athtar arched an eyebrow. "Lord Alric?"

Will sighed in mock exasperation. "Could've at least made me a
duke, right?"

Gissumir smirked. "Come, let's see what sort of finery Urias can
drape us in."

The rooms prepared for them in the western wing of the palace
were nothing short of palatial. High-ceilinged and adorned with
gold-trimmed latticework, silk-draped beds, and marble wash-
basins filled with warm, fragrant water. The hum of the city
drifted faintly through the open shutters that allowed the warm
afternoon light to fill the space.

They rested and talked as they passed the time, waiting for the
evening to arrive. Attendants came and went with the discretion

that palace serving staff are trained in, drawing warm baths, trimming hair, and offering sweet tea with notes of jasmine and spice.

Later in the afternoon, attendants laid out their selections... silks, embroidered tunics, a dozen gleaming clasps he didn't understand the purpose of. He had never felt so out of place. The air smelled faintly of citrus oil and polished brass.

Athtar moved with effortless grace among the garments, her long hair pinned back by a silver clasp shaped like a leaf. "You look as though you'd rather face a room full of trolls," she said lightly, fastening the final buckle of her dark-green sash.

Will managed a half-smile. "At least I'd know where to stand."

She gave him a look that was equal parts amusement and pity. "This is how the powerful fight their wars, with silk and smiles. Keep yours steady, and you'll be fine."

From the adjoining chamber came a low, irritable muttering followed by the snap of fabric. "By the forge, who designed these things?" Gissumir grumbled as he emerged, wrestling with a pair of tight hose that seemed determined to throttle his legs. "How does anyone fight, walk, or—" he yanked them higher with a grunt, "—breathe in these ridiculous contraptions?" He caught sight of Will's smirk and jabbed a finger at him. "Laugh it up, lad. When the enemy comes calling, I'll still be the only one who can swing a hammer without splitting a seam."

Athtar hid a smile behind her hand. "You look very dignified, Gissumir."

"Aye," he grumbled, tugging at the fabric again. "Dignified as a trussed up fowl."

Will shook his head, chuckling as the dwarf stomped back toward his chamber, muttering darkly about "courtly nonsense" and "the downfall of civilisation by tailor."

He let the attendants fuss over him, tightening a collar here, straightening a hem there, while his thoughts drifted to the southern roads ahead.

When at last they were left alone, Athtar stepped closer and adjusted the clasp at his shoulder. "You clean up better than you think," she said quietly.

Will looked at her reflection in the mirror. She stood poised and perfectly composed. "Let's hope the same can be said for Urias when this is done."

Outside, a bell tolled the hour. The murmur of carriages echoed through the courtyard below.

"It seems the hour approaches," Athtar said.

Will straightened his jacket and glanced at the mirror, forcing his face to adopt the same mask that he presented to his own world.

Eventually, the moment broke with a polite knock at the door.

An attendant entered, bowed, and addressed them with gentle formality. "Honoured guests, the banquet is soon to begin. If you would please make your way toward the Great Hall, the court awaits your presence."

Will nodded, glancing one last time at the city bathed in golden light before turning away.

"Showtime," he murmured.

The towering golden doors of the banquet hall opened with a sonorous groan, revealing a chamber bathed in amber light and decadence. A hush swept across the hall as the herald raised his voice with ceremonial grandeur.

"Announcing... Lord *Alric of Batlon* and his esteemed retinue."

The name, though completely fabricated, carried a gravity that rippled through the crowd. Whispers ignited like sparks among the gathered nobles. Heads turned. Fans twitched. Goblets paused halfway to lips.

Will strode forward with calm confidence, wearing the mask of his new identity with ease. Each of the others had adopted the guises they had discussed whilst preparing for the evening. They entered as one, but quickly went their separate ways as the herald resumed his announcements and new guests began filtering in behind them.

Will drifted toward a well-lit alcove where minor nobles gathered around a table, engaged in idle chit-chat. He smiled faintly, taking a seat, listening more than speaking.

Athtar let herself be drawn into a circle of elegantly dressed court ladies who couldn't resist her striking presence. She responded with grace, adopting a light, easy manner that immediately put those around her at ease.

Eldran moved along the hall's perimeter, sipping wine only occasionally, nodding respectfully to those who greeted him but saying little. He concentrated instead on watching the entrances, the exits, looking for anything suspicious.

Gissumir grunted through introductions and half-heartedly engaged a minor merchant baron in a strained conversation about coastal trade. He had never been comfortable in these kinds of social gatherings, but he could, when the occasion demanded it, adopt the persona of a courtier.

As the music swelled and the laughter grew louder, the trap was slowly being set. Somewhere among these perfumed dignitaries, Malrec's agents walked freely, still unaware that tonight was to be their last at Edarn's court.

As the evening wore on, the mood in the banquet hall had grown heady and thick, many of the revellers having consumed far too much alcohol. The music rose and fell in complex, lilting phrases, and the scent of perfumed oil mingled with the smell of sweat from the ever-growing crowd filled the air. Will and his companions continued to move among the revellers, subtly avoiding King Edarn himself, who was putting on a fine performance of merry hospitality, ensuring that the ones they hunted wouldn't suspect a thing.

Every half hour or so, the four of them would cross paths and exchange murmured updates, each one increasingly less hopeful than the last.

"I think we've missed it," Will muttered to Athtar, who lingered near a cluster of chatting nobles.

"Or Edarn's intelligence was flawed," she replied softly. "There are too many people. No one would attempt anything like this in such a crowd."

They were just about ready to pull back and call the night a loss when Will, sipping at a goblet of wine he hadn't really wanted, noticed it. It was so subtle that he wondered at first if he had imagined it. Two finely dressed men across the room stood un-naturally rigid and made a strange gesture to one another.

Moments later, the men turned and quietly slipped from the hall.

As he watched, the phenomenon spread like a contagion through the room, and each time, the strange gesture would be followed by people abruptly leaving.

Will's eyes widened. He signalled to the others with a subtle tilt of the head, and within moments they'd reconvened near the periphery of the room. "I think this is it," he said under his breath.

"I saw," Athtar confirmed. "We mimic it. Follow one."

They waited until a group of two women and a tall, broad-shouldered man made the gesture and turned toward a side corridor. Without a word, Will repeated the sign. The man looked back briefly, nodded, then resumed walking. The group followed.

Down twisting stone corridors and past silent guards who notably looked the other way as they passed. As they descended beyond the ornate upper halls, the path became colder, darker. The floor changed from polished marble to older, rougher stone. The air thickened with damp and the faint smell of mildew.

They emerged into an ancient chamber, its walls vast and cracked with age, its high ceiling supported by squat stone columns. Smoke from the torches filled the room with a haze that stung their eyes and settled in their lungs. Figures continued to filter in steadily for the next few minutes. Some were masked, fearful of their face being recognised, while others stood proudly, almost belligerently, as they waited.

A few moments later, he arrived from a dark recessed doorway at the rear of the chamber. He was tall and lean with hair that was greying slightly at the temples, wearing deep red robes trimmed in gold. His bearing was unmistakably noble, and though he wore no crown, he held himself like one accustomed to power.

He stepped up onto a low platform and raised his arms.

"Brothers. Sisters. Urias sleeps," he said, his voice ringing out against stone and smoke. "But no longer!"

A hush fell. He continued.

"The decay that has gripped our kingdom must be cut away, and we are the blade. For the glory of our ancestors, we shall put an end to that gilded farce upstairs. For the strength of Urias reborn."

Cheers rippled through the crowd. He went on, decrying weakness, invoking the honour of the old dynasties, painting Edarn's reign as a slow infection rotting the essence of Uriasan pride. The speech swelled into a monologue filled with fury and nostalgia, steeped in hatred and feeding off the weaknesses of his audience, whose eyes all gleamed with reverence.

Malrec's eyes burned with a wild, fevered light, and his words tumbled out in a breathless, near-apoplectic torrent, each claim more outrageous than the last. The crowd hung on every word, drawn by the strange gravity of conviction in his madness.

Realising that they had seen enough, the four motioned silently to one another and slipped out quietly, retracing their path, making for the banquet hall, weaving swiftly through the crowd, searching for Edarn.

They found Edarn deep in performative conversation with an older duchess and two younger nobles, his face frozen in a mask of cordial amusement. But the moment he caught sight of Will and the others approaching with urgency in their steps, his smile melted away, his interest in the conversation coming to an abrupt end.

"Did you find them?" he asked.

Will nodded grimly. "We did. They're gathering in the old dungeons. We followed a group down. At least fifty of them, maybe more?" he asked the others, looking around.

They all nodded their agreement.

Edarn's eyes narrowed. He turned slightly, beckoning a nearby attendant who seemed to melt from the shadows at the edge of the hall. "Fetch Captain Renlor. Now."

The attendant vanished.

Edarn turned his full attention back to Will. "What did you hear?"

"A speech," Will said. "Rousing, full of fire and fury. The speaker... whom I assumed was Malrec, talked for some time about you. He said some less-than-flattering things about your ineffective rule. He doesn't like you much, does he?"

The king didn't flinch, but a tremor of weariness passed through his shoulders. "That sounds like his usual rhetoric. No one else would dare use language like that in the presence of so many nobles."

Moments later, a tall man in a silver-trimmed uniform approached and gave a brief bow. Edarn pulled him aside and issued hushed but urgent instructions.

Captain Renlor nodded, saluted, and vanished into the crowd as swiftly as he'd come.

Edarn turned back to Will and the others. "You've done Urias a great service tonight. And you've likely saved lives."

He glanced toward the massive doors at the back of the hall, where laughter and music still spilled in from the adjoining rooms. "Tomorrow, everything will change."

At the end of the festivities, Will lingered at the huge window behind the throne, watching as the last of the nobles drifted out into the torchlit courtyard below. The air felt heavier now, the echo of the night's confrontation leaving them all a little on edge.

King Edarn walked up behind him, looking out across the city. "Malrec's words have poisoned more ears than I dared believe."

"You have taken steps to put an end to that now," Will replied. "That's what matters."

Edarn turned, passing a weary hand across his face. "What matters is what comes next. Urias stands on the edge of something it may not survive. If my own court can be swayed so easily, how many beyond these walls have already fallen?"

Will said nothing.

Edarn exhaled. "You've straddled worlds, Will. You know how quickly faith turns to fire. If you can help me hold the line—"

Will nodded once. "I'll do what I can."

The king offered a faint smile, but it faltered almost immediately. "I pray that will be enough." He turned away again, gazing out toward the city's sleeping rooftops.

Will's eyes followed his, and for a heartbeat, he thought he saw movement beyond the window... a ripple of darkness shifting across the courtyard below. But when he blinked, there was nothing.

Chapter 12

The following morning, they awoke early, itching to be back on the road. They dressed in their travelling clothes and hastily ate the breakfast provided for them by the ever attentive staff, before gathering their belongings and making their way to the throne room to meet with Edarn, who was being briefed by a very tired-looking Captain Renlor.

Edarn looked up as they entered, flashing them a broad smile and beckoning them over. "The Captain here was just telling me that they managed to arrest all those who attended Malrec's side show last night," he said in breathless excitement. "They will now permanently reside in the dungeon they were so fond of spending time in."

Will grunted in satisfaction. "So it seems to have been a complete success then?"

Edarn nodded his head enthusiastically, still grinning. "I am eternally grateful. As soon as Malrec makes an appearance, we will discuss how I can repay you."

They didn't have to wait long, as a few moments later, the towering doors to the throne room burst open and Malrec strode in, his eyes aflame with fury.

His gaze locked on Edarn with unrestrained contempt, and when he spoke, his voice rang through the chamber like rolling thunder.

"Where are they, Edarn? What have you done with my friends?"

Edarn didn't flinch. He remained seated on the throne, hands resting lightly on the arms of the ornate chair, a study in calm composure. Captain Renlor took an instinctive step forward, but Edarn held out a hand to stay him. He rose smoothly, his tone measured and cold as morning steel.

"Your 'friends,' cousin," he said, "have been taken into custody on charges of treason. They plotted in secret beneath my roof, conspiring to turn Urias into their personal playground of power," he said, taking a step forward, his voice growing firmer. "They will face trial... or whatever justice their treachery warrants."

Malrec's face darkened with fury. "Treason? How very dare—" he spluttered.

"You were spared, Malrec, out of respect for our shared bloodline. But if you press me further, if you push this any more, I may reconsider my position on that."

A hush fell over the throne room, broken only by the sound of Captain Renlor sliding his sword halfway from its sheath suggestively. Malrec's chest heaved, his hands clenching and unclenching at his sides. For a moment, it looked as though he might strike Edarn right there, but after a sideways glance at the nearby captain, he stopped, the fire in his eyes flickering. The game had changed, and Malrec realised he no longer held any cards. He stood still for another moment, then, without another word, turned sharply on his heel and stalked out.

Silence lingered after his departure until Captain Renlor murmured, "What should be done with him, my king?"

Edarn didn't answer at once. He turned back to Will and the others, his expression sober now. "Let him go," he said finally. "Let him carry the weight of failure with him. For him, that will be punishment enough."

Another moment passed in the wake of Malrec's outburst, and then the king took a deep breath, straightened his shoulders, and turned to face Will and the others. "And now... let's talk about that debt I owe you."

Eldran stepped forward, his voice respectful. "Your Majesty, if we are to make for Strada, I would ask that we travel under the cover of another merchant caravan, as we did last time I was here. It proved to be an effective cover."

Edarn nodded thoughtfully, already anticipating the request. "I will have word sent to the merchant quarter immediately to see which caravans plan to leave today."

He turned to one of his aides and murmured instructions. The man bowed and quickly departed through a side door.

A short time later, the aide returned, bowing low. "Sire. A silk and spice merchant named Fennick intends to leave before mid-day, bound for the trading camp at Alesia. He has agreed to take on a few additional 'guards' for the journey."

The king allowed his gaze to sweep over them once more. "You have done more for this realm than I could have asked. Urias owes you a great debt, and you will always be welcome here."

Will inclined his head, offering a respectful nod. "Thank you, Your Majesty."

Eldran lingered a moment longer. "Your hospitality is deeply appreciated. I ask only one thing more...that you consider strengthening your borders and fortifying your defences. If what we suspect comes to pass, Urias will be among the first to stand in the path of the storm."

Edarn's expression sobered. He looked past them for a moment, as though seeing some distant shadow on the horizon. "I've dismissed too many warnings already," he said finally. "No more. There's a darkness stirring in the south, I can feel it. Perhaps it is time I begin listening with more than just courtesy. A little precaution, as you say, may soon prove wisdom."

Leaving the throne room felt like stepping out of one world and into another. The air outside was heavy with dust and spice, thick with the noise of the city. Everywhere they turned, there were hawkers calling, wheels creaking, the bark of dogs echoing from the narrow lanes. Will squinted into the sunlight, a low ache pressing behind his eyes. He told himself it was just fatigue, but something in the way the wind shifted; sudden, dry, carrying the faint tang of metal, set his nerves on edge. He glanced once at Athtar. She had already noticed it too.

The attack came so swiftly that it almost took them completely off-guard. A rush of armed men from a narrow side street launched at them, rust-splotched swords in their hands and garments that were torn and patched. Immediately before the attack, Will felt a tingle down the back of his neck that set him on edge. Just enough of a warning to shift his footing and cry out a warning to the others.

The street burst into chaos. Nearby citizens screamed and scattered, scrambling to get away from the violence. Will had his sword free in a heartbeat, steel ringing as he deflected a wild swing from the nearest attacker. Athtar ducked low, her hands flashing as she drew a pair of daggers from the tops of her boots. She slipped between two of the assailants and left one howling, clutching at a deep gash along his ribs.

Gissumir bellowed, swinging his heavy axe in a wide arc that drove the remaining attackers back a pace. One lunged in, only to find himself staggering away with a shattered forearm. Eldran, still weak from the lingering effects of his brush with the shadow realm's infection, didn't engage directly. Instead, he muttered under his breath, casting thin wards of light that shimmered into place just in time to turn a blade aside from Gissumir's exposed back.

It didn't take long. The attackers were untrained, likely desperate, and completely unprepared for the ferocity of the resistance they encountered. Within moments, several were on the ground groaning, and the rest were already fleeing, clutching their injuries and vanishing into the narrow, winding alleys that threaded the lower tiers of the city.

Will, his senses still flooded with adrenaline, started after them, blade still in hand, but Gissumir caught his arm.

"Let them go. We've got an appointment with Lyra to keep."

Will blinked, snapping back to the present. Gissumir didn't look all too astute at times, but he'd known exactly what to say to ground him. Will nodded, lowering his sword and letting the tension drain from his limbs.

"Who were they, do you think?" he said.

"I saw Malrec's crest on one of their tunics," said Eldran, frowning. "Edarn may have cut the head off the snake, but it seems the body still has a little life in it."

Athtar looked up and down the street to make sure there were no reinforcements coming, but eventually relaxed and moved back towards the others. "Why attack us, though?"

Eldran squinted as he considered her question. "I suppose word could have reached his people about our involvement. Maybe they were expecting their liege to be on the throne by today and blame us for finding themselves on the wrong side of things."

Will slid his sword back into its scabbard. "Whatever it is, we should keep our eyes open until we're far from Anhai."

They made the rest of the journey through the city's outer districts with weapons close to hand and eyes scanning every alleyway. The mood had shifted. Gone was the relaxed banter, replaced now with quiet vigilance. Though the streets remained crowded with morning traders and vendors calling their wares, the companions moved through them in tight formation, alert for any further signs of danger. But no further attack came.

At the South Gate, they found the caravan already assembling. Wooden carts loaded with tightly lashed goods sat lined in a row, their wheels creaking slightly under the strain. Mules snorted and stamped impatiently. The air smelled of leather, dust, and the faintly sweet scent of the spices that were packed for trade with the south.

Fennick spotted them from atop his mount and grinned broadly. He slid down from the saddle with surprising grace for a man of his age and came toward them with arms outstretched. "Ah, my friends! You made it. The king sent word ahead to inform me of your arrival," he said, wrapping his arms around them, and quickly turning to wave down his partners.

Fennick's business partners, five other men of middle years with weathered faces and watchful eyes, were dressed in flowing silks dyed in ochres, deep reds, and greens. Their heads were wrapped in turbans to shield against the sun. Though they had the easy manner of men long accustomed to travel, there was nothing soft in their expressions. These were veterans of the road.

The guards who had been hired for the journey were a more eclectic mix. Some wore the garb of the men of northern Anther, others bore the tattoos and weaponry of desert clans of the borderlands of Urias. All looked capable. None looked talkative. Like Will and the others, each was leading a mule, loaded with cargo.

Fennick gestured toward a few spare animals. "Got one for each of you. Keep them calm and moving. They're better than horses for the terrain ahead."

He gave Will a knowing look, then added, "I don't expect any trouble between here and the border, but once we're into Strada... keep your eyes up. Things aren't what they used to be down there."

Will exchanged a glance with Athtar, then reached for the reins of the nearest mule. "Thanks for the warning," he said.

The borderlands to the south of Anhai were predominantly large stretches of arid, red rock and coarse sand. The road was straight and monotonous, and there was absolutely nowhere to find shade from the unrelenting heat of the sun as it beat down mercilessly. Fennick and his men gave Will and the others cloth scarves to wrap around their heads, to shield from the sun, and when necessary, pull over their mouths to protect them from the dust. They distributed water sparingly and on a strict schedule to ensure they would have enough to reach their destination. At night, they set up camp and sat together by the campfire, eating spiced meats and talking. The nights in the open desert were as cold as the days were hot, and after a couple of days of gruelling travel, Will longed for the comfort of a hot bath and a comfortable bed.

He shifted closer to the fire, holding his hands out to the flame and watching the orange glow flicker across his dirt-smeared fingers. The chill of the night seeped into his bones even through layers of fabric. Gissumir, seated opposite him, had his axe resting across his lap as he chewed silently on a strip of jerky, eyes half-lidded and staring into the fire.

"You're quiet tonight," Will muttered, pulling the scarf down from his face.

Gissumir shrugged. "I miss trees."

Will let out a dry laugh, hoarse from days of breathing in the sand-choked air. "You and me both, my friend."

The others were similarly quiet. Eldran looked like he was bearing the desert with quiet endurance, though the lines around his eyes hinted at lingering fatigue. Athtar had taken to polishing her daggers in the evenings like a ritual, though tonight she simply sat cross-legged with her eyes closed, the firelight painting her still expression in flickering amber.

Fennick and his men, by contrast, seemed completely at ease in their surroundings. They moved through the routines of life on the road, their soft conversation in a language Will didn't know drifting through the camp like smoke on a gentle breeze.

Will was about to roll out his sleeping mat when Gissumir looked over at him, his face half-shadowed by the flickering firelight.

"I've been meaning to ask, Will," Gissumir said, his voice quieter than usual.

Will glanced up, pausing with the blanket half-unfurled. "Yes?"

"My people talk with great reverence of the hero, Lolmig Nightforge. Is it true that you travelled with him?"

Will didn't answer immediately. His gaze dropped to the fire, watching the slow dance of the embers as they pulsed and popped. He smiled, but the expression was tight, pulled askew by the knot of grief that tugged at his throat.

Athtar, who was sitting nearby, opened her eyes and looked over with interest as she drew her whetstone and resumed her nightly ritual of sharpening.

"It is true," he said at last. "And it's good to hear that he's being honoured as he should. Lolmig was the most steadfast friend a man could ever ask for... a hero, in the truest sense of the word."

The fire popped, sending a plume of embers towards the night sky, lighting Gissumir's features, and Will saw the reverence there... the quiet awe of a man raised on tales of valour and sacrifice.

"He stood against the darkness in Shadowmoor," Will said, almost to himself, lost in the memory. "He gave his own life fighting one of the cursed creatures there... to ensure I could reach Malakar and end the curse."

Athtar looked over, silently lowering her whetstone.

Will blinked once, then again, trying to swallow the heaviness rising in his chest. The fire blurred a little at the edges. "He was my anchor when everything started to fall apart. And when we lost him... I didn't know how to carry on," he said, looking over at Gissumir. "We never talked about what came after. There wasn't time. There never is."

The dwarf nodded solemnly. "In the lowlands, we carve the names of the fallen into ironwood. Lolmig's name is etched into nearly every town I've visited. Children learn it before they know their letters."

Will gave a quiet laugh, though it came out more like a sigh. "He'd have hated the fuss. Said all he ever wanted was a quiet forge and a mug that never emptied."

"He has both now, in the songs," said Gissumir, earnestly.

They sat in silence for a while after that, the fire continuing to crackle, casting long shadows across the sand. Above them, the stars stood as silent witnesses to all that had passed, and all that was still to come.

When the fire burned low, Will rolled out his blanket and lay down on his side, drawing his cloak tighter around himself. The mule he had come to half-respect was lying just a few feet away, snoring softly.

He wasn't sure if it was the cold, the hard ground, or the thoughts gnawing at the edges of his mind, but sleep didn't come easily.

Somewhere out there, beyond the dark horizon, was Lyra, and as he stared at the pale moon, he wondered what she was doing right now.

Chapter 13

By late afternoon the following day, the low walls and outer buildings of Alesia had come into view, rising from the horizon that shimmered in the heat of the day. Rather than continue on into the city, the caravan veered west and made for a stretch of flat ground just beyond a small rise where a makeshift market had sprung up over the past few weeks.

Once they reached the trading outpost, Fennick dismounted with a groan and waved for his men to start unpacking. "This is where we part ways for now," he told Will, wiping his brow with a sleeve. "We don't go into Alesia anymore."

As the others dismounted and stretched, Will surveyed the scene. Fennick's men were rapidly erecting his marquee and displaying the spices in front. As quickly as the carts were unloaded, people came to trade what little they had for the things they needed.

Will and the others lent their hands, unloading the mules and driving in the tent poles. As the sun began its final descent, Eldran set down a crate and dusted off his hands. "I think we should head into the city before nightfall," he said, looking over at the others, who all nodded in agreement.

They gave Fennick their thanks and gathered their belongings and began making their way towards the city.

They passed through the outskirts, moving toward the main gates as the first evening shadows stretched across the road.

Eldran drew his scarf across his face as they approached the outer gates and spoke low to the others. "Cover up. Keep your heads down and your hands near your belts."

Eldran had described the squalor that he had discovered here, but the city within the walls was worse than any of them had expected. Once-proud buildings of carved stone and painted plaster stood faded and cracked, their colours long since scoured away by sand and sun. The tiled streets were fractured and uneven, half-buried beneath drifts of sand that whispered through the alleys with every hot gust of wind. Roof beams jutted from collapsed buildings, bleached white by years of relentless sun, and doorways gaped like open wounds, leading only into darkness and emptiness.

The people lingered in doorways, huddled in broken window frames, or leaned against sagging walls, their clothes little more than filthy and threadbare rags. Their eyes were hollow, filled with hunger and suspicion, and a fury that had become their sole motivation, allowing them to keep moving forward.

Will tried not to meet their gaze, but it became impossible to do so. A child stood barefoot in the street ahead, staring with such intensity that Will instinctively reached for the pouch at his side. Eldran caught his wrist before he could offer anything.

"We can't help them," he said gently. "Not like that."

Will swallowed hard but let his hand drop. A man passed by, dragging a wooden cart piled with clay pots that the locals took to market to trade with, while an elderly woman leaned against a crumbling doorway and spat into the dust as they passed.

They continued to move cautiously through the streets of Alesia. Eldran led them deeper into the rabbit warren of residential homes that resembled a patchwork shanty-town, his wits sharp, his eyes alert. At one point, they had to duck into a side alley at the sound of booted feet marching through the streets, waiting until the soldiers had passed before continuing their journey. "Things are a lot more tense than when I left," Eldran muttered to them as they crept stealthily through the narrow streets.

Will began feeling a heaviness in the pit of his stomach. With this much military activity, could Lyra have remained safe here? He tried to push those thoughts down as he pressed on, keeping one eye on Eldran and one looking for patrols.

Eventually, Eldran paused, peering both ways down the street, before ducking under a dirty tarpaulin and into the shadowed interior of what might once have been a workshop. The room was dim, lit only by narrow shafts of sunlight that slipped through cracks in the wooden slats above. Old tools hung from pegs on the walls, and in one corner stood an old kiln that still contained the ashes of its last use. Eldran gestured for them to stay close and moved toward the back, pushing through a narrow hallway.

Will's hand hovered near the hilt of his sword, his every sense on high alert in this place.

At the end of the hall, Eldran knocked three times on a section of the wall. There was a pause, then a sharp click, and a hidden panel opened, revealing a small room lit by a flickering oil lamp. A woman stood inside, her expression hard until her eyes fell on Eldran.

"Surah," he said with quiet relief.

She stepped forward, eyes narrowing at the others before wrapping Eldran in a brief but firm embrace. "You're late," she said, pulling back, eyeing the others with suspicion.

Eldran caught her gaze and looked back at the others. "Don't worry, they're with me."

Surah gave a tight nod, her gaze sweeping over the group, lingering a moment longer on Athtar before turning back to Eldran. "The streets aren't safe anymore. Not for anyone, and definitely not for people like you."

She closed the panel behind them once they were through, securing a latch with a soft *click, and* Will let out a quiet breath.

"Sit," she said, gesturing towards a couple of mismatched chairs and some crates at one end of the room, "and I'll bring you up to speed."

As they sat, a murmur of soft, indistinct voices drifted in from deeper within the dilapidated building. Will's eyes flicked to the shadows beyond the lamplight, wondering how many more people were hiding in the gloom. The air was thick here. Cooler than in the streets, but so heavy it was almost difficult to breathe.

Surah knelt nearby, pushing a stray hair back out of her face. For an instant, Will looked past the dirt and the hard look of defiance on her face. Her dark skin and slightly angled eyes held an exotic beauty that no amount of grime could obscure.

Surah's voice was low, her words edged with fatigue. "Since you left, things have only gotten worse. We're under martial law now. Soldiers on every corner... stopping people, breaking into homes. No one sleeps easily anymore."

She glanced toward the door, as if expecting boots on the stairs, then forced herself to go on. "At first, people welcomed their arrival. The recruiters, I mean. Oberith's talk of unity lit something in them. We hadn't felt that in years. The young men lined up to enlist, and the rest cheered them on." She hesitated, her jaw tightening. "But not everyone wanted war."

The room went still.

"That's when the red robes came," she said finally.

Eldran's brow furrowed. "The red robes?"

She met his gaze, unblinking. "Oberith's priests. Mages. Dangerous ones. They don't answer to the generals or even the governors. Only to him."

She crossed her arms, eyes drifting to the shuttered window. "When the soldiers first marched in, there was a city-wide celebration. Flowers, banners... people calling them heroes." Her voice hardened. "Then came the disappearances. Anyone who spoke out... anyone who asked too many questions. Families, whole streets, some nights. Gone before dawn."

Her voice dropped to a whisper. "Now we don't speak at all. We keep our heads down, and we pray we're not next."

A long silence followed. None of them knew what to say. Will felt a chill at the cold certainty of what it meant if Oberith's armies reached the north.

Eldran's eyes went distant as a thought suddenly struck him. "This might explain the shift in the light-source, though."

"How so?" asked Will.

"If Oberith has an order of magic users who haven't trained at Thorn Island, that would account for the disruption in the source," he said as he stopped pacing and looked at Will. "When you were moving about in Aruna a decade ago, we could all feel it. You were very powerful, but completely unrefined, like a toddler."

Wills looked abashed. "Thanks."

Eldran waved a hand. "I mean no offence, but you had that role thrust upon you and didn't have the time to study the years it takes to master the delicate ways of energy manipulation."

Will nodded, begrudgingly. "I suppose so. But what has this got to do with the red robes?"

Eldran paused his pacing, and his eyes went distant again momentarily. "What is that damn noise?"

The others all looked around, baffled. "You mean the voices from the other room?" Will asked.

Eldran shook his head, still looking slightly distracted, but eventually continued. "Assuming that Oberith became active at about the time you left Aerinthos, Will. And assuming he has grown a significant force of these red-robed mages, all stomping about like toddlers... This would account for the growing disruptions we have been experiencing."

Eldran stamped his foot, his expression angry. "There it is again... are you telling me none of you hear that?"

The room fell quiet as the others strained their ears.

Will frowned. "I hear the others talking in the back room, maybe someone moving about down the hall—"

"No, no, not that," Eldran snapped, his frustration growing. He closed his eyes, brow furrowed in concentration. "It's beneath all of that. A hum... of sorts. I feel it at my core."

After a moment or two, they all gave up trying to hear whatever it was Eldran was hearing. "Sorry, old friend," said Will, "but I hear nothing."

Will turned then back to Surah. "So when are you expecting Lyra back here?" he asked, suddenly eager to get to the point of their visit.

There was a momentary flicker of...something. Something Will couldn't quite put his finger on in Surah's expression, but as quickly as it crossed her face, it was gone again. She smiled at him, "She has been working as a servant in the old city hall. She is usually back here before midnight."

Will's face lit up.

Surah stood up, suddenly moving towards the door. "I have some business to attend to in the city this evening," she said. "You're more than welcome to stay here and wait for your friend, just stay inside and out of sight."

Will gave her a grateful nod. "Thank you, Surah. For everything."

She paused with her hand on the door, her eyes sweeping over each of them in turn. "Just... be careful. Soldiers don't patrol this area often, but that doesn't mean they never come through." Her gaze lingered on Will for a fraction longer before stepping out and pulling the door shut behind her.

Gissumir leaned back in his chair with a low grunt. "Anyone else get the sense she wasn't telling us everything?"

Athtar's golden eyes flicked to the door. "It did seem like she was choosing her words carefully."

Eldran didn't respond. He stood near the window, fingers tapping absently on the sill, his eyes distant again. Will stepped toward him.

"You still hearing it?" he asked quietly.

Eldran didn't look at him, just nodded slowly.

Will didn't like the sound of that, but silently gripped his friend's shoulder and backed away, keeping an eye on him.

Something Eldran had said before was gnawing at Will. He sat chewing it over for a while before finally trying to engage Eldran again. "You mentioned earlier that when I wielded the light in Shadowmoor, you could sense my power?"

Eldran's gaze took a moment longer than it should have to focus back in the room, but finally, he nodded. "Oh yes, you were quite powerful. We could all sense it."

Will's shoulders slumped. The implication was clear in Eldran's use of the past tense. A few moments passed in silence; the only sound was the continuing murmurs from down the hall. Eventually, Will sighed, "Do you think I will ever be able to use it again?"

But as he looked at Eldran, he realised that not a word of what he'd just said had gone in. Eldran's stare was almost completely blank, his head tilted to one side, listening to whatever noise was troubling him. Will watched for a moment, troubled. He gestured to the others who shared his look of concern.

"Eldran, are you okay?" asked Gissumir, moving slowly towards the old mage.

Eldran suddenly stood up straight and looked straight at them, the sudden movement breaking the silence and startling them.

"I think I know what this sound is. I must go and investigate," Eldran said.

Will began standing from the chair, but Eldran motioned them all to remain seated. "I won't be long... and I'll be able to move around easier by myself. I'll be back before midnight, and then we can all get out of here."

Will wasn't sure, but Eldran left them no time to deliberate before stepping out of the door and disappearing into the soft evening light beyond.

"That was bloody strange, even for him," said Gissumir, his bushy eyebrows raised.

Athtar nodded. "Do you think we should follow him?" she asked, looking at Will.

Will shook his head. "I doubt you would even catch him now... besides, if he doesn't want to be found, you won't find him. He knows how to take care of himself."

The minutes crawled by as Will, Athtar, and Gissumir settled in to wait. The low murmurs from deeper within the building continued. Will assumed it was just others like Surah, sympathisers, or perhaps refugees hiding from the patrols.

Athtar spent the time peering out of a high-level window that looked out onto the street, her ears flicking slightly with every distant sound. Gissumir remained near the door, arms crossed, eyes unmoving. Will could do little but pace, his mind circling endlessly.

Then a sound cut through the silence. The sound of dozens of booted feet striking the cobbled street outside in unison.

Athtar was the first to react, motioning sharply with one hand. Will snuffed out the lamp with a pinch of his fingers and dropped to a crouch beside the others. They waited, expecting the rhythm of the patrol to continue down the street. But the steps halted just outside the building.

Gissumir's expression darkened as he reached for the hilt of his axe. Athtar drew a dagger from beneath her cloak, her stance shifting, weight balanced on the balls of her feet. Will barely dared to breathe, his heart hammering in his chest.

They could hear people moving about in the room down the hall, and then came the unmistakable sound of a door handle turning. Slow, deliberate.

Will quickly gestured toward the rear of the building. They moved like shadows, slipping through a narrow corridor and deeper into the structure. At the back, they found a rickety stairwell and a crumbling exit into the adjacent building, little more than a ladder leading through a torn canvas sheet.

They didn't speak. Just before they slipped through, Will whispered, "If we get separated, meet back at Fennick's camp."

The others nodded.

Then the door behind them burst open, wood splintering, the remnants of it bouncing off the wall.

Shouts followed them as they scrambled through the passageway and into the next building. It was abandoned, barely more than a frame with a collapsed roof, but it connected to another set of buildings beyond.

They ran.

Through low hallways and tight alleys, ducking under beams and leaping over fallen rubble. Behind them came the clatter of pursuit. Armoured soldiers barking commands, the dull clink of blades striking walls as they tried to force their way through the narrow paths.

At one junction, a soldier rounded the corner too fast and Athtar struck like lightning, her blade flashing once across his throat before she darted ahead again. Gissumir turned and dropped another with a brutal swing of his axe, but the delay cost them. More boots slammed the stone behind them.

Will skidded around a corner, nearly losing his footing, and was met with a soldier lunging from the shadows. He twisted, grabbing the man's wrist and driving a knee into his gut before slamming him against the wall. The soldier went limp, and Will ran on.

The three of them darted through the twisting maze of Alesia's ruined underbelly, scattering debris, knocking over crates and barrels behind them to slow pursuit. They climbed over shattered walls and ducked beneath broken beams, breath ragged, muscles burning.

At last, after what felt like an eternity of pursuit, they tumbled out into a wide, derelict courtyard. The boots were no longer behind them. The soldiers had either lost them or chosen not to follow further into the broken maze.

They stood there, gasping, drenched in sweat.

Will leaned against a cracked stone column, trying to calm his racing heart. "What the hell was that? That was no random search."

Athtar turned slowly, checking the shadows. "No. They knew where to look. They came directly for us."

Gissumir spat to the side and rolled his shoulder. "I'd say someone just gave up our position. And there aren't too many candidates."

Will didn't answer. His thoughts were already spinning toward the worst-case scenario.

Chapter 14

When they arrived at the camp, Fennick whistled as he looked them up and down. "I assume you've been upsetting the locals," he said.

Will looked at the others, now that they were in the circle of firelight, and realised they were all a little scuffed up, their faces smudged with dirt and dried blood from their encounter with the patrol inside the city. He gently pressed a hand to his ribs that he now realised were quite badly bruised.

Will cast Fennick a sheepish smile. "It seems we have a habit of doing that."

They settled down by the fire, cleaning their wounds and talking to Fennick and his men about what had transpired inside the city.

"So where is your Eldran mage now?" he asked suddenly, looking around.

"He…urm…" Will started, but faltered, looking briefly at Athtar and Gissumir, before turning back to Fennick. "Something came up," he said finally.

Fennick tilted his head, the stem of the pipe he was smoking bobbing between his teeth. "…that timing is a little suspicious, no?"

Will bristled, but before he could answer, Fennick waved a hand to soften the edge of his words.

"I mean no offence. Just… I have seen many betrayals in my years; it teaches you to squint sideways at the timing of things."

Will looked at Athtar, who gave him a faint shrug, and then at Gissumir, who didn't bother hiding the suspicious frown creasing his brow. He wanted to reject the thought outright, wanted to insist that Eldran would never abandon them, would never sell them out.

But the truth was… he didn't know for sure.

He stared into the fire, troubled. "He wouldn't betray us," he said at last, but even as the words left his mouth, he could taste the bitterness of uncertainty in them. "He wouldn't."

Fennick didn't press the issue. Just gave a grunt and leaned back, exhaling a long plume of smoke into the air. "I hope you're right, Will."

The campfire popped. Somewhere in the distance, a dog barked once and then fell silent.

* * *

Will arose early the following morning to the sounds of the camp waking up, hoping that Eldran might have turned up during the night. When it became apparent he hadn't, Will prepared to go back into the city.

"Don't cause too much trouble today," Fennick said, laughing. "I don't need you getting us chased out of the city for good."

Will smiled, shaking the man's hand firmly. "We won't. I promise," he said. "If all goes well, we should be back here by sundown."

Fennick nodded, bending down to double-check the peg on a guide rope. "Well then, I will see you later. If for some reason you are delayed, you should know that we return to Anhai with the rising sun tomorrow... with or without you."

Will drew his brow together. "Why so suddenly?" he asked.

"These people don't have much to trade, but their pottery is highly sought after in Anther, and I can make a fortune there. There is a big festival coming up soon and I will be able to charge double if I make it in time..." he paused a moment, looking pained. "Also, honestly, this place has started giving me the creeps."

"I understand," said Will.

The light of a new day had washed Alesia clean of shadow, and for a moment, the streets seemed almost bright with promise. There were subtle differences from the cities of the north, but Will could almost imagine this was a normal city, going about its day. The signs all remained, but the living tide of the city masked them with a thin veneer of vibrancy.

The soldiers on the gate barely gave them a second glance as they passed through, just another trio of travellers returning from the trade enclave.

Will glanced to the side as a man passed by with a loaded cart. He smiled politely, but his eyes were dull, fixed forward. The reality of it struck Will then. The city wasn't free. It had just learned to live with its chains.

What little conversation they dared when they were walking through the busier parts of the city stopped as they re-traced their footsteps from the day before and into the rougher, more impoverished area of the city. They didn't have Eldran to guide them this time, so they took several wrong turns, but eventually found themselves back in the familiar street outside where they had met Surah.

The building looked different in the daylight. Less mysterious, more run-down. The faded, flaking paint, the crumbling stonework, the broken shutters, all painfully visible in the light of the rising morning sun.

They entered the building and found the concealed entrance to the room where they had met Surah. Will knocked twice, firm but not loud.

They waited.

Nothing.

He knocked again, a little harder this time. Still nothing.

"Maybe she hasn't come back yet," Athtar said quietly, though there was doubt in her voice.

Will tried the handle. It creaked open, unlatched. He shared another glance with the others, then pushed it open all the way and led the way to the room.

Inside, the room was dark and still. Dust hung in the shafts of sunlight slicing through the boarded windows. There was no sign of Surah. There was no sign that anyone had been there since their departure.

Will stepped in carefully, senses sharp. "Stay close," he said quietly.

They moved through the building slowly, methodically checking each room. Everything was completely undisturbed, and they soon realised no one had been back here.

Realising they were there alone, Gissumir looked at Will. "What now?"

Will's eyes went distant as he gazed blankly at the boarded windows. "We wait until noon. If no one comes... then we'll figure out what to do next."

They made themselves as comfortable as they could and sat in near silence, listening intently to the distant sounds of the city, but whether it was the natural aftermath of the attack by the patrol last night, or whether the people who inhabit this part of town don't routinely spend the day here, the entire street remained almost silent. The hours slipped by agonisingly slowly, but eventually Will peered out between the boards covering the window.

"The shadows are pretty short out there, I would say it's about noon," he said, a note of disappointment in his voice.

Athtar stood from where she had been crouched, back pressed against the wall. "So do we head back or ask around?"

Will knew that the safest course of action would be to retreat to the relative safety of the camp again and carefully consider the next step, but the idea of wasting any more time inflamed his senses and overruled rational thought. "We should ask around," he said, scratching at his beard. "Let's be smart about it, though."

Gissumir nodded in approval. "Sounds good. Let's go and find Eldran and Lyra and then get out of this forsaken place."

The three of them slipped back into the street, moving casually enough to avoid the suspicion of those they hoped to question, but with enough care that they could make a quick exit if they needed to. The eerie atmosphere in this part of the city left them all feeling quite uneasy.

They moved cautiously, heading toward the nearest cluster of open doors and sagging laundry lines. A hunched old woman sat on a crumbling stoop, shelling a bowl of pale beans into a cracked pot. Her eyes flicked to them with guarded suspicion as they approached, and Will offered her a polite nod.

"Good day, elder," he said, stopping a respectful distance away. "We're looking for a friend who lives nearby. Tall woman, quiet voice. Name's Surah. You wouldn't happen to know where she's gone?"

The woman stared at him with eyes gone cloudy with age, and for a moment, Will thought she hadn't heard. Then her fingers resumed their slow work, and she spoke in a voice like dry leaves. "She don't live here no more."

Will frowned. "Since when?"

The woman shrugged, lips folding inward. "She knew better than to linger when the wind turned foul."

"What do you mean, the wind turned foul?" Athtar asked, pressing for more.

The woman only shook her head and returned to her beans, indicating that as far as she was concerned, the conversation was over.

They waited for a moment, looking at one another, but the woman seemed oblivious to their continued presence, so they moved on.

The next few attempts yielded little more. Some shrugged and hurried away. Others glanced about nervously and claimed not to know anyone by that name. It wasn't until they reached a skinny man crouched outside a butcher's with a bloodstained apron that they got anything more.

"Surah?" the man repeated, wiping his hands on a rag. "Aye, I know her. Kind soul. Always kept her head down. You say you're friends of hers?"

Will nodded. "We were meant to meet her today. We heard she might have left?"

"She cleared out sometime last night," the man said, glancing around before leaning in a little closer. "Didn't even stop to say goodbye. That's not like her."

"Any idea where she might've gone?"

"Not a clue. But if she left in the night without a word, something must've spooked her."

The three exchanged uneasy looks.

"Thank you," Will said, slipping the man a small coin.

They stepped away, their frustration growing with every encounter.

Will exhaled slowly. "If Surah ran, she must have had a reason. At this point, I am more concerned with why Eldran never returned, and why Lyra didn't show."

From where he was still sitting, the skinny man overheard their conversation. "You know Miss Lyra?" he said, a note of adoration in his voice.

Will looked at him sharply, moving towards him a little more aggressively than he'd intended, causing the man to recoil slightly at his approach.

Will stopped, forcing his posture and expression into something more relaxed and holding up his hand to the man to indicate that he meant no harm. "It is Lyra I need to find. Surah was meant to help me find her. How do you know her?"

The man's face lit up again. "Miss Lyra is good people. She helps us poor folks, bringing food back from the city hall and helping folks who don't want to be a part of Lord Oberith's war."

Will's heart swelled with pride. That was the Lyra he remembered.

The man kept talking, warming to the subject now that the tension had eased. "She never talks much about herself," he said, glancing about. "But folks around here trust her well enough...for an outsider at any rate. Most nights, she comes back through the south alley, near the old well."

Will looked to Athtar and Gissumir, the familiar rush of excitement tightening in his chest. "Then that's where we'll wait."

The man leaned in slightly. "If you're looking for her, do it quiet... and stay out of sight. There's eyes everywhere now. People have been disappearing. Some don't come back. Some do, but they're... not the same."

"What do you mean, not the same?" Athtar echoed.

He nodded grimly. "Like they left their souls behind somewhere and only the shell made it home."

Will's jaw tensed. "Thank you. You've helped more than you know."

The man gave a small nod and ducked back inside the butcher's.

As they stepped away, Gissumir muttered, "That didn't sound ominous at all."

They located the old well that the butcher had described. Nearby, tucked between crumbling walls and a collapsed archway, they found a hidden spot where they could wait out the rest of the day. Few people passed through this part of the city, but they remained cautious, keeping low and out of sight.

They spoke only in hushed tones, passing the time quietly as the sun descended. The heat was merciless, baking the stone around them and filling the air with dry, choking dust. They did what they could to find shade, but by the time the sky began to deepen and the shadows stretched long across the streets, their lips were cracked and their throats parched.

As night fell, Gissumir crept to the well and returned with their water-skins refilled. The cool night air brought welcome relief, and the fresh water did the rest. Refreshed, they settled in once more, keeping their vigil under the gathering stars.

The moon that night was bright and full, casting a pale silver light over the streets of Alesia. It lit the world with a clarity that made the details of everything almost more vivid than they had been during the daylight hours. Just before midnight, they were speaking in low murmurs when the sound of approaching footsteps brought them all to stillness.

Tense from the ambush the night before, they instinctively melted into the shadows, ready to run, hide, or fight depending on what came around the corner.

From the southern alley emerged two women wrapped in the traditional robes of the region, their faces and hair covered by layers of cloth. Their movement was graceful, familiar... something about that image froze Will in place. His breath caught in his throat. He didn't need to see the flash of silver hair to know that it was Lyra approaching.

He raised a hand, motioning for Athtar and Gissumir to hold. He didn't yet know who the second woman was or if they were being followed. But as the pair drew closer, Will realised that if he waited any longer, the moment might pass them by.

He stepped into the moonlight.

The women gasped, instinctively drawing back. Their hands went to the scarves covering their faces. Then, as recognition widened their eyes, they slowly, cautiously, lowered them.

After all these years, Lyra stood before him. The moonlight caught her features, soft and unreal. She stared at him as though the world had just opened up before her. Neither of them spoke.

They simply stood there, in silence, lost in the impossible truth of what they were seeing.

Will took a hesitant step forward, afraid that if he moved too quickly, the moment would shatter. "Lyra..." he said, his voice thick with emotion.

She didn't answer at first. Her eyes scanned every inch of him, unable to reconcile the reality in front of her with the years of grief she'd carried. Her hands trembled at her sides. "How?" she breathed, the word barely more than a whisper.

Will smiled, his own eyes beginning to well up with the turbulent sea of emotions that he suddenly found himself in. "It's a long story."

Her mouth opened again, closed, then opened once more. "I thought I would never see you again," she said, her voice cracking.

Will stepped closer, lifting a hand as if to touch her but stopping just short. "I have been trying to get back since the moment I left."

Lyra finally reached out, her fingers brushing his. It was all the invitation Will needed. He stepped into her arms, and she into his, and they held each other like people who'd been drowning in separate oceans and had just found the same shore. Her arms were tight around his back, his hands buried in her silver hair, and neither of them could quite speak for a while.

"I thought it would get easier with time," she murmured against his shoulder. "But I never got used to being here without you."

"I'm here now," Will whispered. "I'm not leaving again. Not unless you want me to."

She suddenly pulled back slightly to look into his eyes, her face wet with tears. "You idiot," she said, half laughing, half sobbing. "You absolute fool."

Will chuckled, wiping a thumb across her cheek. "Guilty as charged."

Behind them, Athtar and Gissumir stood respectfully silent, while Surah gave them a knowing smile.

For a moment, neither of them spoke. The night was so still it felt as though the world itself had stopped to allow them this perfect moment, only the faint rustle of fabric and the whisper of their breathing breaking the silence. The full moon hung above the shattered rooftops, silver light spilling across the empty square. Then, from somewhere down a side street, a dog barked, the sound carrying far in the still air. The moment shattered, reminding them that they were still in enemy territory and desperately needed to find cover.

"We should move," Surah said quietly. "The night patrols will be moving through this area soon. The safehouse you were in has been compromised, but there is another nearby."

Will nodded, finally stepping away from Lyra but keeping her hand in his. "Lead the way."

She pulled her hood back up and turned into the shadows of the alley. Lyra lingered for one last look at Will, her fingers tightening in his before she followed.

Chapter 15

Will felt suddenly elated, as if nothing could suppress his euphoric state of mind. He couldn't help but steal sideways glances at Lyra as Surah continued to lead them through the dark streets. Every so often, she caught him looking and smiled, teasing him gently. "Stop staring," she whispered, though her voice held no real protest. When he chuckled and made a show of pulling his hand away, she only gripped it tighter, drawing him closer. Even the others were lifted by Will and Lyra's reunion, leaving everyone smiling and walking a little lighter.

Eventually, Surah led them into a building that looked much the same as the last safehouse where they had first met her, quickly ushering them all inside, before securing the opening and lighting a lamp.

"I am sorry, but I have no food to offer you. I have not been able to prepare this place with provisions yet," she said.

Athtar immediately rounded on Surah, arms folded, fixing her with a piercing gaze. "Where were you last night? One moment we're lying low, the next a full patrol bursts in like they knew exactly where to look."

Will remained silent, watching Surah closely.

"I told you, I had an errand to run," she said, shifting uncomfortably under their scrutiny.

Athtar narrowed her eyes. "At the exact moment we were ambushed?"

Surah's jaw tensed. "I didn't set you up, if that's what you're suggesting," she said, her voice cracking slightly. "I was late meeting my contact because of your arrival. The guard patrol passed me as I was making my way back to you. I saw them breach the building from a distance, but by that point, there was nothing I could have done, so I ran."

Gissumir glanced at Will, then back to her. "And Eldran?"

Surah exhaled slowly, sitting down on an upturned crate. "I don't know exactly where he went, but... my contact shared something. Something that might at least explain his strange behaviour, if not his absence."

The room fell still, all eyes now on Surah.

"My contact had called to meet me last night because the red robes were abuzz about a breakthrough they had made," she said.

Noting that the tension had eased slightly and she had their full attention, Surah continued. "They have developed... a weapon. I didn't really understand everything that he was telling me, but apparently, mages have a certain signature... a mark. Knowing that the order has infiltrated the city, the red robes have developed a kind of psychic trap that targets the order's signature and lures them."

Will's eyes darkened. "You think that's what happened to him?"

Surah nodded slowly. "It would explain his strange behaviour last night."

Athtar rubbed her forehead, frowning. "Then he's surely been captured. That would explain why he's not been in touch."

"It's likely," Surah said quietly. "If that's true, then he's in grave danger. They'll try to break him. It could well be that it's he who gave up your location, even unwittingly."

Will slammed his hand against the wall, frustration at this new development building up inside him. It seemed that no matter how far they got, the universe always found a new obstacle to put in their path.

Surah leaned her head back against the wall, closing her eyes briefly, her weariness etched deeply on her face.

Lyra moved over to her with a glass of water. "Are you alright?"

Her eyes opened slowly, unfocused at first, then settled on her. "Just tired," she murmured, smiling a wan smile as she took the glass off Lyra. "I didn't sleep last night. After the raid on the old safehouse, there was too much to do."

Silence fell across the room again. Surah's lethargy, seemingly contagious, spread across the room; everyone's eyes suddenly heavy as the events of the day caught up to them all. Lyra curled up in Will's arms, and he held her close, resting his chin gently on the top of her head. For a while, they simply sat in the stillness, enjoying that brief reprieve.

Then Gissumir stirred, glancing up from where he'd been studying a crack in the floor. "So what do we do about Eldran?" he asked. "We can't just leave him."

"I think I might know where they have taken him," said Lyra quietly from her position in front of Will.

"Mmm?" mumbled Will, fighting against the compulsion to fall into sleep's welcoming embrace.

Lyra sat up slightly, the movement disturbing Will's moment of peace, bringing him back into the room. "There was a level below the city hall where the serving staff were not permitted to go, but I saw red robes coming and going from there a lot. I don't know what they do down there, but if they are holding Eldran, I'll bet that's where they have him."

Surah exhaled slowly, rubbing her eyes with the heel of her hand before speaking. "The city hall is the heart of the military operations here in Alesia. If Eldran is being held there, he's in the most heavily fortified place in the city."

A silence settled again, heavier this time.

"So we sneak in," Will said, meeting her gaze. "There has to be a way."

"There might be," she nodded, though her voice was hesitant.

She glanced over at Gissumir, her expression apologetic. "You'll have to remain outside. I'm sorry. Your presence would raise too many questions. A Dwarf here in Alesia draws attention, and if you're spotted inside the hall, it's over."

Gissumir frowned but didn't protest. "Someone has to watch your back anyway. I'll guard the exit and make sure there's a clear escape route in case you come out hot."

Surah nodded before continuing. "The rest of you will dress in local clothing... I'll find something for you all. They'll conceal enough to keep us from being recognised, and the head scarf should conceal Athtar's heritage."

Athtar gave a dry smile. "I have been hiding my heritage for a long time now in Will's world... one more day won't hurt."

Will glanced at Lyra. "You said the staff were barred from that level. Any idea how to access it?"

She shook her head. "Only that the red-robes always used a specific door near the east wing, but it is guarded most of the time."

They exchanged a look. The plan was forming, but the potential for risk was high.

"Do we go tonight?" Lyra asked quietly, looking from Surah to Will.

Surah hesitated, the weariness dragging at her again. "There's a shift change in the guard at first light," she said. "It's the only window where the watch is distracted. And I—" she caught herself, then softened. "I need rest. If I go in there half-awake, I'll get us all killed."

Will gave a small nod. "Then we wait for morning."

Will had so much he wanted to say to Lyra, questions and confessions that had waited years to be spoken. But as they all settled down to rest in the few hours before dawn, he knew this wasn't the time.

For now, she was here. In his arms.

He could feel the steady rhythm of her heartbeat against his chest and breathe in the soft, flowery scent of her hair.

A small smile tugged at the corner of his mouth as the last of the tension melted from his shoulders. His eyes drifted shut, and for the first time in a long while, his mind slipped peacefully into sleep.

* * *

The sky was still a deep shade of blue when they slipped out of the safehouse before sunrise. They moved in silence, cloaked in layers of coarse fabric, moving on silent feet as they made their way through the winding streets of Alesia.

When the great dome of the city hall finally rose into view, its dark silhouette lit by the faintest edge of morning, they stopped short.

Rows of soldiers patrolled the perimeter, some wearing the light, weathered garb of local militia, others in the darker, tighter-cut uniforms of southern forces from Mor'Dan.

They huddled near the corner of a quiet alley as the city slowly stirred around them. Surah took a moment to go over the plan again, keeping her voice deliberately low to avoid being over-heard by any nearby guards.

She turned to Gissumir. "You stay close, but not too close. In that alleyway across the street, there's a recessed stairwell. It'll give you cover and a view of the entrance. Wait there and be prepared to cover us if we need it."

Gissumir nodded grimly, absently hefting his weapon.

The first blush of sunlight tipped over the city walls, and with it came a shift in tempo. The plaza in front of the hall stirred to life as the day's staff began to arrive, all merging in quiet lines with those exiting from the long night shift.

Now was their window.

Will tugged the scarf tighter over his face, glanced once more at Lyra beside him, then stepped into the slow-moving crowd. Athtar stepped confidently into position behind them alongside Surah, her hood pulled low.

He could feel the eyes of the soldiers on him, but tried to maintain a relaxed, confident stride, hoping that his lack of confidence wasn't written so plainly on his face that it exposed them. But none of the other workers who were approaching the city hall gave them a second glance as they all continued to shuffle their way, slack-jawed, across the plaza.

As they reached the main entrance, they were stopped by a guard who turned to Will. "I don't recognise your face," he said bluntly. "What is your work detail?"

Will's heart dropped as fear coiled in his gut, and his mind raced, trying to react, but being stubbornly sluggish. For a split second, the instinct to reach for the sword hidden between the folds of his robe took hold of him, but he quickly suppressed it, realising that it would be the end of their rescue attempt.

As he stood there, slack-jawed, for what felt like minutes, Lyra stepped forward, pulling down her scarf and flashing a tired but familiar smile at the guard to get his attention. "Don't worry about him," she said, her tone light and familiar. "He's new…. and a little slow. I've got him on cleaning duties today, helping me out in the general's wing."

The guard didn't look convinced at first. His eyes lingered on Will, narrowing slightly before flicking to Lyra. Recognition sparked there, and after a pause, he gave a short grunt.

"Alright. But don't let him wander off if he's slow. This isn't a care centre."

Lyra offered a mock-sympathetic sigh, shooting the guard another smile. "Trust me, I know."

With a dismissive wave, the guard stepped aside and let them pass.

As they slipped through the heavy wooden doors, Will released a breath slowly, allowing the tension to release with it.

"I thought we were done before we started there," he said, looking at Lyra with pride. "If it wasn't for you, I would have been done for."

She smiled at him and looked down at the ground, pushing back a stray hair that fell across her eyes.

She continued leading them through the halls, the others trying to keep up as she confidently made her way towards their destination. After a few moments, she led them into a small room just off the main hall and closed the door behind them.

"We should be safe in here for a moment," she said in a whisper. "The door to the lower level is just across the way. This is our last chance to abort."

They all exchanged glances, weighing up the risk they were about to face. Will eventually spoke up. "Eldran wouldn't leave us behind," he said simply.

Athtar mumbled her agreement.

"All right then. What's the plan from here?" Lyra asked.

Will gently twisted the door handle and inched it open, pressing his eye to the crack to peer out and get a better look. He watched the movement of people in the hall outside for a few moments before gently pressing the door back into its opening, the latch clicking as it closed.

"Looks like two guards on the door. We could probably rush them, but there are a lot of others moving around out there, so there is a chance we get caught before we can hide them... and then of course, the question of where the guards are," he said.

Lyra looked at him pointedly. "Okay... I assume you have another idea?"

He smiled. She knew him so well... even after all these years. He did have a way of over-explaining, and she tended to pull him up on that. "I suggest we lure a red robe in here. Do you think you could manage that Surah?" he asked.

She looked afraid, but nodded silently. Bracing herself, she slipped out the door, leaving them in silence. Will stood by the handle, ready to act the moment she returned, every muscle in his body taut with anticipation.

Seconds dragged. Then came the sound of approaching footsteps... two sets. Surah's voice filtered through the wood.

"No, just in here. The general specifically told me to come and find you and—"

The door creaked open.

The red-robed figure barely had time to register their presence before Athtar was on him, swift and silent. She knocked the man off balance with a hard shoulder, sending him stumbling into Will's waiting grip. With one arm around the man's throat and the other yanking his arm behind his back, Will wrestled him to the ground. The mage thrashed, muttering the beginnings of an incantation, but Lyra was faster. Her fist cracked across his temple, cutting the words short.

The man went limp.

They all stood frozen for a moment, catching their breath.

"Well," Athtar muttered, peeking through the door, "that went better than expected."

Will quickly stripped the unconscious man's red robe and donned it over his clothes. It was a little short in the sleeves, but it would have to do. Athtar wrapped the man's wrists with a length of cord, and Lyra stuffed a scrap of cloth in his mouth to keep him quiet when he came to.

"Let's go," Will whispered.

Together, they stepped out into the hall, falling into a casual formation behind Will, who took the lead with the confident stride of someone used to authority. They crossed the polished floor quickly, making their way to the guarded door.

"Halt," one of the soldiers said, holding out a hand. "No staff allowed below."

Will didn't stop walking until he stood directly in front of them, pulling his hood back just enough to show his face and give them a clear look at his irritation. "There's been a spill," he said coldly, voice heavy with disdain. "Something foul. Unless you're volunteering to scrub it off the stones, I suggest you let the cleaners through."

The guards hesitated, glancing at each other. One of them sniffed. "What kind of spill?"

Will scowled. "The kind that melts boot leather and sours your breakfast. How do you think these ones end up assigned to cleanup detail?"

After a tense moment, the guards stepped aside, bowing their heads.

Will offered a tight smile and pushed the heavy door open, motioning the others through before stepping inside and letting it close behind them with a dull *thud*.

Beyond the door was a series of stone corridors and descending stairwells, leading deep into the bowels of the city hall. They didn't know which way to go, but the passages didn't really give them many options anyway.

As they continued deeper, something else intruded on Will's senses. As they continued their descent, he tried to identify it. He'd felt something similar once. Standing in the heart of Thorn Island, within the Chamber of the Nexus. There, it had been like standing beside an ancient river of light, flowing with wisdom and memory. The energy there had been vast, but calm.

This presence was not like that.

He could feel it now, humming just at the edge of his perception, like fingers brushing against the back of his mind. Curious. Probing. But where the Nexus felt like it was seeking harmony, this presence exuded hunger.

The further they descended, the more disturbing the presence became. What disturbed him the most was the whisper of familiarity. A low current stirred within him, like a tether tightening in his chest, and for a moment...just a moment, he felt the faint pulse of the power of his magic again. Real and tangible. And yet it felt *wrong*. It was like staring into a mirror and seeing something that *almost* looked like him, but not quite.

He slowed his steps, placing a hand against the cold wall to steady himself as the continuing presence began making him feel light-headed and queasy.

The corridor they were in finally opened up into a galleried balcony, overlooking a large stone hall. At the far end of the hall on a raised dais stood a grotesque statue of a horrific, demonic form, carved from onyx and exuding an unholy radiance. As they emerged onto the balcony, the energy of that presence hit Will, and he knew immediately that this was the source of the energy he was sensing, as wave after wave of that dark malevolence washed over him. In front of the effigy stood an altar of sorts, adorned with a heavy black cloth and assorted accoutrements, and in rows before the altar knelt red-robed mages, all prone, with their faces pressed to the floor in worship. The air was thick with the stench of burning incense, and...something else more putrid.

At that moment, a huge brass gong sounded in the room, and the four companions crouched down, startled by the sound. Staying close to the ground, they inched their way as close to the edge as they dared.

A procession of clerics made their way from the area below the gallery, all wearing grotesque masks that mirrored the demonic effigy behind the altar. The ones at the fore of the procession led a new chant that was taken up by those prostrating themselves before the altar, whilst the ones to the rear dragged a dirty, struggling captive. The man seemed to be a local and definitely did not want to be there. He was kicking and moaning, animal-like guttural sounds of terror spilling from his mouth as they dragged him towards the altar.

Surah inhaled sharply, but caught herself quickly to avoid making a sound. She had a look of shocked horror on her face. "That's Omar... he and his whole family went missing days ago," she said in a low whisper, her voice quivering slightly.

Unable to proceed across the balcony for fear of alerting those below to their presence, all they could do was stay low and witness what was unfolding. When the procession reached the altar, the four who restrained Omar ripped off his clothes, his naked body showing evidence of days of abuse at the hands of his captors. They took him and contorted him over the altar, holding him there while the high cleric turned to face that statue and began incanting his sermon over the terrified moans of his victim.

"Hear me, oh great one. We, your most faithful servants, stand before you to offer homage for the bountiful gifts that you bestow. Accept our gift with grace, and we pray that you find it pleasing."

With that, he withdrew a cruel-looking ceremonial dagger from a dark cloth on the altar and performed a macabre dance, extracting the organs of his victim with chilling speed and precision. So quick and precise were the cleric's incisions that Omar witnessed the removal of all but the last of his organs, each cut causing the man to let out blood-curdling screams of agony that cut through the air. When they were done, the air was thick with the metallic tang of blood and the stench of death. Omar's life force ebbed away in a crimson tide, the last of his screams echoing through the chamber until they were silenced forever.

With a fanatical reverence bordering on madness, the cleric offered the freshly harvested organs to burning braziers that stood on either side of the altar, their flames casting flickering shadows across his horrific visage, now drenched in Omar's blood. He joined the other clerics in a cacophony of chants that reverberated through the chamber, making the stones vibrate.

Suddenly, all chanting came to a complete stop, and the chamber fell into a silence so absolute that Will wondered for a moment if the ceremony had concluded, but the clerics all remained prostrated as though waiting for something. And then, they received their answer. The braziers roared to life. Flames, two feet tall, roared, consuming the sacrifices, and at the same time, the statue behind the altar glowed in time.

"Our lord is pleased. Rejoice!"

And with that, the chanting resumed as the procession left the room through an archway to the rear of the altar, and Omar's body was dragged from the room.

The four remained frozen, crouched in silence as the last echoes of the chanting faded beneath the vaulted stone ceiling. Will could feel his heart hammering in his chest so strongly that he worried irrationally that it might give away their location.

Surah had buried her face in her hands, though she didn't weep. Her body shook with the effort of holding it in, the grief and rage radiating off her like heat. Lyra put an arm about her shoulders in an effort to comfort her grieving friend.

He risked another glance down at the altar. The red-robes slowly rose to their feet again, straightening their garments, resuming their places like actors preparing for the next act. The masked clerics had already vanished through the archways behind the dais, dragging the last traces of their cruelty with them.

"Let's move," Will said quietly. "Before another offering is dragged in."

They moved stealthily along the gallery, hugging the shadows, moving as quickly as they dared. On the far side, they found themselves once again descending a stone staircase. Will carefully tried to gauge their direction, trying to make sure they weren't about to enter into the midst of that room full of red-robes, but a few moments later, they found themselves emerging into a wide open space that Will surmised was somewhat behind the altar room. The room was lined with heavy, barred, wooden doors. The smell of blood and faeces filled their nostrils, and Will was more thankful than ever for the scarf across his face. Behind some of the doors, they could hear whimpers of the cell's residents, and he had to resist trying to help the hapless souls trapped inside, recognising that would only result in them all getting caught.

"This has to be where they're keeping him," said Lyra, breathless with tension.

None of them talked about it, but the scene in the hall behind them had deeply unsettled them all. They knew they were in danger, but the sight of such a carnal, visceral display of human suffering had shaken them badly.

As they moved deeper into the dungeon, Will felt that resonant energy stirring in his chest again, faint at first but quickly swelling, alive with a dark pulse that seemed to echo through the stone. The awareness rippled through him, drawing his attention toward the far end of the corridor. Something was there.

The realisation hit him with a pang of shame. This was the darkness inside him, reaching out, recognising its own. For a heartbeat, he considered saying nothing, afraid of what they might see in his eyes.

Instead, he forced his voice steady, choosing subterfuge. "Wait," he said, nodding toward the far cell. "I thought I saw something move... down there, at the end."

The others all looked unsure, but without any better ideas, were happy to follow his lead.

The barred wooden door was heavy, reinforced with blackened iron, and sealed with a thick lock. Will crouched, peering through a crack in the slats.

"Someone's in there," he said softly, then louder: "Eldran?"

A groggy groan answered him.

Lyra was already reaching for the lock, her fingers fumbling in haste. "Do you see a keyhole?"

Athtar crouched beside her. "Step back."

She reached into her satchel and retrieved a slim, bone-handled dagger. She slipped it into the lock and whispered a word under her breath. The dagger shimmered briefly as ripples of flame seemed to pulse down its blade, then twisted with an audible *click*, and the lock fell open.

"Handy," Will muttered with admiration.

"I'm not just here for my charm," she said dryly.

They eased the door open, wincing at the heavy, creaking groan as it swung ponderously on its rusty hinges.

Inside, huddled in a heap of torn robes and dried blood, was Eldran.

He blinked at them blearily, a slow recognition dawning on his face. "Will...? Lyra?" His voice was hoarse, his lips cracked, and his skin deathly pale beneath a mask of grime and bruises.

"We've got you," Lyra said, already at his side, helping him sit up. "We came as fast as we could."

Will knelt opposite her. "Can you walk?"

Eldran tried to rise, then winced, collapsing back with a groan. "Not well," he said in a shaky voice. "They... they took something from me. I can't feel the light anymore."

Will's stomach twisted. "We'll deal with that later. Right now, we need to get you out."

Surah slipped out of the cell, returning a moment later with another red robe she had discovered hanging in a nearby cloak room. "We pass him off as having been injured by a struggling prisoner, maybe? If we move quickly, no one will have time to question it."

Will glanced behind them, the shadows seeming to lean in closer now that they had found what they came for. He had a knot at the pit of his stomach that he couldn't shake. It had all been a bit too easy. The moment they tried to lift Eldran, however, the air shuddered. A ripple of black energy flared around him, jagged and cold, hurling his body back to the centre of the room like a rag doll. He hit the stones with a sickening thud, a strangled cry escaping his lips.

"What—?" Lyra started forward, but as she did, the snare revealed itself. Thick, inky tendrils of shadow coiled from the floor and walls, knotting themselves around Eldran's limbs. They pulsed with a malign rhythm, as though feeding on his weakness.

Athtar's bow clattered to the ground as she thrust out her hands. Fire roared from her palms, a brilliant surge of white-hot flame that seared the cell in sudden light. For a heartbeat, it seemed to bite into the shadowy binds. Just as Will started to feel a surge of hope, the flames guttered, smothered as if drowned in tar. The snare recoiled, then tightened its grip, dragging Eldran back down with a violent jolt.

Athtar staggered, sweat beading on her brow. "It won't break."

Eldran writhed, his voice raw with pain. "It's entwined into my essence. You can't—" His words dissolved into a hoarse cry.

Will's pulse hammered. He could feel it too... the same sick resonance that had haunted him since his return, the whisper of shadow threading through his veins. For a moment, he hesitated, then stepped forward.

"Maybe I can," he said quietly.

He knelt beside Eldran, pressing a trembling hand to the writhing black cords. The darkness stirred at his touch, recognising something in him. It recoiled, then yielded, threads unravelling like smoke. Will focussed on the dark tendrils, not seeking to attack them, but asserting his will on them instead, commanding them by force.

The snare pulsed and screamed, fighting him at first, but then gave a final shiver before collapsing entirely. Eldran slumped into Will's arms, the room falling deathly still.

Everyone was staring at him, open-mouthed, but Will didn't have time to explain, nor did he really have any explanation to offer. Instead, he helped Eldran to his feet once more and draped the pilfered red robe over his shoulders, leading him from the cell.

They moved as quickly as they dared, remaining vigilant. Outside the cell, Surah and Lyra took over helping Eldran as Will led, still cloaked in the red robe, head bowed low in case they encountered others, Athtar by his side.

When they reached the base of the stone stairs that led up toward the gallery, Will paused, listening.

Silence.

They continued to meet no resistance as they climbed back towards the upper halls. *They had surely triggered some sort of alarm*, Will thought to himself, tension building as they got closer to the more populated parts of the city hall.

They reached a junction.

Will started forward, then stopped suddenly, throwing an arm out. The others froze.

They waited a moment, and then they all heard it; cloth brushing stone. The flap of sandals against the stone floor. Voices.

They ducked into a recessed alcove, half-hidden by a decaying tapestry. Will pulled the corner across them and pressed them all back against the cold wall, barely daring to breathe.

A pair of red-robes rounded the corner at a casual pace, deep in hushed conversation.

"...feel my power growing with every sacrifice."

"The dark lord's gifts are incredible," agreed the second one. "By the time our campaign in the north begins, we will—"

They suddenly stopped directly in front of where Will and the others were concealed.

Silence.

Will's heart pounded in his ears as he tried his best to hold his breath. He could feel Lyra tense beside him.

"Did you hear something?" one of them said.

A pause.

"No. Rats, probably."

The other one grunted, apparently satisfied, and the footsteps resumed, shuffling away towards the dungeon.

As soon as the two red-robes had moved away and they could no longer hear their footsteps, the group peered out from behind the tapestry, before cautiously continuing.

Just before they reached the heavy wooden door that would lead them back out into the upper city hall, Will turned to address them.

"Let me speak," he said under his breath. "Keep your heads down. Look tired. Like we've been hauling filth."

Will pushed the door open.

Two guards stood on the other side, dressed in black leather uniforms with red trim, bored expressions on their faces. They weren't the same guards that had seen them going down in the first place, so their re-emergence startled them.

"Hold up. What are you lot doing up here?" the guard asked, stepping forward.

Will didn't hesitate. He let annoyance seep into his voice, curling his lip. "I dare you to question me again," he said, his voice carrying the promise of imminent violence.

The guard stepped back, his eyes suddenly wide with panic. "I meant no disrespect," he said, shrinking back.

The two guards stepped aside, and Will led the others through without another word. He didn't look back. His shoulders burned with tension, but he didn't let it show.

They slipped through a storage courtyard lined with broken crates and rusted barrels. Before leaving, they disposed of the robes, stashing them behind a stack of crates in the hope that it would be some time before anyone found them, and slipped out unnoticed.

Once outside, they quickly melted into the dense crowds, keeping their hoods up. Lyra and Surah led the way now, leading them back towards the side street where they had left Gissumir. Eldran now stumbled less, though each step still looked painful. Sweat beaded on his brow, and his skin had a sickly pallor, but he didn't utter a word of complaint.

"Well, I'll be damned," Gissumir muttered as they approached.

Surah helped Eldran sit against the wall. He slid down with a groan, his back hitting stone. He didn't speak, didn't even look at them. Just stared forward, hollow-eyed.

Gissumir looked at Eldran, his brow furrowing with concern, before looking back at the others. "What the hell happened in there?"

Will shook his head, looking out across the skyline of the city. "No time now. We'll explain once we're on the road. They'll know he's missing soon, if they don't already."

"Then let's vanish before they start looking," Gissumir said, already shouldering his pack.

They had barely taken a dozen steps when Eldran stirred against Will's shoulder. His breathing raspy with the effort of moving, and then, suddenly, his hand shot up, gripping Will's sleeve with surprising strength.

Will froze. The old mage's eyes were glassy, unfocused, but there was something alive behind them. Eldran pulled him closer until Will could feel the heat of his breath against his ear.

"I saw it..." he whispered, voice raw and trembling. "Down there... in the dark. It was you, Will."

Will stiffened, unable to answer.

Eldran's hand trembled, still clutching his arm. "It knows you," he murmured, the words almost lost to the sounds of the city. "It knows your name."

Then the strength left him as suddenly as it had come. His grip slackened, his head dropping against Will's chest.

Will swallowed hard, staring straight ahead. He looked about to see if anyone else had heard, but if they did, they gave no indication.

Chapter 16

They made their way north in short, easy stages. Surah taught them that the locals find it easier to make shelter and rest during the heat of the day and then travel as the sun sets, making travel during the cooler night more bearable. She also taught them how to find water to drink in the desert, harvesting succulent plants for their moisture.

Eldran's physical condition slowly improved as they continued north towards Anhai, but it was his emotional state that had Will most concerned. Eldran hadn't really spoken much about what the red robes did to him back in Alesia, but he had a permanent haunted look in his eyes.

Lyra, for her part, never strayed far from Eldran. Will didn't understand the bond that had formed between them in her role as his acolyte, but he could see it in the way she looked at him that she cared for him very much.

Some days, Will would wake and find Eldran already up, staring at nothing, his hands resting flat on the sand as if trying to reconnect himself to the energy of the universe. There was a war happening behind those eyes. One Will couldn't see, couldn't fight, and didn't dare interrupt.

They reached Anhai just after sun-up, a few days later. After the long, arduous journey through the desert, they were grateful to feel the cobbled streets of Anhai under their feet.

A small host of court functionaries awaited them just inside the palace complex, bowing respectfully and leading the weary travellers through familiar corridors to the quarters they had used on their previous stay.

The last attendant bowed low at the doorway as he prepared to leave, his robes brushing the polished stone floor. "His Majesty King Edarn bids you welcome to Anhai once more," he said, his tone formal. "He has instructed me to say that the throne room is open to you whenever you are ready. The king would be most delighted to receive you."

With that, the man slipped away, leaving the companions alone in the high-ceilinged chamber.

Will sank onto the edge of a low couch, rubbing a hand through his dust-caked hair. "I'd forgotten how good this place smells," he murmured.

Eldran didn't speak, only sat in silence near the window, staring out over the waking city. The golden light gently bathed his face, but it couldn't mask the terror in his eyes.

Lyra had already poured water into a basin and began washing the grit from her arms. "Let's not keep the king waiting too long. He needs to know what we've learned."

Will nodded, glancing again at Eldran. "A few minutes to wash and catch our breath. Then we go."

Once refreshed, they gathered themselves, sharing only brief looks and unspoken nods before heading straight for the throne room.

They reached the towering, ornately carved doors of King Edarn's throne room just as they began to open, their hinges groaning softly in welcome. The doormen, already alerted to the group's approach, stood aside with respectful nods. As the doors parted, the throne room came into view, and they saw the king himself rising from his seat to greet them.

A broad grin spread across Edarn's face as he stepped down from the dais. "It's good to see you all back in one piece," he said warmly. "When Fennick returned without you, I feared the worst."

The king's eyes swept over them as they stood before him. "You look like you've been through a lot," he said with a nod. "Come. Let's move through to the next room, where we can be a bit more comfortable."

Edarn led them through a side archway into the more intimate, high-ceilinged conference room where a long, polished table dominated the centre. The walls were lined with bookshelves and tapestries, and the dusty scent of the city outside was carried throughout the room from a breeze that passed through the latticework windows on this side of the building. Cushioned chairs surrounded the table, and the soft furnishings gave the room a more inviting, comfortable atmosphere than the formal furnishings of the throne room.

With a relieved sigh, Edarn slipped off his ceremonial mantle and crown, placing them neatly on a small side table that was clearly meant for that purpose. He sank into his chair with a relaxed air and gestured for the others to do the same.

"Please," he said, his voice softer now. "Tell me everything."

The others took turns recounting the events of the past week, sparing no detail. King Edarn listened with rapt attention, his expression growing darker with every revelation. He didn't interrupt once, absorbing their words with increasing concern. The scale of Oberith's mobilisation and how alarmingly close his forces had come to the southern borders of Urias clearly unsettled him. But it was the grim description of the sacrificial ritual that drew a visible shudder from him, his face paling visibly. Only when they finished with the story of their narrow escape did he finally lean back, exhaling heavily.

His gaze drifted to Eldran, who sat unmoving, his vacant eyes fixed on a distant point beyond the window. "Will he be alright?" Edarn asked softly.

Will followed his gaze and sighed. "I honestly don't know," he said. "Physically, he's recovering, but..."

He trailed off, shaking his head, trying to imagine the torment that could hollow a man out like that. "We'll know more once we get him back to Thorn Island. I'm hoping the healers there will know more."

Edarn nodded, a quiet sorrow in his eyes. "Oberith has done what no warlord has managed in generations in uniting the southern clans. We always thought their endless infighting would keep them too fractured to ever pose a threat again."

Will's expression hardened. He sat forward slightly, voice edged with restrained anger. "Forgive me, Your Majesty, but... have you ever been to the south? Have you seen what was left of it after the Hundred Year War?" he said, shaking his head. "They didn't tear each other apart because they were savages. They did it because they were abandoned... forced into survival, forced to fight for scraps while the rest of the continent moved on, and prospered. Oberith didn't create the conditions that made his rise possible. The north did."

A heavy silence fell over the chamber. Edarn looked as though he'd been struck, his usual composure giving way to shock and something akin to shame. He bowed his head, as if weighing Will's words carefully.

Eventually, he looked up. "You're right...of course," he said gently. "But now we must deal with the repercussions of those conditions. Hopefully, this time we can handle things better."

Realising that he had probably overstepped, Will took the opportunity to back down gracefully. "I hope so, Edarn. Whatever happens, we're in this together now."

Edarn's smile returned at Will's friendly response. "Will you stay for a while, or do you wish me to have the portal room made ready today?" he asked.

Will looked at the others, a questioning look on his face, his gaze finally resting on Eldran. "I think we should get our friend back to Thorn Island as soon as we can. I am sorry to leave so quickly, but we really should go."

Edarn waved his hand, dismissing Will's apology. "Say no more. I should have assumed that would be the case. I will have an attendant lead you there immediately. Please know that you will always be welcome here in Anhai, my friends."

He paused a moment, his eyes settling on Surah. "Surah...I wonder if I might ask something of you."

Surah raised a brow, overwhelmed at being addressed by royalty. "Of course, Your Majesty."

"I would be honoured if you stayed in Anhai a little longer. We in the north know too little of Strada beyond the old histories. But

I see in you a representative of your people. Perhaps, by spending some time here, you might help us understand your people better... and in turn, carry a fuller understanding of Anhai back with you."

There was a moment of silence. Surah looked uncertain, surprised by the request. "I hadn't planned to stay behind," she said carefully, glancing at Will. "But... if you think it might benefit our people... I'll remain. For a time."

Edarn smiled warmly. "Thank you. I think we both may gain more from the exchange than we realise."

At his signal, an attendant slipped away and returned moments later to confirm the arrangements had been made. The group all rose to their feet, gathering their belongings and thanking the king once again for all his help.

Edarn moved among them, clasping hands and embracing them in turn. When he reached Lyra, he paused.

"I regret that we didn't have more time to speak, Lyra. I've heard much about you. Your man here," he gestured gently toward Will, "would've moved heaven and earth to be reunited with you. I suspect there's nothing he wouldn't do."

Lyra gave him a warm hug and smiled over at Will. "He certainly is determined. Once he sets his mind to something, very little can stand in his way," she said, turning back to the king. "I hope one day we get that chat, Your Majesty."

"It would be my pleasure," Edarn replied, bowing his head slightly.

As they moved toward the doors, Will turned to Surah. "You're sure about this?"

Surah gave a half-smile. "No. But it seems the right thing to do."

"Then we'll see you soon," Will said.

The attendant gestured for the rest of them to follow, and they made their way out through the sunlit halls of the palace. Will smiled as they walked the palace halls. There was something about Anhai that had begun to settle into him, smoothing the edges that months of turmoil had left behind. The air here always seemed warmer... not stifling like the heat in the desert to the south, but softened by the cool stone of the palace itself, carrying the faint scent of jasmine from the inner gardens. Sunlight poured through the buttressed and latticed openings, washing the stone corridors in gold.

He didn't know whether it was the quiet murmur of the court-yards, the gentle sound of fountains trickling somewhere beyond, or the way the palace seemed to breathe in time with its people, but he found himself at ease here.

The court functionary bowed deeply to them after leading them into the portal room, before melting away back into the palace.

As they made their way towards the dais where the portal stood, a horrible thought washed over Will as he glanced sharply at Eldran, who was still staring absently. *Who would activate the portal*?

He turned to Athtar. "Do you know how to activate the portal?" he asked suddenly, a note of urgency creeping into his voice.

She took his meaning, following his gaze to Eldran, who was still staring blankly at a wall, and shook her head.

Will swore under his breath and threw his head back in exasperation. "Why?" he said to no one in particular. "Why can't something just go right for once?"

Lyra looked at him, confused. "Why don't you just do it, Will?" she asked.

His head snapped toward her, a flicker of anger passing across his face until he reminded himself that she didn't know about... his current condition. His face relaxed into one of weariness, his shoulders slumping slightly.

He hesitated, then met her eyes. "Since I returned... I haven't been able to access the light," he said. The disappointment gripping his throat, carved from weeks of frustration and shame.

But Lyra didn't flinch. She only tilted her head and shrugged, a small smile playing at the corners of her mouth. "Well, I assume you're not just going to give up," she said simply. "You are the most powerful mage I've ever seen. I doubt opening a portal is beyond you."

He stared at her, perplexed by her calm confidence. His emotions flared. Confusion, hurt, defiance, and finally, as he realised what she was doing, all of it dissolved into laughter. She was pushing him on purpose. Just like she used to. And it worked.

"Well," he said, smiling in spite of himself, "I can try."

Lyra stepped in and wrapped her arms around his neck, drawing him close. Her lips brushed his, and in that kiss, all the darkness he'd been carrying these past weeks, the grief, doubt, guilt, all melted away, and in that moment, he felt suddenly lighter. Then, like bubbles slowly rising to the surface, he could sense the edges of it stirring within him. It felt different than before, but the unmistakable warmth of magic was flowing once more through his veins.

Without another word, he turned and led the others to the pedestal at the heart of the dais. He raised his hand over the polished stone, closing his eyes as he focused. Thorn Island.

He hesitated, staring at the pale markings etched into the stone. For a moment, the quiet hum of the chamber seemed to fade, replaced by the echo of every failure that had brought him to this point. He lifted his hand, then paused, leaving it hovering just above the pedestal. The old fears started to creep back in through the cracks of self-doubt. *What if the light still wouldn't answer?*

Then he felt Lyra's presence beside him, calm and reassuring. Her fingers gently brushed his arm, her presence a soothing balm to his weary soul.

He exhaled slowly, set his doubts aside, and reached for the light.

The surge came fast, rushing up through the stone, into his hand, through his chest. Runes etched into the portal ring pulsed to life. The air shimmered, twisting and folding in on itself until the portal whooshed into being, its surface settling into that calm, luminous veil that belied the chaos of its birth.

When he finally opened his eyes, the chamber shimmered faintly with reflected light, and Lyra was watching him, smiling, her eyes bright with pride.

He looked at each of them in turn, trying hard not to get overwhelmed by the waves of emotions that were suddenly crashing over him.

"Let's be on our guard. Stay close. We go through fast, and we come out together."

They nodded, gathering near. Will gave the portal one last glance, then turned to the others.

With a shared breath, they stepped into the light, and Anhai faded behind them.

Chapter 17

Their feet had scarcely touched the stones of the portal dais when a shrill siren split the air, its wail reverberating through the vaulted chamber. A moment later, a shimmering energy barrier flared to life around them, locking them inside a translucent dome of golden light. They were still reeling from not suffering the expected detour through the shadow realm, and this new development left them standing there, stunned.

Before anyone could speak, the side doors burst open and two dozen battle mages swept into the room, robes flaring, hands already alight with glowing offensive elements. The air bristled with latent power as enchantments were summoned and held at the ready, each mage poised for combat, their eyes fixed intently on the figures within the containment field.

Then, from behind the advancing line, a familiar voice cut through the chaos. "Hold your fire!" Lucian's commanding voice reverberated throughout the chamber. He pushed his way to the front, robes trailing behind him as he stepped into full view.

He raised a hand and muttered a quick incantation. The energy field surrounding them flickered, then dissolved into nothingness.

"It's alright," he said, his voice quieter now but still clear. "Stand down."

The mages hesitated only a moment longer before lowering their hands and allowing the enchantments to fade. A ripple of relief passed through the room.

Lucian let out a breath that was almost a laugh and strode forward, arms outstretched.

"You have no idea how glad I am to see you all in one piece."

Will stepped down from the dais and approached Lucian. "What's with the warm welcome?"

Lucian's expression softened. "We have much to discuss, my friend," he said, glancing at the others behind Will. "A few days after your departure, the portal began activating without warning. A few nights ago, a pair of spectres slipped through. Several mages wound up in the infirmary trying to send them back. The emergency protocols you just witnessed were put in place to defend against that happening again."

Will nodded slowly. "I'd hoped the situation was starting to resolve itself," he said. "Especially since we managed a clean portal connection this time."

Lucian's brow furrowed. "You didn't pass through the shadow realm?"

"We didn't," Athtar answered from where she stood, just behind Will. "Which, given Eldran's condition, was a mercy."

Lucian's gaze shifted to Eldran, who still stood motionless near the dais, eyes unfocused, expression blank.

Lucian's expression stiffened slightly. "What's wrong with him?" he asked cautiously, as though speaking sternly would shatter the fragile man he called brother.

Will followed Lucian's gaze and sighed. "He was taken," he said quietly. "Captured by Oberith's followers. They had a weapon of some kind... he says it severed his connection to the light."

Lucian's eyes darkened. "At least you were able to recover him," he said, turning back toward Eldran again. "We will do everything we can to help him."

He summoned two acolytes who were in attendance nearby, giving them brief instructions to lead Eldran to the infirmary.

After Eldran had been led away, he turned to the others. "Come. You all look like you've been through hell. I know you probably need rest, but... could we go to my study first? You can fill me in there."

Though their limbs were heavy with exhaustion, no one protested. Silently, they fell into step behind him, passing through the winding halls of Thorn Island.

Once inside Lucian's study, Will walked toward the huge panoramic window instinctively. The view was as breathtaking as he remembered. From this high vantage, he could see the dramatic, jagged peaks that encircled the basin like the ribs of some ancient creature. The namesake thorn-vines, thick as tree trunks and armoured in bark-like hide, twisted through the landscape, some rising in arches while others slithered like petrified serpents over the cliffs.

The sunlight streamed through the clouds in brilliant shafts, casting long shadows that danced along the rocks and foliage. Beyond the ridge-line, where the mountains broke, the sea stretched endlessly to the horizon, where waves smashed against the rocky coastline in rhythmic violence.

He didn't realise how long he'd been staring until Lucian cleared his throat directly behind him.

"I forget sometimes," Lucian said, stepping up beside him, "how rare that view really is."

The door to Lucian's study creaked shut behind them as the others finally entered and joined them.

Lucian gestured for them to sit, settling himself into the carved chair behind his desk. He leaned back, hands steepled. "Alright... Tell me everything."

Lyra was the first to speak. "Alesia still stands," she said quietly, "but only just. When the armies from the south arrived, the people welcomed them as saviours. They were tired, hungry, desperate. They believed Oberith's men would bring food, order, something better." She paused, her eyes distant. "Now they tolerate them out of fear. The soldiers patrol every street. Anyone who questions them vanishes."

Lucian's expression hardened. "And the army itself? What did you see?"

"The Stradan troops from Mor'Dan are the core of it," Lyra replied. "They're Oberith's elite. Disciplined, well-armed, utterly loyal. However, most of his forces are comprised of local militia. Poorly trained, barely equipped, yet bound to him by belief and fear. They call it service; it's really conscription."

Gissumir gave a low grunt. "And the Yagerians?"

Lyra shook her head. "None in Alesia. But I heard them mentioned by the Mor'Dan officers... always with contempt. They see them as unreliable, soft."

Lucian leaned back in his chair, a spark of calculation in his eyes. "Good. Division breeds weakness. That might yet serve us."

Will spoke then, his tone grim. "It's not just the soldiers, Lucian. They have a large force of mages who can wield a corrupted form of energy. The locals there refer to them simply as 'red-robes'."

"They answer only to Oberith," Lyra said. Her voice faltered slightly as memory crept in. "They call themselves his priests. They use their power to keep the people obedient."

"We saw one of their ceremonies. A sacrifice," she said, shuddering in revulsion at the memory. "A man was dragged to the altar. He was screaming, begging for mercy. The red-robes chanted as if it were a celebration."

She closed her eyes as if she could blot out the memory of what happened.

Will saw her struggling and took over. "The ritual was grotesque," he said, shaking his head. "The poor man was disembowelled... his organs burned in braziers before the massive statue."

A heavy silence filled the room.

After a moment, Lucian rose from his seat and crossed to one of the high shelves. "The rite you described... sounds like a very specific kind of demonic ritual," he said, his fingers brushing across a row of cracked leather spines until he found the one he wanted.

He returned to the desk, flipping through the fragile pages with care. "Here," he said after a moment, turning the book toward them. The page showed an archaic diagram etched in blood-red ink, surrounded by notations in a script none of them could read.

"It's a ritual of subjugation and offering, used to curry favour with one of the old demons of the underworld. This kind of suffering... inflicted deliberately, ritually, is tied to a single name—"

Will could feel the tension building in his chest as he could almost sense what was coming.

Lucian met their eyes. "Moloch."

Will flinched. A subtle, involuntary motion. Barely perceptible, but not missed by Athtar, who glanced at him sharply, eyes narrowing slightly.

Lucian went on. "It's believed Moloch grows stronger with each soul consumed in agony. That's what Oberith is doing. He's feeding his master, and it's safe to assume that Moloch is in some way rewarding him... and his followers."

Will stared at the page, his heart thudding. He could feel it now, the shadow stirring at the edge of his soul. The whisper of her presence, always just behind the veil.

"We need to assume," Lucian continued, "that this is more than just conquest. It's a preparation. Oberith is paving the way for something worse to come. If we don't stop him soon..."

Will stood abruptly. "Then we *will* stop him," he said, voice firmer than he felt. "No matter what it takes."

Lucian regarded him with a wary look. "We'll need allies," he said. "Many more than we have. But for now, you should rest. All of you. I will bring this information to the attention of the other elders and we will devise a plan."

* * *

No one spoke much as they entered their familiar living quarters in The Hive. The exhaustion had sunk deep into their bones.

Athtar peeled off her torn cloak, revealing the worn leathers beneath. "If I don't get this dust out of my skin, I'm going to start shedding like a snake," she muttered, heading toward the bathing area at the rear of the space.

"Join the queue," Gissumir grunted, already unbuckling his greaves. "I can still smell the south on me."

Lyra chuckled softly as she passed Will, giving him a faint, sidelong smile. Her hair was loose again, fallen to her shoulders, and even with the days of hard travel through the desert, she seemed radiant to Will. He nodded to her, heart ticking faster.

After bathing and changing into light, comfortable garments, they gathered again at the table, now set with a modest meal.

The conversation was light as they all enjoyed the opportunity to relax. There was laughter, genuine and light. Athtar mimed a dramatic rendition of one of the young soldiers who had pursued them through the first safehouse, knocking himself out cold on a low-hanging timber, which made Lyra snort wine through her nose.

Will sat beside her, shoulders brushing hers as they leaned together to reach for plates. The warmth of her thigh pressed against his own, a steady, pulsing heat through the fabric of their clothes. Every time she leaned in to speak, he caught the curve of her mouth, the scent of her skin, and his senses became inflamed. His stomach was full, but a deeper hunger began to stir.

She turned toward him mid-conversation and their eyes met. For a second, the world fell away. She smiled faintly, eyes lidded, and rested her hand briefly on his leg beneath the table. It was a simple gesture, but full of quiet promise.

Eventually, the meal wound down. Athtar pushed her plate away with a groan. "That's it. If I eat one more thing, I think I'll burst."

"We should go see Eldran tomorrow," Lyra said, glancing around the group. "He'll want to know we're safe."

Everyone nodded in agreement.

"Yes," Will said softly, not looking away from her. "First thing in the morning."

As the others began drifting off toward their sleeping spaces behind the curtains, Will and Lyra lingered.

Will leaned back slightly in his chair, feeling quite content for some rest and a meal.

She turned toward him, her dark eyes catching the soft lamplight. "You've been quiet," she said gently.

Will looked at her, his breath catching in his throat. "Just thinking how long I've wanted to be exactly here."

Her shy smile melted his heart, and when he reached up to tuck a strand of her hair behind her ear, her hand caught his wrist. She leaned in and kissed him, slow at first, then deeper, more urgent. His arms slipped around her waist as hers wrapped behind his neck, drawing him in with a kind of hunger that had long waited to be sated.

They stood without a word, fingers intertwined, and Will led her through the curtain to the private alcove beyond. The room was simple, but their surroundings melted away as each of them only saw the other.

Lyra's hand lingered on his, steadying him as though she could quiet the storm inside. When she leaned in, her lips met his with a softness that stole his breath. The world seemed to fall away, leaving only her warmth, her scent, the fire in her touch.

His hands found her, tentative at first, then surer as the space between them dissolved. She drew him closer, her nails grazing his skin, her body yielding and insistent all at once. Every heartbeat thundered through him, every breath a plea.

When they finally broke apart, her eyes searched his with an intensity that felt like both a question and an answer. He held her gaze, knowing words would fail.

After, they lay tangled in each other's arms, the sheets wrapped loosely around them. Their bodies were slick with sweat, breathing deep and slow, skin still tingling with the memory of each touch. Will rested his forehead against hers, eyes closed, indulging in her presence.

As he drifted off to sleep, Will's final thoughts were that he had never been as happy as he was in this exact moment. But as he sank into oblivion, he found himself in the now all-too-familiar hellscape of the underworld. *Or was it?* There was screaming and suffering and fire, but this time things seemed different. Will tried to focus, despite the familiar wave of terror that was rising up in him, threatening to blot out all rational thought. He tried to calm his racing pulse and still his mind long enough to figure out what was going on.

He was walking through the streets of a city. He couldn't quite put his finger on it, but it felt familiar, maybe back home...or somewhere here in Aerinthos, he couldn't tell. Fires raged in every building, and people were running terrified, screaming. Some were burning, others were horrifically maimed; terrible mortal injuries, their wounds pumping their lifeblood. Everywhere he turned, he was surrounded by death and suffering.

Just when he thought he couldn't bear it any more, he heard the voice that he had anticipated. Moloch's deep chuckling reverberated from the horizons, everywhere and nowhere all at once.

"Why do you take such pleasure in my suffering? When will this end?" he screamed at the uncaring sky.

"Soon, Will," replied her voice in a sibilant, almost soothing tone. "Believe it or not, I aim to put an end to all this suffering, and I will need your help to do it.... And then you will be free of your obligation."

He was suddenly jolted into wakefulness by Lyra, who was leaning over him, shaking him awake, her hair falling across his chest, her eyes full of concern.

Will shot upright with a gasp, his body slick with sweat, heart pounding in his chest. For a moment, the dream clung to him, but Lyra's hands on his shoulders pulled him back from the edge.

"Will," she whispered, brushing damp strands of hair from his brow. "You were yelling in your sleep..."

He stared at her, wide-eyed and trembling, his throat dry and tight.

"I'm sorry," he murmured hoarsely, pulling her close and pressing his face to her neck, as if her warmth could banish the cold that had crept into his soul. "Just a dream."

But he knew it wasn't.

Lyra wrapped her arms around him, wordless, holding him until his breathing slowed. She didn't press him for answers, only held him as he gradually lay back down, his body curled around hers like a shield against whatever haunted him in the dark.

Chapter 18

Though no sunlight touched the underground lair of the order, there was a morning calm Will had grown fond of. The sconces glowed with a dimmer light, the corridors hushed, most still at rest. Will rose quietly, careful not to stir Lyra as she slept, one arm draped loosely across where he had been. Her face was peaceful, utterly still, with strands of silver hair spread across the pillow.

He hesitated a moment at the threshold, watching her chest rise and fall in a steady motion, and he smiled. But the moment passed, and with it came the whisper of that persistent thought that had found him in the haze between dreams and waking.

He dressed swiftly, lacing his boots with steady fingers before slipping from the alcove and into the hushed corridors of the Hive.

Thorn Island was quieter at this hour. The distant sounds of movement echoed faintly, but in the hive, all was still. As he walked, he wondered about the plan that had been so clear to him upon waking that morning. He had not spoken the name aloud in years, and yet it pulsed now like a buried splinter pressing through the skin.

Valenor.

Once as close as brothers until Valenor's betrayal had ripped apart their bond all those years ago.

If he was still here on Thorn Island... still rotting in some forgotten cell deep beneath the Order's stronghold, then he might also be the only soul who could help Will understand what had taken root within his own.

Because Valenor had touched the dark. Lived in it. Embraced it.

He reached the stairwell that led to the cells, pausing at the top. The air was cooler here, tinged with the faint metallic scent of iron and damp stone. For a moment, he considered turning back. Telling Lucian. Telling Lyra. But he feared their reaction. If they knew what he had done, what darkness he had allowed in... would they be able to look at him the same again? Would they immediately imprison him? No... he couldn't tell them.

So instead, he started down.

He searched the cells for a long time, most of which were completely empty. He was about to give up when he felt something from the far end of the chamber. An energy barrier hummed in the silence. Realising that must be an active cell, he quickened his pace and moved towards it.

Will stopped in front of the shimmering barrier. The cell beyond was dim, lit only by a faint glow that emanated from the barrier itself. Within, seated against the stone, was the figure he had once called brother.

"Valenor," he said softly.

The man stirred, lifting his head. The years had not been kind to him. His once-proud posture was slouched, and his eyes, once sharp, were now dulled and consumed with an overwhelming bitterness.

"Well," Valenor rasped. "Look who finally came crawling back."

Will paused a moment, a retort hovering on his tongue, but instead he chose kindness. "I was hoping we could talk. I could use your help to understand something."

Valenor pushed himself up, coming to stand just beyond the barrier, wrists bound in front of him in shackles that glowed with the same energy as the barrier. "Years. Years locked in this pit, treated like a traitor, abandoned by those I fought beside. And now you need something from me. How convenient."

"I didn't put you here."

"No, but you didn't stop them either. You stood by and watched them drag me away, and you said nothing."

"What could I do? You sided with Malakar. You betrayed everything we were."

Valenor's eyes glinted in the dim light. "You look at me like I'm a traitor. But what was I meant to be loyal to? Masters preaching Light while closing their eyes to the suffering of the people at the hands of those sworn to protect them?"

Will's jaw tightened. "So you followed Malakar."

A crooked smile cut across Valenor's bruised face. "He had vision, Will. He didn't flinch from the hard truth... he dared to act. While everyone else bowed to corrupt kings, he fought to break the cycle."

"You call that vision?" Will shot back. "He wanted dominion. He slaughtered without mercy in his rise to power. And when I finally confronted him, it was all a trap to lure me here. He never cared for you... You were a pawn. He would have let this whole world burn to get what he wanted."

Valenor paused for a moment. Maybe Will's words had struck a chord, or maybe his years of confinement had slowed his mind so much he couldn't come back with a suitable retort, but for a moment, they just stood eyeing each other.

Then Valenor's eyes narrowed, his head tilting slightly as though he was noticing something for the first time. Then his face broke out in a wide, sickly grin, and he let out a low chuckle. "Oh...

now I see why you have come. You have let the darkness in? Oh, this is too rare."

"I can't reach the light anymore," Will said, his voice cracking slightly.

"Yes. The light recoils from darkness."

Will's hands curled into fists. "Then tell me how to *get rid* of it."

"You can't get rid of it... not without killing part of yourself. That shadow is rooted in you. Stop resisting... let it serve you."

"No," Will said, recoiling in horror at the suggestion. "I won't. I don't care what it costs me. I will *never* give in to the darkness."

Valenor gave a hollow laugh. "Then you'll remain half-alive, chasing ghosts of what you used to be. You'll watch your strength fade, and your enemies surpass you. All because you were too afraid to adapt."

As Valenor's words sank in, Will desperately tried to cling to his belief that he would never give in to the darkness. But the seed had already been planted, and it dug deeper with every echo of that mocking laugh. What if Valenor was right? What if the darkness had already claimed too much of him? A cold dread took hold, whispering that he could no longer tell where his will ended and the shadow began. He drew a slow breath, forcing the thought down. Fear was the chosen vessel of darkness... It's primary language. He would not speak it. Whatever the cost, he would keep his own mind, his own soul.

He exhaled slowly, letting the fear fall away. He looked at the man behind the barrier, his voice quieter now. "For what it's worth... I'm sorry, Valenor. For how things turned out. For what we lost. You were once like a brother to me."

Valenor's expression softened... just for a moment. "I, too, have regrets."

They stood in silence, the humming of the energy field the only sound.

"Maybe," Will said, turning to leave, "in the next life, things can be different."

Valenor didn't answer right away. But just as Will stepped away, his voice echoed from the cell, softer than before.

"Maybe."

A hollow pressure tightened in Will's chest as he climbed the stone steps back toward the upper chambers. He hadn't known exactly what he expected to hear from Valenor, but the exchange had left him feeling somehow more vulnerable than before.

Crossing the great chamber beneath the shimmer of the nexus light, he barely registered the robed figures drifting past him. His thoughts twisted, tangled. Surely Valenor had lied. There must be a way to sever his connection to the darkness... There must be.

But the doubt quickly gave way to anger. Not at Valenor, but at the cruel design of fate, at the ever-narrowing path he'd been forced to walk. The impossible choices. The cost of each step forward. But what were his options? Every decision seemed to be a poor one, but it wasn't his fault. It wasn't. What more could he do?

Hope crept in for but a fleeting moment, but then, like the sudden silence after a storm, the truth snuffed out that hope. There would be no easy way out.

His shoulders sagged, his steps growing slower as he approached the hive. The weight he carried was no longer sharp; it was dull and familiar. The heavy fog of resignation.

When he stepped into the hive, he didn't speak. His thoughts no longer raced. They drifted, directionless.

It was the quiet numbness of despair.

Will hadn't made it five paces into the hive before he heard her voice.

"Will?"

He froze. He hadn't even noticed her there, seated by the table, cupping a small teacup between her hands, arms wrapped around her knees. She rose when he didn't answer, placing the teacup down on the table and crossing the room.

"Are you alright?" she asked gently, reaching up to brush his hair from his eyes.

"I'm fine," he said, too quickly, pulling away from her touch.

"You don't look—"

"I said I'm fine, Lyra!"

She flinched at his harsh outburst, her lip trembling slightly. "You weren't there when I woke up. Where did you go?" she asked finally, breaking the brief silence.

"Nowhere important."

"Don't do that," she said, her brows knitting together in frustration. "Don't shut me out."

Will exhaled sharply through his nose, running a hand through his hair. "I'm not shutting you out. I just... don't want to talk right now."

"Will, talk to me," she pressed, stepping closer. "If something's wrong—"

"I said drop it!" His voice rose, a sharp edge of anger, the echo biting into the stone walls around them, much harsher than he'd intended.

Lyra recoiled a step, stunned. For a breath, neither of them moved.

Her eyes searched his, pain quietly blooming beneath the surface.

"Fine," she said, her voice barely above a whisper. "If that's what you want."

She turned from him without another word and crossed the room in silence, her back straight, but her shoulders drawn in tight.

Will stood motionless, watching her walk away. He didn't want to hurt her, but his mind was so consumed with his own problems, he didn't know how to put this right. He felt the shape of his anger hollow out inside him, leaving only regret in its place. But as he turned away, he said nothing. The words he should have said caught in his throat and died there, unspoken.

* * *

In the days that followed, his thoughts gnawed at him like an old wound. At first, the others tried to be there for him, but he kept everyone at arm's length. His refusal to open up, coupled with a growing tendency to snap at even the mildest of questions, gradually wore them down. One by one, they began to give him space, hoping he would come around in his own time.

But that space only deepened the divide. Will saw their distance not as mercy, but confirmation that he was becoming exactly what he feared. The isolation fed his self-loathing, and that loathing became a lens through which he viewed everything. Every silent glance, every quiet conversation that paused when he entered the room was taken as signs of abandonment and judgment. And so the self-fulfilling prophecy of his own creation continued to unfold. The more he pulled away, the more alone he became. The more alone he felt, the more certain he was that he deserved it.

Time lost all meaning in those dark days after his visit with Valenor. He didn't know how many days had passed in the cold embrace of his own dark thoughts, but one afternoon, something changed.

A single idea pushed through the fog. Fragile, faint...but sharp enough to pierce the cloud that was lingering in his mind. It latched onto something still living inside him, and for the first time in days, he stirred.

He rose from his cot and crossed the chamber, walking over to Lyra. "Do you have a minute?" he asked her gently.

She looked at him with a grateful smile, happy to see him up and talking. "Of course," she said, setting aside a tunic she had been mending.

He gestured to their sleeping quarters, and she followed, intrigued.

Once there, he began to pace restlessly, unsure how to begin. She watched and waited patiently, not wanting to shatter his apparent first steps towards recovery.

Eventually, he stopped where he was standing and turned back to look at her. "I love you... So very much. You do know that, right?"

Her face softened, her smile full of warmth. "I know. And I hope you know I love you too, Will."

His eyes flickered as he tried to process how best to approach the next part. His mind was still sluggish from his days of melancholy.

He rubbed his palms together, staring at nothing. "Maybe... maybe we shouldn't be here. I could... Candleford. I could take you back. Let Lucian and the Order... handle the rest."

Lyra's eyes narrowed, her voice taking on a note of concern. "You'd just walk away? You'd leave our friends to their fate?"

"I... I don't know." He shook his head, words stumbling. "I came back here for you. That's all I knew. But now... It's like... everything's slipping. Every day... I'm drowning deeper."

Her face softened, but her voice remained firm. "And you think leaving will stop that?"

"I don't know." His voice cracked, raising slightly. "I don't know anything anymore. Just... staying here—" he broke off, looking down at the floor. "It's breaking me."

His mind was moving so sluggishly that he didn't know how long he had been staring at that one spot on the ground, thinking of nothing. His eyes slowly rose to meet Lyra's sympathetic gaze.

She stepped forward and cupped his hand between both of hers, her voice soothing. "Will... I know you're tired. We all are. You've carried more than anyone should for so long. You've always felt the weight of all our lives on your shoulders. No wonder you want to run. Anyone would."

She leaned closer, her eyes searching his. "But leaving now... abandoning our friends... that isn't you. You're stronger than this. You just need rest, time to heal. That's all it is."

Will's head snapped up, his voice rough with anger. "No, Lyra. You don't understand!"

She blinked at the sudden fire in his words.

"I want to understand," she whispered. "But I can't get close enough, Will. You keep pushing me away."

"I'm not pushing you away," he growled. "I'm trying to *save* us!"

"No," she said, her voice breaking. "You're trying to run."

He flinched, as if struck, but said nothing.

Lyra looked at him for a long, heart-wrenching moment, then turned and fled the room, a sob escaping her as she left.

Will stood frozen, the silence left in her wake amplified by the sudden absence of her light. Slowly, he sank to the edge of the bed, head in his hands. As he sat alone with his thoughts, the familiar numbness crept back in, constricting his heart.

Chapter 19

Over the next few days, Will's mood grew darker, and as if summoned by the storm of thoughts within him, the frequency and intensity of his nightly torment at the hands of Moloch increased. Each time his eyes closed, he found himself back in some desolate hellscape, flames licking the sky, screams echoing through ruinous corridors, and always her voice, sultry and serpentine, whispering the words of madness that burrowed deeper into his thoughts. He would wake gasping, drenched in sweat, his fists clenched as though he'd been fighting something in his sleep. Sometimes he screamed. Sometimes he wept. But always, he awoke exhausted.

He took to wandering the corridors and halls of Thorn Island, circling the great nexus chamber without really seeing it. There were moments when he nearly broke down and told someone about Valenor's warning, about the dark mark blotting his soul. But every time he opened his mouth, something stopped him. Pride? Shame? Fear that saying it aloud would make it real? He couldn't say. All he knew was that the darkness inside him was growing.

The others had all been to visit Eldran during those days, but Will, so wrapped up in his own battles as he was, had not yet been. While wandering the halls alone one afternoon, he found himself near the infirmary and, on a whim, decided it was about time.

His old friend was sleeping when he entered, but opened his eyes and smiled at Will's approach.

"I am glad you came," Eldran said, his voice sounding stronger. "The others tell me you've not been well either."

Will glowered at that, angry that the others had been talking about him behind his back.

"I am alright," he said.

Eldran studied him for a moment, his face turning serious.

"You and I both know that's not true, my friend," he said finally. "I've lived long enough to recognise when someone's wrestling with demons, and you, my friend, show all the classic signs."

The word demon had been at the forefront of Will's mind a lot, so hearing it said out loud piqued his interest.

"And what advice would you give to someone who was wrestling 'demons'?" he asked Eldran in a quiet voice.

"Well, I would tell them to learn that some things need to be accepted. Stop fighting battles you cannot win and learn to accept the things you have no power over," he said, smiling gently.

Eldran's words seeped through the fog of his thoughts, but the message Will heard was not the one Eldran had intended: Stop fighting the inevitable, when fate's hand had obviously chosen his path? Why fight the light's judgment when the dark offered power without penance?

Something in Will's eyes made Eldran squint at him, realising the smile on Will's face wasn't a natural one, but he couldn't quite put his finger on what exactly was bothering him. He simply sighed and moved on.

"How are you feeling now?" Will asked, turning the conversation around.

"I am feeling much better. I can even feel the light again. Later today, I will return to my own quarters, and then tomorrow I will begin rehabilitation to build up my strength again."

"That's great news. I'm happy for you," said Will, although his insincere smile and hollow tone spoke louder than words. That happiness for his friend came with an unhealthy dose of jealousy.

Eldran was beginning to feel uncomfortable with the conversation, so he feigned tiredness, asking Will if he could return and see him another time. Will, too, had other things on his mind and willingly parted ways, wishing Eldran a continued recovery before going in search of Valenor.

Something had shifted in Will during his visit with Eldran. The suffocating weight of bitterness and self-loathing had eased. He felt more at peace with his decision now, if not proud of it. There was clarity in the path he had chosen, a grim kind of purpose. And yet, beneath that newfound calm, a flicker of something else stirred. A grief for that part of himself that he was letting go.

As he approached the cell, Valenor stood waiting, cloaked in gloom, his face adorned with an oily smirk.

"I thought I would be seeing you again," he said, his voice dripping with smug satisfaction.

Will didn't slow his approach. His expression hardened, the last traces of the gentle, uncertain man now burned away.

"You'd do well to think about what that means," he said coldly. "Be very careful, Valenor. You'll find I'm not so patient anymore."

Valenor chuckled low in his throat, but there was an uncertainty behind it now. "So... you're ready," he said. "You've felt the power clawing through your veins, haven't you?"

"I didn't come here to listen to your gloating," Will replied. "I want to know how to harness it, how to control it. If I'm going to use this power, I won't be at its mercy."

Valenor tilted his head back slowly, a shrewd glint in his eye. Calculating. "Then it seems we have a problem," he said, his words measured. "I can't show you anything from inside this cell."

Will folded his arms, taking a small step backwards, his guard going up as he realised Valenor was trying to play him.

Valenor leaned forward slightly, voice lowering. "Tell them I've agreed to talk... to give up everything I know about the enemy's strategy in exchange for leniency. If you vouch for me, they'll listen."

Will's eyes narrowed, his jaw clenched. "It's not a terrible plan," he admitted. "But hear me, Valenor... and hear me well. If you so much as *think* about betraying me... if I so much as sense that you're playing some deeper game..."

He stepped closer, the air around him suddenly dense, almost humming with his dark potential.

"I *will* end you. Slowly. And without mercy."

Valenor's smile returned, thinner this time. "Of course," he said smoothly. "I wouldn't dream of it."

Will knew that it would be a tall order to convince the order to release Valenor. He petitioned directly to Lucian rather than going to the whole council of elders, knowing that as the new Elder of Light, Lucian hadn't been involved in Valenor's incarceration and would be the most likely to see the strategic benefits of having inside information. Lucian was suspicious at first, but Will was at his persuasive best.

In the end, Valenor was released under strict conditions, bound by a magical tether that would alert the Order should he step out of line and alert them to his location should he try to run. But Will knew, even as the terms were spoken aloud to Valenor, standing before the council in the nexus chamber, that it was all a formality. The real leash would be fear...fear of him.

Will hadn't uttered a word of his plan to the others, and so it came as a huge shock, especially to Lyra. She had been with them aboard the ship when Valenor had called down Malakar's wrath upon them, causing the vessel to wreck upon the rocks. She had been witness to the death of their friend Lolmig on their trek across the wastes of Shadowmoor. All suffering inflicted at the hands of Valenor's master.

"How could you, Will? After everything he did?" she demanded of him when they were alone later that day.

Will met her eyes, unflinching. His expression was cold, unreadable. "Because the situation has changed. Because we need him."

Lyra shook her head, taking a step closer, her voice rising. "We don't need *him*. We need each other. We need to trust the people we fight beside. Or does that mean nothing to you anymore?"

"Trust won't stop what's coming," Will replied. "Knowledge might. Power might."

"You sound just like *him*," she spat.

Will turned away from her, pacing the small chamber. "Maybe that's what it takes now. Maybe your way, *our* way... isn't enough."

"So you've just... what? Decided to throw your lot in with him? Everything we fought for?" Her voice cracked. "What happened to the man who carried the light across the dark wastes of Shadowmoor? Who stood up for what was right, even when it nearly killed him?"

Silence fell between them. A cold, suffocating stillness.

He turned then, and the look in his eyes made her take a step back. Not rage. Not sorrow. Just... emptiness.

"I'm not asking for your blessing," he said. "I'm doing what needs to be done."

Lyra stared at him, her mouth trembling, the words she wanted to say dissolving into silence. She shook her head, blinking back tears, and without another word, she left the room.

Will didn't follow.

The door shut with a quiet finality, and the air seemed colder for it.

He stood for a moment, a pang of... something, maybe guilt, washed over him, but he didn't have too long to examine it, as it passed quickly. He shook his head... he had work to do if he was to be ready in time. Lyra would have to understand that sometimes you need to fight fire with fire.

He quietly left their room and went in search of Valenor. He found him in another of the alcoves further up in the honeycomb structure of the hive, sitting alone at a simple wooden table. Valenor looked up warily as Will entered. He had clearly thought Will to be the same naïve man that he knew from a decade earlier, and this new Will had taken him off guard.

"Twice in one day," Valenor said, his tone guarded. "Should I be flattered, or worried?"

Will didn't respond immediately. He pulled the stool opposite Valenor and sat down, folding his arms across his chest, his gaze hard. "Let's get something clear," he said. "This isn't a partnership. You're not my equal, and I'm not here to be your pawn. If you cross me, *once*—"

"I know, I know," Valenor interrupted, raising a hand. "Obliteration, wrath, darkness incarnate. You've made your point. Quite dramatically, I might add."

Will didn't blink. "Good. Then let's begin."

Valenor eyed him for a long moment, then nodded slowly, the flicker of a grin curling at the edge of his lips. "Very well," he said, tapping a single finger on the wood. "You've already taken the first step. You've accepted the truth."

He leaned back in his chair, easing into his subject. "You still think the light will save you," he said softly. "That it forgives, that it redeems. But the light doesn't care. It only takes... your strength, your will, your hope, until there's nothing left but obedience."

He leaned forward, the shadows seeming to bend toward him. "The darkness doesn't demand worship. It gives. It rewards hunger, passion, desire. It doesn't ask you to kneel... only to act."

Will said nothing, but his pulse quickened.

"You've felt it," Valenor continued, his voice low, hypnotic. "The power that answers when the light turns away. You think it's corruption? No... it's clarity. It's truth stripped of weakness. Do you know why the light recoils from you?" He stepped closer, eyes gleaming with feverish conviction. "Because you frighten it. Because it knows what you could become if you stopped begging for its approval."

The words hit Will like a blow. He wanted to deny them, to shut his ears, but the echo of them coiled through his mind. Dark, terrible, and seductive.

Will said nothing, but his eyes burned with his willingness to hear more.

Valenor stood. "Come," he said, beckoning Will to follow. He led him away from the Hive, down a narrow, spiralling corridor lit only by the occasional sconce embedded in the walls.

"Where are you leading me, Valenor?" he asked, suspicion creeping into his voice.

"Somewhere we can test you without the order feeling what we're doing," he said cryptically.

They eventually emerged into a hall that branched off into sealed chambers... practice cells of sorts. Entering one and sealing the door behind them.

Valenor gestured toward the centre of the room. "Let's see what you've got, Will. Let's see what we're working with."

Will stepped forward. He closed his eyes, reaching deep within himself and channelling all the fear, frustration, and rage that seemed to have consumed him his entire life. The same darkness that had crippled him with anxiety in his younger years, the frustration that had destroyed every meaningful relationship he had ever had, and the anger at the hands of fate that always seemed to be steering him onto this inevitable course towards ruin. And for the first time since returning to this world, he stopped holding it back and *let it all in*.

The air chilled, the shadows in the corners of the chamber thickened, and a quiet slithering sound filled the room, like the low vibrations of a storm building just beneath the surface of the world, that pulsed with such latent power that the walls shook and fine silt sifted down from the ceiling.

Valenor's smile widened.

"Yes," he whispered. "This will do nicely."

Over the next few days, Will's instruction in harnessing the power of darkness continued. At first, he felt a strange mix of shame and excitement at being able to wield magic once again. The familiar pulse of power coursing through his body was intoxicating. But each time the darkness responded to his call, it left behind a faint bitterness, like ash in his mouth. The peculiar combination of triumph and self-disgust left him confused and exhausted by day's end.

As he watched the shadows curl to his will, bending with brute force rather than graceful coaxing, the shame began to fade. In its place grew a creeping sense of satisfaction, but that newfound confidence gradually transformed into pride, which in turn blossomed into ego.

He no longer second-guessed Valenor's instructions, no longer flinched at the raw brutality of the magic. The recoil that once tugged at his conscience was gone, buried under a swelling belief that this was the strength he had always lacked.

At first, his friends seemed happy to see him up and about again, no longer drifting listlessly from one sleepless night to the next, or wallowing in his sleeping chamber, unwilling to join them. There were even smiles, tentative though they were, and for a moment, Will had almost believed things might return to how they once were. But it didn't last.

As the days wore on, his tongue became sharper. Conversations grew shorter. He no longer laughed at Gissumir's jokes or entertained idle chatter as they sat together over their evening meal. He would disappear for hours, returning with the scent of scorched stone clinging to him and a cold gleam in his eyes that hadn't been there before.

They tried to be discreet, but he caught them often enough. Hushed voices talking about him when they thought he couldn't hear, the sudden drop in conversation when he entered a room, the glances they exchanged behind his back. It gnawed at him, though he told himself it didn't matter. They didn't understand. They weren't carrying what he was.

But worse than any of that was how distant Lyra became with him. She had pulled away from him in ways that went beyond words. She looked at him with apprehension in her eyes. She no longer tried to reach out to him. She didn't even argue with him anymore; she simply avoided him.

He had crossed worlds for her. Given up everything to return. And now, when he needed her most, she recoiled like his presence was a sickness.

He told himself it was fine. That she'd come around. That once he had become powerful enough to save them again, she'd understand. She had to.

Chapter 20

The dark no longer resisted him; it came when called, flowing through his hands like water. A flick of thought birthed coiling tendrils across the chamber wall. Another, and the light around him thinned to a suffocating murk.

He should have felt triumph. Instead, his gaze slid to Valenor, sprawled across a chair, muttering to himself. Always muttering. Always watching.

A dangerous thought coiled in Will's mind: *How simple it would be to silence him.* A subtle whisper of shadow across his throat. A surge of darkness in his lungs, just enough to stop his breath. Or perhaps something slower, like a withering curse, let him rot from the inside until his bitterness ate him whole. Will blinked hard, the visions scattering like startled birds, but the aftertaste clung to the back of his throat.

The door creaked. Will jerked upright, cold dread flooding him. Athtar stood in the threshold, eyes darting from the dark tendrils fading at his command to his guilty expression.

"Athtar—" His voice cracked, shame burning in his throat. "I didn't—"

Valenor laughed, sharp and mocking. "Didn't what? How precious... You still worry about what they think of you."

Will could sense Valenor gathering the shadows, his eyes trained on Athtar, and instinct took over. Darkness exploded from his hand, hurling Valenor into the stone wall with a sickening crack. He crumpled, unconscious.

Athtar's face hardened, horror filling her widened eyes. She spun and bolted.

"Athtar, wait!" he shouted after her. His terror spiked. This wasn't how it was supposed to happen. He was going to tell them... one day, when the time was right, when he could control the story. Not like this.

He ran so hard that his muscles burned and stars began dancing before his eyes, but he knew that he had little chance of catching her.

As he entered their living quarters, he could hear Athtar's voice cutting through the air, still raised from the adrenaline. "He's using dark energy. I saw it with my own eyes!"

The others turned sharply as Will stumbled in behind her, chest heaving.

"It's not what she thinks!" His words came too fast, too desperate.

Gissumir was the first to recover from the shock of the revelation and approached Will calmly. "If it's not what she thinks, then tell us lad... what is it?"

Will took a few deep breaths to try to calm his racing heart as his eyes darted about in panic. "I didn't choose this... It came to me. I needed to learn to control it... to protect us."

Athtar's hand went to her blade, knuckles white. Her face was flushed with rage. "Protect us? Will... it's dark magic. It doesn't protect, it consumes."

Athtar looked back at the others. "I saw him use his power to attack that Elf he's been spending time with, too."

Will felt his throat tighten. "You think I wanted any of this? Valenor was going to attack you, and if I hadn't—"

"You struck him first!" she snapped, her voice raw. "Don't twist it. Don't lie to us now. We trusted you, and you've been hiding this all along."

Lyra's eyes brimmed with tears as she stepped forward, her voice trembling. "Will... please. Just tell me it isn't true. Tell me she's wrong."

Her words struck harder than Athtar's fury. Will opened his mouth, closed it again. His voice cracked when it finally emerged. "I can't."

The silence that followed was shattering.

Lyra shook her head, tears spilling freely as her eyes searched his face for any trace that this might all be a huge mistake.

He reached for her hand, but she pulled away as though burned. "Lyra—don't you see? The light abandoned me. I tried, I begged for it, but it wouldn't answer. The dark did. And it saved me. We need the power for what's coming."

Athtar barked a bitter laugh. "Listen to him. Justify it, dress it up however you like... darkness doesn't save, Will, it corrupts."

"I am still me!" Will's shout rang in the chamber, sharper than he intended. Shadows rippled around him, stirred by his fury. "I am still me, and I'm fighting for us! Can't you see that?"

Gissumir's face had dropped. He shook his head, voice thick with disappointment. "In Hent-Taui, they still tell your story. The traveller who fought the darkness, who gave everything to protect this world. I thought you were that man." He paused, his expression hardening. "Now I see the darkness wasn't something you fought. It was something you brought with you."

The words pierced deeper than any blade. Will staggered under them, shame clawing at him, but his anger boiled up hotter still.

"So that's it? After everything I've done... you're all going to turn on me the first time it doesn't fit neatly into your little story of heroes and monsters?" His voice cracked into a near scream. "You don't know what it's like! To be cut off from the light, to feel the incredible pressure of expectation. I had no choice!"

Athtar spat the words. "There is always a choice."

"No!" Will snapped, his voice breaking. "Not for me. Not anymore."

Lyra whispered, almost pleading, "What have you become, Will?"

Will's chest heaved, and for a moment, he had no answer. Then, softer, ragged: "I've become who I had to, in order to ensure our survival... Even if you all hate me for it."

Silence again, thick and suffocating. No one moved. Will could feel the bond between them shattering, seemingly beyond repair.

Athtar's eyes lingered on him, cold and sharp. Distrust was written plainly on her face. Lyra's tears glistened in the dim light, torn between love and fear. Gissumir could not even look at him.

Will pressed a shaking hand to his brow, forcing his voice lower. "Please... just listen. I never wanted this. I don't even know what's happening to me half the time. But I'm still me... I swear it. Don't turn away from me now, I beg of you."

His words hung in the air, brittle as glass, as he left his fate in their hands and waited for their verdict.

Lyra brushed at her tears, her gaze fixed on him with a love she no longer knew how to reconcile. Gissumir shifted uncomfortably, unable to meet Will's gaze.

They all glanced sideways at one another, the weight of that decision resting heavily on them. None of them knew what to say or what choice to make.

Finally, Athtar broke the silence. "We're due in the nexus chamber. The elders are waiting. We should... bring him before the council."

Will's stomach knotted. "Athtar—"

She held up a hand. "We could plead for leniency. Say Valenor corrupted you, twisted you into this. It would be a mercy, compared to what they'll think if they hear it from anyone else."

Gissumir shook his head. "Mercy? The council will imprison him. Or worse. You know their judgment in these matters."

Lyra stepped between them, her hands trembling. "No! I won't let you hand him over like a criminal. He's not lost. He's still Will," she said, her voice cracking with a note of desperation.

The echoes of her plea died in a tense silence that followed.

Will swallowed hard, shame gnawing at his insides. "I'll prove it," he said, his voice steadier than he felt. "I'll prove I haven't changed. That I'm still the man you believe in."

Begrudgingly, they agreed, but as they walked towards the nexus chamber in a tense, uncomfortable silence, Will could feel Athtar's eyes boring into the back of his head. As they approached, they could hear that the meeting was already in session; the elders' voices were distorted by the hard stone walls.

"—that said, we will need to send the battle mage squadrons immediately to Anhai," Lucian was saying as they rounded the stone outcropping that separated the main chamber from the council floor.

He paused as he saw them enter.

"Ah. Glad you could join us," he said with a brief smile, directing them towards their seats. "I was just informing the other Elders that Oberith has begun his march north. There are troubling reports coming from the first towns he's taken in the borderlands."

They all filed into one of the galleries that encircled the five thrones of the elders and took their seats.

Lucian continued. "I was just saying that the situation in the south has developed quickly. Oberith seems to be making his move, and we believe Anhai will serve as the primary defence against the advancing southern hordes. We'll establish our staging area there and prepare to meet Oberith head-on. He won't be able to bypass it. If he tries, we'll strike his rear guard and cut him to pieces. He'll have no choice but to attempt to take the city."

Will was no strategist, but the plan sounded solid. "Sounds good. When do we leave?"

"Immediately," Lucian replied. "I've sent word to the northern rulers, trying to convey the severity of the threat against all the kingdoms of the north, but whether they'll listen this time... remains to be seen."

The meeting went on for some time, but after that, it was mostly boring logistical details about troop movements, so Will tuned out, his mind wandering over the events of the day. He cast a sideways glance at the others, who were all listening rapt to Lucian as he continued to explain the plan. He knew that things were far from okay with them, but he was happy that, for now at least, disaster had been averted.

Feeling his eyes on her, Lyra turned and met his gaze. He smiled, a tentative smile, unsure how it would be received, but the smile she returned filled his heart, as it always did. He reached out his hand, and they locked fingers.

At that moment, Lucian said something that broke through the haze of distraction that left the rest of his announcement muffled.

Will snapped out of his daze and shook his head. "I'm sorry, Lucian... I missed that?" he said.

"I said that the survivors of the attack on the first border towns have turned up at Anhai with the most troubling reports. If they are to be believed, after demanding their surrender, Oberith allowed them ten minutes to deliberate. At precisely ten minutes, he summoned the most horrific creatures of the underworld who decimated the town in a matter of minutes, pulling back when only a few survivors remained to tell the tale," Lucian said, pausing to allow the gravity of that to sink in.

Gissumir let out a noise that indicated that he wasn't entirely convinced. "Small town folk the world over are all the same... tall tales and excuses for cowardice," he said.

Lucian tilted his head to the side. "I am not sure. According to Edarn, the reports have come from several towns, and they all tell the same tale. We will, of course, need to investigate, but we should be prepared for anything."

Will considered this troubling development a moment before clearing his throat. "So Oberith is destroying everything in his path?" he asked finally.

Lucian shook his head. "Apparently, his strategy of allowing a few survivors to spread the word has worked well for him. After the first few towns he took, the others all abandoned their homes at his approach. The streets of Anhai are packed with refugees, and hundreds more arrive each day."

Another of the elders stood. Her hair was steely grey and her skin weathered, but there was a keen light in her eyes that made her seem younger than her years. The green mantle she wore over her white robe identified her as the elder of Empathy.

"What about wards?" she asked. "Can we reinforce Anhai's perimeter?"

Lucian gave her a curious glance. "It's been discussed, Eldara. The southern perimeter is already being etched with fortification runes, and your empath mages will bless them when we arrive. But if these creatures are as powerful as the stories suggest, it may not be enough."

Eldara nodded and returned to her seat. Lucian straightened, signalling the close of the meeting. "We leave later today. Prepare yourselves. The battle for Anhai may well decide the fate of the north."

They all sat a moment as the mages stood and shuffled from the room. Finally, when they were the last to remain, Will took a deep breath and stood, the others following suit, and made their way back through to the hive. As they reached their shared apartment, Athtar finally broke the silence. "I'll be glad to be out of this place. I'll meet you all back here within the hour. I have to go and check on my students before we leave."

She avoided eye contact with Will as she said it, cutting him deep as he realised the rift between them was vast.

Will muttered a brief acknowledgement, then turned off down the corridor toward the chamber he shared with Lyra, Gissumir leaving without a word to go and pack his things.

As he reached their private room, Lyra's voice spoke softly behind him. "Will."

He turned.

She stepped closer, reaching up to tenderly touch his face. "You don't have to carry this alone. You know that, right?"

He wanted to believe it. Desperately.

But all he could do was nod.

She studied him a moment longer before they each turned to the task of packing their belongings.

When they returned to the communal part of their alcove, they found Gissumir standing by the exit, fully prepared to leave, pack on his shoulder.

"We don't leave for a couple of hours yet, Gissumir," said Lyra.

He shifted uncomfortably, avoiding their gaze. "About that," he said awkwardly. "I won't be joining you in Anhai."

Will looked at him sharply. "Why not?"

Gissumir glanced at Will for a moment before looking back at Lyra. "Things are changing very quickly. The situation in the south is developing quicker than I think anyone expected."

"That's exactly why we need you there," said Lyra, squinting as she tried to understand what he was getting at.

He nodded. "I know, but I think it's about time the dwarves of Hent-Taui finally shake off their isolationist ways and recognise that we all live in this world together. I will go and try to convince my brother to send reinforcements."

Will clasped his friend by the shoulders. "Well then, we wish you the very best of luck, my friend," he said.

Gissumir looked up at him, a cloud of uncertainty hanging just behind his eyes as he regarded Will. "Are you sure you're okay?" he asked finally.

Will smiled ruefully. "I am not sure any of us are truly okay... But I will be," he said.

Gissumir gave a short, thoughtful nod at Will's words. "Good," he said, though the tightness in his voice betrayed his doubt. Then he turned to Lyra, his expression softening. "Watch each other's backs. I've grown quite partial to your company," he said, his eyes misting up.

Gissumir stepped forward and pulled Lyra into a one-armed hug, then slapped Will on the back of the shoulder.

He stood for a moment, looking at each of them as though recording the details of their faces one last time. "I will try to meet you at Anhai before the fun starts."

When he turned back to Will, something more serious lingered in his gaze.

"If the path gets dark... remember that you're not walking it alone. Even if it feels like it at times."

Will opened his mouth to reply, but Gissumir was already turning away. With his pack slung high, he strode out of the alcove.

They stood in silence a moment after he left, trying to adjust to the void left in the wake of his departure.

Lyra was the first to break the silence. "He's right, you know. We *do* need the dwarves. And if anyone can talk sense into that brother of his, it's Gissumir."

Will nodded absently, still watching the empty corridor.

He considered looking in on Valenor before leaving, but on reflection, he realised that he now owed Valenor nothing. The order would still never let him leave the island, but at least he had a more comfortable life now, outside the cells.

They spent the next couple of hours tending to their weapons in silent preparation. No words were needed... they all knew what lay ahead. When the time arrived, they all stopped to take one last look at the small alcove they had called home during their time here, realising that this might well be the last time they saw it, before gathering up their things and making their way to the portal room.

Lucian was already there, deep in conversation with Eldara when they arrived, but he looked up as they approached.

"Good," he said simply. "You're just in time."

Athtar glanced around the staging area. "Is this all we're sending?"

"For now," Lucian said. "More will follow once we set up our operations in Anhai. We will set up a staging area in the Anhai portal room with the advance group, and then we can maintain an active portal indefinitely to move our people through in larger numbers."

Will stared into the still surface of the glowing portal a moment longer before turning to the others. "I suppose this is it then," he said.

Lucian nodded. "This will be decided soon, one way or another."

Chapter 21

It always took him by surprise how much drier the air in Anhai was, but this time it was also notably more tense. As he looked around, he felt Lyra and Athtar materialise behind him on the raised platform.

The portal room buzzed with activity. Mages in robes of various hues moved between crates of supplies and stacks of enchanted armaments, a low hum of quiet conversation filling the air as they checked the contents of the crates against manifests.

A young mage broke away from a nearby group and approached them. He nodded sharply to them. "We've been expecting you," he said, turning to sign a form a nearby acolyte passed him.

"Is there anything we can do to help?" Athtar asked.

The mage hesitated, glancing around the room at the organised chaos. "At the moment, we have things under control here."

Will nodded once. "Then we'll find King Edarn."

The mage pointed down a wide corridor. "You'll find him in the conference room adjoining the royal hall. Do you know the way?"

"We know the way," Will assured him.

The council chamber was heavy with the heat of Anhai's afternoon, the air thick with dust and pride. A long table dominated the room, strewn with maps, troop manifests, and half-drained goblets of wine.

At the head sat Edarn himself, sleeves rolled up, listening to a thick-necked general pointing at a southern map. When he saw them enter, Edarn waved a hand and gestured toward the seats at the far end.

"Good. Sit," he said without pause.

They obeyed, slipping quietly into their seats.

General Harth, a grizzled veteran with a scar splitting his cheek, jabbed at the parchment with a calloused finger. "Their numbers are impressive, I'll grant that," he said with a wry grin, "but they fight like farmers. Peasants with pitchforks and stolen blades. My men will cut through them like grain before harvest."

A ripple of laughter circled the table.

Another commander leaned back in his chair, armour creaking. "We'll have them routed before dusk. They'll come shouting and waving their rusty swords, but the first charge will break them."

Edarn sat quietly at the head of the table, watching them through hooded eyes. He let the noise of laughter and bravado build a moment longer, before speaking.

"Tell me," he said finally, his voice measured, "how many of your 'peasants' have you actually faced in open battle?"

The room fell still.

Harth shifted in his seat. "None, Your Majesty. But reports—"

"Reports," Edarn cut in softly, "don't bleed on your sword. These are desperate men, driven by hunger and hatred. That combination is often a far deadlier weapon than fine steel."

Harth's smile faltered. "With respect, my king, this city has never fallen. A rabble like this—"

"—has already taken half the southern borderlands," Edarn said. He leaned forward, the lamplight catching the sharp edge of his expression. "They may be untrained, but they are united and desperate. And desperate unity can topple empires."

No one laughed after that. The silence that followed was thick, broken only by the uncomfortable shuffling of papers and clearing of throats.

Edarn folded his arms. "Update me on the situation in the city," he said finally.

A moment of hesitation.

"The city is at capacity," one of the generals said. "The refugee flow has slowed, but barely. Every town between here and the border has emptied. They're all here, packed into the lower wards. Resources are stretched. Tempers are short... We're doing what we can."

Lyra leaned closer to Will. "You're quiet," she murmured.

Will gave a slight shake of the head, attempting a smile. "Just tired," he said.

But the truth was heavier than that.

He wasn't sure what he believed anymore. He had glimpsed too much of the darkness that lay ahead, and worse, the darkness that now lived within him. The fire that had once driven him felt dimmed, if not entirely extinguished.

Let them talk.

Will closed his eyes and leaned back in his chair as the meeting settled into the nitty-gritty of mundane issues like how much grain stores remained within the city and how the management of sewerage was being handled for such a burgeoning population, but these things were of no interest to him, so he let his mind wander. He looked out the window and at the sun, which was blazing high in the sky. There was still so much day remaining and so much to do, he sighed and rubbed his face. He was roused from his day-dreaming by the clattering of chairs as the generals all stood to leave, the meeting evidently having come to an end.

Edarn remained seated, his hands steepled beneath his chin as he stared down the table in thought. When he finally looked up, it was to Will, Lyra, and Athtar.

"You three, stay a moment," he said.

The generals paused at the door, glancing back uncertainly, but Edarn waved them off. One by one, they filtered out, boots echoing against the polished stone until the door closed behind them with a heavy thud.

For a long moment, no one spoke. Then Edarn leaned back in his chair and let out a sigh that seemed to carry the weight of the entire city with it.

"You heard them," he said. "Confident as cocks in spring. But it's not going to be that simple, is it?"

Will shook his head slowly. "I doubt it."

Edarn nodded grimly, as if he'd expected the answer but still hated hearing it aloud.

"We've seen Oberith's soldiers," Will continued. "His forces are well trained and work well together," he paused a moment. "and that's not even taking his army of red robes into account, or the reports that he has access to dark creatures of the underworld."

Edarn was silent a moment longer, fingers tapping lightly against the armrest. Then he stood and crossed to the window, looking out over the rooftops of Anhai where the streets below teemed with people, soldiers, carts of grain, and the ever-present murmur of a city on the edge.

"We'll need every advantage," he said without turning. "And every honest voice. You think of something the generals won't want to hear, I expect you to say it anyway."

Will blinked at that. "Even if it undermines morale?"

Edarn turned to face them, eyes flinty. "If morale rests on delusion, it's already broken."

There was a long pause as Edarn continued surveying the city. Then he turned and gave a tired, half-hearted smile, gesturing toward the door.

"Go get some rest. Or a drink. Or both. I suspect none of us will be resting much once Oberith reaches the walls."

After leaving Edarn, Athtar went back to the portal room to assist with the arrivals from Thorn Island, and Lyra went down into the city in search of the empaths who were already enchanting the walls to fortify them. Will hadn't really thought about it much since his return, but Lyra's position within the order was one she took very seriously. She was different than the others, though. The acolytes they had come across in the past had always been demure and submissive, but Lyra had still retained the fire...

the passion that had always been at the core of her spirit, and Will loved that about her.

He wandered the halls of the palace, basking in the warm, dusty afternoon air that hung still and heavy in the open corridors. He walked around in a bit of a daze, the accumulation of weeks of pressure and frequent nights of interrupted sleep having left him burned out and hazy. His wandering brought him to an open inner courtyard at the heart of the palace. The gardens were full of desert flora, and he marvelled at these most resilient of blooms that survived in the most extreme conditions. He stood there for some time, enjoying this rare bubble of calm in an otherwise hectic city that was preparing for battle. The long shadows cast by the high walls and spires that surrounded the courtyard protected the plants from the unrelenting heat of the sun for most of the day, and given his recent internal struggles, Will found that to be quite a poetic perspective on light and shadow.

He lowered himself onto a stone bench, its surface warm beneath his hands. For a while, he just sat, eyes half-closed, letting the dry breeze carry the scent of sun-warmed herbs and desert flowers. The sounds of the city beyond were distant, softened by the walls and the high towers that loomed like watchful sentinels.

He couldn't say how long he sat there, but a part of him wanted to stay in this quiet corner forever, away from the pressing demands of life. But he knew it was borrowed peace. A soft rustling among the hedges drew his attention. He looked over, half expecting a gardener or a passing soldier, but there was no one, only the leaves shifting lazily under the touch of the wind.

Finally, he stood, exhaling slowly, and continued his wandering.

The lack of any particular direction brought with it a strange catharsis that healed his troubled soul a little. He shouldn't have been surprised, therefore, that his feet carried him down into the southern wards where Lyra was still assisting the empaths. He stood for a time, just watching her work. He loved the serious expression and the way she would occasionally try to blow a stray hair out of her face, only to have it fall back to exactly the same position it had started.

A few moments later, she spotted him and smiled, waving him over. "I didn't expect to see you down here," she said.

Will shrugged, the corners of his mouth tilting in a weary smile. "Neither did I," he said.

Lyra tilted her head, her smile lingering but coloured now with curiosity. She brushed the rogue strand of hair behind her ear in a way that made his chest ache for simpler days. "You alright?" she asked, low enough that the nearby empaths, still hard at work tracing sigils into the sandstone, wouldn't hear.

He glanced around at the enchantments forming in pale threads of light along the walls. "Better than I've been," he replied, after a pause. "It all feels so real now that we're here. This place..."

Lyra nodded, following his gaze. "This city is incredible... It's people, even more so. Whatever happens here, we're a part of momentous times once again."

Will looked at her then, really looked, and saw the fire in her eyes hadn't dimmed at all. "You've changed," he said, not meaning it as a judgement.

She smiled again, softer this time. "So have you."

They stood there for a moment, just breathing in the dust and sweat and subtle hum of magic in the air.

"Want to help?" she asked eventually, gesturing to a fresh wall space where a younger empath was preparing one of the etched runic symbols to be enchanted.

Will raised a brow. "You're trusting me with this?"

"You once stood face to face with the cursed creatures of Shadowmoor, and you're still here to talk about it. I don't think this is beyond you."

He chuckled, and for a moment, the weight on his shoulders felt a little lighter. "Alright," he said, stepping forward. "Show me what to do."

Lyra laughed, a musical sound to Will's ears, clean and bright against the din of voices and distant hammering. Without another word, she led him to a nearby table where several other acolytes were preparing a thick, silvery compound in shallow stone bowls.

"We take this mixture," she said, dipping her fingers in and scooping out a small amount, "and work it into the etched runes, ensuring there are absolutely no gaps or air bubbles."

"That's it?" Will asked, watching the slow, deliberate motion as she spread the mixture along a waiting glyph.

"That's it," she replied. "The mages come along and enchant them after we've finished this section and move on to the next."

He nodded, then picked up a small, worn spatula, and got to work. The compound was grainy, like wet sand mixed with ash, and it gave off a faint, metallic scent that stung his nose. He pressed the mixture into each line and swirl with quiet concentration, smoothing the surface as best he could.

It felt good to be doing something. For too long, he'd felt so completely useless. Powerless. Disconnected. But here, with dust on his boots and grime under his nails, surrounded by others who gave their all in small ways, he remembered something he'd long forgotten. That help didn't have to come in the form of raw power and grand gestures.

Sometimes the little things, done by many hands, held more weight than any spell or sword. Sometimes it was these quiet, unremarkable acts that turned the tide. There was something profound in that, something healing.

And as that realisation sank in, something shifted. It was subtle at first, like a string pulled taut within him. Then it grew. A warmth rose in his chest, threading through his limbs like a slow-burning fire. He stiffened, his hands frozen mid-movement, heart thudding.

He could feel the pulse of light energy in his veins once again. It embraced him like an old friend... Like it had simply been waiting for him to remember who he was.

He stood slowly, wiping his fingers clean on a nearby cloth. The world felt sharper, more alive. The air seemed to almost vibrate with energy. On an impulse, he turned toward the wall, lifted his hand, and extended it palm-forward. His fingers trembled with excitement and anticipation.

He closed his eyes.

Light gathered in his palm, soft and silver-white, and with a breath, he released it. A wave pulsed outward, sweeping across the wall in a quiet rush, stirring up the dust on the ground as it passed. The compound shimmered, drank it in, and every rune along the wall lit up in turn.

He opened his eyes to silence.

The empaths and acolytes had all stopped what they were doing. Lyra stood a few steps behind him, her eyes wide.

Will let out a slow breath, hand falling back to his side. "Well," he said, voice rougher than he expected, "That felt good."

Lyra stepped forward, her smile warm, eyes gleaming. She didn't say a word, but simply wrapped her arms around him and kissed him.

Will glanced at the glowing wall, then down at his now completely unremarkable hands. But he could feel it now, humming beneath the skin like a current beneath calm waters. The power was back, yes, but it wasn't the same as before. Something fundamental had shifted.

There was a balance now. The light didn't surge through him as it once had, pure and unyielding, a blade of righteous fire. Nor did the darkness curl and claw with the same hunger it had shown in his worst moments. Instead, he felt both. Present. Co-existing.

He closed his eyes and let his awareness sink inward. There, at the centre of his being, he could feel them, the tendrils of light intertwining with the slow, patient coils of darkness. Two serpents circling each other in a slow and measured dance. Not battling, just... existing. A delicate spiral, neither force claiming dominion.

His mind drifted back to that final moment atop the basalt monolith at the heart of Shadowmoor. The stone had been cracked and smoking beneath his feet, the world split open in every direction. When the dust settled, Malakar's essence was drawn into him. The curse slithered away, releasing its grip on the land. In that stillness, he had understood... light and dark were but two sides of the same coin. The two were bound to one another in a cycle older than time. One could not define itself without the presence of the other. In those precious moments, he'd understood the universe in a way few ever had.

But then came the fall. The loss of Lyra. The exile from Aruna. The empty years that followed. The years of obsession, of chasing whispers and fragments and in that desperate search, he had forgotten. Forgotten the truth he had grasped on that cursed monolith.

Until now.

He exhaled slowly and looked at Lyra, who was watching him with a strange expression, equal parts awe and quiet understanding. She'd seen the worst of him and hadn't turned away. That had to mean something.

"I forgot," he said softly, more to himself than to her.

Lyra stepped closer, her eyes flicking down to his hands before meeting his again. "Then it's good you remembered," she said, smiling, her eyes full of warmth.

Chapter 22

The air shimmered once more, and then the light of the ancient gateway sputtered and died, leaving Gissumir standing in the gloom. For a long moment, he simply breathed, pulling the familiar damp air deep into his chest. The smell of stone and lichen, the faint metallic tang that lived in the rock itself, the unmistakeable scent of home.

The portal chamber of Hent-Taui lay in a long-abandoned part of the cave network, but Gissumir knew every inch of this place like the back of his hand. It had been centuries since this portal had seen true use. Most of his kin scarcely remembered it existed. He tightened his cloak around his shoulders and set off, instinctively moving towards the main cavern at the heart of the mountain kingdom.

As he pressed deeper, the silence changed. A low pulse vibrated through the walls and floor, growing in intensity as he got closer. The floor trembled beneath his steps, and a deep roar welled up in the stone around him. Gissumir slowed, a smile tugging at his lips.

The Falls.

His chest swelled. By the gods, how he had missed that sound.

The tunnel ahead bent sharply, and suddenly light spilled into the darkness. Gissumir emerged blinking, and the sight struck him like it always had, with awe that stole the breath from his lungs.

The grand cavern of Hent-Taui opened vast and immeasurable before him. Walls arched high overhead, lost in shadow, their surfaces glittering with threads of crystal. All across the stone clung forests of bioluminescent fungi, casting emerald and sapphire glows that painted the cavern like a dream. Swarms of glow-flies floated in great drifting clouds, their pale yellow light shifting like stars trapped under the earth.

At the cavern's heart, the waterfall roared. It plunged from towering cliffs, crashing down into the lake far below. A natural shaft of daylight speared through a break high above the mountain, striking the water and mist in a blazing column of gold. Rainbows shimmered in the spray, arcing across the cavern in colours so vivid they seemed alive.

The lake spread outward in a glassy expanse, its surface rippling with reflected light. Bridges of stone and steel spanned the waters, leading toward clusters of towers carved directly from the cavern walls. Balconies, arches, and staircases rose like frozen waves, a city sculpted seamlessly into the living rock.

And commanding the very centre, rising from the lake's shore as though grown from the mountain itself, stood the Citadel. Its foundations merged with the plateau it rested upon. Bannercloths streamed in the mist, colours marking the great clans of Hent-Taui.

Gissumir slowed, heart tight in his chest. He had grown up here, played as a child along the lake shore, trained in those courtyards, and learned everything he knew in the halls and libraries of the great citadel. Yet still the sight humbled him, as though the mountain itself reminded him who he was.

Crossing one of the great arched bridges, Gissumir made for the Citadel. The guards at the gate spotted him long before he approached. They saluted smartly and stepped aside.

He almost faltered then. Just beyond the gates, a side street wound toward the residential terraces, and beyond that, he knew, lay his own dwelling. He thought of Sizzuli and almost decided to delay seeing his brother in favour of the comfort of home and being in the arms of the woman he loved.

But time was short, and his friends and the people of Anhai needed him now. As much as his heart yearned to be reunited with his wife, he knew that would have to wait a little longer. He clenched his fists and strode for the Citadel.

When he arrived in the main royal halls, the functionaries left him in an antechamber that was draped in all the finery that royal visitors usually craved: velvet cushions, tapestries of past kings, gilded fixtures. Gissumir sank into one of the seats and immediately regretted it; the cushion scratched his skin, too soft, too indulgent. He shifted uncomfortably, muttering to himself.

Minutes passed. He drummed his fingers on his knees, rising and pacing, then forcing himself back into the seat. By the time the functionary appeared, he almost leapt to his feet, smoothing the creases from his tunic with fumbling hands.

The functionary led him down a wide hallway, chandeliers dripping with crystal light. Massive doors swung open, and the throne room yawned before him.

Everything in Hent-Taui was built for grandeur, and the Citadel was no exception. Columns soared high into the shadowed ceiling, each etched with the deeds of dwarven kings long gone. Tapestries hung heavy on the walls, and the floor shone with polished stone.

At the far end, upon a dais of black stone, sat King Dhongrolir. His crown gleamed in the torchlight, and his cloak of sable fur spilled down the steps. Advisors and courtiers filled the hall, all of them fawning bootlickers in Gissumir's opinion, always puffing up his brothers fragile ego and toadying up to him.

Gissumir bowed low as he approached, deeper than he wished. *Steady. Show no weakness.*

"Gissumir," Dhongrolir said, his voice deep, resonant, and tinged with disdain. "At last, my wandering brother returns. Tell me…

what brings you scurrying back from your games with humans to the halls of real power?"

Laughter rippled through the courtiers.

Gissumir rose, jaw tight. His heart hammered, but his voice rang clear. "I come to speak of war."

A ripple of unease passed through the courtiers, but Dhongrolir only leaned back, one hand toying idly with the hem of his robe.

"War?" His lip curled. "I know well enough what war is. Do you take me for a fool, brother?"

"No," Gissumir said quickly. "I take you for a king. And as king, your duty extends beyond these caverns. Our allies cry out for aid—"

"*Our* allies?" Dhongrolir cut across him, the words sharp as a chisel on stone. "Do not mistake your own friendships for oaths binding Hent-Taui. I owe nothing to men or elves. I will not spill dwarven blood for their folly."

A murmur of approval rippled through the court.

Gissumir's hands clenched. "Folly? Oberith has risen. He commands abominations from the underworld itself. If Urias falls, do you truly think the darkness will halt at our gates?"

Some of the courtiers shifted uneasily at that. But Dhongrolir's gaze never wavered.

"You speak like an elf," he said, his tone dripping disdain. "Soft with fear, your years among them blinding you to the strength of our own walls. Hent-Taui has endured since before their kind had even mastered fire. We are no one's shield."

"By the gods, Dhongrolir, open your eyes!" Gissumir's voice cracked with frustration. "This is not a war that can be ignored. You think to wall yourself in, but walls cannot keep out what festers in the heart of the world. If we do nothing, the dark will devour us as surely as them."

A silence fell, broken only by the rush of water echoing faintly from beyond the walls as the great falls continued its journey. For a heartbeat, Gissumir dared hope he'd reached him.

Then Dhongrolir laughed. A harsh, ringing sound.

"You speak as though we know not of war," he sneered. "Fool. We are already at war."

Gissumir froze. "...What?"

Dhongrolir rose from the throne, cloak spilling across the steps as he descended. His eyes burned with a cold light.

"Did you think I idled while you wasted time among surface folk? No, brother. Our cousin, Kasarlum of the northern Ma'yan, has raised banners against me. Against *us*. He names me usurper, claims the old oaths broken, and he has marched. Even now, his armies test our borders, bleeding my warriors in the northern tunnels."

The words struck like hammer-blows. Gissumir staggered, heart thundering. "Kasarlum? No... he would never—"

"He *has*," Dhongrolir snapped. "Declared war. Claimed king-ship of Ma'yan and declared it a sovereign nation. He burns our holds, slaughters our kin. While you dally with humans and play at prophecy, our own blood makes war upon us."

Gissumir shook his head, unable to reconcile the words. "Not unprovoked. Kasarlum is proud, yes, but no fool. He would not plunge the clans into ruin without cause."

He looked hard at his brother. The years had etched lines of pride into Dhongrolir's face, but beneath them, Gissumir still saw the boy he had grown up with... the boy who had always hungered for more, who had fought to be first in every contest, who could not abide being denied.

"What did you do?" Gissumir asked softly.

A ripple of shock went through the courtiers. Some gasped, others hissed in outrage. Dhongrolir's expression darkened.

"Careful," the king said, voice low and dangerous. "You stand in my hall, before my throne. Choose your next words with wis-dom."

But Gissumir would not be cowed. "If Kasarlum rose against you, it was not without reason. Did you insult him? Seize his holdings? Tell me, Dhongrolir—what did you do?"

Then Dhongrolir smiled. Cold. Unyielding. "Accuse if you will, little brother. It changes nothing. War is upon us. If you crave battle so dearly, then fight here, where your kin bleed. Leave your human toys to their fate."

The reality of it settled on Gissumir like the weight of the mountain was pressing down on him. He thought of Will, of Lyra, of the desperate struggle against Oberith. He thought of Sizzuli, of the halls of his childhood, of kin dying in the northern tunnels.

Two wars. Both were crying for him. He could not fight both.

Slowly, painfully, he bowed his head. "Very well. You are right, brother. My place is here. But know this, Dhongrolir: your pride may yet cost us all. And when it does, no walls will save you."

Dhongrolir waved a dismissive hand, already turning back to his advisors.

* * *

The preparations of the city continued throughout the night. The people of Anhai, along with the countless refugees from southern Urias who had sought shelter within its walls, worked side by side with the silent understanding that their very survival hung in the balance.

Bakers who had once fed the morning markets now hauled sandbags to reinforce the inner gates. Children too young to fight fetched water for the exhausted, wide-eyed, and solemn as they moved through the crowded streets. Mages lit the night with steady orbs of light, casting long shadows across the courtyards.

They worked in shifts, taking turns to rest when they could, curling up in corners or on makeshift pallets. Everyone knew that the days ahead would hold few opportunities for sleep, and those who weren't resting now were urged to do so.

It was strange, Will thought, how unity always seemed to rise out of adversity. There was a kind of nobility in it, something quiet and honest. He could feel it in the air, in the shared glances, the clapped shoulders, the exhausted laughter that broke out now and then as a small act of rebellion against the fear that stalked them in the quiet moments.

The following day, the preparations slowed somewhat as they neared completion. The city took on a more quietly vigilant air and everywhere you went an unnatural stillness had descended as people quietly prepared themselves for the inevitable. Later that afternoon, a series of ringing bells sounded across the city, breaking that calm. People knew the drills, but the fear still filled the air with the sounds of wailing as they ran to seek shelter, and soldiers took their positions.

Will found Edarn making his way quickly through the halls of the palace, escorted by a full detail of guards, and fell in step beside him. "Is this it?" he asked.

Edarn wore a serious expression as he turned to Will. "I don't know, but if it is, he's well ahead of schedule."

Once outside, the two men descended into the streets of the western quarter, where civilians scrambled to shelters, clutching children and bundles of possessions, their faces pale with terror.

Soldiers snapped into formation at key intersections, directing foot traffic, helping the infirm, shouting orders above the din. Every citizen knew where they were meant to be. Still, fear did not heed discipline so easily, and Will saw it in every wide eye and trembling hand.

As they neared the gatehouse, the noise shifted. The wails and shouts of fear gave way to something different... cheering.

It started as a ripple, distant and uncertain, then surged into a roar. Soldiers atop the battlements had begun raising their weapons and fists in celebration. Voices shouted from the towers, and a great cheer erupted among the defenders who moments before had stood braced for the worst.

Will exchanged a glance with Edarn, who frowned, confused, and quickened his step. They climbed a short flight of stone steps to reach the parapet.

Edarn approached a nearby captain standing near the signal platform, his hand resting on the hilt of his sword. "Report," the king barked.

The captain turned, grinning beneath his helm. "My lord, riders approach... riding under banners of crimson and gold. Cervian banners."

Will moved to the edge and looked out over the wall. Sure enough, an armoured host was cresting the horizon; a wedge of gleaming steel and red cloaks, their standards snapping in the breeze. The sun caught on their helmets, glinting all along the horizon.

The good news continued as a few hours later, word arrived from King Haelyn that he would be sending a regiment of archers to help fortify the walls. Throughout the remainder of the afternoon and evening, they began arriving from the crystal city through the portal room.

Once King Torvahn had seen his knights and their mounts were suitably quartered, he presented himself in Edarn's throne room, as was protocol. He approached the throne warily, past tensions between the nations leaving him tense, but as he approached, Edarn got up and walked to him, hesitating only briefly, before embracing him as a brother. "Thank you, my friend. I hope you know how much this means to me and the people of Urias. This day, our two great nations will forge a new bond and rewrite our story in the history books as allies and friends."

Torvahn, tall and broad-shouldered in his ceremonial plate, stood motionless for a moment. Then he returned the embrace, clasping Edarn's back with gauntleted hands. There was a murmur of approval from the attending nobles and advisors who lined the throne room.

There was a moment of silence, then Edarn gestured to the table in the adjoining conference room, where a sprawling map of Urias and its borderlands was spread. "Then come. Let us plan together, and may our unity give the enemy pause."

As the kings leaned over the table, their generals and advisors closing in around them, a quiet shift rippled through the room. For the first time in weeks, there was more than just grim determination in the air... There was a real sense of hope.

The city, already stretched to capacity, was suddenly at breaking point, but everyone was thrilled to see the new arrivals, and a celebration broke out in the streets that night. Everyone pitched in, bringing tables into the streets and filling them with food and drink. Bonfires were lit and musicians played into the night.

When the meeting concluded, Edarn moved to the window and gazed out over the city, where the glow of bonfires lit the streets and the sound of music and laughter rose into the air, and smiled.

"It seems the people of the city have had the right idea," he said, turning back to the others. "Let us also take advantage of this rare opportunity to celebrate."

At his gesture, the ever-watchful servants along the edges of the chamber slipped away and quickly returned with food and wine.

Moments later, a lute player and harpist entered, their soft melodies beginning to fill the room.

Will and Lyra grabbed drinks from a passing server and drifted toward the edge of the room, away from the bustle near the thrones, where courtiers swarmed the two monarchs in the hope that some spare nobility might rub off on them.

Will chuckled, shaking his head. "They're the same in every world," he murmured.

Lyra turned toward him, brow arched. "Who are?"

"The ones who hover near power," he said, nodding toward the crowd and tilting his drink toward them. "They share a universal belief that proximity to those in power somehow elevates them."

Her face took on a sympathetic expression, but she said nothing.

Will looked about for Athtar, hoping to steal this moment to spend with those nearest him on the eve of battle, but he couldn't see her anywhere.

"Have you seen Athtar?" he asked Lyra.

She shook her head, sipping from her glass. "I think she went to greet the elves when they arrived. She might still be with them."

Will nodded, though a flicker of disappointment tugged at him. Things hadn't been right between them since they had left Thorn Island. He'd hoped to find a moment tonight to bridge that distance, before... whatever unpleasantness was about to befall them.

As those darker musings stirred, he felt Lyra slip under his arm and lean into him. He looked down, smiled, and pressed a kiss to the top of her silvery hair. Closing his eyes, he exhaled a long, quiet sigh and held her tighter.

"Any word from Gissumir?" Lyra asked.

"I haven't heard anything. Maybe Edarn has," he suggested, reluctantly releasing her from their embrace, and grabbing her by the hand to lead her through the dense crowd.

Edarn saw them approach and welcomed them, introducing them to Torvahn, much to the consternation of the courtiers, still swarming around in an attempt to be noticed.

"You approached like a man with a question," Edarn said.

"Very astute, Your Majesty," said Will. "I just wondered if you had received word at all from Hent-Taui?"

Edarn's expression dimmed. "I'm afraid not. And with Oberith's forces drawing closer, I fear time has all but run out. I know Dhongrolir well, and I suspect Gissumir's efforts to change his brother's mind may be in vain."

Torvahn chuckled dryly. "Ah, yes, Dhongrolir. The only thing thicker than his stubborn streak is his cowardice."

As they continued to talk, Will felt a shift in the energy beyond the tall windows. The music and laughter from the streets below had turned into something sharper. Shouts. Screams. Panic. At the same time, a tremor of magic pulsed at the edge of his awareness. The runes embedded in the southern wall had activated.

Edarn broke off mid-sentence, catching the change in Will's expression. His eyes followed Will's to the vast open window overlooking the city.

"What is it, Will?"

The question brought him back to the room. He turned to the two monarchs, suddenly all business.

"You should gather your generals. It's begun."

Chapter 23

The mood in the throne room shifted dramatically as word spread. The bright music halted, strings falling silent mid-note as the first shouts carried through the hall. Guests pressed together, wide-eyed, straining to catch each new fragment of rumour as fear paralysed them in place.

Edarn was on his feet first, his throne scraping back against the dais with a screech that cut across the din. Beside him, Torvahn rose, his voice booming over the crowd as he barked orders at the guards. Steel clattered as men and women moved into position and began ushering civilians toward the exits.

The kings did not linger. They had planned for this moment, and with only a glance to one another, they gathered their generals and strode into the adjoining conference chamber that had become a makeshift council of war.

Will lingered by the massive window overlooking the southern quarter of the city, Lyra's hand still in his. He couldn't see the enemy beyond the wall, but he felt it. An unease in the flow of magic festered under his skin, leaving him with a restless feeling.

Lyra gave his hand a gentle tug. He turned, just as she pulled him down into a firm kiss.

"I have to go and join the others," she said. "I'll send word when I can, but I have to go."

He looked at her helplessly. He was torn, not wanting to be separated from her, but he understood and respected the sense of duty that drove her. He met her gaze and held it, then leaned in and kissed her once more.

"Please be safe," he said. It was all he could manage as fear constricted his throat.

She smiled, squeezed his hand one more time, and then turned to leave.

Will suddenly found himself once again without purpose, and the helplessness clawed at him. He didn't like the feeling. Frustration welled up inside, hot and directionless. He could feel the balance within shifting, light giving way to shadow as the tendrils of dark magic stirred, fed by those rising emotions. But just as the swell of power began to overtake him, a voice from the next room cut through his thoughts, breaking his spiral.

"I need information, damn it! Who makes their primary attack at night anyway?" Edarn's shout rang out clearly from the war room, the strain and panic creeping into his voice.

The distraction was enough to snap Will out of his building wave of rage and self-loathing, and as he did so, an idea came to him. He didn't know if it would work, but closing his eyes, he reached inward, drawing on both the light and the dark now woven through his soul. He focussed his energy and channelled his awareness into his shadow. He felt an abnormal tugging sensation as his awareness dislodged from his body. The sensation was unnatural and left him feeling momentarily disorientated, but a moment later, he found himself hovering somewhere nearby.

He could see his own body standing there, still facing the window, eyes vacant. He looked down and lifted a hand out before him, suppressing a shudder at the sight. There was the merest outline of an appendage, formed from a gently swirling shadow.

Everything looked different now. The world was draped in dim, desaturated tones. Shadows pulsed with subtle movement, rich in depth and detail. Torchlight burned like acid in his eyes, its radiance too stark for this form.

Now he was free of his corporeal form, and he knew he could move freely, but he found he was limited to slipping from shadow to shadow. With uncanny speed, he descended the tower, slipping through alleys and across rooftops where the torchlight didn't reach. The south wards were dark and quiet, the perfect conduit. It didn't take long for him to reach the southern wall.

There, he hit his first obstacle.

The runes. Glowing with enchantment and flanked by evenly spaced torches, they lined the top of the wall like a warding fence. The combined light formed a barrier that seared at his senses, creating an impassable threshold to his shadow-born form.

He cast about frantically, searching for any breach that might grant a view beyond the wall, but found none. *It had seemed such a good plan,* he thought to himself as disappointment welled up.

From his vantage in the shadows behind a stack of crates, he caught a flicker of movement. A detachment of Elves sprinted toward the wall, ascending the stone steps with a swift, fluid grace. They fanned out into a defensive formation, drawing their bows and sighting down the arrows. Among them, one figure stood out.

Athtar.

She stood with bow drawn, an arrow nocked and ready, her cloak catching the wind in the wake of her charge. Seeing her sparked an idea, but he couldn't enact it in his current form.

He immediately pulled his awareness back. The world streaked past in reverse as he snapped back through the streets. The reentry of his consciousness felt like running headlong into a wall, leaving him disorientated and nauseous, but he braced against it, breathing through the dizziness until his mind cleared.

He'd barely caught his breath when he reached inward again. Not for shadow this time, but for light.

He searched his soul for the emotional connection he shared with Athtar. In his mind's eye, countless ribbons of light stretched outward from him, binding him to the people who mattered most.

He sifted through his memories of Athtar, searching for the correct ribbon. He remembered the days before their return, when she had sought him out and helped him find his way back to Aerinthos, always being a steady guiding light. And that moment in the realm between portals when shadow wights were closing in, their shrieks like tearing metal, until Athtar's flames erupted from her hands, driving them back, defending him when he could not defend himself. She had never faltered. Across worlds, across dangers he barely understood, she had stood beside him, loyal beyond question, steadfast when others may have walked away.

He clung to those fragments, let them burn like stars within him, and reached out through the light, seeking the ribbon of pale gold that vibrated faintly with the energy of their shared bond.

This time, when his awareness left his body, the journey was swift and radiant, like falling through the heart of a star. The ribbon became a highway of light, and he travelled its length in the space between one heartbeat and the next.

Then, he was there, lodged gently in the back of Athtar's mind. He could see what she saw, hear the sounds of the city mobilising through her ears, smell the sharp tang of oil and torch-fire.

He could feel the unease rolling off the others stationed along the wall. There was an expectant tension that seemed to shroud everyone there, a silent dread that passed from one soldier to the next, every breath held in anticipation of imminent violence.

"What the fuck are they waiting for?" muttered a male voice nearby, fraught with anxiety.

He heard the creak of bows being held, half drawn, the sputtering of the flames on the torches behind them that lined the wall on the inside of the city.

The elves were the first to see it.

From their vantage atop the southern wall, their keener eyes pierced the gloom that shrouded the fields beyond the torchlight. Athtar raised her voice to the archer who stood next to her. "Movement. There...do you see?"

A silent ripple moved down the line as arrows were nocked and spells prepared.

Then the darkness broke.

A sudden, violent cacophony shattered the stillness of the night air. From the darkness beyond the wall, the war horns howled, drums thundered, and a chorus of distorted voices chanted in unison. A wave of lightly armoured infantry surged forward, shrieking as they came. Some ran on all fours like animals, while others clutched rusted swords and spiked maces, their bodies unnaturally fast and twitching with Oberith's dark enhancements.

Behind them came the red-robed mages.

In unison, they raised their arms, and the world changed.

The sky above the south quarter shimmered, and suddenly, the city seemed to be under siege from every direction. Entire phantasmal armies shimmered into being across the landscape, siege towers rolled forward from the east and west, and monstrous shadow-beasts prowled around in the gloom, just barely visible.

Several of the human defenders cried out, backing away from the parapets, their eyes wide with terror.

"Stand your ground!" Athtar shouted. "They are illusions!"

The true attack came seconds later.

Crude grappling hooks arced over the wall's edge, their iron teeth biting into stone. Scaling ladders followed, slammed against the wall, chipping the sandstone corners. The twisted infantry were already climbing, shrieking in a frenzy as they climbed, heedless of the arrows raining down from above.

Athtar loosed her bow. Her first shot punched through a skull. The second struck an enemy square in the chest. Around her, elven and human archers released volley after volley, sending climbers hurtling backwards into their own comrades. But no matter how fast they fired, the ferocity of the attack meant that a few made it to the top.

The first over the wall was barely human. Pale and sinewy, eyes red with madness. He lunged at the nearest defender, a young Uriasan guardsman who barely managed to raise his sword. The thing sank its teeth into the man's throat before Athtar drove an arrow through its spine, snapping it like a broken puppet.

More followed.

Screams and the clash of steel rang out along the parapet. One of the elves was dragged screaming over the edge. Another twisted his spear through the gut of an attacker, only to have his leg crushed beneath a spiked mace from a second climber. Blood sprayed against the stone. A Uriasan swords-master battled three at once, her blades flashing as she spun and carved through limbs and torsos with graceful savagery, expertly parrying the clumsy attacks of the invader.

Athtar was a blur. Firing, drawing, firing again, her arrows precise and merciless.

Beyond the front line of the attacking infantry, Athtar could hear as the red-robes intensified their chant, focusing their power toward a single point near the central section of the wall. Runes along the stone guttered and flared as a focused magical bombardment pounded at the base of the wall.

With a crackling roar, the ancient stones burst outward in a cascade of rubble and flame, the force of the explosion shaking the wall above. Dust and smoke billowed into the air from an old abandoned aqueduct, as the mages stepped aside and a fresh wave of infantry surged forward, howling as they poured into the newly opened breach.

The defenders focussed their attacks on the advancing infantry to try and keep them away from the breach, but they continued to surge forward, clambering over the bodies of the fallen to reach their goal. Dozens crammed into the narrow tunnel, scrambling over shattered stone and broken iron, even as arrows and spells rained down from above.

But the Order had anticipated this.

Suspecting Oberith might be aware of this weakness in the wall, they had warded the aqueduct with a powerful enchantment, one buried deep within the tunnel itself. When the vanguard reached the halfway mark and clustered at the rusted iron grate, the trap sprang.

A searing blast of flame erupted from within, incinerating everything in the passage. The shockwave ripped back toward the opening, flinging scorched bodies and debris in all directions and sending the remaining attackers into a panicked retreat.

Back on the wall, the last of the probing force was falling back.

Seeing their losses mounting and no breach made, Oberith's forward commanders blew a single, low horn. The surviving foot soldiers disengaged, shrieking as they retreated into the night, dragging wounded and corpses alike. The red-robed mages dropped their illusions with eerie synchronicity and melted back into the shadows.

Silence followed, punctuated only by the groans and wails of those waiting for death to take them.

Smoke drifted lazily along the battlements. The defenders stood among the bodies, panting, bleeding, shaken, but not broken.

Athtar lowered her bow, her eyes scanning the gloom beyond the light of the torches.

"That was just the beginning," she said, her chest heaving. "Everyone, take a moment to breathe, but remain vigilant."

Having seen enough, Will released the strand of light tethering his consciousness to Athtar. His awareness whipped back through the city like a coiled ribbon, and a moment later, he stood once more in his own body, blinking against the torchlight in the throne room. He took a calming breath, steadying himself, then turned and strode toward the war chamber to brief the gathered generals on what he had just witnessed.

Edarn stood rigid at the head of the table, Torvahn looming beside him, both kings grim and wordless. Their officers hovered like men drowning, searching for orders that would not come.

Then the doors opened, and Will stumbled in. The room snapped to attention. All eyes turned to him.

"The southern wall still holds," Will said, his voice shaking with adrenaline. "We've repelled the first assaults, but just barely. The red-robes illusions turned men on each other; half the line was swinging at shadows. The minute everyone was distracted, they went straight for the aqueduct, as we'd expected. The trap worked, but it left a hole in our defences."

Edarn's knuckles whitened against the table as he struggled to hold on to his composure. "And their numbers?"

"Hard to tell... but I get the feeling that wasn't their main force anyway," Will replied. "It felt more like a probing attack."

Edarn exhaled, the first trace of relief touching his face. He looked to Will. "Thank you. Information is what we need more than anything right now."

For the first time that night, pride swelled in his chest... at last, he had purpose.

Edarn turned to his generals. "Begin immediate reinforcement of the positions Will mentioned. We need more eyes on those sections of wall, and get a messenger to the mages on the west wall. Tell them we need some of their number on standby to counter illusions."

Orders began to fly, the room suddenly crackling with energy and movement. Will stepped away, quietly excusing himself.

As he made his way back through to the vast south-facing window in the throne room, he could already hear the monarchs' voices rising behind him, continuing to issue sharp commands.

This time, when he reached the window, he knew exactly who he wanted to look in on next.

Drawing a steadying breath, he reached deep within, focusing on the light at his core, searching once again for his connections. Dozens of luminous tethers shimmered in his mind's eye, each one pulsing with its own unique hue. He searched for hers.

It didn't take long. Amongst the golds, blues, and soft greens, one strand blazed pure, brilliant white. It sang to him. He reached for it, fingers closing around the radiant filament with reverence, and held it fast, both in his hands and in his heart.

A smile, small and involuntary, curved his lips as the familiar warmth of her presence washed through him. It soothed the tightness in his chest. But then his eyes snapped open, sharp and focussed.

His consciousness surged forward.

Out through the open window, it shot like a comet through the night, diving over rooftops and snaking down the winding streets of the western quarter.

The energy there was very different from that in the southern quarter. The mounted knights of Cervia were there, clad in burnished steel, mounted on their armoured mounts, who pranced in nervous anticipation as his consciousness passed by.

When he finally took up residence in the back of Lyra's mind, he found her and the other Acolytes in preparation for something the others spoke of as becoming a "relay conduit". Will listened as they prepared, slowly picking up bits and pieces, finally understanding that the mages intended to raise a magical barrier along the western wall and hold it in place. In order to maintain that in the long term, they would use the acolytes as an energy relay when one mage became tired and needed to trade places with another, allowing them to step away for a moment without creating a weak spot in the enchantment.

In the wide open courtyard area where the knights prepared for battle, mages moved among them, handing out charms that would allow them to pass through the barrier when the time came for them to ride out.

When the horns sounded once more, the mages called the acolytes into position, and Lyra climbed to the top of the wall. Will could feel her heart racing, but he also felt her fierce determination as she stood side by side with the other acolytes, preparing to serve the greater good.

Once again, a huge wave of infantry rapidly approached, this time from the south-west, roaring and beating their shields. The mages who stood along the parapet alongside the acolytes all raised their arms in unison at some unspoken command, and a shimmering wall of light energy rose up from the ground, arcing up and over them in a half dome. Will could almost see the strands of light tethering each of the acolytes to the enchantment, passively channelling the mage's power.

Behind the advancing infantry units, a large group of red-robed mages appeared from the shadows. Sensing the magical warding that had been raised by the order, the red robes began bombarding the wall with inky black tendrils of dark energy. The projectiles hurtled through the air at incredible speed, dissipating with explosive impact on the shimmering wall of light. The first strike made Lyra jump as the concussive blast shook the ground, but she held firm. As the attacking infantry line got closer to the wall, the red robes' barrage of projectiles became more focussed and intense as they realised their infantry was about to meet an impenetrable wall of energy, but that was the least of their worries.

As the howling front line reached the halfway mark, another horn sounded. This time, from the knights inside the wall. At that signal, the portcullis raised as the knights snapped down their visors. They rolled out through the open gate, forming up into a phalanx with parade-ground precision and, in one fluid motion, began thundering towards the enemy, the hooves of their mounts kicking up a huge cloud of dust in their wake.

Seeing death bearing down on them, the approaching infantry's nerve broke, and they turned tail and bolted back towards the main army, trampling red-robed mages to the ground as they passed.

Another horn call sounded from the knights, and in another beautifully choreographed movement, they wheeled around and returned, passing through the wall of warding and in through the open gate, which was lowered once again once the last knight was safely inside.

A cheer went up from the citizens inside the wall when the knights returned, but the mages held firm. Will felt a sense of pride well up in Lyra's chest as she looked up and down the line of mages and acolytes.

Will took that moment to return to his own body, whipping back through the western quarter and scaling the palace tower at dizzying speed. This time, he barely had to take a moment before returning to the war council to make his report.

The night went on like this, hour after hour. Will maintained a vigilant watch on both fronts, his consciousness flickering between minds, locations, and moments like a lantern casting light in the dark. Oberith continued his relentless probing, launching attack after attack in calculated waves, testing for weakness. But with Will's real-time intelligence, the monarchs were able to deploy and re-deploy their forces with astonishing speed, often reinforcing positions mere moments before impact.

Chapter 24

As the sun slowly crept over the eastern horizon, bathing the battlefield in warm morning light, the full extent of the carnage became apparent. Smoke drifted lazily across the southern and western quarters, rising from shattered siege towers, scorched bodies, and smouldering patches of earth where fire and magic had collided.

The probing attacks had slowed, then ceased entirely with the coming of dawn. The bloodied remnants of Oberith's advance forces lay in broken heaps near the walls, some still twitching as the last of their life drained into the scorched soil. The dead numbered in the hundreds, and among them lay a handful of brave defenders who hadn't survived the night.

Inside the city, Empath mages moved between the wounded, triaging where they could. Runners passed messages between watch stations, while soldiers not actively on duty were rotated off the walls and down into the city for food, rest, or, where needed, grief.

Inside the war chamber, Will stood with the two kings and their generals, all of whom shared the same weathered look of exhaustion.

"Given what we've learned of Oberith and his forces, it seems the strength of his red-robed mages is diminished in the light," said Torvahn, rubbing his tired face. "That may be the only reason the attacks have halted with the rising sun."

"Which means they'll probably return at sundown," Edarn added grimly.

A schedule was quickly established where defenders would rest in shifts, and the fortifications would be reinforced where they'd been tested hardest. Mages began rotating out, leaving their acolytes to meditate and recharge. Supplies were hauled to strategic posts, and watchmen were ordered to report even the slightest sign of renewed activity.

Realising that there would be little for him to do here now that the efforts had shifted from defence to logistics, Will excused himself and went looking for Lyra.

Making his way through the streets, he was once again overwhelmed with the powerful sense of unity. The city, for all its scars and weary faces, felt more alive than he'd ever seen it. In the quiet hours after the battle, something unspoken had bound its people together.

There were no titles here, no class divisions. Merchants worked beside beggars, nobility side by side with blacksmiths.

As he approached the western wall, he passed a group of Acolytes moving supplies and paused to ask one of them if they had seen Lyra. The girl smiled and pointed him toward a chapel that had been turned into a makeshift infirmary.

Will thanked her and continued on, his desire to see Lyra pushing him on even though the exhaustion in his legs protested.

The chapel was quiet, save for the low murmurs of voices and the occasional pained groan. Morning light filtered through high stained-glass windows, casting gentle hues across the rows of bedrolls and makeshift cots. Will stepped inside and immediately spotted her.

She moved among the wounded with a purposeful, attentive grace, her face pale beneath streaks of sweat. Her hands were steady, wrapping clean bandages around a soldier's arm, murmuring soothing words as she tied the last knot. The soldier nodded his thanks, and Lyra gave him a tired smile before straightening and scanning the room for her next patient.

Her eyes landed on Will.

A slow, radiant smile spread across her face, cutting through her exhaustion like sunlight after a storm. She crossed the room without a word, and he stepped forward to meet her, drawing her into a quiet antechamber just off the main hall. As soon as the door closed behind them, she rose to her toes and kissed him, deeply, passionately, all the words they didn't have the strength to speak pouring into that moment.

When their lips parted, they held each other close, Will pressing his cheek to her hair, breathing her in.

"I saw you," he said softly. "On the west wall. Holding the line with the Acolytes. It was... incredible. You were incredible."

She pulled back just enough to meet his eyes, confusion flickering across her features. "You saw me? How?"

Will smiled and brushed a strand of hair from her face. "It's a long story. But I've found a way to monitor the battlefield and give real-time intelligence to the kings. It was incredible to see you work though... I've never been prouder of anyone in my life."

Lyra's eyes shimmered, and she buried her face in his shoulder, holding him close for a long moment. No words passed between them... none were needed.

Eventually, he pulled back gently. "They think the attacks will pause until nightfall. Everyone's being ordered to rest where they can. I was hoping... maybe you'd join me?"

Lyra shook her head with a tired smile. "I can't yet. There are still a few more who need care."

Will opened his mouth to protest, but she touched a finger to his lips.

"Go," she whispered. "You look worse than some of the men I'm treating. You go and rest, and I'll join you when I can."

He chuckled softly, kissing her again, tenderly, full of warmth and gratitude. "Don't be long."

"I won't," she promised.

He lingered a moment longer watching her walk back to tend the wounded, then turned and made his way back through the city streets.

By the time he reached the door to their room, he was barely upright. Inside, the room was still and warm, the sheer muslin curtains diffusing the morning light into a soft glow. His eyes fell on the bed. Large, inviting, draped in soft linens, and a wave of intense longing washed over him. He barely had the presence of mind to kick off his boots and shrug out of his tunic before he crossed the room in a staggered shuffle.

He fell into the bed like a stone into deep water, the mattress rising to meet him with merciful softness. The cool sheets wrapped around his tired limbs, and the moment his head touched the pillow, he succumbed to sleep's sweet embrace.

When he awoke, the sun was low in the sky and Lyra lay sleeping soundly next to him. He rolled towards her, wrapping one arm around her and kissing the back of her shoulder gently, allowing his lips to linger a moment on her soft skin. He lay there for a short time, enjoying this beautiful moment of peace.

Lyra began to stir, and he watched as her eyes began to flutter. When she awoke and saw him looking at her, she smiled sleepily and leaned forward to kiss him. "Morning," she said. "... or good afternoon, I guess."

Will smiled, brushing a strand of hair from her face as he gazed at her. "Afternoon works," he said softly, his voice still hoarse from sleep. "Though I wouldn't mind pretending it's morning, if it means we get to stay like this a little longer."

Lyra gave a quiet laugh, her fingers tracing lazy patterns on his chest.

For a few blissful moments, the war outside the walls didn't exist. There was only the hush of the room, the fading warmth of daylight on the stone floor, and the indulgent comfort of their embrace.

They remained like that for a moment longer, but then Will sighed deeply. "I suppose we should get up and go to see what fresh hell awaits."

Lyra smiled at him, but rolled out of bed without saying another word. They both quickly got ready and then walked, hand-in-hand, to the throne room.

As they reached the huge, ornately carved wooden door, they met Athtar, just leaving. She looked tired, and Will wondered if she had managed to get any rest.

Lyra stepped forward to greet her, embracing her warmly. Athtar returned her warm smile, but the uncomfortable look she gave Will spoke volumes. She was still unsure how to behave around him, and that hurt deeply.

"How are you doing?" Lyra asked, stepping back and looking at Athtar.

Athtar hung her head wearily. "It's been a long day. I will go and try to grab an hour or two now before dark."

"Make sure you do. We don't need you making silly mistakes and getting yourself killed because you go out tired tonight."

Athtar nodded. "Are you okay?" she asked, before parting.

Lyra tilted her head to the side, forcing a smile. "It was a tough night, but we came through it well enough. Better than some anyway."

Athtar reached out and gripped Lyra's shoulder in silent reassurance before turning to leave. There was much more that could be said, but both women knew that too many words of hope would be hollow, and they had conveyed their meaning in a hundred gestures.

Lyra started to open the door to the throne room as Athtar turned to leave, but Will held back.

"Actually, can I just borrow you for a moment, Athtar? I'll catch you up, Lyra," he said.

Athtar paused, her back still half-turned. Will saw the tension ripple through her shoulders before she slowly turned around to face him. Her expression was guarded, but she nodded. "Of course."

Lyra gave them both a hopeful look, but didn't press. She touched Will's arm briefly in passing. "I'll let them know you're on your way." Then she slipped inside the throne room, the heavy doors easing shut behind her.

Will and Athtar were left standing in the corridor, the afternoon sun cutting through the high windows in bands of gold and shadow. Dust drifted lazily between them, suspended in the still air.

For a long moment, neither said a word. They looked down the hall or at their feet. Anywhere, but at each other as they tried to carefully consider their words.

Finally, Will drew a breath. "I know things haven't been right between us," he said softly. "But I don't want it to stay that way. Not with what's happening. If... if this is to be our last chance to make things right, I couldn't leave it unsaid."

Athtar's arms folded across her chest. "I don't mean to be distant," she said, her voice quiet, almost weary. "It's just... hard to unsee what I saw that day. You were—" she stopped, shaking her head. "You weren't you. You looked like something else entirely. And now, when I look at you, part of me still sees *that*."

Will flinched, guilt flickering across his face. "I know, and I hate that I gave you reason to see me that way. I made mistakes—" he exhaled heavily. "So many mistakes. But I'm really trying."

Her gaze softened, but she said nothing.

He hesitated, searching for words that wouldn't sound hollow. "The truth is... I'm not the man the stories made me out to be. I'm flawed. Human. But I'm trying to be better. I just... I need the chance to prove that to you."

Athtar let out a slow breath, her eyes finally meeting his. "You were more than human once," she said quietly. "At least to me. You were proof that light could overcome anything. But that image... it's hard to look at it now without seeing the cracks."

Will nodded. "Then maybe it's time you stopped seeing me as something perfect. I am far from it. I am just someone who is still fighting, still trying to choose the right thing."

For a heartbeat, neither moved. Then Athtar gave the smallest nod, her voice rough but sincere. "Maybe that's enough."

Will smiled faintly as the spark of hope flickered to life. "Then that's all I can ask for."

It wasn't what he'd hoped for, but it was enough... for now.

"Go and get some rest. We'll talk more when you're not half-dead on your feet," he said, chancing a smile.

A faint smirk tugged at the corner of her mouth. "I'll hold you to that." Then, without another word, she turned and walked away, her footsteps echoing down the stone corridor.

Will watched her leave for a moment, filled with regret over the damage his actions had done, but eventually sighed and turned back towards the throne room door. When he walked into the war chamber, he found the kings there in much the same positions he had left them in hours earlier. They both looked haggard, but the room was buzzing with activity.

"What have we missed?" asked Will as he entered and sat down.

Edarn cast him a weary smile. "Not much, my friend. We have just been trying to decide what to do with the bodies piling up outside the wall. This hot climate doesn't lend itself well to long-term storage of bodies."

Will nodded, grunting in agreement. "I take it you've not come up with a solution?"

Torvahn shook his head. "Nothing good."

Edarn snapped his fingers. "Ah... I almost forgot. We sent out a scouting party a couple of hours ago. We should have a better picture of what we're up against before tonight's festivities."

Will nodded again. "There's been no more attacks today?" he asked.

"Thankfully, no," said Edarn.

A quiet knock came at the chamber door, and a messenger stepped in, panting slightly.

"Sire... the scouts have returned. They're in the courtyard."

"Well... don't keep us waiting. Send them in, man," Edarn snapped.

The messenger slipped away and returned moments later with a small detachment of soldiers who loitered uncertainly near the threshold.

"The scouts, your majesties," said the messenger before bowing deeply and leaving again.

Edarn eyed the men, tired and road-worn, their lips dry and cracked. "Someone bring these men something to drink, please," he called.

Cups of mead were passed around quickly, and the scouts drank deeply.

"Well... what did you find?" Edarn asked at last.

The scouts took turns reporting on the general size of Oberith's army, camped roughly a mile to the south. They estimated the numbers in the tens of thousands, but clarified that the attackers they'd faced so far weren't part of the main force.

"They weren't soldiers, not really," one of the scouts explained. "Just armed civilians, barely trained. Oberith's holding back a real army; fully armoured Stradans and Yagerians."

Another added, "They've set their encampments apart. The two forces... don't seem to mix. Could be some bad blood there."

"What about the red robes?" Torvahn asked.

The scouts exchanged uneasy glances and looked down at their feet.

Torvahn waited a moment, his gaze sweeping the room. "Well?" he demanded.

One of them cleared his throat, his face colouring. "They have a...um... a fortress, my lord."

"A fortress?" Torvahn repeated.

"Yes, Your Majesty," another confirmed. "A floating fortress. A black citadel, massive... just floating above the ground on a cloud of shadow. That's where the red robes come and go from."

The looks from the generals and monarchs around the room ranged from incredulous to outright sceptical at the revelation.

Torvahn paused, troubled, before turning back to the scouts. "Perhaps another one of their illusions?" he offered, though without conviction.

Will stepped forward. "It wouldn't make sense for it to be an illusion," he said. "If Oberith's forces had no idea they were being observed, they wouldn't waste the energy required to maintain such a powerful illusion."

Edarn folded his arms. "So what do you suggest, Will?"

Will paused before answering. "I suggest it is exactly as the scouts report. The red robes might lack the discipline or refinement of the mages of the Order, but they have one undeniable strength... numbers. If enough of them combined their will, I believe they *could* achieve such a feat."

A heavy silence followed.

Then Lyra's voice broke through the quiet. "But, why?"

Will turned toward her, puzzled. "Why what?"

She met his gaze. "Why would they bring a floating fortress with them?"

An uncomfortable silence fell over the room as they all considered her question, but no one came up with any answers.

Eventually, Edarn cleared his throat, breaking the uncomfortable silence that had settled over the room, turning to the scouts who were still waiting nearby.

"Thank you for your service. Please go and find some food and rest. I fear we're in for another long night."

The scouts bowed, then turned and left.

With a fuller picture of the situation beyond the wall, the meeting descended once more into strategy planning, but Will couldn't concentrate. There was so much going on, and his tired mind struggled to keep one coherent thought from running into the next.

He was brought back to the present by chairs clattering as a few of the generals rose to leave, the meeting having concluded as his mind wandered.

As they all began making their way towards the exit to pass on orders to their subordinates, Edarn piped up over the scraping of chair legs and shuffling of feet.

"Let's just stay light on our feet tonight. We will continue to provide feedback on any real-time intelligence we get. Be ready to adapt strategies quickly to the changing moves of the enemy."

The sky outside was just turning from the vibrant colours of sunset to dark blue, the light fading fast. In the distance, they heard the warning bells chiming throughout the city, indicating that the enemy was attacking once more.

"The peace was nice whilst it lasted," said Will.

Lyra stood beside him, turned to give him a lingering kiss. "I'll see you later," she said.

Chapter 25

Far across the moonlit plains, the horizon caught fire.

A line of torches burned like a wound in the darkness, spreading wider, brighter, until the whole night seemed to bleed flame. Then came the sound of drums and horns and the ceaseless grind of wheels and armour. Oberith's army was on the move.

From the walls of Anhai, the defenders answered in kind: beacon-fires flared to life, bells tolled, and mages gathered on the ramparts, their hands already weaving enchantments of light.

Among the defenders stood Seloria, one of the younger mages of Thorn Island. Her hands shook as she prepared for battle. She had studied the light source for years and specialised in earth, but nothing in her training had prepared her for the surge of fear that threatened to overwhelm her when faced with the roar of an army charging through the night, the ground trembling under the weight of a thousand boots. For a moment, her resolve wavered. She could feel the tremor in her chest as much as under her feet, and her breath came ragged with fear.

But then the fear sharpened. Adrenaline surged, burning away hesitation. She inhaled deeply, centring herself, and the trembling earth no longer felt like a threat... it was the rhythm to a song she knew how to conduct.

She raised her hands and called, and the earth answered.

The battlements beneath her feet vibrated with power as cracks raced along the ground below. The earth split and heaved upward, jagged ridges erupting before the first wave of infantry. Soldiers stumbled and fell as the ground pitched beneath them, shields clattering. With a cry, she thrust her palms forward, and the stones themselves bucked free, tearing upward into a volley of jagged shards that rained down into the advancing ranks.

The screams of men mingled with the thunder of falling rock. Dust and splintered stone choked the air, but Seloria's focus only deepened. She felt the flowing energy of the light source moving through the earth, and for the first time that night, her fear gave way to fierce exhilaration.

And still the tide came on. Oberith's numbers seemed endless as they threw themselves relentlessly at the defenders, but as relentless as the attacking army was, the defenders met each attack with a fierce tenacity.

Just when it seemed that they might make it through the night without any major surprises, a deep tremor rumbled through the earth beneath the city, so subtle at first it might have gone unnoticed, had it not been accompanied by a low hum that vibrated in the bones of every soul within the walls.

From where he stood, at his usual spot, overlooking the city, Will felt a powerful shift in magic and his attention snapped toward the south. He now instinctively reached out, his mind seeking refuge with Athtar, who was still stationed there with the Elven archers. From her elevated vantage point, he saw a squadron of red-robed figures forming a perfect ring beneath the floating fortress, barely visible in the darkness but for the unholy glow emanating from it. Shadows curled upward from their hands, coalescing into the dark energy that suspended the impossible mass of the fortress. Then, with a thunderous roar that split the night, the sky above the fortress cracked open, and from within it descended a weapon unlike anything Will had seen; an enormous inverted spire, pulsing with umbral energy that was increasing in intensity the closer it got.

As the fortress reached a position less than a mile beyond the southern wall, the spire pulsed and discharged a concentrated beam of dark energy that screamed through the sky like a comet. It struck the wall with devastating force, rocking the stone foundations and causing several of the magical runes to flicker and collapse. The defenders atop that portion of the wall were obliterated, seared viscera flying through the air and raining down on those beneath, who were scrambling to reinforce the enchantments before another strike could follow.

Simultaneously, the trained reserve forces of Strada and Yager began to march. Unlike the untrained civilian mob who had previously been thrown against the walls, these soldiers no longer approached in scattered waves, but in precise, coordinated formations. Shields locked, spears bristling, they moved with chilling discipline toward the weakened section of the wall.

For the first time that night, Will felt gripped by real fear. He realised, too late, that their unearned confidence in their success thus far was flawed, based on the assumption that Oberith was giving them his best shot.

All around them, Will could hear the sounds of panic. Athtar looked back over her shoulder into the city. He saw civilians running about, terrified. Some were weeping, others had been horrifically injured by the impact of the blast from the deadly weapon.

Will quickly pulled his awareness back to his own body and sprinted through to the Monarchs.

"You need mages and reinforcements on the south wall immediately," he yelled, before sprinting from the room.

He knew that he needed to do something quickly... but what? Projecting his consciousness into someone's mind only allowed him to observe. He remembered once transporting himself during his fight with Malakar atop the monolith in Shadowmoor, but that was a very short distance, and he could see his destination. He didn't know if it would work, but he had to try.

He gathered as much focus as he could muster, forming up an image of the section of the city near the west wall. He tried to remember as many details as possible, forming as complete a picture as he could in his mind before unleashing the enchantment.

He felt a sudden tugging sensation, just behind his navel, and a rush of wind moving at a speed so intense that he felt suddenly nauseated. When he felt the movement stop and his form re-materialised, he dared to open his eyes. He looked around in dismay, realising that he had appeared some distance above the town. Once the enchantment had concluded and he was fully materialised, he plummeted like a rock, crashing through a warehouse roof and landing on a huge pile of flour sacks, winded and surrounded by a cloud of flour that erupted from the sacks upon impact.

He lay coughing and spluttering, his body stunned from the impact, his mind screaming at him to move. As soon as he was able, he forced himself to roll onto his knees and, with a groan, forced himself into an upright position.

As he staggered out into the street and tried to get his bearings, there was another concussive blast from the direction of the southern ward.

The square between him and the wall was tightly packed with Cervian soldiers, and Will realised that he would never be able to physically force himself through. He was able to see his destination this time, so he concentrated his energy once again. Between one blink and the next, he moved from the far side of the square to the top of the west wall. He cast about, trying to find a mage and quickly saw Eldara standing a short distance away, focussed on holding the energy barrier in place.

He moved down the wall, lungs burning, pushing past mages that lined the parapet, their hands raised in shimmering unison as they fed power into the energy barrier.

"Eldara!" he shouted, his voice piercing the night. "The south wall is breached… we need reinforcements there immediately!"

She spun toward him, eyes widening in alarm. "By the light… how did they—?"

"There's no time!" Will cut in. "If we don't move now, they'll punch through before dawn."

Eldara's hesitation vanished. She turned sharply, voice rising over the storm. "Acolytes! Circle formation… two-thirds remain here, the rest with me. Keep the barrier stable as you transition!"

Even before she finished, Will saw movement ripple through the line as mages began peeling away in coordinated bursts of light, their chants overlapping in a rising crescendo. The air shimmered as the formation split, half the defenders pivoting toward the stairways that led south.

A moment later, Eldara looked back at Will. "Go. I'll follow with whoever I can spare. Just hold the line until we get there."

Will nodded once, drew in another sharp breath of cool night air, and vanished.

He moved across the city in a sequence of short bursts, always keeping his destination in sight, not wanting another warehouse incident, but within a minute or so, the jagged silhouette of the south wall rose before him, and as he neared, the chaos hit him like a wave.

If he'd thought the west wall had been frenzied, it was nothing compared to the south. The street below boiled with panic. Screams echoed between the buildings. Soldiers shouted over one another. Fires smouldered in gutters where the intense heat of the energy beam had ignited anything remotely flammable.

He sprinted up the stone steps to the parapet and quickly scanned for Athtar.

He spotted her crouched behind the battlement, loosing arrows at a rate so fast her movements seemed a blur. Her hand was already reaching back for the next shaft before the last one found its mark.

"What's the situation?" he shouted over to her, trying to be heard over the din from the streets below.

She glanced at him from the corner of her eye, then her sight shot back to the front as she released another arrow, finding her mark directly between the eyes of an advancing Stradan soldier.

"Well... we're being overrun. I'm nearly out of arrows. And that huge bloody weapon out there has almost broken through the wall. So I'd say—" she loosed again, "—we've been better."

"Hold on a while longer, reinforcements are on their way," he said. "What can I do for now?"

"I could use a fresh bundle of arrows... there." She nodded to a stack some distance down the wall. "And grab a pike while you're at it. We've got ladders coming."

Will nodded and sprinted off, returning moments later with the bundle and a pike in hand. For a time, he stood beside her, helping hold the line. The waves of attackers just kept coming, but together they fought them back, inch by inch.

The minutes stretched, each skirmish blurring into the next. Between clashes, Will would glance westward, searching the shadows for any sign of Eldara and her mages. Nothing. Just smoke and the steady drum of boots on stone.

Then a roar went up as a pack of Stradan soldiers had made it over the wall. Will dropped the pike and drew his sword, hurling himself into the melee.

"Here we go again!" Athtar called behind him, raising her dagger.

Will turned just in time to see what she meant.

The umbral energy beneath the floating citadel was gathering again. The inverted spire beneath it throbbed with power, pulses of shadow magic flaring faster, harder, as if charging for a final, decisive blow.

But then, there they were.

Eldara and her mages emerged at the far end of the wall, already moving in tight formation. They raised their hands in unison. A half dome of luminous energy rippled into being, arcing over the defenders just as the spire loosed its weapon.

The collision was deafening. Light met shadow in a blinding cascade that lit the sky, and the very wall beneath their feet shook to its foundations. But the shield held.

A cheer went up from the defenders. Where moments before they had been losing hope and growing weary, they now fought back with renewed tenacity, pushing back against the advancing line. In the distance, Will saw the citadel withdrawing as the first blush of dawn light imperceptibly brightened the horizon. As soon as the citadel was clear of the field, a series of horn blasts sounded, and the enemy began their retreat, the rising sun signalling the end of their offensive.

Will raised a hand to his shoulder, examining a heavy laceration he'd picked up in the last skirmish. It was shallow, barely worth noticing, but his entire body ached. Every muscle throbbed with fatigue.

As he staggered past Athtar, he reached out, silently clasping her shoulder. She raised her own hand, gripping his firmly. No words passed between them, but none were needed. In that brief gesture, something unspoken was reaffirmed; a deep, unshakable bond re-forged in the crucible of survival.

Around them, infantrymen moved along the wall, methodically checking the fallen enemy. Steel blades punched into chests, and the lifeless bodies were heaved over the parapet to join the ever-growing mound below. Already, the stench was rising from bloated corpses that fed clouds of flies that buzzed incessantly in the morning heat.

Will turned, descending the stone steps that led back into the city. What met him below tightened his chest.

The south quarter had suffered. Smoke curled listlessly above broken rooftops. Entire sections of the street were strewn with rubble. People wandered through the devastation, some dazed and bloody, others calling out names that would never be answered.

He saw one woman kneeling in the dirt, rocking back and forth with a bloodied form of a child cradled in her lap, her wails rising sharp and thin into the smoky air.

He tried to block it out, to shut off the flood of sorrow pressing in from all sides, but he couldn't. The grief was too loud. Too overwhelmingly intense. And it squeezed his heart like a vice.

He briefly considered using magic to return to the palace, but dismissed the thought almost instantly, the idea of expending that energy making him realise that he was running on fumes. Instead, he trudged through the battered streets, pausing now and then to lend a hand wherever he was able.

By the time he reached the palace, every bone in his body ached with the simple longing to collapse into bed and sleep for a week. But he wanted to check in with Edarn before seeking rest. As he staggered into the war chamber, he was met with a familiar and welcome face.

Lucian had arrived. He sat near the head of the table, speaking in hushed tones as the kings brought him up to speed.

"—ward this chamber against magical incursion. We can't risk the enemy breaching the command through sorcery—" Lucian broke off as Will approached, his expression softening into a rare smile at the sight of his friend.

"You're a sight for sore eyes," Will said, pulling out a chair beside him.

"What news from the Wall, Will?" asked Torvahn, leaning forward slightly.

Will let his head fall back against the chair, closing his eyes for a moment as he exhaled. A long, slow release of tension. He rubbed his face with both hands, trying to shake off the fatigue.

"That siege weapon... whatever it is, was seconds away from breaching the wall. The order arrived just in time to raise a barrier."

He paused a moment, gathering his thoughts. "At least we know what the fortress is for now."

There was a murmur of agreement from the others around the table.

Will went on. "We lost more people than last night. The damage to the city was worse. A lot of buildings in the south ward were hit by the shockwave. People are still pulling bodies from the rubble. Civilians are terrified, scattered."

He looked up then, his eyes bloodshot.

Lucian shifted slightly beside him, his face unreadable. "Sounds like quite the night."

Will grunted, not quite sure how to respond and too tired to think of something witty.

"We expected you here days ago, Lucian," said Edarn. "What kept you?"

Lucian pushed himself up in his chair, trying to find a more comfortable position. "I had hoped to come with the first wave from Thorn Island, but I received a message from our friend at Hent-Taui."

That caught Will's attention. "What news from the Dwarves?"

"Hent-Taui will not march to our aid."

The words fell like stones into still water. A ripple passed through the assembly you could hear a pin drop as everyone waited for Lucian to continue.

Lucian's gaze swept the room. "Dhongrolir has turned inward. The mountain kingdom is at war with itself. Their northern cousin, Kasarlum, has declared open conflict, and the clans battle in their own halls," he said, his eyes shadowed.

The silence deepened, and for a long moment, no one moved. Then Edarn pushed back from the table, his jaw set. "Then we make do with what we have."

They moved on to discussing how they might adapt their defences to accommodate the vulnerability of the south wall.

"I am fresh, so I will go down there and assess today. I will do what I can to fortify and reinforce it with magic, but it might not be a bad idea to distribute a few more forces there tonight," said Lucian.

Torvahn studied the map on the table for a moment and then stood, pointing. "If my men and I take up strategic positions here... and here. I think we can hold the west wall. Pull all other reserves to the south," he said.

Edarn raised an eyebrow. "You'll be joining your troops?"

Torvahn smiled. "I have lamented them having all the fun these past nights," he said with a small chuckle. "Besides, it's good for morale for them to see me out there."

Will found himself beginning to nod in the quiet lulls in the conversation. Realising that his time in the waking realm was short, he stood up sharply. "I am afraid I must leave you, gentlemen. If I don't get to bed soon, I will be sleeping here."

There were a few murmured words in response, but Will barely heard them through the haze of the rapidly descending slumber that was threatening to claim him.

Will offered a tired nod, placing a hand briefly on Lucian's shoulder as he passed. "It's good you're here, my friend," he said.

Lucian nodded once in reply, patting the back of Will's hand, and flashing him a quick smile.

Will shuffled out into the corridor, the murmuring voices of the others fading behind him. When he finally reached his chambers, he didn't even recall his getting undressed or getting into bed, but sleep claimed him swiftly.

The dream came softly, like a slow tide.

Will found himself standing alone in a vast expanse of soft, ashen grey. The ground was neither stone nor sand. Just a flat, endless surface without texture, stretching into a sky the same colour, seamless and empty. There was no wind, no sound, no horizon, only a strange still peace.

He felt no fear standing in that featureless landscape. The stillness, though unnatural, was oddly soothing.

Moloch suddenly appeared beside him without a sound, but even that didn't startle him.

Her form was, as always, tall, graceful, a woman of impossible beauty. She wore a gown of deep crimson that shifted like smoke around her feet. Her presence felt intimate... gentle, almost.

She offered him a small, knowing smile. "The time has come, Will," she said softly, as if breaking a long silence. "After tonight, your debt will be repaid."

He turned to her, sceptical, but with her words came a wave of hope and gratitude that almost brought him to his knees. "Just like that?"

"A trifling favour," she crooned, her voice smooth as silk. "Nothing at all in the grand weave of fate. And then... You will be free of me."

Will frowned, his suspicion growing. "What do you want?"

Her fingers brushed the sleeve of his tunic as she spoke.

"Tonight, before the hour of midnight, you need to ensure the Cervian knights are gone from the west wall. That's all. How you manage it, I will leave to your creativity. You've always been resourceful."

Will recoiled, staring at her. "No. Absolutely not."

Her tone shifted, just slightly. The warmth faded like dying coals.

"Refusal would be a breach of your oath. You know the consequences."

"I'll face them," Will said firmly, though his voice trembled. "Do to me what you will, Moloch. I won't serve up the city to Oberith like that!"

Moloch tilted her head, amusement flickering across her features. "You misunderstand. It won't be *you* who pays alone. You swore your soul... and hers."

His heart turned to ice.

"No," he said. "You wouldn't."

"Oh, I would. And it seems fate would reward me with a bonus soul for my trouble. Three souls would be ample recompense."

Her smile widened as he stared at her, horror blooming in his chest.

"Three?" he said, parroting her words in confusion.

She gave a mock gasp, covering her mouth delicately with one hand. "Oh... I thought you knew."

"Enough of your games, tell me what you mean," he said, growing irritated.

She turned from him, wandering across the grey like a cat gliding across silk sheets. Her voice floated back to him, thick with glee.

"Why, Will... I thought you knew. Lyra is with child."

The words struck him like a hammer. His legs buckled, and he fell to his knees, the world around him spinning even though nothing moved.

"No..." he whispered, but he knew it was true. Somehow, he knew.

"You must choose," Moloch said, crouching beside him now, her voice once more quiet, coaxing. "Pull the knights from the wall. No more death. No more screaming. You'll spare the city far more pain than if you fight. This is the cleaner way, Will. The gentler way. And your debt... wiped clean."

Will didn't answer. His thoughts were no longer thoughts but fragments that seemed to scatter like dust in the wind. Lyra. A child. The west wall. The price of silence. The blood of betrayal.

Her voice followed him as the grey around them began to dissolve into shadow.

"Your answer by midnight, Will. If you agree to my terms, then you know what must be done. If not... You know the cost."

The dream faded, but her words lingered in his mind like smoke.

The sun filtered through the curtains in a warm, golden haze, but Will felt no warmth. He sat bolt upright, his chest heaving, skin slick with sweat. His heart was pounding like a drum behind his ribs, his breath shallow. His mind remained trapped in the echo of the dream's final words.

He blinked a few times, trying to pull himself free from the haze of sleep and nightmare. Slowly, his senses returned as his breathing returned to its normal rhythm.

Lyra lay curled toward him, one arm folded beneath her head, strands of silver hair cascading over the pillow like moonlight spilled from a dream. She looked untouched by the world's pain, serene in a way Will couldn't comprehend. And more than anything, she looked *safe*.

He reached out with trembling fingers, placing a hand gently against the subtle curve of her abdomen. He held it there, barely breathing. There was no movement... too early for that, but in his mind, he imagined he could feel a spark, a warmth, a pulse of life. Something beautiful and pure. Something worth giving everything for.

"I'll protect you," he whispered, barely a sound, but the weight of a vow behind it. "No matter what it costs me."

He closed his eyes and lowered his head, tears welling up and gathering at the corners of his eyes. His hand remained pressed to her stomach, not for comfort, but as a seal. A covenant. In that quiet moment, everything became clear.

The sickness swelled in his gut like a tide of ash, because the choice had already been made. His mind may have wavered, his conscience may yet cry out in protest, but his heart had anchored itself to one truth:

He would betray them all.

Chapter 26

Will slipped quietly from the room he shared with Lyra, pausing in the doorway to glance back at her sleeping form. Even the sight of her slumbering peacefully couldn't break through the haze of dread that had descended upon him in the wake of Moloch's ultimatum. He pulled the door closed and let his feet carry him aimlessly through the corridors of the palace. Each familiar turn led nowhere; every hall looked the same.

He pressed a palm to the cold stone, attempting to ground himself, but the chill of the stone did little to steady him. He turned the problem over and over in his mind, searching for an angle, a way to save them all without yielding what the demon demanded. But the more he fought the thought, the clearer it became. Every imagined escape folded back on itself, leading him down the same bleak path.

There was no way of saving them, without damning himself. And if that was the choice fate demanded of him... then so be it.

A strange calm washed over Will as the sun finally crept over the horizon, ushering in twilight and the slow descent into darkness. From his usual place in the throne room, he let his mind drift outward, threading itself into the folds of shadow that blanketed the city. His awareness moved like smoke through alleyways, over rooftops, along battlements. All was quiet. Too quiet.

Unlike the nights before, when Oberith's forces struck with ruthless precision the moment darkness fell, this night, the defenders were instead met with an unsettling stillness. Just the occasional whistle of wind through broken stone and the restless shifting of boots on stone from the defenders who were growing more anxious with every passing moment.

The defenders held their positions, their eyes straining against the darkness, their muscles tight with expectation. At first, the silence was met with heightened vigilance. But as the minutes dragged into an hour, then two, tension began to curdle into unease. There was no relief in the stillness, no respite in the calm.

On one occasion, when he returned to his own body, Will overheard an outburst from the war chamber behind him. Edarn's voice rose over the general din of the palace as he addressed his generals.

"What kind of tactic is this? I need someone to get me an update on their troop positions... and I need it now, if not five minutes ago," he bellowed out at the room, his voice fraught with the tension everyone was feeling.

The generals issued orders, and runners were dispatched to carry out the king's command. Will hung his head, wanting to run and warn them, but knowing that he wouldn't. Oberith knew what was coming, and he wouldn't make his move until the right moment. Hearing the king's last command, though, gave Will an idea.

He stepped through to the next room, and Edarn's head shot up in anticipation of an update… any update.

"Tell me you have some news?" Edarn said tensely.

He spread his hands and shook his head. "Sorry… there's still no movement out there. I am going to go down to the wall and see what I can find out. I can be there and back before you know it."

Edarn nodded wearily, throwing himself down into the chair at the head of the table. "Do whatever you think best, my friend. Just update me the minute you get news."

"I will," Will promised, even as his soul cried out in pain.

When he reached the Cervian army, he asked about for Torvahn, eventually finding him atop the wall with a number of his generals.

He walked over to where they were animatedly debating what Oberith might be planning and stood waiting. Torvahn noticed him standing there.

"Greetings, Will…What brings you to the wall? There's no action yet, my friend."

Will smiled. "I know, Edarn sent me to see if there have been any sightings yet."

Torvahn shook his head. "Nothing yet. This is a strange tactic indeed."

Will gave a slow nod, feigning thoughtfulness as he stepped closer, peering out over the parapet. "It doesn't sit right with him. He's worried they might be repositioning somewhere out of our line of sight."

Torvahn crossed his arms, brow furrowed. "We've had scouts doing sweeps at intervals, but so far nothing."

Will kept his voice calm as he continued to try steering the conversation. "That's what worries me. Edarn wants eyes in every blind spot before midnight. He thinks this might be a feint… an attempt to draw our attention here while they strike somewhere else."

One of the generals scoffed lightly. "They'd be mad to shift focus away from the south wall after last night. That's where they made the most ground."

"True," Will agreed, "but it might be *because* of that. We reinforced the south heavily after last night. Maybe too heavily. Edarn's wondering if Oberith is baiting us."

He turned to Torvahn more directly. "He asked me to pass on the message that he wants your troops to make a pass. He wants a quiet sweep a mile out, all the way to the northern quarter. I'm told your men are the sharpest and least likely to spook if they come across something unusual."

Torvahn arched an eyebrow. "You want to pull my men *off* the wall? Now?"

"I'm sure there'll be nothing to it, but let's try and appease Edarn," Will said, calm and persuasive. "In and out. If there's nothing, you'll be back before the moon reaches its peak. If there *is* something, we need to know before it's too late."

The general to Torvahn's right frowned. "This smells off to me. Why not use local militia?"

Will met his eyes. "Because this mission might involve contact. We may need to act fast, and you know as well as I do, the Uriasan city guard aren't ready for that."

Torvahn studied Will's face, searching. Will forced himself to hold the man's gaze. Just long enough. Not too long.

Finally, Torvahn exhaled through his nose and gave a short nod. "Alright. We can make a sweep. If you spot even a hint of enemies approaching, though..."

"I will call you back immediately," Will said sincerely.

The guilt clawed at his throat even as the plan took root. The very words escaping his lips caused a deep pain in his heart, but he pushed it down, mustering all the energy he could to hold his confident smile in its place.

As the Cervian captain began shouting orders, Will stepped away, unable to watch it unfold. He stared out across the darkness of the city and whispered under his breath, to the night and the stars and the life he swore to protect:

"I'm sorry."

He watched the soldiers leave, the portcullis being raised and then lowered behind them. He heard the thundering of hooves receding off into the distance as the darkness swallowed them.

He knew that he had a very finite window to enact the remainder of his plan. The timing had to be perfect. Too soon and Oberith's forces might not be ready... too late and Torvahn might return.

He turned to the knight standing to the side of him, peering out into the darkness. "I never did get used to how cold the nights are here, considering how hot the days are," he said, attempting to make small talk.

The knight smiled, his features softening slightly. He knocked on his burnished breastplate. "The benefits of wearing all this steel. I have multiple layers under here."

Will chuckled, a mirthless laugh as he was once again reminded of the humanity of those he was about to betray.

"Would you say we're approaching midnight?" he asked the young knight.

The young man looked up at the sky for a moment and then turned back to Will. "I would say so."

Will closed his eyes, steadying his resolve a moment before forming up the enchantment that would seal his fate and the fate of this whole city.

Off in the distance, in the direction that the Cervian scouts had ridden, he formed a simple illusion, but one which he knew would force the remainder of the troops to abandon their posts.

"Did you see that?" he said sharply to the young knight.

The knight looked out into the darkness. "I did. What was it?"

There was a glint of moonlight, and then another, and another. Moonlight reflecting off the armour of thousands of troops.

"Enemy troops!" yelled Will in feigned panic. Raising his voice in an effort to instil that same feeling in those around him.

"Do they approach?" asked a voice from further down the wall.

Will shook his head. "I think they are pursuing the scouting party."

That idea only took a moment to sink in before an elderly general nearby bellowed from the bottom of his lungs, filling the night air. "The king is in danger! Everyone to your mounts, immediately!"

The entire Cervian force, fearing for the safety of their king, mounted up into formation and thundered through the gates. A few moments later, the western quarter was deathly silent, the walls manned by just a few local guardsmen who remained, faces bewildered.

Will stood in silence, the noise of the hooves vanishing into the distance, swallowed by the night like the last breath of a dying man. The few remaining guards paced uneasily along the ramparts, none of them trained for what was coming.

The illusion shimmered for a few moments longer before he let it unravel into smoke. There was no need to sustain it now. The trap was set.

He exhaled, long and slow. He had done it.

Every breath now felt tainted, cursed. He leaned on the wall, suddenly aware of the weight of his limbs, the trembling in his hands. The silence around him wasn't peace. It was the awful, breath-held stillness before a scream.

He slowly began stumbling down the stone stairs into the city. He knew what was coming, but he didn't need to witness it. As he walked away, he heard the clink of grappling hooks biting into the stone at the top of the wall, followed by the startled exclamation of the local militia who were awkwardly patrolling there. There were the sounds of scuffles and grunts, and a few moments later, the sound of the portcullis being raised. Oberith's troops had secured their entrance without so much as a murmur. He saw one of the guards running past him in the street to raise the alarm, for whatever good that would do them. Will's heart broke in that moment, and as he slowly walked back towards the palace, he openly wept. He couldn't stop the tears, nor did he try. With every silent sob, he whispered apologies that would never be heard and never be enough.

By the time he reached the palace, the first fires had begun. He never understood why an invading army would immediately begin destroying the very thing they had fought so hard to seize. In the distance, he could hear screams and shouts rising above the bells that were now ringing out, raising the alarm, but he tried to block them out, resolutely marching forward.

The guards at the palace gates barely registered him as he passed, too busy scrambling to their posts, shouting for orders that no one seemed to be listening to. Inside, the corridors were a flurry of motion as servants and palace guards ran about, flustered and stressed, often colliding in doorways. But Will moved through them like a ghost, untouched and unnoticed.

The turmoil in the halls was only surpassed by the devastating levels of chaos unfolding in the war chamber. Voices were all raised as everyone tried to grapple with how the enemy had found their way inside the walls. He overheard a dozen speculations as he approached, each one more wild than the last. It was clear that no one had a clue... no one but Will, that is.

"Will," came Edarn's voice, cutting through the crowd. "Bloody hell, please tell me you know what is going on."

Will froze, like a trapped animal. His face was still streaked with tears, and all he could do was numbly shake his head, unable to find his voice. "I'm sorry," was all he could say.

Edarn's brow softened slightly as he took in Will's tear-streaked face and hollow expression. "Of course," he muttered, more to himself than anyone else.

The war chamber erupted again around them, generals barking at one another, arguing over phantom scenarios.

Will stood in the eye of the storm, numb, silent, letting their wild theories wash over him.

Then a scout burst through the doors, breathless and bloodied, his uniform tattered and torn. "The western quarter burns," he gasped. "They came from inside the walls—" he paused a moment, gasping for breath, "—we don't know how. Civilians are being slaughtered. The streets are running red."

For what felt like an eternity, a stunned silence followed.

Then the room erupted into a fresh wave of chaos; orders were barked to dispatch reinforcements, accusations of sabotage, and frantic calls for updated troop reports filling the spaces in between.

Will backed away from the table, the heat of guilt rising in his chest like bile. But underneath it all, a small fire had ignited. A fire that took hold and began to grow and grow into a raging inferno. She had promised that it would be an end to the bloodshed, an end to the suffering. If there was even a shred of truth in these reports from the city, it seemed that Oberith's forces were slaughtering indiscriminately.

He turned without a word, leaving the room, his rage feeding into the darkness at his core, fuelling it to explosive proportions. When he reached the large window in the throne room, he instinctively reached for the energy at his core and folded into the shadows, transporting himself down into the city. His mind was on fire now, but he had a single purpose, and it consumed him entirely.

The city welcomed him with screams.

He stood amid the chaos, his boots crunching over shattered glass and loose stone as he took in the devastation he had enabled.

A woman stumbled from behind a nearby building, blood streaking her dress, her eyes vacant with horror. A moment later, a Stradan soldier stepped out from behind the same building, securing his britches and grinning foolishly.

Will's fury consumed the softer parts of him, shoving them deep into the shadows of his mind. He raised a hand, and black tendrils shot from his fingertips, coiling around the soldier and lifting him off the ground. The man twisted in the air, thrashing, shouting for his squad.

With a single decisive motion, Will clenched his fist. Bones cracked and splintered, joints snapping one after another as the man's body folded in on itself. Blood poured from his nose and ears, and his eyes rolled back in his skull.

He turned to look about for another target, even as he sharply lowered his arm, opening his hand. The twisted remains of the soldier hit the ground with concussive force, kicking up a cloud of dust.

He moved like a blade now, fast and silent, shadows trailing behind him as the darkness itself bent to his will and coalesced around him. He didn't need to ask where the enemy was. He could feel them, sense them, drawn to them like a predator to its prey.

Moloch had lied, and Will's rage would not be satisfied until he had destroyed every last invader.

There would be no clean end. No quiet surrender. She had used him... used Lyra's life, their unborn child to manipulate him into opening the gates of hell.

Now hell would pay.

He turned a corner and found the first wave of them. Oberith's soldiers were swarming through a collapsed barricade, dragging civilians from homes, cutting down anyone who resisted.

Will raised a hand. The air rippled.

A whole squadron suddenly stopped in their tracks, gasping, shrieking, frozen mid-step as their bodies began to boil from the inside. Their innards liquefied. One by one, they collapsed, limbs twitching, silent mouths stretched in agony as they fell to the ground.

A scream tore through the night; raw, primal, broken. For a moment, he wondered where it had come from. Then he realised it was his own.

Chapter 27

Athtar beckoned a nearby comrade to relieve her from her post, who stepped quickly into her place, patting her shoulder before drawing their own bow. As she stepped back from the parapet, she rolled her neck, easing the tension that had settled there. Slinging her bow across her back, she strolled away, trying to work out the kinks left by hours of tense waiting.

She used the walk to double-check the supply crates for the coming night, exchanging a few quiet words with those stationed nearby. But her steps, almost unconsciously, drew her toward Ilbryen's post farther down the wall.

"Any signs of movement yet?" she asked as she approached.

He glanced back at the sound of her voice, then returned his eyes to the horizon, arrow nocked but loose against the string. "Nothing yet," he said. "I think I hate this waiting more than the chaos."

She nodded. There was a real sense of camaraderie among the defenders now; those who had survived the last few nights of bloodshed had forged a deep brotherhood. All along the wall, people who had never met until a few days ago passed one another with murmured jokes, shared waterskins, or quiet touches to the shoulder.

"I should probably get back," she said at last. "Do you need anything before I go?"

Ilbryen smiled faintly. "Just stay alive tonight... I have grown accustomed to your company."

She dipped her head, hiding the shy smile tugging at her lips, and glanced at him from beneath her lashes. "I'll see what I can do. But only because you asked nicely."

As she turned to walk back to her post, a sudden flare of orange lit the sky to the west.

"What the hell?" she whispered, stopping in her tracks.

All along the wall, defenders turned to look. Another burst of fire bloomed a moment later, casting eerie shadows over the rooftops.

Then the bells began to ring out, urgent and discordant, carried on the night air, and the distant sound of voices raised in panic.

The mood on the wall shifted instantly. Every soldier scanned the darkness beyond the parapet, half-expecting an attack to surge from the south, using the chaos to strike. Confusion rippled through the ranks. Minutes stretched agonisingly as they waited, the tension building in their muscles until it hurt.

Then, cutting through it all, came the bark of a general's voice.

"Skeleton crews to remain only... everyone else, move! Get to the western wards! The enemy is *inside* the city!"

There was no time for questions. They gathered what supplies they would need and fell in with the others, racing down from the battlements and into the streets, heading toward the flames.

The people they passed were terrified, their wails echoing through the air as they fled blindly into the night. As her squad pushed deeper into the city, they passed dozens of wounded allies stumbling in the opposite direction, horrifically injured, but still alive. They were the lucky ones.

Rounding a corner, they entered a wide plaza. The buildings around it were fully ablaze, casting everything in a flickering orange glow and filling the square with thick, acrid smoke that seared the lungs.

Across the square, the Yagerian soldiers advanced in tight formation, their faces grim, weapons at the ready. Shields overlapped, spears bristled, their march steady despite the carnage underfoot.

Athtar raised her bow, shouted for her line to hold, and braced herself as the distance between them and the approaching force vanished.

The charge hit like a tidal wave. The physical impact was only equalled by the thunderous sound as shields slammed and splintered. The man in front of her barely had time to scream before a Yagerian axe split his helm. Blood sprayed hot against her cheek.

The world narrowed to movement and sound; thought itself was a luxury. Athtar fell back, allowing the infantry forward as she sought higher ground. Around her, men and women on both sides shouted, the sound already breaking into panic.

Then the lines began to grind, neither side giving ground. The screams rose again; the ragged sound of survival.

The dead and dying piled up between the lines, but neither side relented. Reinforcements kept coming from the rear, feeding the inferno that continued to intensify at the front line.

Athtar paused only briefly, drawing breath and scanning the scene before turning back to the fight, loosing another arrow. All around her were faces carved with fear and desperation. They knew they were outnumbered, each coming to the realisation that they probably wouldn't make it out of this, but none of that mattered now.

They would fight to their last breath, if only to buy the citizens of Anhai a few more moments to flee the slaughter.

* * *

Lyra walked beneath one of the sandstone arches of the upper city with a detachment of mages. They had all spotted the smoke rising above the western quarter as they made their way down through the city, preparing to relieve those holding the energy barrier on the west wall, but none knew its significance yet.

As they reached the southern wards, the air suddenly rang with the clamour of bells, loud and jarring. Everyone came to a complete halt and waited, listening.

A moment later, a young runner sprinted towards them from the direction of the palace, breathless. He bowed quickly and thrust a parchment into Lucian's hands. As he scanned it, his brow tightened.

"They're inside the city," he said grimly. "The western quarter is overrun."

Finally, he looked up. "We need to head back. A force of red-robed mages is cutting a path directly toward the palace. We need to intercept them."

He turned to the assembled mages. "I want elemental shields up before we engage and support spells ready to cast on arrival."

They moved as quickly as they dared, expecting to meet the detachment of red-robes, but when they reached the palace gate, there was no sign of them.

A lone palace guard jogged the expanse of the courtyard to meet them as they arrived.

"Thank the light, you've arrived. Scouts report the red-robes are approaching rapidly from the west, but we need time to secure the palace. Can you hold them while we work?" he asked.

Lucian nodded. "Leave it to us. You get the palace secured, we'll keep them off your back."

The guard smiled gratefully, only a hint of fear showing in his eyes as he returned to the huge open gate at the front of the palace, whilst Lucian turned to face the detachment of mages now fanning out in the courtyard.

"This is what we've trained for. Everyone... take your positions. Acolytes, I know your training is untested, but we're going to need all hands on the task if we're to stand any chance of success here tonight."

The first shadow fell like a whisper. Then came another. Then dozens.

Red-robed figures materialised out of the gloom, stepping through veils of darkness like phantoms born from the night itself. Their hands moved in unison, dark sigils glowing in dull crimson light. Without warning, lances of black energy tore through the night, narrowing beams of seething dark magic, slicing through the air toward the mages of the Order.

"Shields!" Lucian barked.

A half-second later, radiant walls of shimmering gold flared into place. The beams struck them with a sound like thunder, tearing through glass, splintering the light into arcing tendrils, but the shields held.

Lyra took a position near the centre, her arms raised, focusing on the rhythm of her breathing and trying to ignore the pounding of her heart. A gust of freezing wind burst forth from her hands, scattering several Red Robes like autumn leaves. To her right, Eldara had driven her staff into the earth, sending silver pulses of energy that burst up through the flagstones and detonated beneath a cluster of enemy mages, scattering them in a bloom of rubble and screams.

The Red Robes countered with unrelenting force, weaving through the shadows at impossible speed. They flitted between columns and tree cover, emerging from pools of darkness like wraiths. Wherever they struck, black fire seared through Order ranks, turning men and women to ash in a blink.

"They're drawing power from the night itself!" one of the acolytes shouted in terror, clutching a bleeding arm as he scrambled back behind the front line.

"We draw from the flame!" Eldara called in response. She spun her staff in a wide arc, casting a ring of white fire around their position. The shadows hissed and recoiled where the flames touched them.

Lucian moved like a man carved from light and fury, each gesture of his hands hurling forth sweeping waves of energy; glistening silver bolts that exploded mid-air, disrupting the enemy's stealth enchantments and revealing their positions. "Push forward!" he shouted. "Drive them from the gates!"

The air was thick with smoke and the stench of scorched stone and seared flesh. Elemental attacks streaked through the night. Waves of flame roared across the gardens, shards of ice tore limbs from bodies, and vines surged from the soil to strangle and hold. Where mages of the order fell, others closed in, dragging the wounded back behind cover.

Lyra's fingers bled from raw overuse of her magic, but she didn't slow. Her eyes burned with luminous fury as she sent a spiral of lightning crackling across the courtyard, tearing through two Red Robes who had broken through the line. Their charred bodies crumpled into the ferns that surrounded the courtyard.

They fought for what felt like hours. The red-robed mages gave no quarter and asked for none. For every one that fell, another two surged forward, and the Order's line thinned with every passing minute.

Finally, with a rallying cry from Lucian, the surviving mages gathered what remained of their strength, hands trembling, eyes hollow but burning with resolve. Threads of light arced between them until the air itself hummed with power that coalesced around Lucian.

Then Lucian thrust his staff forward.

The explosion of brilliance was blinding. It erupted outward in a wave of light, sweeping across the plaza like a divine tempest. The red-robes were caught mid-incantation, their voices breaking into shrieks as the radiance consumed them. Some burned to ash in an instant; others staggered blindly into the open, their robes smouldering, only to be cut down by the archers lining the palace walls.

Silence fell, broken only by the groans of the wounded and the crackling of smouldering ferns.

Bodies littered the courtyard, many of them draped in the crimson robes of their foes, but too many others wore the white robes of the order. Lyra lowered her arms, trembling, her face streaked with ash and blood.

They moved quickly now, carrying the wounded between them as they crossed the scorched threshold of the palace. They had bought the palace guards the required time, and as they moved towards the palace interior, they heard the portcullis boom shut behind them. With a flick of Eldara's staff, a fresh barrier shimmered to life, as the echoes of the battle rumbled closer from beyond the walls.

* * *

Edarn had always considered himself a man in full command of his emotions. As a ruler, that control was essential to ensure the stability of the kingdom. Showing weakness was a luxury he had never allowed himself.

But tonight, with the enemy inside the walls, Edarn felt completely adrift for the first time since taking the throne. Not even the day his father died, or when he had been crowned amid the mourning and unrest, had shaken him like this.

He sat in the war chamber, dazed, while voices clamoured around him. Generals barked reports and theories, their words overlapping in a cacophony he could no longer process. Snippets reached him, jagged and disconnected:

"—lost the western quarter—"

"—red robes marching on the palace—"

He heard them, but nothing settled. Nothing made sense. His thoughts scattered like leaves in a storm. He had gone completely numb, sitting slumped and motionless as the room spiralled deeper into chaos, but no one seemed to notice his silence. They were too busy shouting over each other, too consumed by their own panic to see their king unravelling before them.

Suddenly, he noticed Will's absence. He was certain the man had been there just moments earlier. Edarn looked up, his eyes sharpening as he scanned the chamber. Although he'd only recently entered Edarn's orbit, Will had proven himself time and time again to be a rock that Edarn could depend on. And right now, he needed people like that around him more than ever.

He stood, weaving through the still-bickering crowd, his mind drifting to the throne room. Will had taken to lingering near the tall windows in recent nights, watching the city from above. But when Edarn entered the room, it was empty. No sign of him.

His shoulders slumped slightly. *Why did that bother him so much?* he wondered. The realisation that no one else was coming to pull him back from the edge was like a cold splash of water. He took a breath, straightened, and turned on his heel.

When he re-entered the war chamber, he clapped his hands sharply. The sound cut through the noise.

"Enough! One at a time. I want status reports... what's happening in the western quarter, and what's going on with the red robes?"

Silence fell over the room immediately. Edarn strode back to the head of the table and sat, his gaze sweeping the gathered officers like a commander stepping back into his own skin.

A broad-shouldered, red-faced general near the front exhaled and undid the top button of his tunic before sitting beside the king.

"The situation in the western quarter is dire, Your Majesty. We've redeployed as many defenders from the southern wall as we could spare. They're fighting valiantly, but the enemy outnumbers us significantly."

Edarn gave a short nod, absorbing it as he tried not to let his mind succumb once again to the creeping numbness.

"And the red robes?"

Another squirrelly-looking middle-aged man, recently promoted to general and looking very much out of his depth, stepped forward.

"We've just had word from the palace guard, sire. A detachment of mages from the Order has arrived and is defending the front gate as we speak."

"Good... that's something at least."

Edarn paused, weighing the options, then looked back at the generals.

"Cards on the table, gentlemen. Can we hold the city with the numbers we have?"

Silence. The generals glanced at one another, waiting for someone else to speak.

"Good Lord, men!" Edarn snapped. "I need your honest thoughts... before the enemy breaches the gates would be better."

The red-faced general at his right shifted uneasily and cleared his throat.

"It's my belief, sire, that we cannot. If we try to hold the entire city, we will surely be defeated."

Though he'd suspected as much, the words struck Edarn like a blow to the chest. He allowed himself only a moment to recover before continuing.

"So, what do we suggest?"

"Pull all forces back within the palace walls. With the troops we have, I believe we can hold the palace itself."

Edarn took only a moment to contemplate that suggestion before he realised the critical omission in the plan. He looked sharply at the general, horrified as the realisation hit him.

"Do you mean to abandon the people to the invaders?" he asked, voice rising in anger. "Did you miss the reports about what these savages are doing to the people?"

The general raised a placating hand. "Hear me out, my lord. I understand the cost. But you are the king. The seat of power must be protected. If the palace falls—"

"Enough!" Edarn cut the man off. "We will not abandon the people. I wouldn't even be worthy of the crown if I allowed such a thing!"

At that moment, the heavy doors opened. Lucian, Eldara, and Lyra entered the room, flanked by a dozen mages and acolytes trailing in from the throne room beyond.

Edarn took a moment to stand and greet them, looking them up and down, taking in their dirty and bloodstained clothes and their weary faces. He raised his brow slightly. "I assume the defence of the gate went in our favour?" he asked, slightly hesitantly.

Lucian nodded. "For now."

Eldara stepped forward. "Forgive me, your majesty, but as we entered, we overheard your current dilemma, and I think I may have a solution."

Edarn looked up sharply, "Go on," he said, intrigued.

"If you send out word for your troops to pull back to the palace, as your general suggested, but with the instruction to bring the citizens of the city with them."

Edarn offered her a soft, indulgent smile. The kind given to a well-meaning child who doesn't fully grasp the reality of what they've just suggested. "We don't really have the space to house the entire population within the palace walls."

Eldara returned his indulgent smile. "I am aware of that, your majesty. I didn't mean for them to stay here. We could open a portal to an old temple site in Graltum. Send as many supplies as we can afford and send your people to safety."

Edarn blinked a moment, stunned by the beautiful simplicity of the solution. He turned to Lucian as if seeking confirmation that the plan was viable, and Lucian nodded.

Turning back to face his generals, he started barking commands. "Well... you heard her. Let's get people moving."

Runners were dispatched immediately, slipping down into the city like arrows loosed from a bow. The command spread quickly, and within ten minutes, the withdrawal had begun.

Chapter 28

Will continued to stalk the ruined streets like a man possessed, wreathed in a shifting aura of shadow and seething energy. The rage that poured from him had become almost sentient, bound to his will, feeding off his fury and growing more violent with every second that passed.

He stepped into the next street without slowing, and the first ranks of Yagerian soldiers barely had time to react before he unleashed his wrath.

A sweeping gesture from his hand, and the ground split beneath them, ribbons of obsidian-black energy erupting like serpents, coiling through the air and lashing into flesh. Screams tore through the night as the tendrils struck home. One man convulsed mid-step as his chest caved inward with a sickening crunch, ribs snapping and piercing through his heart before he collapsed, twitching, to the ground. Another was lifted high into the air, his limbs flailing wildly before his body imploded, blood spraying in every direction.

A column of enemy archers raised their bows and attempted to draw a volley... too slow.

He swept his arm across the air again, and a wave of shadow burst outward, distorting the light and warping reality in a sudden, nauseating pulse. The magic struck the archers like a scythe through wheat. They crumpled to the ground as dark fire consumed them from the inside out, eyes boiling in their sockets, and molten tears of viscous fluid poured down their cheeks. Finally, they dropped, clawing uselessly at the stone.

He moved like death incarnate through the smoke-choked streets. The enemy fled, but there was nowhere for them to run. There was no escaping his wrath.

The faces of the dead blurred together. Young, old, terrified. He no longer saw them, no longer recognised them as people. Their cries were muted echoes in his ears. The fire inside him hungered, and the betrayal he carried was a wound that would not close.

He passed a cluster of retreating soldiers trying to help their wounded. One of them turned to look at him, eyes wide with fear. Just a boy. Maybe seventeen. Blood smeared across his cheek, a trembling hand gripping the shoulder of a fallen comrade, trying to drag him to safety, whimpering in terror. Will hesitated for the briefest second.

But the darkness surged again, howling through his mind, and the boy's face was swallowed in a tide of red.

Will exhaled slowly. The rage still burned, but in its wake came emptiness. A void that only seemed to grow with each life he took.

The savagery he unleashed had served, momentarily, as a salve for the betrayal that had torn through him. But as he stood amidst the sea of twisted bodies and scorched stone looking for the next enemy to dispatch, the face of that young soldier resurfaced in his mind. The humanity of the terror on his face, the silent plea in his eyes. That image served as a mirror into his soul that pushed through the fury like a shard of glass, and he didn't like what he saw there.

But the darkness in his heart didn't care. It only knew hunger. And why *shouldn't* he punish them? These weren't innocents; they were invaders. Murderers. Servants of the demon who had dared to threaten Lyra. The demon who had threatened *his child*.

He staggered as that thought hit him, the inferno inside faltering for the first time since he had let the rage consume him. The pulse of dark energy that had been surging around him hiccuped violently and thinned, drawing back like a tide receding from the shore.

He stood in the middle of a street choked with corpses, the cobbles beneath his boots slick with blood and ash. The torrent of rage that roared in his ears subsided, and the silence that settled in the wake of his rampage was deafening. Somewhere, distantly, the war still raged, but here... it was only him, and the dead.

His hands trembled.

The image of her face came unbidden. He'd left her alone to indulge his rage. Left her to face the red-robed cultists and their demonic masters while he turned into something else. Something monstrous. He told himself it was for her, for their child. But standing there, surrounded by the shredded remains of men who'd died screaming, he wasn't so sure anymore.

He looked down at his hands, still crackling with residual magic, slick with gore.

What have I become?

The air around him shimmered, the last of the darkness pulsing like the heart of a dying star, flickering with the last defiant effort to seek the fuel it needed to sustain itself.

The world tilted, and suddenly his body rebelled against him. He stumbled to the side and doubled over a low gulley, retching until there was nothing left to give. The bitter taste of bile mixed with the copper tang of blood that already ran through the channel, turning his stomach all over again.

When it passed, he stayed there a moment, trembling, the stench of death and smoke clinging to him like a shroud. He wiped his mouth with the back of his hand, his chest still heaving. The echo of his own question haunting him.

He clenched his fists and turned, forcing himself to move.

There would be time later to reckon with what he had done.

Right now, he needed to find Lyra. He needed to make sure she was alive. Because if he lost her... No force in this world or the next would be enough to contain what he would become.

He began to shiver as he wandered the empty streets, the adrenaline that had sustained him now bleeding away, leaving his limbs weak and trembling. The darkness that had wrapped around him like armour had receded, and in its absence came a creeping numbness, as though his very soul were frostbitten.

The bodies he passed were silent witnesses to what he had done, twisted wrecks of men and women, their faces frozen in expressions of terror, their final moments scrawled across the cobblestones in crimson streaks. He tried not to look at them, but they were everywhere. He had wrought this, but the reality of that was almost too much to bear.

He had no idea how long he had been in his murderous trance, but he had lost all sense of time. Sometime during the night, the invading forces had apparently pressed further into the city, and he was now deep behind enemy lines. As he moved deeper through the now silent streets of the western quarter, trying to figure out where the front line of the invasion now lay, the silence around him began to fade. The distant clang of steel and the low boom of spells detonating like distant thunder reached his ears, and his senses sharpened.

Had they really progressed that far? The sounds of the battle raging in the distance appeared to be coming from the centre of the city. From the district that surrounded the palace.

As he got nearer to the city centre, the sounds of the battle raging ahead grew louder, and so he almost missed the telltale sound of marching boots approaching from a side street until it was too late. He considered fighting, but since letting go of his rage, a deep weariness had settled over him that made him almost want to weep at the thought of mustering up that energy again.

Instead, he ducked into the hollowed-out husk of a half-wrecked building, pressing his back against the cool, crumbling stone as the muffled tramp of boots echoed down the street outside. He breathed gently, listening to the rhythm of approaching enemy soldiers.

A low rustle made him snap his head to the side.

In the dim interior, half-shrouded by dust and shadow, stood a Uriasan soldier. Young, barely more than a boy. His uniform was torn, his helmet missing, and dried blood crusted in a dark line from his temple down to his jaw. The soldier raised his sword in trembling hands, panic flaring in his wide eyes.

Will immediately raised both hands in a calming gesture and took a slow step forward, then placed a finger to his lips. The young man hesitated, then gave the slightest nod, lowering his blade just enough to show he understood, and they both waited in silence for the sound of marching boots to pass.

It was then, as his eyes adjusted to the gloom inside the darkened building, that Will noticed the others. Behind the soldier, crouched in the far corner of the rubble-strewn room, were two or three families, maybe more. Their faces were streaked with soot and ash, their clothing torn and filthy. Children clung to their parents in utter silence, eyes glassy and vacant, the kind of stillness that only true horror could imprint.

Will's breath caught in his throat. For all the slaughter he had seen that night, for all the violence he had *inflicted,* this moment pierced deeper than any other. It reminded him sharply that in any war, regardless of who was right or wrong, it was the innocent civilians, trapped in the crossfire, who paid the price, and it was they who deserved it the least.

He crouched beside the soldier, trying to keep his voice steady. "How long have you been here?"

The soldier's eyes flicked to the families behind him. "Since the order came down to retreat to the palace. I got separated from my unit in the retreat and found these folks hiding in a nearby alley. I was leading them back to the palace when we got cut off."

Will looked him over. The soldier was hurt, clearly. Bleeding from a gash in his side, breathing shallow, but he was holding it together, somehow.

Outside, another enemy squadron passed by, their boots loud against the cobblestones. Will glanced to the doorway and then back to the soldier. "I am making my way towards the palace now. Let's get these families to safety... can you walk?"

The soldier nodded once, grimacing as he moved, the pain from his injuries obviously quite severe, but he refused to give in.

"Good... You lead these families. Keep them quiet, but keep them moving. I'll scout ahead and find us a safe path."

The young soldier gave a tight nod, his jaw clenched as he prepared to move his injured body. Will stepped toward the threshold and paused, glancing back once more at the group. A mother gently urged her daughter to her feet, clutching the child's hand and preparing to lead her from the building. Others were already preparing to move, helping the wounded and grabbing what few possessions they had managed to salvage.

Will took a breath and peered out through the jagged opening in the stonework. The street beyond was still. No sign of enemy troops. He turned back, gave a single sharp gesture, then slipped into the street, disappearing into the night.

He moved like smoke, here and then gone, slipping between collapsed walls and heaps of debris, eyes constantly sweeping for signs of movement. Every so often, he would pause and look back, catching a glimpse of the group following at a distance. The wounded soldier was keeping them steady, moving them through the shattered remains of Anhai like a thread stitching together what was left of hope.

As they approached the streets adjacent to the palace, they started meeting enemy troops in greater numbers. In one square, he watched as red-robed priests worked on constructing an altar, similar to the one he'd seen in Alesia, and he shuddered, the reality of what was in store for the people of Anhai sickening him. He steered clear of them, opting instead for the alleys and old servants' paths that criss-crossed the district.

Eventually, he reached the edge of a broken wall overlooking a narrow bridge that crossed one of the city's canals. On the other side lay the outer wards of the palace district, still contested, but not yet fully fallen. He scanned the route carefully, but didn't spot any patrols.

He turned and made his way back toward the group, who waited in a shadowed area behind a half-collapsed smithy. The children sat against the wall, silent and shivering, while their parents stood watch. The soldier raised his head as Will approached, a quiet hope in his eyes.

"There's a path," Will said, voice low. "I didn't see any patrols, but it is quite open once we reach the bridge. If anything happens, scatter and hide. But we stick together for as long as we can."

He looked down at the children, then back up to the soldier.

They carefully made their way towards the bridge and then Will paused raising a fist. The others halted immediately behind him, crouching in the deep shadows of an overturned market cart. His eyes narrowed. On the far side of the bridge, where an intersecting street met the square beyond the palace, a furtive movement caught his eye.

"Pull back a bit," he said, gesturing them backwards. "I will go and check ahead."

He frowned and reached out with his mind, slipping his consciousness outward, weaving through the ink-like veins of shadow between the stones.

There, less than a block away, he found a detachment of Stradan soldiers. Dozens of them, setting up a forward command post. He spotted red robes among them and two supply wagons being offloaded as the command post took shape with terrifyingly efficient speed.

He snapped back to his body, drawing in a sharp breath. "We're hidden for now," he whispered to the wounded soldier beside him, "but once we start to cross the bridge, they'll see us."

He stared at the palace gates on the far side of the square. Frustratingly within reach, but so inaccessible it may as well have been the far side of the moon.

He clenched his jaw. Time was against them. Reinforcements would arrive at that outpost soon, and when they did, their odds would plummet.

"We'll have to make a run for it," he said at last. "No better option."

The soldier nodded grimly. Around them, the families quietly readied themselves. Parents hoisted children into their arms, tightening straps on makeshift satchels, looking at him through wide, terrified eyes. Despite everything, they trusted him. He could see it in their faces.

And it tore at him.

He didn't deserve their trust.

But he said nothing. He couldn't.

He turned to face the plaza. "On my mark. Fast and quiet. Stay low and out of sight for as long as we can. Don't stop."

They crept from their place of concealment, moving across the bridge as quickly as they dared. Will took the lead, the others close at his heels. The sound of their footsteps echoed unnaturally in the still night air.

They were halfway across when the first shout came from the far street.

"Movement! On the bridge!"

Will's blood ran cold.

He didn't look back, not at first. But the sudden chaos from the far side of the square told him everything he needed to know. Orders were shouted. A line of armoured soldiers surged into motion, boots pounding, gaining ground with terrifying speed.

"Run!" Will shouted. "Faster!"

As they ran, Will shot a glance across the square to gauge the position of the troops.

Red-robed mages emerged from behind the Stradan vanguard, their hands already raised. One of them began to chant, and a great orb of crackling crimson lightning surged into the air, illuminating the entire courtyard in an unholy red glow. Shadows danced violently across the faces of the fleeing civilians, panic erupting in terrified whimpers and sobs.

Will's lungs burned. His legs felt like lead. For a moment, it seemed like they were going to make it to safety before the soldiers reached them, but as they got closer, the gates loomed in front of them, shut.

His stomach dropped. *No. No, no, no—*

"The gates!" he cried out, pure desperation in his voice.

Booted footsteps thundered behind them now. The clang of weapons bouncing against armour. The enemy was nearly on them.

Will skidded to a stop and turned, throwing up a protective wall of light, planting himself between the civilians and the oncoming tide. His hands flared with dark energy. He could already feel the red robes drawing from the same current, latching onto the surrounding darkness with greedy familiarity.

He braced himself for the final stand.

Then a voice shouted from above.

"Hold on!"

Will looked up. The palace wall was suddenly alive with defenders. A row of elven archers emerged like ghosts, stepping from their positions atop the ramparts with bows already drawn. Mages of the Order began materialising in flickers of golden light to either side of him, conjuring shields and readying offensive spells, as a squadron of Uriasan soldiers poured from the gate and moved to the front, lining up into battle formation.

A hail of arrows streaked from the wall, arcing overhead before plunging into the advancing enemy ranks, felling the first line and slowing the approach of those behind.

"Get them to safety!" Will barked at the young soldier, pointing to a shattered section of outer wall to their left, a remnant from an earlier battle. "Keep them safe until we can get the gates open."

The wounded soldier didn't hesitate. He guided the civilians toward the edge of the bridge, shielding them with his body as arrows whistled overhead.

Will watched only long enough to ensure they were safe, huddled behind the broken wall. Then he turned and stepped forward, joining the mages of the Order at the gate's base.

His hands flexed. His eyes narrowed.

The rage still burned inside him. But now he was back in control. He forged his will in the combined power of light and shadow. No longer limited or constrained by the rules of either, but channelling something greater.

The Stradan soldiers had hesitated, momentarily stunned by the sudden shift in the battlefield dynamic, but that pause had allowed them to prepare and form up.

Will raised one hand, tendrils of energy already dancing between his fingers, and spoke in a low, deathly growl.

"Let's end this!"

Chapter 29

Will stood at the front of the line of mages, his sword drawn and gleaming faintly in the dim light. Rank upon rank of Stradan infantry and red-robed mages waited across the plaza, silent and still, like wolves gathering before a kill.

Then came the sound of boots and clattering steel as more reinforcements began pouring in from the streets behind the enemy. The Stradan lines surged, their confidence swelling with their numbers. A horn sounded, shrill and triumphant, and then they began to advance.

Will reached into himself, finding the wellspring of energy at his core. The warmth of light and the churning torrent of the shadow, and wove them together. Radiance laced with darkness coiled up his arms as he lifted his blade and poured power into the steel. It sang in response, a haunting hum of opposing energies held in tension as the weapon rippled with the potential energy it was now imbued with.

There was something comforting about the weight of the sword in his hand. Magic had answered his rage too readily earlier that night, erupting from him with a savagery he hadn't thought himself capable of. It had thrilled him in the moment, filled him with a sense of godlike purpose... and then left him hollow, shivering in its wake. He hadn't quite come back from that yet. But now, standing at the edge of another bloodbath, he dared not lean on it too heavily. He didn't trust what might happen if he opened that door again.

So he gripped the hilt of his blade tighter and focused on what he *could* control. Muscle, memory, discipline. He let the magic course into the steel rather than into himself, letting it enhance rather than define him.

Channelling the darkness, he slipped through the shadows, moving around the battlefield like a wraith. His blade danced with lethal grace, cleaving through steel and flesh alike. Wherever he struck, enemy lines faltered. One of the nearby Stradan's took a broad swing at Will, but the blow was met with empty air as he vanished, materialising a moment later immediately behind his would-be attacker, cleanly driving the blade through his back, its tip reappearing through the soldier's chest.

Across the courtyard, Lyra stood amid the defenders, shoulders tense. Sweat slicked her brow, and her hands trembled slightly as she gripped her daggers. As the battlefield erupted into chaos, she became immediately overwhelmed—*she wasn't ready for this, she was just an acolyte*—but as a bolt of shadow hurled from the opposite side of the courtyard bore down on her, she reacted instinctively. The ground before her blazed briefly with radiant light, just in time to intercept the attack. The impact rattled her to the bone, but the shield held.

She stared in disbelief, then the shock turned to fierce, trembling pride.

There was no time to celebrate. A Stradan soldier broke through the defensive line, sword raised high. Lyra ducked under the swing, her daggers flashing as instinct took over where skill still lagged behind. The blade slipped between the plates of his armour, and he fell to the ground with a clatter.

Another surge of dark magic swept across the courtyard. This time, she didn't flinch. She thrust out her hand, letting instinct guide her. The light answered. It was wild, imperfect, but entirely hers, and burst outward in a crackling wave that sent two red-robes reeling.

The effort nearly dropped her to her knees. Her chest burned, her thoughts scattered, but she forced herself upright. Around her, the defenders were falling back, and she moved with them, weaving between mages, deflecting strikes, her magic flaring in stuttering bursts. Each cast grew surer, steadier. Each breath came with a little less fear.

Lucian and Eldara stood side by side at the rear of the formation. They formed the anchor of the Order's power. As red-robed mages hurled torrents of dark flame and red lightning, Lucian raised a shield of golden force that shimmered like sunlight through glass. Eldara answered with a blast of energy that scattered incoming projectiles.

Lucian raised his arms, voice booming with ancient incantation. The enemy's morale wavered as fear clawed at their minds and a wave of lethargy weakened their limbs. Eldara followed, weaving a web of empowerment for their allies, precision for the archers, and resilience for the wounded.

High atop the palace wall, Athtar loosed arrow after arrow, her movements smooth and unerring. The wind carried her fletching true, each shot finding its mark, each kill precise. She barked orders between volleys, rallying the defenders as Stradan ladders began to rise against the outer parapets.

"Stand your ground!" she cried. "For Anhai!"

A ladder crested the wall, and she loosed three arrows in rapid succession, dropping the soldier before he could clear the ledge. He tried to hold on to the ladder, causing it to topple backwards into the ranks of the enemy, crushing dozens as they clamoured below, trying to be the next to climb.

Although the Stradan and Yagerian forces held the advantage in sheer numbers, and the red-robes outnumbered the mages of the Order tenfold, the defenders of the palace began to turn the tide. Inch by bloody inch, they pushed back against the encroaching enemy. What the defenders lacked in numbers, they made up for in unity and in an unshakable will to protect what remained.

Amidst the chaos, a beautiful rhythm developed between the various elements of the defending forces. Sword strokes and spells aligned as if choreographed. Shields of light flared up the instant before a dark bolt would strike, while volleys of arrows arced in perfect tandem with bursts of elemental fury.

The enemy line began to buckle under the weight of the resistance, their cohesion fraying as hesitation spread like a crack through glass. Cries of retreat began to ripple among the Yagerian ranks, and even the red robes seemed shaken, their spells more and more often cast in haste instead of precision.

Seeing this, a roar of determination surged through the defenders. They fought harder, faster, with every drop of energy they had left, fuelled by the growing belief that they might actually hold the line.

But then something strange happened.

It was so sudden that it took several moments for anyone to notice. One by one, the enemy ranks behind the front line began to pull back, not in a frantic retreat, but in a measured, almost unnatural synchronicity. In an almost fluid ripple of motion, the entire force pulled back, like a wave receding from the shore. All but the very foremost attackers vanished into the smoke and darkness as if summoned away by some silent, unseen command, leaving behind a thin shield wall of soldiers doomed to die.

The defenders wasted no time. They fell upon the remaining attackers with renewed fury. The outnumbered soldiers fought like cornered beasts, but it was clear they had been left behind to buy time. One by one, they were cut down, and when the final one fell, a strange, echoing silence settled over the field.

Then came the cheer.

A thunderous roar erupted from the defenders, ringing off the palace walls. Even inside, it could be heard, a raw, jubilant sound of victory. There were claps on shoulders, bloodied grins exchanged, and sagging stances finally relaxing. The reason for the withdrawal remained a mystery, but in that moment, none of them cared.

Suddenly, the wind changed, making the hairs on the backs of their necks stand on end, and a deep, bone-rattling tremor coursed through the ground, growing steadily in strength. Dust sifted from the palace walls as stones groaned under the strain of the quaking earth. Slowly, the cheering subsided as the defenders all began looking about, trying to find the source of the rumbling.

From the smoke-choked western avenue, it emerged. The creature towered as tall as the palace walls themselves, its silhouette monstrous and shifting as if reality strained to contain its presence. Its limbs were long and spindled, tipped with talons that gleamed like obsidian scythes, dripping with a viscous, sickly green ichor that hissed where it touched the ground, scorching stone and soil alike.

Its body was a grotesque amalgam of muscle, scale, and something far worse. All along its underbelly writhed with hundreds of twitching, lidless eyes. They blinked independently, gazing in all directions at once, their movements jerky and erratic, as though each was seeing a different moment in time.

The creature had no visible mouth, but the air around it shuddered with a low, wailing sound that burrowed into the minds of those nearby, a sound that made thoughts scatter and courage falter. Every step it took sent cracks spidering through the ground and collapsed nearby buildings in its wake. It was as if nightmare itself had taken form and strode into the waking world. Behind the beast came a large force of red-robes, all grinning oily smirks of absolute confidence as they unleashed their secret weapon.

Panic swept through the defenders. If not for the bone-chilling appearance of the beast inexorably bearing down on them, the immense scale of it filled every heart with terror.

Will's shoulders slumped in resignation. It seemed no matter how many seemingly insurmountable obstacles they overcame, there was always another, larger one, just around the corner. This was the last straw. He suddenly found himself irrationally infuriated at the fickle shifting sands of fate. All around him, he could sense the wavering resolve of the men and women who were suddenly faced with this horror, but he knew that if they were to stand a chance, he needed to snap them out of it.

He turned to face the assembled defenders, lifting his blazing sword into the air. "Just another enemy... Who's with me?" he roared.

He didn't know why he chose those particular words, but they seemed to do the trick, as one by one the defenders refocussed on him, rather than the approaching horror, and then as one, they each raised their weapons. Swords, bows, and staffs were raised high over their heads, and they all roared in defiance. Defiance of their would-be oppressors, defiance of the monster, but mostly, defiance of the fear that threatened to completely disarm them if they gave in to it.

Hearing their roar, the beast stopped, focussing all of its eyes on them, and let out a horrific bellow of its own. That bellow shook the very ground beneath their feet, and caused a wall of putrid air to blast across the plaza towards the waiting defenders, thick with the stench of rot and sulphur. Several of the defenders doubled over, coughing and retching, but still they held their ground, weapons raised, eyes fixed on the abomination advancing toward them.

Lucian and Eldara were already moving, calling out coordinated magical commands. Walls of shimmering energy crackled to life as layers of protective light and arcane barriers flared into being between the defenders and the oncoming horror. Athtar barked orders from the wall, already releasing arrow after arrow, each one searching for a spot that might cause the beast to react, though it was impossible to tell if it had any real effect. The Beast didn't flinch. It didn't even slow.

Lyra appeared at Will's side, her daggers drawn and glowing faintly with residual light energy. "Do we have a plan?" she asked, voice tight.

Will glanced at her, offering the ghost of a grin. "Not dying is top of the agenda... beyond that, I am winging it."

Then the Beast struck.

Its claws slammed into the shield wall like battering rams, sending sparks and shards of magic flying. The force of the impact sent shock-waves through the plaza, throwing some of the defenders off their feet. Those hideous eyes on the beast's underbelly suddenly began to glow with malignant energy, and beams of darkness lanced out in every direction, searing into stone and flesh alike.

Screams erupted from the flanks. The first lines buckled.

Will surged forward, blade flaring brighter as he poured both light and shadow into its edge. He struck low at the nearest limb, and his blade met the beast's thick hide, ancient and armoured, like obsidian plated in sinew. It resisted his strike, but the surge of his magic left a crack, and that was enough.

"The legs!" he shouted. "Bring it down!"

Lucian and Eldara joined the call, and all across the battlefield, the defenders rallied, launching everything they had: fire, light, stone, ice, at the monster's limbs. The Watcher Beast bellowed again, its many eyes now writhing about in chaotic, dissonant rhythms. For the first time... it stumbled.

The stumble might not have seemed much, but for the defenders, it was a revelation. Something that colossal, that nightmarish, could be made vulnerable. What had moments before felt like a death sentence now sparked with a flicker of hope. Determination surged through the ranks, bolstering resolve where fear had nearly taken root. Cries of fury and defiance rang out as the line pressed forward again, weapons and spells aimed with renewed focus.

The huge beast, enraged by the pain, let out a guttural bellow that reverberated through the bones of every soul present. It had approached the battle with the lazy menace of a predator sure of victory, but now that assurance had soured. It struck out with a savagery borne of a newfound and unfamiliar fear of vulnerability.

Its massive, bladed limbs swept across the frontline with devastating force. Where it struck, men and women were hewn in half, torsos flung like rag dolls into the air. Some had just enough life left to register what had happened. To watch their legs crumple beneath them as their organs spilled out in steaming ropes across the cobbles. Behind them, those still standing flinched and gagged at the sight, some breaking rank for a split second, but the collective roar of their comrades and commanders pulled them back into formation.

"Keep on that leg! Watch for the claws!" Will bellowed, his voice hoarse from shouting, his blade gleaming black and gold with infused energy.

He saw Lucian and Eldara off to the flank, directing a group of mages into position. Their hands were blazing with light as they unleashed attacks designed to weaken and confound the beast.

On the wall, Athtar's arrows sang through the air, each one aimed precisely at one of the beast's eyes. Some buried themselves deep into the shifting underbelly. A few even exploded on impact, spraying viscous, stinking fluid that hissed and steamed where it landed.

Lyra darted between fallen bodies, her daggers a blur as she carved through red-robed sorcerers who were trying to shield the beast. One of them caught her with a glancing blast of dark fire, enough to burn the sleeve from her arm, but she pressed on despite the searing pain of her injury, flinging one dagger with pinpoint accuracy and watching the mage crumple in a heap.

Will dropped back slightly to get an overview of the battle. He watched carefully, trying to gauge the beast's movement, noticing it seemed to be favouring its right side, shielding its left. He took a moment to re-centre himself, re-focussing his energy back into the blade until the air around it seemed to ripple and distort, waiting for the right moment. That moment came at great cost.

The beast, now fully enraged, made another powerful attack that devastated another large swathe of their troops, but that was the opening Will had been waiting for. With a roar of absolute defiance, he charged the now exposed left leg, launching himself high into the air off an outcropping of tumbled wall, and raising his sword in two hands above his head. As he plummeted back down towards the creature's leg, he swung the blade with all his might, aiming for the spot he'd previously injured and striking it true.

The impact made a satisfying crunch as it cut deep into the creature, the superheated blade slicing through sinew and tendon with ease. The creature let out a horrifying sound that echoed all around the city, almost deafening those nearest, before staggering and beginning to topple forward.

Will's heart leapt at first, thinking them victorious, but as the mammoth creature began its irreversible descent, he realised with dismay it was collapsing towards the outer palace wall. Defenders scattered to avoid being crushed, but the ground shook as it slammed through stone and parapet, leaving an opening at least ten men wide. Huge chunks of sandstone skittered down into the plaza, smashing through nearby buildings, decimating the ranks of red-robes who were still in the area.

Will had thrown himself in front of Lyra, tucking his head down, for all the good it would have done, but when the dust cleared, he looked up. The watcher beast's form had unchained, its cursed essence slithering down through the shadows, returning to the underworld, leaving behind a residue that leached into the ground. Will watched in horror as a creeping infection spread outward from that residue. Stone withered to dust, moss and lichen shrivelled, and even the air tasted acrid, like sulphur and rot.

He opened his mouth to cry a warning, but the words stuck in his throat. The nearest mages, still cheering their narrow victory, froze as the corruption reached them. Their cries turned to screams as their flesh darkened and split, eyes sinking into pits of shadow. Within moments, their flesh had withered from the bone, and they collapsed, their screams silenced.

Will staggered back, heart hammering.

And then, before he could call out again, another sound rose above the silence... a deep, steady drumbeat. The measured thunder of thousands of boots, marching in perfect time.

Chapter 30

Will and Lyra burst into the palace entrance hall, lungs burning, boots skidding on marble. Chaos reigned inside the palace walls. Everywhere they looked, there were servants crying out for lost kin, courtiers scrambling in blind panic, and soldiers shouting conflicting orders over the thunder of boots and armour that were heard by few, and ignored by most.

Lucian was shouting orders when they reached him, his voice hoarse, his staff hammering the floor with each command. The doors shuddered under another impact. Splinters rained down like hail. Will caught his sleeve. "It's over, Lucian... the south wall's gone."

Lucian looked around at the chaos, slowly taking it all in. Eventually, he reluctantly nodded and drove the butt of his staff against the stone. When he spoke, his voice carried unnaturally, booming through every passage of the palace:

"Everyone! To the portal room! Leave everything!"

The command rang out through the halls, cutting through the panic. For a heartbeat, there was silence, and then a sudden surge of movement as people streamed toward staircases and side doors, urged on by the hope of escape and the fear of being left behind.

The four of them drove forward with the flood, forcing their way up the grand staircase. Behind them, the splintering crack of wood made Will whip his head around. The great doors exploded inward, the hinges torn from the walls, crushing dozens of terrified stragglers beneath. Screams filled the hall as Stradan soldiers poured through the breach like a tide unleashed.

When they reached the upper level, Lucian halted mid-stride. "The king," he breathed, eyes darting toward the throne hall.

Will turned back. "What?"

"The protection wards," Eldara said, her voice tightening. "They'd block your summons. He won't have heard your command to evacuate."

Lucian's gaze flicked between them, and then to the chaos surging up the stairwell behind them. For a heartbeat he seemed torn between duty and survival. Then the hesitation hardened into resolve.

"Go," he said, his voice rough, final. "Get to the portal. I'll bring him myself."

Eldara reached for his arm. "Lucian—"

He pulled free, already moving against the tide of bodies rushing past. "There isn't time to argue!"

Will seized Lyra's hand and pulled her onward, Eldara falling in beside them. They pounded up the next staircase as the clash of steel below rose to a deafening crescendo, accompanied by the guttural roars of invaders, the desperate cries of defenders, and the metallic scream of blades meeting.

As they reached the upper landing, Athtar appeared from a side passage, staggering under the weight of a limp form. She half-dragged, half-carried an elven archer, her cries raw and broken. "Help me! Please...help!"

The noise of battle seemed to fall away for an instant. Only the sound of Athtar's ragged breaths filled the corridor.

Will and Lyra rushed to her, but they knew before they got there that there was nothing they could do to help. The archer's head lolled lifelessly, his skin an ashen grey, chest unmoving, and his tunic soaked through with blood that flowed no more.

"Athtar," Lyra whispered, her voice cracking. She wrapped her arms around her friend, gently pulling her away from the body. "He's gone. I'm so sorry."

Athtar's sobs broke into shuddering gasps. "No... Ilbryen!" she cried out, her hands clawing toward the fallen elf even as Lyra held her fast.

Will dropped to one knee beside the body, resting a hand against the cooling brow. He whispered an incantation, the words trembling in his throat, and a faint glow wrapped the corpse in a spell of protection. "I'll take care of him," he said softly, his chest tight.

From below came the clash of steel, the guttural cries of men, and the occasional piercing scream as the lower halls buckled under the weight of battle. The sound of boots hammering stone grew steadily louder, surging up toward them like rising flood waters.

Will stood, jaw set. "We have to move. Now."

Still weeping, Athtar let Lyra guide her forward, leaving behind the shrouded form of her comrade. Together, the four pressed on toward the portal chamber, the roar of the enemy swelling behind them.

Mages and soldiers surged past them in a frantic tide, their faces hollowed by exhaustion. The air was alive with tension and voices raised in panic.

As they rounded the final corner, the great arch of the portal chamber came into view, blue light spilling into the hallway in shimmering waves. Inside, chaos reigned. The mages of the Order worked in perfect, desperate rhythm, some maintaining a perimeter, others guiding soldiers and refugees toward the portal's glowing surface. The surface of the portal rippled with every soul that passed through, absorbing them into its embrace and sending them far from the nightmare that had overtaken their home.

Will slowed, chest heaving, and took in the scene. He peered back down the hallway, noting that the surge of bodies approaching was now thinning. "That's almost the last of them," he said, voice barely audible over the din.

Eldara nodded, moving to the perimeter where the mages were intently watching for any signs of imminent attack. "You're relieved, evacuate now with the others," she told them. "Lucian is yet to return with the King, but we'll make sure the way stays open. We will hold the portal until he returns and then follow."

The mages at the perimeter looked uncertain, but finally nodded, following the last of the Uriasan soldiers into the portal chamber.

The four of them took their places, guardians of the threshold, while the last of the Uriasan soldiers and the remaining mages hurried past.

Then, at last, the stream began to thin. The hum of the portal filled the chamber, steady and mournful. When the final mage stepped through, the noise dwindled to near silence, leaving only the distant echoes of fighting below. The dying clashes that came fewer and farther between.

Will exhaled slowly, his pulse drumming in his ears. The stillness after so much chaos felt unnatural, like the pause before the world remembered to break again.

He pressed his back against the cool stone of the wall and slid down until he was resting on his heels. Athtar sat on the edge of the dais, quietly sobbing, now that the initial wave of grief had run its course.

Will became restless and paced up and down the portal room anxiously, occasionally peering down the corridor beyond, looking for signs of Lucian approaching.

"Shouldn't they be here by now?" he asked, breaking the silence.

Eldara looked up from where she was sitting on the dais in front of the portal, a look of concern creasing her features as she looked towards the door.

"Yes. They should."

Will looked back down the hallway one more time. "I'll go and see where they got to," he said.

Lyra stood up to join him, but he gestured for her to stay. "I'll move quicker by myself, and you guys should stay here in case Oberith's men find the portal. If that happens, you need to go through and close it. We can't let them find the people we sent through."

Lyra looked at him, her reluctance written plainly on her face, but she was unable to give any reasonable excuse for refusing.

He smiled at her, noting her reluctance.

She stared at him for a moment longer, her brows pulled together in quiet worry. She opened her mouth to protest, but stopped herself. He was right. They couldn't risk losing the escape route; instead, she stepped closer and gripped his hand.

Her fingers lingered in his. "Don't be long," she whispered.

"If I'm not—" He stopped himself, forcing a smile. "I'll be back before you know it."

Chapter 31

Lucian took a sharp turn, the thick scent of burning timber and dust already seeping into the corridor as the shifting winds outside the open galleried halls pulled the smoke in from the burning city below.

He came to the heavy oak door of the throne room and pressed it open. The guards that would normally have been on duty there were conspicuously absent, making Lucian slow his approach, pausing a moment to glance up and down the hallway.

Seeing no immediate danger, he quickly made his way through the empty throne room and into the adjoining chamber where Edarn stood near the central table, surrounded by his generals, who continued to study the map of the city.

"You took your time," said Edarn, looking up as Lucian approached. "How goes the defence?"

Lucian shook his head, stepping forward quickly. "The palace is breached, Edarn. We're evacuating through the portal."

Murmurs rippled through the room. One of the generals bristled. "We still have men holding the inner wards—"

"All gone, my lord," Lucian cut in. "We suffered huge losses in that final assault, and those who made it to the safety of the palace are helping escort the remaining survivors to the portal."

Edarn's expression darkened. He looked around the room, at the faces of his closest advisors. Lucian stepped closer.

"We're defeated, Edarn," he said quietly. "Our only move now is to evacuate. To save as many lives as possible. We fight another day, or we die in the ashes of a fallen city."

The words landed with a heavy intensity. Then, slowly, the king gave a single nod.

"Very well," Edarn said. "Lead the way, my friend."

Lucian exhaled, his breath catching ever so slightly as he did.

The generals moved swiftly, gathering scrolls, maps, and ledgers, stuffing them into satchels and cases. But Lucian's voice cut through the flurry of motion.

"Leave it," he commanded.

The room went still for a moment.

"The enemy is already inside the palace... I don't know how much time we have."

Several of the generals hesitated, looking toward the king, uncertainty written plain on their faces. Edarn gave them a single, solemn nod.

At his command, they let their burdens fall back to the tables, the scrolls rolling loose across the polished wood as they turned their full attention to preparation. Swords were belted, cloaks fastened, and then they turned, preparing to follow Lucian from the room.

And then—

BOOM.

The throne room doors swung back heavily against the stone walls, and chaos poured through the opening. A surge of Stradan soldiers burst in, their eyes scanning wildly. They were looking for something. Or someone.

Lucian's hands were already in motion.

Arcane syllables rolled off his tongue as he extended both arms toward the doors of the war chamber, forcing them back with a wave of shimmering energy. The air cracked with force as he sealed the breach and placed a warding enchantment across it, the door glowing faintly with sigils of containment.

The generals didn't hesitate, drawing their weapons and stepping in front of the king, forming a shaky, protective half-circle. Their stances weren't perfect, most of them having not seen a training ground in many years, but in their King's moment of need, their instincts kicked in nevertheless.

The red-faced general turned toward him, blade held firmly in his grip.

"Will that hold?" he asked, his voice rough.

Lucian's gaze flicked back toward the glowing doors. The enchantment pulsed faintly under the strain.

"Against these troops?" he said. "Yes. But if they bring red-robes up here..." he didn't finish the sentence. He didn't need to.

King Edarn stood pale and trembling behind them all, face drained of colour. His voice, when it came, was small and cracking. "Can you get a message to the others?"

Lucian's eyes met his. "Unfortunately, no. The protective warding we used to shield this room blocks all incoming and outgoing magic. If I lower it, those troops would be in here before reinforcements could arrive anyway."

He looked back at the doors where the sound of muffled hammering was coming through as the Stradan soldiers attempted to break through in vain.

"I can hold them off for now," Lucian said grimly. "But we need a plan... and we need it fast."

The room erupted in a sudden cacophony of raised voices as the generals tried to devise a plan to get through, but the limitations of their military backgrounds led their plans to lean heavily in the direction of direct confrontation.

"Gentlemen, if we knew how many troops are beyond that door, your ideas might have some merit, but as it is, we might open those doors and be faced with hundreds of trained soldiers to wade through," said Lucian.

As he spoke, he noticed a sudden change in the atmosphere and paused, tilting his head to the side.

"Do you hear that?" he asked in a half-whisper.

The generals all looked at one another in confusion before one of them replied. "I hear nothing."

"Exactly," said Lucian.

He crept slowly towards the door, gently placing his fingertips against the smooth timber, followed by an ear as he tried to figure out what was going on in the room beyond that would make the banging come to a sudden halt.

He could hear nothing at first, and as he tried to pinpoint faint noises beyond the door, his eyes darted about. Everyone else in the room was holding their breath, waiting for news.

Lucian heard a low, droning of voices chanting in unison, and a sensation of a huge amount of energy being drawn in. He realised at the last minute what was about to happen, his eyes going wide.

"Get back!" he yelled as he tried to put as much distance as he could between himself and the door.

Lucian's warning hadn't even finished echoing when the throne room doors detonated inward in a brilliant, blinding flash of crimson light. The ward shattered with a high-pitched wail, splintering into shards of energy that screamed like banshees as they flew across the room. The blast wave hit with a thunderclap, throwing several of the generals off their feet and sending loose papers and debris flying like shrapnel.

Lucian barely managed to conjure a protective sigil in time, a glowing dome flickering into existence around him and the king, shielding them from the worst of the explosion. Even so, the force of it staggered him, sending him to one knee.

When the light cleared, the doors were gone. So was most of the frame. The doors now hung in charred fragments, the wall blackened with soot.

And in the jagged opening stood three red-robed mages, flanked by a platoon of Stradan soldiers. One of the soldiers raised a single, gloved hand and pointed directly at the king. "Take him."

"Lucian—!" Edarn cried, his voice shrill with panic.

Lucian surged to his feet, drawing on his light-source with raw desperation. His hands glowed gold and silver as he thrust them forward. A beam of searing light shot out, slamming into the floor in front of the advancing force and erupting in a wall of radiance. The soldiers stumbled back, momentarily blinded, but the red-robes moved forward and began casting again.

"We're out of time!" Lucian barked. He turned to the surviving generals, three of whom were already limping to their feet, blood running from scalp wounds and torn uniforms.

"You! Form up around the king. Move with me... now!"

Weapons were drawn again, their blades gleaming in the light of the newly risen sun streaming through the window. There would be no strategy here. Only escape, or death.

Lucian raised a protective ward around the king and cast a quick repulsion spell toward the doorway, forcing the attackers back once more. He didn't know how long he could hold them off, but he knew that staying here was no longer an option.

They inched through the press of invaders in the throne room like swimmers pushing against a crushing tide. For every soldier cut down, two more surged in to take their place.

Lucian moved at the King's side, every nerve in his body alight with tension. His hands glowed with the soft gold of his protective enchantments, erecting shifting planes of magical light to block blows and spells alike. Each time a crimson bolt screamed toward them, he wove another shield into place, gritting his teeth as the impact rocked his arms and sent sparks flying.

Ahead of them, the generals fought with a desperate fury. Their swords were now stained dark. Red-faced, gasping for breath, they hacked and parried like men who had resigned themselves to death but refused to go quietly.

One Stradan soldier slammed into a general with a roar, steel flashing. The older man pivoted awkwardly, barely deflecting the strike, then responded with a brutal pommel to the face that sent teeth scattering across the polished marble. Another soldier lunged in from the side, only to catch the full force of a magical bolt from Lucian's outstretched hand, the impact hurling him backwards into a pillar with a sickening crunch.

Lucian didn't pause. His eyes were locked on the red-robes now moving methodically through the breach behind the soldiers, their hands working in smooth, practised gestures. Inky tendrils coiled around their wrists like snakes, power humming in the air as they readied another coordinated strike.

He hurled another bolt of his own, not to kill, but to disrupt and scatter their thoughts.

The nearest red-robed caster flinched as the blast grazed her shoulder, the sudden force unbalancing her just enough to break the casting chain. The other two staggered, losing their rhythm.

That's right. Look at me, Lucian thought grimly. *Not at him.*

He shifted his stance, planting his feet as another torrent of dark energy rushed toward him. The shield flickered, but held... barely. A lance of pain stabbed through his temple, the impact of the magical blow transferring to a physiological injury.

Behind him, King Edarn stumbled, and Lucian reached back with one arm to steady him.

"Don't stop," Lucian growled. "We've got to keep moving."

Hope fluttered in Lucian's chest, barely daring to take wing as they reached the edge of the throne room. Just a few more steps. If they could break through to the hallway, they might outrun the pursuit, maybe even get a message to the others. Just a few more steps...

But as they got closer, the temperature in the room plummeted. Breath frosted in the air, and the torches along the walls guttered low, their flames shrinking back as if recoiling in fear. A sudden weight pressed against Lucian's chest, a suffocating pressure that curled around his soul.

A shadow passed over the chamber, crawling like spilled ink across the stone floor. The heavy door creaked open of its own accord, revealing another contingent of red-robed mages. But it was not them that stole the last dregs of hope from Lucian's heart.

At the centre of the formation strode a towering figure clad in shadowy black armour so dark it seemed to drink the very light around it.

The figure didn't speak.

He didn't need to.

The very air around him whispered of dread.

Lucian staggered back a step instinctively, his mouth suddenly dry, his fingers twitching with restrained magic. The generals around him faltered at the sight of the new arrivals.

King Edarn gasped, voice barely more than a whisper. "Who is that...?"

Lucian didn't answer. But he *knew*. Deep down, in the marrow of his bones, he *knew*.

Oberith had come to claim his prize.

The figure raised a single gauntleted hand. The red-robes moved in perfect synchronicity, beginning to chant in low, guttural tones, the air warping as dark magic began to coalesce between their palms.

Lucian stepped in front of the king again, his shields flaring to life with renewed force, golden arcs rising like wings around them. "Fall back!" he shouted to the generals.

But there was nowhere for them to go. They had been effectively flanked and were now trapped between the two groups.

The force of red-robe mages with Oberith released their enchantment, and a volley of projectiles flew through the air at great velocity towards them. Lucian instinctively cast a barrier up in front of them, but the generals who were standing at the outer edges were not protected. The projectiles passed through them as if they were made of thin paper.

Lucian's breath caught in his throat as he watched the generals fall. Beside him, Edarn cried out for his fallen generals and reached out, but Lucian grabbed him by the arm. "Stay behind the shield, your majesty."

There had been no screams, only that sickening, fleshy sound as the magic tore through them, followed by the quiet, almost graceful slump of their armoured bodies collapsing to the stone floor. The spells had passed clean through them like shards of glass through smoke, but the result was all too real. Their expressions were frozen in that final instant of disbelief; eyes wide, mouths slightly parted.

From behind the obsidian visor, Oberith let out a slow, mocking laugh. It reverberated through the hall like the tolling of a funeral bell, and it chilled Lucian more than the killing spell had.

"Your defiance was always admirable," Oberith said, his voice finally emerging, distorted by the helm.

Lucian didn't reply. His mind was racing, calculating, searching for anything that might buy them a few more moments. As his mind struggled with the problem, a sense of familiarity intruded into his thoughts. That voice... he knew it.

"We need to move!" Edarn hissed from behind him, his voice tight with panic, breaking through Lucian's thoughts.

"We *can't*," Lucian said, eyes still locked on the enemy. "They've boxed us in."

Chapter 32

Lucian's eyes darted about the room as his mind grappled with a way to get them out of this situation. Behind him, the generals formed a loose semicircle around Edarn, blades trembling in bloodied hands. They were battered and breathless, their uniforms torn and scuffed from their skirmishes. The haunted look in their eyes said louder than words that they were readying themselves for the final stand.

Across the throne room, Oberith loomed menacingly, but said nothing. He simply hovered at the edge of the room, watching them squirm in fear with a look of mild amusement on his face, savouring the moment, and then, with a faint motion of his hand, lifted with elegant cruelty, he gave the command to his mages without saying a word, never breaking eye contact with Lucian.

A whisper of dark words from the red-robed mages, and the air turned to ice.

Lucian's eyes flared wide as the first volley came; a dozen streaks of roiling shadow hurtling towards them at lightning speed. He reacted on instinct, throwing up a shimmering barrier of golden light. The arc held, barely, but one projectile slipped through a gap and caught one of the generals in the throat. The man didn't cry out. His eyes twisted with fear, and then he simply dropped where he stood, his weapon clattering beside him as his lifeblood pumped from the wound.

"No—!" Lucian pushed the shield wider, forcing himself to draw on the light beyond what his exhausted body could maintain.

But it still wasn't enough.

Another shadow-laced bolt struck home, and a second general crumpled, clutching his chest as the dark magic sapped the life from his veins. One by one, the defenders fell, deliberately, methodically, each death more agonising than the last. Lucian tried to cover them all, to be everywhere at once, but they were doomed from the start. Oberith was simply toying with them now. Prolonging the agony.

Finally, only Edarn remained. His face was ashen, eyes brimming with disbelief and heartbreak.

"My people..." he choked, rising slowly to his feet. "You didn't have to—"

He never finished the sentence.

A final shadow spear shot across the chamber and struck him in the chest. He staggered backward, eyes wide, mouth agape, looking down at the gaping hole in disbelief. Then, with the gasp of his final breath, he fell to the ground in front of the throne.

Lucian's knees buckled. He dropped to the floor beside the king's lifeless body, the golden glow around his hands dimming to embers. The silence that followed was suffocating.

Lucian knelt amid the dead, drenched in failure, his strength spent and his soul on the verge of breaking.

Oberith stepped forward slowly, the black steel of his armour drawing the eye like a void. Though his face was hidden behind the cruel sweep of a jagged helm, Lucian could feel the his gaze boring into him.

"You disappoint me, old friend. I expected a more interesting resistance," came a voice distorted by the helm's visor, but familiar.

Lucian's eyes narrowed. The tone was unmistakable. Rougher now, older, hollowed out by years of hatred and bitterness, but beneath it was a cadence he remembered well.

"...No," Lucian whispered, the word slipping past his lips without thought.

Oberith chuckled, and the sound was cold.

"Is that all you have to say to me, after all this time?"

Lucian's voice found its strength again. "Orick?"

The figure in black armour tilted his head.

"Orick is dead," the man said coldly. Then, as if peeling off the last remnants of illusion, he reached up and slowly lifted the visor of his helm. "I am known as Oberith now."

The face revealed beneath was gaunt, drawn tight across high cheekbones, aged far beyond its years. But the eyes... the eyes were the same. Piercing, intelligent, full of fire.

"Gods, Orick," Lucian breathed. "It is you."

Oberith's face darkened. "I told you. That name has no meaning to me now," he said, his voice turning into a growl

"Why, Orick? Why do all this? The slaughter... so much senseless death? What happened to you?"

The man who was once Orick took a slow breath, as he looked down upon Lucian.

"You want to know what happened? You happened. The Order happened. The Northern Alliance happened. While you sat in your ivory tower at Thorn Island debating theory and doctrine, I was stationed in Anhai. Remember? They thought me an easy choice for a token posting. But when I arrived, I saw the truth. I saw what our 'civilisation' had done to those people."

He began to pace, his voice growing more intense with every step.

"The people of Strada and Yager weren't savages. They weren't monsters. They were survivors. Survivors of years of subjugation. Of famine, poverty, and forced servitude. And all of it sanctioned, even encouraged, by the Northern Alliance. I marched with trade convoys that spat on children, burned their crops for sport. I watched so-called nobles call them animals."

For a heartbeat, Lucian almost believed him. There was conviction in Oberith's voice and the same fire that had once driven him to heal. But beneath it now, Lucian sensed something twisted. The passion that once sought to save the world had curdled into hatred; what burned in Oberith's eyes was not hope, but hunger.

He felt sick, and turned away from his old friend. "So you sold your soul to demons."

"I gave those poor souls in the south purpose!" Oberith shouted, his eyes wild with madness. "I gave them something to believe in. A unifying force. A future that didn't involve them licking boots in the mud. And yes, Moloch showed me what I needed to see. Power enough to change the world. Power enough to punish those who built their kingdom on the bones of a civilisation they'd helped destroy."

Lucian's face darkened. "You betrayed your oaths. You gave yourself to darkness."

Oberith came to a stop, facing him. "Do not preach to me of oaths. You swore to protect the weak, and yet you serve a king who turns a blind eye to suffering as long as it doesn't cross his palace gates. I lost faith in you long before I lost faith in the Order."

Silence hung between them.

Lucian looked up at his old friend, sadness in his eyes as he realised that whatever had existed of his old friend was gone, burned away by years of hatred and the influence of the demon he has consorted with. With that realisation came a calm resolve. He looked into Oberith's eyes and realised that once again he was being studied.

Then, without warning, both men moved.

Lucian raised his hands, and light flared to life between his palms, taking shape as a shield of translucent brilliance. Across from him, Oberith's laughter echoed as tendrils of shadow writhed into form, condensing into jagged blades that pulsed with malignant energy. The chamber seemed to tighten, the air alive with the charge of two opposing forces meeting after decades of divergence.

They met with a clash that detonated in a shockwave so violent it forced even the red-robes to retreat, hands raised against the searing wind of raw power. Torches guttered and died. The throne itself groaned under the strain of the energies tearing through the air.

Lucian's movements were measured, controlled as he shifted his shield smoothly into a spear of light, then dissolving it into a storm of radiant shards that streaked across the room like a meteor shower. Oberith swept an arm, and the shadows coalesced into a wall of black glass, absorbing the brilliance before shattering outward in a hail of obsidian fragments that hissed like venom as they struck the marble floor.

The atmosphere was suffocating, alive, every breath heavy with static energy that made the small hairs stand on end for every person in the room. Each surge of power bent reality at the edges, causing walls to bend and the floor itself to crack beneath their feet. Soldiers and mages alike dared not intervene, caught between awe and terror, their eyes wide as two titans wrestled with the essence of creation itself.

Lucian lunged, his body encased in a corona of light. Oberith answered with blades of shadow spinning around him like a crown of thorns, each strike probing, slashing, and tearing at Lucian's defences. Their energies collided again, light and darkness knotting together before exploding outward in a burst that left afterimages burned into the retinas of all who watched.

"This ends now!" Lucian shouted, thrusting his hands forward, a beam of radiance splitting the room like dawn breaking through storm clouds.

Oberith staggered but only for the briefest moment... then his grin widened. With a guttural snarl, he dragged the darkness into a lance of pure void and hurled it forward. The two beams met mid-air, and the throne room became an inferno of warring brilliance and abyss. The ceiling rained dust and fractured marble.

Every feint, every parry pushed Lucian further out of position, until Oberith had placed himself between Lucian and the huge window that flooded the room with morning sunlight.

Lucian suddenly realised... too late. Oberith hadn't been pressing the attack blindly; he'd been steering Lucian, step by step. Oberith unleashed a volley of attacks that left Lucian reeling, and with a final flourish, unleashed an enchantment that completely shrouded the window, blocking the incoming sunlight.

The red-robes moved then, hands raised, chanting in unison. Sigils flared beneath Lucian's feet, and he cried out as the magic snared him, binding his limbs, suppressing his connection to the light.

"No!" he roared, struggling, golden light flaring and sputtering as he realised what was happening.

Oberith approached slowly, step by deliberate step. "You should be honoured, Lucian. You were always the strongest of us. I couldn't have opened the door without you. And now that I have you, the future belongs to me."

Lucian fought. He screamed. But the sigils tightened.

One by one, his senses dulled as his connection to the light-source was completely subdued.

* * *

Will made his way down empty corridors, now completely devoid of life. It was eerie to see the place this way. Even in the dead of night, there would normally be a certain hum of activity about the palace as servants went about the task of making the place ready for the following day. He could still hear the sounds of clattering and running feet from the lower levels as the invaders methodically ransacked the palace, but even those were so faint that it was almost like the distant rustling of leaves in a gentle breeze.

As he approached the wider, more ornate corridors surrounding the throne room, he felt a strange prickling sensation crawling up the back of his neck, the telltale sense of magical activity nearby.

Then he heard the concussive sounds of combat coming from the direction of the throne room.

He froze.

For a moment, instinct nearly took over. He started to sprint toward the doors, his hand drifting to the hilt of his sword, but something stopped him. Charging in blind could be suicide. He needed to know what he was walking into.

He glanced around, searching, and spotted a service alcove, tucked away behind a heavy velvet curtain along the side of the corridor that he knew led up to the narrow gallery balcony that ringed the throne room from above.

He slipped behind the curtain and ascended the narrow staircase, being careful to place his feet as silently as possible so as not to alert those in the room below.

At the top, he emerged behind a carved balustrade, crouched low to avoid drawing attention, and saw the scene unfolding below.

What he saw turned his blood to ice.

The throne room was in ruins. Fires flickered in small patches where soft furnishings had been set ablaze by the exchange of magical energies, and broken chunks of marble and golden masonry lay scattered like bones. At the centre, a ring of red-robed mages stood in eerie stillness, encircling two figures locked in ferocious combat.

Lucian.

Will's breath caught. His friend fought with the last shreds of strength he had, light flickering from his hands, but the expression on his face told Will that he was tapping the last reserves of his will. Across from him stood a figure clad in jet-black armour, moving with terrifying grace and ferocity.

Will's eyes scanned the rest of the scene, and his heart dropped even further.

The king lay dead, slumped at the base of the throne. The generals, every last one of them, had fallen. Their blood painted the marble floor in vivid streaks. Only Lucian remained, defiant and alone, a single flame defiantly flickering against a storm.

Will clutched the railing, muscles coiled and heart thundering, every instinct urging him to leap into the fray. But the throne room below was awash in magic so thick it made the air shimmer. To wade into the middle of that could be devastating, causing an unstable reaction that would obliterate everyone present.

From the shadows above, helpless, he watched as they subdued his friend. Lucian sagged to one knee, caught in a complex lattice of binding sigils that spiralled around his limbs and throat, dimming the light within him until only the faintest glow remained.

Will staggered as if struck himself. The air around him rippled with unseen pressure, the light-source within him keening in resonance with Lucian's pain. It was as though a thread that bound them had been severed.

The room fell deathly still.

The black-armoured figure moved toward him, the sharp sound of his steps echoing through the broken chamber. Will could see the rise and fall of his chest beneath the plates, slow and deliberate as though savouring this final moment of triumph.

He came to a stop before Lucian and stared down at him for a long moment, saying nothing.

Will tensed, his hand on the hilt of his sword. If it looked like Oberith was going to strike... if it looked like Lucian's life was about to end, he would act. Consequences be damned.

But then the figure lifted his sword in a formal salute, the blade held upright before his face.

"I regret that it has to be this way, old friend," came the voice, deep and resonant. "But the Order must be stopped. And to do that... I need you."

Lucian raised his head. Blood streaked his brow, and sweat soaked his tattered robes, but his eyes burned with defiance. With fury. With something not even defeat could extinguish.

"You may have defeated me, Oberith," he said, his voice hoarse. "But you will never stop the Order."

The words landed like a blow. Oberith said nothing at first. He turned, slowly, the faint sneer creasing his lips. He paused at the foot of the throne dais and then gave a short nod to his mages.

"Take him to the tower," he commanded. "Secure the rest of the palace. And someone send for the executioner... We'll begin dispatching the survivors at first light tomorrow."

Chapter 33

Will burst into the portal chamber, lungs burning, and a wild look in his eyes. The others stood as he entered. Lyra's eyes lit with hope at the sight of him, only to darken to worry as she saw he was alone.

"Where are the others?"

Will's throat felt raw as he forced the words out. "Gone. Edarn... the generals... Oberith killed them. Lucian's alive, but... They're holding him in the tower. He means to execute him. At dawn."

The silence that followed was deafening, pressing down on them so hard it almost made their knees buckle. They were all pale, their eyes bloodshot, their hands unsteady from exhaustion after the physical and emotional beating they had suffered the past night. Will knew his own body was failing too... every muscle screamed, his mind dulled by weariness, but the thought of Lucian in chains kept him upright.

"We need a plan," he said. The words rang hollow. They stumbled through ideas, but nothing held. Their minds moved sluggishly under the weight of the exhaustion, like wading through thick mud trying to chase the ideas that always just flitted out of reach.

Finally, Athtar cut through the noise. "If we stay here, the soldiers will find us. We need somewhere hidden. Somewhere they won't look."

They all agreed and prepared to leave. Before they moved, Eldara stepped to the portal dais. She pressed her hand to the activation stone, whispering a sharp incantation. The light guttered, then folded in on itself until the archway stood empty and inert. With care, she prised the stone from its cradle and slipped it into her pouch.

"No one follows," she said firmly. "Whatever happens, at least the refugees who made it through are safe."

They slipped from the portal chamber into a side corridor, keeping their heads low, ears straining at every echo. Somewhere deep in the lower halls, they could hear the enemy as they continued to claim their prize.

Athtar led the way, her bow clutched in her hand, eyes searching the dim passages with the instinct of a hunter.

They pressed on, each step taking them further from the sounds of movement in the lower halls, until at last, Athtar pushed open a plain wooden door and motioned them inside. The room beyond was small, with basic bunks lining the walls, broken crockery strewn across the floor, and a faint smell of mildew. But it was shelter.

"What is this place?" asked Lyra, looking around.

Athtar propped her bow in the corner, turning to secure the door behind them. "It's the servant's quarters. No one will think to check here for us."

Will slumped onto one of the intact benches, his body trembling with exhaustion. Lyra sank down beside him, resting her head against his shoulder. Athtar stood for a moment, staring at the ruin of the room, before dropping heavily to her knees, her grief finally quiet, but no less raw. Eldara set the activation stone on a ledge, wrapping it in a scrap of cloth before lowering herself to the floor with a sigh.

The silence grew. Outside, the sounds of distant movement continued, but for the first time in hours, they were still.

"We wait until nightfall," Will said at last, his voice a rasp. "Then we move."

* * *

Despite his racing mind, Will found himself in an extremely deep sleep that passed in the blink of an eye, and before he knew it, night was upon them. They prepared to leave in silence, needing no words. They all knew what needed to be done, and as impossible as the challenge seemed, they all knew that they would die trying if they had to.

They carefully looked out of the door, peering up and down the corridor, before stepping out into the cooler air of the open space beyond.

Will closed his eyes and reached outward with his senses, letting his shadow magic flow from him like tendrils in the dark. It blanketed the area around them in a light distortion field, bending their outlines and swallowing their sounds. It wasn't perfect. If someone looked directly at them, or if a red-robed mage was nearby, they'd be noticed. But it was enough to move more easily.

"This way," he whispered, leading them back toward the western halls.

They moved in near silence, their boots crunching on fragments of shattered tile. Will led the way, hand hovering near his blade, his other arm brushing the wall for balance as they turned a corner that opened into the servants' hall. Pots lay scattered across the floor, their contents long burned dry.

They crossed the hall quickly and slipped through a side passage that led into one of the inner courtyards. Moonlight filtered through the smoke above, catching on the leaves of the ornamental trees and the shallow pools that now reflected only flame. The garden had once been serene; now it felt like a tomb.

At the far end, a door hung open. Faint chanting drifted through it, the memory of the altar room back in Alesia resurfacing in Will's mind. Eldara raised a hand, halting them. "Red-robes," she mouthed.

The voices were distant, somewhere along the eastern wing. Will nodded and motioned them onward. They took the western passage instead, slipping into a long gallery lined with shattered statues. Dust motes danced in the flickering light, and each echo of their steps felt too loud.

They passed through what remained of the library, stepping over scorched books that crackled underfoot. At the far end, a staircase spiralled upward, half-collapsed. Behind a row of bookshelves, they discovered a squadron of Stradan soldiers had made camp and were sleeping in rows. The doors at the far end of the room guarded.

Will ground his teeth. "Turn back," he mouthed. "We need to find another route."

They wasted precious time zigzagging through hallways and corridors. Each path seemed to yield nothing but more patrols, more locked doors, more layers of magical protection. The tower had become a fortress within the fortress.

Hours slipped by, and frustratingly, their destination continued to elude them.

Once, they came within fifty feet of the base of the tower. From their hidden position behind an archway, they were met with yet another patrol.

"We could try to draw them off," Athtar whispered.

"No," Will said, eyes narrowing. "They'd call for backup. Too many eyes. Our element of surprise is our only advantage... we can't afford to spend it without a guarantee of escape."

Again, they waited. And again, nothing changed.

Eventually, they fell back to the now-ruined war chamber, which seemed to be uninhabited... for now. The great table stood split in two across the centre of the room, the remnants of their plans, scattered across the floor in piles of scorched parchment. They found a quiet corner and sagged to the floor.

"We can't get to him," Lyra said, almost on the verge of tears.

There was a long pause. Then Athtar spoke. "Maybe... maybe we wait. Let them bring him out for the execution. That will be our chance."

Will looked up sharply, nodding in approval. "Grab him in transit?"

"Better than this," she said. "Were being blocked at every turn. But if he's on the move..."

"We'll only get one shot," Eldara warned. "If we fail, there won't be another."

"We're failing now," Lyra said, her voice raised with a note of panic.

Will gave her a tired look but nodded. "Then it's settled. We regroup, rest for an hour, then find a route to the courtyard. They'll bring him there…. And that's when we make our move."

They tried to rest. Will closed his eyes but found no peace. Every time he drifted, he saw Lucian's face, bloodied, bruised, still standing. Still fighting. And he knew they were wasting time.

Eventually, as the eastern sky began to show the first blush of approaching dawn, they prepared to leave, going over their plan one more time.

* * *

Lucian tossed and turned on the hard cot, its stuffing long since worn into uneven lumps. The cold stone walls wept with condensation, and in the deeper shadows of the cell, thin sheets of ice had formed during the night. That chill had seeped into his bones, his thoughts, and even his spirit. He wrapped his arms around his knees and sat up with a frustrated groan, swinging his legs to the floor.

He stood and crossed to the narrow window slit, rising on his toes to peer out. A faint line of grey touched the horizon, signalling dawn's approach.

There would be no sleep tonight.

He sat back on his cot, leaning against the wall and closing his eyes. His mind, as it had all night, replayed every choice, every order, every moment that led to the fall of Anhai. He had believed... truly believed that they could hold the city. That faith now mocked him, echoing hollowly in the silence of his cell.

The thought of what would follow, of what Oberith would do now that the last great defence of the North had fallen, tightened in his chest like a vice. The people who had fled north weren't safe. Not truly. They were only delaying the inevitable. Anhai had always been the lynchpin.

Tears burned behind his eyelids. He pressed his palms against them, but it did nothing to block out the images, the dead, the dying, those he'd failed. Faces frozen in pain and fear.

And somewhere among them, the king. His friends. All gone.

The first rays of dawn spilled in through the window like a blade of gold across the floor. Lucian turned away.

He couldn't just sit here.

Drawing in a slow, steady breath, he knelt on the cold stone and closed his eyes again, drawing in his focus. Somewhere beyond the suffocating murk that subdued his power, the light still waited for him... he knew it. But each time he reached for it, the enchantments tightened like a noose, pulling him back into darkness. He gritted his teeth, forcing every sinew of his being against it, sweat trickling down his brow despite the chill.

A hiss of pain escaped him. He collapsed forward, palms braced on the damp floor. The bindings didn't just cut him off from the light. They fed on him. Drank from his attempts, leeching his strength, gorging itself on every ounce of defiance.

Despair threatened to crush him. He pressed a hand over his face, fighting the tears. His chest heaved once, twice... then he forced the grief down, locking it beneath the same discipline that had carried him through countless challenges. He would not give in.

But then, through the haze of exhaustion, an idea began to form.

Not an escape but a way forward. A plan.

Simple. Risky. But maybe, just maybe, enough.

A flicker of hope sparked within him, and for the first time since the tower door slammed shut behind him, a smile tugged at the corners of his mouth.

That was when the air shifted.

An unnatural pressure stole into the room. The shadowy binds around his wrists trembled, as though acknowledging the presence of their master. Lucian straightened, heart thudding.

A voice came from the shadows beyond the bars.

"I fail to see what you have to smile about."

Oberith's voice, deep, rasping, familiar in a way that made Lucian's stomach turn, drifted into the cell like a venomous fog.

From the deeper gloom, two pinpricks of faint light emerged, narrowing as they fixed on him.

"You're wasting your strength, Lightbearer. It's gone. All of it."

Lucian looked up and met the glow of Oberith's eyes beneath his helm. For a heartbeat, he saw the ghost of the man he once knew in that stance. The same proud tilt of the head, now swallowed by the abyss.

"You may have won this battle," Lucian said, leaning back against the cold stone wall. "But you will not win the war."

Oberith gave a cold chuckle. "Still clinging to that nonsense? An-hai has fallen. The king lies dead. Your order is shattered. And you... You're nothing but a broken relic in a cage."

Oberith's words withered Lucian's soul, but he didn't flinch, refusing to give Oberith the satisfaction. "You think you've killed hope, but you don't understand it. You never did."

Oberith chuckled, low, mirthless. "Still clinging to that leash? Hope?" He moved closer, the bars casting his face into stark shadows. "I wore that leash once, old friend. It chafed. Cut deep. But I learned... and so will you."

Lucian stared back, eyes burning with quiet defiance. "If that's your takeaway, then I pity you."

For a heartbeat, silence filled the space between them, taut and electric. Then Oberith laughed again, a hollow sound that reverberated in the stone. "Enjoy the sunrise, Lightbearer," he said, turning. "It will be your last."

The glow of his eyes lingered in the darkness even after his footsteps faded, like embers burned into Lucian's vision.

Chapter 34

Dawn arrived, and with it came the inevitable arrival of the executioner. Lucian was led, shackled in irons, down to the courtyard by two of Oberith's higher-ranking clerics. He smiled slightly at that; even though his essence was bound in warding, Oberith still obviously feared Lucian's power. He kept his pace slow as they descended the tower to the courtyard below, realising that time was not on his side. The delicate spell he sought to cast required precise timing and a connection to the light-source. Since he had lost access to his essence, direct sunlight was his only option, and the high palace walls were casting long shadows over the courtyard this early in the morning.

As they emerged from the heavy doors at the base of the tower, Lucian's eyes darted to the ground as he assessed the progress of the ever-shortening shadows creeping across the frosty cobbles. The leading edge of sunlight was almost there now, but it still had some way to go. Thinking quickly, Lucian decided that a calculated stumble might buy him a few precious moments. He placed one foot directly in front of the other and deliberately tripped, sending himself crashing to the ground with a loud thud. He winced as his uncovered knees met the sharp chill of the frost-covered cobblestones, the shock of the impact jolting through his whole body. Rolling around in only partly feigned pain, he listened to the laughter of the nearby soldiers, their amusement amplified by his convincing performance. All the while, he kept an eye on the shadows, gauging the success of his ploy.

"Get up and stop this foolishness!" spat one of the clerics, "You," he beckoned to one of the soldiers nearby, "come and move the prisoner."

One of the soldiers came over and looked down at Lucian, who was still rolling around, face contorted in apparent agony.

"Get up!" he said, grabbing Lucian roughly by his robes and hauling him to his feet, before marching him towards his fate.

Lucian looked about in panic as he realised he hadn't achieved enough of a delay, and with one desperate last attempt, he very quickly turned and stuck the soldier full in the face with his forehead, hearing a satisfying crunch as the soldiers nose broke and a spray of crimson misted the soldiers top lip. Using the momentary distraction he turned to run, his hands still bound behind him. He knew that he wouldn't escape, but all he needed was a few more moments. His heart was pounding out of his chest by now as adrenaline coursed through his veins, his breath coming in short bursts in his panic. His eyes darted left and right as he saw soldiers closing in on him from all sides, but before they could reach him, he felt the inky black tendrils of the red-robed clerics wrap around him, lifting him off the ground as they physically bound his arms to his side and moved him towards the executioner. The soldier whom he had injured was approaching with a murderous look in his eyes as he slowly levitated across the courtyard. When he reached Lucian, he drew his sword, but the soldier's commanding officer barked an order at him to stop. With a flicker of annoyance, the soldier reversed the hilt of his sword and smashed Lucian in the face, returning the favour of a broken nose.

A sly smile graced Lucian's blood-covered lips as he revelled in the success of his deceit. The executioner's block now basked in the warm glow of the morning sunlight. The irony was not lost on him that this was aided by the gaping hole in the palace wall, a result of the final assault two nights earlier.

Oberith gazed upon his old enemy, who stood bedraggled and defeated in chains before him. "Quite a pitiful display of cowardice there, Lucian. I expected better from you," he said, with a sneer on his face, "Do you have any last words before you meet your end?"

Lucian's eyes glowed with defiance as he turned to face the eastern horizon. With a deep, commanding voice that echoed across the courtyard, he called out to the light-source directly. "Release me from this mortal form and return me to the source," he roared, his words ringing out like a battle cry. "And when the time is right, send my essence back to this world, so I might serve again!" His every word resounded with unwavering conviction.

As his final words reverberated off the stone walls of the courtyard, a hush fell over the soldiers gathered there. They all knew the legends of the immense power of the Lightbearer, and their faces reflected concern and uncertainty as they looked around at one another. Silence fell over the courtyard, as the echoes of Lucian's final words faded into muted silence, only to be broken a few moments later by a sudden burst of laughter from some of the soldiers. The sound of the mocking laughter spread through the crowd like wildfire. Oberith smiled, a sickly and insincere expression that oozed malice. He let the laughter continue on for a few more seconds before lifting a gauntleted fist. The courtyard fell back into a hushed silence immediately.

Oberith's smile widened as he leaned forward, looking at Lucian with amusement and contempt. "What a pitiful, impotent fit of rage," he said, goading Lucian further. But instead of anger, Lucian's face only showed pity. "You never did understand the power of light," he said calmly. "Maybe if you had, you wouldn't have turned from it to become this vile, twisted version of the great man you once were."

Enraged, Oberith turned to the headsman and barked, "I've had enough of this. End him!"

Lucian was thrown to his knees, the hard scaffold beneath him icy cold. His head was yanked forward over the block, exposing the vulnerable flesh of his neck to the deadly blade hovering above. Though he clung to his faith, fear gripped him, squeezing the very breath from his lungs. The deafening thud of his racing heart echoed in his ears, as adrenaline surged through his veins. And then, the heavy axe fell with a sickening thud, severing his head cleanly, ending his life.

* * *

They continued to meet obstacles at every turn as they tried to traverse the lesser palace halls, making their way to the lower halls, reasoning that the executions would likely take place in the courtyard. Each delay chaffed, but they tried desperately to remain calm.

Finally, they found a half-concealed entrance to a service corridor that led down through the kitchens. pans upturned, knives left embedded in chopping blocks, dough half-kneaded on flour-dusted tables. The acrid tang of burnt food hung heavy in the air, though the fires had long since died.

Athtar pressed forward eagerly, her hand brushing past a rusted rack of ladles. "The scullery has an exit that opens straight into the lower courtyard," she whispered. "We're close now."

"When we reach the courtyard, we need to proceed with care," Will said, his voice low. "If Oberith means to make a spectacle of these executions, there'll be a crowd."

Pushing through a swinging door into the scullery, they found more signs of the sudden evacuation. Overturned stools, dishes stacked precariously in cold, murky water, the whole room dim and abandoned.

When they reached the door, they peered outside, pausing a moment to have a look around. They could hear voices on the far side of the courtyard, but the scullery was slightly below ground, so whoever was talking was concealed from view, and the echoes in the courtyard distorted the sound.

"If we run into trouble, defend yourselves, and we'll pull back to here," said Will under his breath.

They all nodded once and then formed up, slowly climbing the stone stairs that would bring them up to ground level. Will once again shrouded them in the shadow aura that would conceal them from most as they slowly ascended.

The warm morning sun was casting long shadows across the courtyard, and the frost was quickly turning to a low-lying mist, the temperature of the air already beginning to climb rapidly.

They blinked against the sudden brightness as they stepped fully into the courtyard, then froze.

Lucian was kneeling on a raised platform, his neck stretched forward over a worn headsman's block. Two red-robes stood to either side. A masked executioner held a massive axe aloft, the blade glinting silver in the sun, poised above their friend's exposed neck.

Horror gripped their limbs like ice. The world around them slowed, sound falling away as the axe hung in the air. Still, dreadful, inevitable.

They tried to move, to scream, to act.

But it was already too late.

The blade fell.

A wet, final thud split the silence as Lucian's head tumbled into a waiting basket below. His body sagged forward, lifeless, folding against the block as blood spilled across the wooden platform in thick, dark ribbons.

For a heartbeat, the world stood completely still.

Then it all came crashing back.

Eldara's scream tore through the courtyard.

"Noooo!"

All eyes turned to look at where the cry had come from. For a moment, no one moved. Dozens of heads swivelled toward the shadow-wreathed figures now frozen at the edge of the courtyard. Will's spell unravelled, torn apart by the shockwave of Eldara's scream and the scrutiny of hundreds of eyes. The shadows peeled away like smoke in the breeze, leaving them fully exposed beneath the harsh morning sun.

There were at least two full squadrons of armed Stradan soldiers lining the courtyard, who all raised their weapons and adopted formation on instinct. And among them, scattered like bloodstains on fresh snow, stood dozens of red-robes.

At the head of it all, flanked by armoured generals and high-ranking clerics, stood the towering black-armoured figure of Oberith.

His helmet snapped toward them.

"Get them!" he roared, his voice booming across the courtyard. He hadn't expected survivors, so was taken aback at the sudden appearance of northerners in their midst.

For a moment, Will's body refused to obey. Somewhere distant, his mind screamed for him to move, but his heart could only break. But then the grief in his chest ignited like dry tinder, flaring into fury. He barely noticed Lyra's hand grabbing for his arm, or Athtar's voice calling his name. His eyes were locked on the man who had destroyed Anhai. The man who had murdered Lucian. The man who had torn their world apart.

Every ounce of rage, every shred of pain, every crushed hope was suddenly given form.

It had a name. It had a face. And it stood within reach.

Will stepped forward, his sword already in his hand, the blade humming with dark fire. The ground beneath his feet cracked with the weight of shadow magic surging from his core.

"Oberith!"

He didn't shout the name. He *declared* it, like a curse hurled across the ages.

The courtyard erupted into chaos.

Before the soldiers could close in, Eldara lifted both hands, her fingers glowing with raw power. Ancient syllables fell from her lips, each one armoured in the raw pain that gripped her. A violet shockwave exploded outward, striking the first ranks of soldiers with concussive force, sending bodies tumbling like dolls across the cobbles, shattering in the intense burst of energy that engulfed them.

More came. This time, a wave of red-robes surged forward, chanting counter-incantations and flinging bursts of inky black shadow-fire. Eldara met them head-on, a cyclone of magic swirling around her like a tempest.

One red-robe dared to charge, dagger flashing. She didn't even blink. Her palm flared, and the mage disintegrated in mid-step, his ashes carried away on the hot breeze.

Still, they kept coming.

Eldara's power surged with each life extinguished. For every shadow-bolt cast her way, she answered with searing light, pure and intense. But she was outnumbered a dozen to one, and already her wards were cracking. Blood dripped from her nose, but she gritted her teeth and stood her ground.

"Shields!" Lyra shouted, throwing her arms outward.

A dome of translucent light blossomed around her friends, creating a time dilation field around them that immediately caught arrows mid air and slowed anything that tried to enter. Charging soldiers found themselves suddenly slowed to a crawl as they entered the field. Weapons swung violently, suddenly arced harmlessly through the air. Sound warped within the dome; the cries of soldiers stretched into drawn-out echoes, arrows whispering past like slow rain.

The strain hit her instantly, the enchantment draining her of her strength. This was more than she had ever attempted, but there was no time to doubt.

Another volley of spears launched from the far wall, and Lyra clenched her jaw and layered the shield again. The weapons shattered against her barrier like waves against rock.

The courtyard entrance erupted with enemy soldiers, and Lyra threw her focus outward. A second dome sealed the gateway shut, a barrier that shimmered like morning frost. No reinforcements would come today.

Through the haze of noise and flame, she saw Eldara beginning to falter under the onslaught of red-robes.

From behind them, Athtar moved like fire incarnate. Her movements fluid, graceful. She focussed her elemental magic on her weapon, eyes closed, she whispered to her bow, running one finger gently down its length as she imbued it with elemental energy.

Opening her eyes, she nocked an arrow, its tip immediately bursting into flame. She loosed it in a smooth, fluid motion, and where it struck, a soldier erupted and moments later detonated in a fiery explosion.

She nocked again. Fired.

Another burst. Another wave of chaos.

Arrows screamed from her bow faster than the eye could follow, each one a blazing harbinger of death, flying through the air, igniting with ethereal brilliance.

Again and again she fired until her quiver was nearly empty. She reached for another, grimacing at the sting in her side from a glancing blade earlier, but she did not pause. She could not.

"I'm nearly out!" she yelled in a panicked voice.

Lyra nodded to indicate she understood. She focussed for a moment and relocated a couple of bushels of arrows from the armoury to appear beside them.

Athtar cast her a grateful smile, quickly refilling her quiver, and continued her brutal rain of fire.

Then she saw Oberith, striding toward Will.

Time seemed to warp around them as Will stepped forward, the chaos of the battle fading to a distant roar. Oberith stood at the heart of it all like a monument to death, his black armour warped the very air around him. Behind them, the battlefield tore itself apart in a symphony of fire, light, and screams, but this space, between the two of them, had gone utterly still.

Will felt the pull of the dark magic within him, feeding on his grief, his anger, his desire for vengeance. It pulsed in his chest like a second heartbeat.

Oberith spoke first. "I sense a great power in you. But you're out of your depth."

Will's eyes narrowed. "We'll see."

Then the storm broke.

They collided in a thunderclap of steel and raw force. Sparks flew with every blow, their swords flashing like twin comets. Will struck fast, moving with fluid precision, testing Oberith's defences. But the dark warlord was a wall of iron. Every slash Will delivered was turned aside by that enchanted armour, which absorbed and deflected blows with unnatural ease.

Oberith retaliated with sweeping arcs of brute force, hammering at Will's defences. The weight behind each strike was terrifying, every block sending shudders up Will's arms, nearly breaking his stance.

A blade of black lightning shot from Oberith's free hand. Will barely rolled aside in time, the energy searing a jagged scar into the flagstones. He retaliated with a burst of shadow magic, tendrils lashing toward Oberith's legs, trying to entangle and trip him, but the warlord stamped one foot down and released a pulse of dark energy that vaporised the spell.

"You fight with anger," Oberith said, circling. "That's good. It will make your fall all the more satisfying."

Will's lip curled, saying nothing, but feeling a sense of distaste at the respect his opponent was showing to his raw, wrathful emotion.

They clashed again. Will ducked under a brutal overhead strike, pivoted low, and drove his blade up toward Oberith's ribs. The blade struck, but the armour once again pulsed a wave of dark energy, and the weapon skidded away as if hitting stone.

Will recoiled, eyes widening.

Oberith grinned beneath his helm. "You cannot win."

Another blow came. Will barely parried, the force sending him flying backward. He landed hard, skidding across the courtyard stones, pain flaring in his side.

He's too strong, Will thought, struggling to his feet. *That armour... I can't break through it.*

Oberith advanced like a god of war, his blade now humming with malevolent energy.

"I've seen stronger men than you broken in these very stones," Oberith snarled. "I will not even remember your name."

He raised his sword.

Will caught his breath... and then let go.

He let the anger fall away. Let the rage, the grief, the guilt... he let go of all of it, let it bleed from him. He closed his eyes for a heartbeat. In that space, he reached down past the dark magic. Past the shadow.

There, beneath it all, was the light.

It responded instantly. The sword in his hand flared to life, a beam of pure radiance that blazed like a newborn sun. The energy surged through him with a beautiful, cleansing clarity.

Oberith faltered. "What... what deception is this?"

Will raised his blade, now incandescent, and stood taller. "I have allowed all my rage to consume me for too long," he said quietly. "But I wasn't made to wield the dark."

He charged.

This time, his strikes rang like bells of judgment. The moment their blades met, the world seemed to fracture. The air burned white, the ground splitting beneath their feet, light and shadow warring not just between them, but through the very air. Oberith blocked the first blow, but his armour cracked. He blocked the second... more cracks. The third cut a glowing gash across the chest plate, causing him to stagger backward.

Will was relentless. Light burst with every swing, illuminating the courtyard in pulses. They moved like dancers, each step driving the darkness back. Will ducked and spun, sweeping low, rising with an upward strike that cracked Oberith's helmet along the jaw.

Oberith retaliated with a brutal punch, sending Will reeling. A blast of shadow magic caught him in the side, knocking the air from his lungs.

"You're still only human!" Oberith roared, charging with a scream of frustration, but his words now held a note of uncertainty that hadn't been there before.

Their blades locked once more, but now the balance had shifted. Will pushed forward, sparks exploding around them, and with a sudden twist, he shattered Oberith's blade in half.

The dark warlord stumbled, eyes wide.

Will stepped in close, reversed his grip, and drove the glowing sword into Oberith's chest.

For a moment, nothing moved.

Light erupted from the wound, crawling through the cracks in the armour like molten gold. Oberith staggered, gasping, his sword arm dropping limp at his side.

"You..." he whispered. "You were supposed to fall."

Will met his gaze. "You forgot one thing."

Oberith collapsed to his knees.

Will leaned in, his voice low. "The light always returns."

Then, with one final burst of radiance, the blade burned through Oberith's chest-plate, and the warlord crumpled to the stones, armour clattering, the darkness finally undone.

Silence fell across the battlefield.

Chapter 35

For a moment, all was still.

Oberith's body crumpled to the ground in a heap of blackened armour, pulling Will's sword from his grip. The sounds of battle all fell into silence as though the world itself was holding its breath.

For a moment, no one moved.

And then, as if a great tether had been cut, the soldiers began to retreat. First in small groups, then en masse, their courage broken now that their black-armoured leader lay slain. Weapons clattered against the stone courtyard as they were discarded in surrender. The red-robes, many of them bloodied and limping, faded back into the fleeing ranks or shadow-slipped away.

Lyra stood in the centre of the courtyard, her hands still raised, maintaining the shimmering barrier around them. As the tide of soldiers reached the edge of her magic, she lowered part of the wall, just enough to let them flee.

The courtyard began to clear. Then they were gone, disappearing into the palace halls or down the city streets, until only the four remained.

Will retrieved his sword from Oberith's body, wiping the blood on the grass, and then slowly turned and approached the execution platform. His shoulders sagged. The fires of vengeance now burned low, replaced by a dull, aching weight.

Lucian's body lay still at the foot of the headsman's block. Will pulled a cloak from the corpse of a nearby Stradan soldier and draped it over the gaping wound where Lucian's head should be, covering the pool of sticky blood as the others approached, sparing them the grisly sight.

For the first time since the siege began, his knees almost buckled. He wanted to sink to the ground beside Lucian and never rise again.

Lyra stood behind him, her arms crossed tightly over her chest, her face a mask of restrained grief as she struggled unsuccessfully to hold back the flood of tears. Athtar looked away, blinking back her grief, her jaw clenched and eyes glistening. Eldara approached last, her footsteps slow, hesitant. The look of raw pain on her face as she approached tore at their hearts once again.

"We should do something," Will said finally. "We can't just leave him here. We can't let the carrion take him."

"But what can we do?" Lyra asked, her voice hoarse from crying.

Will looked up. "We'll carry him. We'll find a way to—"

He stopped. The ground beneath them trembled, subtly at first, like a distant thunder rolling through the earth. Then the tremors grew stronger, the courtyard stones rattling beneath their feet. Eldara gasped, taking a step back as the very air around them seemed to vibrate.

"What's going on?" Athtar said, her eyes wide.

A low, resonant hum began to rise from Lucian's body, and they all backed away quickly.

A faint glow began to pulse beneath his skin, soft and golden. Then it brightened, radiating outward until the entire platform was bathed in light. Lucian's body lifted slowly into the air, his limbs limp. The hum rose into a harmonic chord, vibrating with impossible energy that pressed against their ears until they could hear nothing else.

Rays of pure, dazzling light shot from his chest in all directions, illuminating the palace walls, lancing into the sky like beacons. The brilliance forced them all to shield their eyes, the sheer intensity of it nearly blinding.

And then, just as suddenly as it had begun, the light vanished. Silence fell once more.

When they dared to look back, Lucian's body was gone. No blood stained the wood of the execution platform.

Only a single object lay at the centre of the platform: a perfectly clear, multifaceted crystal. It rested where Lucian's body had been, sunlight passing through it and casting faint, prismatic colours across the oak boards.

Will stepped forward, a look of confused apprehension on his face. He gingerly lifted the crystal and cradled it in both hands as though it might vanish at any moment. "What... what is this?"

"I don't know," Eldara murmured, eyes wide. She looked as shaken as the rest of them, but the serene effect of the crystal seemed to be calming them all.

A moment passed in complete silence as they simply stared at the crystal, absorbing it's energy.

Will finally drew a deep breath and straightened, carefully wrapping the crystal in a piece of cloth and stowing it in his pouch. "We need to get out of here. It won't be long before those troops regroup and realise that they still outnumber us."

They moved quickly now, threading back through the palace's twisting halls, where the corridors buzzed again with life. When a knot of enemy soldiers rounded a corner, they didn't think. They simply moved as one. Blades flashed, arrows struck, spells flared, all without a word, as though exhaustion had burned away hesitation and left only instinct. The clash was over in moments, bodies crumpling soundlessly to the floor. None of them paused to look back. With adrenaline the only force keeping them upright, they pressed on, a single will driving them through the chaos toward the last hope of escape.

By the time they reached the portal room, they had managed to shake their pursuers, and Will ran straight to the pedestal, and after replacing the orb, began channelling the destination for Graltum.

As the portal flared to life, Eldara stepped toward the pedestal, hovering a hand over the activation orb. She closed her eyes, and her lips began moving in a silent chant.

"What are you doing?" Will asked.

"Ensuring none can follow," she said.

The orb began to glow, veins of gold spreading like cracks across its surface, before resuming its previous state.

Eldara looked up, finally, stepping to join them in front of the now glowing portal. "Once we're through, the magic in the portal will overload until it collapses in on itself. The explosion will destroy this entire chamber and take any would-be pursuers with it."

Will flashed her a quick smile and gripped her shoulder before stepping towards the portal.

Without another glance back, they all stepped through together, leaving Anhai and everything that had happened there behind.

* * *

They emerged into cold air and salt mist.

Graltum greeted them without fanfare or celebration, but with grey skies, a biting wind, and the distant crash of waves against a rocky coastline. The northern settlement was no more than a fledgling outpost, a handful of tents and hastily constructed shelters nestled among weathered cliffs. Smoke curled from campfires, and everywhere they looked they were met with the faces of the last survivors of southern Urias.

They asked around and finally found the tent where the elders of the order had set up a temporary outpost while helping the people settle. For the next hour or so, they briefed the assembled elders on everything that had happened since they had sent the refugees through. It had only been a few days, but it felt like a lifetime. By the time Eldara had concluded her report, the other elders had recovered from their initial bout of grief at hearing the news of Lucian's passing. They sat in silence for some time, allowing the weight of the news to fully sink in, before the elder of integrity stood from his chair, walking forward to meet them.

"This stone you mentioned... May we see it?" he said.

Will pulled the stone from his pouch, holding it out in his hand, and the other elders all leaned forward in their chairs, trying to get a closer look, while the elder of integrity reached out a hand to take it from Will.

Will felt a strange reluctance to be parted from the stone, but conceded that the order should be its caretakers until they knew its purpose.

The stone had not dulled. It shimmered even in shadow, refracting light in ways that defied nature. It pulsed gently, like a heartbeat, and radiated warmth.

Over the next few days, the Elders tried everything to breach its depths, to understand its purpose. They tried incantations, relics, spells of sight and revelation, but the crystal refused to yield its purpose. It hovered at the edge of understanding, its mystery always frustratingly just out of reach. Will sat by it each night, hoping for something, anything that would prove to them that Lucian's sacrifice hadn't been in vain.

Then, one night, under the gaze of a pale northern moon, it spoke.

The crystal flared suddenly with blinding light, awakening the entire encampment. Will, Lyra, Athtar, and Eldara were immediately drawn to it, and as they gathered in the makeshift hall that held it, the light coalesced into a column above the pedestal, twisting upward like a funnel of stars. A voice echoed within them. It didn't speak aloud, but in a gentle voice that spoke at the very core of their being, beneath the skin, within their soul. It was not Lucian's voice, and yet it held something of him. It was the voice of the nexus. The voice of the Light-source itself.

"When the Crown of Stone is broken, the tide of shadow shall swell.

The Bearer of Light shall be unmade, his flame scattered yet enduring.

From taken lands shall rise the one who walks between,

a hand in darkness, a heart in light,

whose choice shall bind the fate of all realms.

Seek well and guide the chosen one, whose path is yet undecided.

The dark lord shall rise again at his master's command, but through ruin the dawn is born,

and only the nameless sacrifice shall open the way."

And then the crystal dimmed again, returning to its gentle, quiet pulse.

For a long time, no one spoke.

Then Will stepped forward and placed his hand on the crystal's surface. It no longer burned. It was warm now. Familiar.

He looked up at the others, the golden light of the stone refracting across his cheekbones.

"Was that—," he began.

Eldara nodded. "We have just been witnesses to the birth of a new prophecy."

Lyra's brows pulled together as she wrestled with what they had just heard. "What did it all mean, though?" she asked.

Eldara spread her palms, shaking her head. "I understood some of it... The crown of stone is Anhai...I think. The bearer of light, Lucian—" she paused here, choking down her grief at the thought of him.

"... And the rest?" asked Lyra.

"We will need some time to study and understand that, but I think it was giving us instructions on how we can push back the darkness," said Eldara.

Will's face had grown dark. "I don't like the sounds of the line about the dark lord rising again."

Eldara shook her head. "No... that can't be good."

Athtar had been apart from the others during this exchange, leaning over a desk. Finally, she stood up and came to join them, holding a parchment in her hand. "If we're to study this prophecy, I figured it would be best to write it down while it's fresh in our minds," she said, holding the parchment out.

They stood in a circle around the crystal, four remnants of a broken world. Outside, the cold wind swept across the cliffs of Graltum, but inside, the light of Lucian's stone cast soft prisms across the walls.

The night ahead would be long.

But somewhere on the horizon, though none could see it yet, the dawn was coming.

THE END